Also by Jack Ramey

Eavesdropping in Plato's Cafe

The Future Past

Burnt Almonds

Death Sings in the Choir of Light

Eurydice's Kiss

Turtle Island: A Dream of Peace

Turtle Island

A Dream of Peace

Jack Ramey

Springwood

PRESS

First Edition

Copyright © 2015 by Jack Ramey

Library of Congress Control Number: 2015949810

ISBN 978-1-943112-20-3

Printed in the United States of America

Cover Design by Rick Lostutter

Springwood Press, LLC
302 Fairmount Drive
Madison IN 47250

springwoodpress.org

Dedicated to

the spirit of

Leon Shenandoah

and the Iroquois people

"What you call the United States,
we Indians call the Great Turtle Island.
This is where the Creator planted us
and when He did, He made us free.
Europeans were not planted here,
but you came here because
you wanted to be free like us.
In our original Instructions
we were told that
nobody owned the land
except the Creator.
That's why we welcomed you."

Contents

Part I

Sorcerer's Moon

Chapter One

I first heard this story many years ago when I was a small boy on my grandfather's knee. He heard it from *his* grandfather, who heard it from his, and so on back into the dim reaches of time, back to one who was there. His name was Orios, and although he was only a boy at the time, he played the flute like no other in his day. They say he could charm the birds of the air and the creatures of the forest with the magic of his music. He saw these things happen, and here is the story that he told, a story that has echoed down throughout the generations.

It all began one summer morning in the land of the Onondaga, what you now call the lake region of the state of New York. Long before the white people came to our land, before the man called Columbus "discovered" Turtle Island and gave us all a new name: *los indios*. But we were not *indios*. We were Onondaga, the people. On this one summer morning, a morning that would forever change the lives of so many people—those living and those who would come to live on Great Turtle Island—a long, elm-bark canoe glided through the fog across a great silver lake. The sun was beginning to break through the early morning mist, leaving blood-red streaks in the V-shaped wake the canoe made on the lake's surface.

In the canoe sat the great chieftain of the Onondaga, Hiawatha. The muscles on his strong arms swelled with each stroke of the paddle slicing through the waters on either side of the canoe. Hiawatha's symbol, a bright golden-yellow sun, was painted on either side of the curved prow of the canoe. A single eagle feather hung down across his back. He was naked except for a deerskin loincloth. The skin of his body gave off a brilliant *orenda*, a glow that bathed the other occupants of the canoe in its golden light. With Hiawatha on this early morning adventure were his treasures, his four daughters. Daughters born of a wife now gone, these girls were his comfort and solace.

Sovana, the oldest, reminded him most of Tamora, his gone wife. She sat upright in the prow of the canoe paddling in time with her father's strokes, a serious and determined look on her handsome face. Her strong arms moved within the folds of her fringed deerskin dress, a dress that had belonged to her mother. Hiawatha remembered the night he first met Tamora, how he was thunderstruck by her beauty and dignity, and now this fringed dress fit their first-born so well some thirteen years later. He had presented it to his eldest daughter five days ago, and Sovana had worn it ever since, proud of the memory of her mother, the newly developing curves of her woman's body fitting perfectly inside the supple garment.

Between Hiawatha at the stern and Sovana at the prow, Seawa, Memoha, and Tiwi sat and reclined. Seawa, a girl of eleven summers, watched intently as an osprey dived into the water some thirty yards away and emerged with a writhing fish in its talons. The sight of the bird of prey's bloody claws and the dying fish gave her pause and made her think about the strange ways of the Great Creator. Tiwi, only five summers old and the youngest, leaned over her father's left leg and the edge of the canoe, dangling her hand in the water and watching the bubbles her tiny fingers made in the flow of red, blue, and white foam. She laughed in delight, and Hiawatha, as he smiled down on his smallest girl, thought that her bright laughter sounded like the ripples of the shining lake water. He looked up from his reverie and scanned the horizon. The fog had lifted, making the distant shore visible. Memoha, nine years old and full of curiosity and raw energy, held her small black-and-white spotted dog and, pointing at the shore, turned to look at her father.

Hiawatha nodded at his daughter as the sweet vibrato from a cedar-wood flute broke through the silence of the morning air. Sovana turned in the direction of the sound, her large brown eyes searching through the lifting fog. An expression of rapt attention molded the delicate features of her smooth and beautiful face.

"Orios," she half sighed, half whispered. An unmistakable note of longing colored her voice.

Hiawatha smiled. "Orios," he whispered in mock secrecy to the other girls. "Orios, the dreamer, Orios, the charming music maker."

"His music is wonderful," sighed Sovana. She absently placed her hand on her breast as she peered through the fog. She was a radiant young girl, one of those rare creatures whose mere presence could light up a longhouse on a dark winter night. Her face gave off a silver light and her voice was as pleasant to hear as a songbird's trill.

Another canoe appeared behind them. Makahwah, large and sturdy matriarch of Hiawatha's longhouse and the Turtle Clan, sat in the middle of the canoe with Orios, a slender youth of fourteen playing delicate, romantic airs on his flute. The notes seem to glide on the morning air like winged creatures, and the birds on the shore answered his song, making intricate harmonic patterns ebb and flow in counterpoint around the two gliding canoes.

Kewahtawa, Makahwah's husband, stopped paddling for a moment and scanned the horizon through the slits of narrowed eyes whose corners were as creased with lines as the wrinkled brow below his thick silver hair. Kewahtawa's cousin, Teom, a lean, middle-aged man with a narrow face and twin braids that fell down either side of his thin chest, rested his paddle across the struts of the prow and smiled at the girls in the other canoe. Sovana pretended not to notice Orios.

"Look, Grandmother. We are almost there." Memoha pointed

her puppy's nose in the direction of the distant shore. "Can you smell the strawberries from here, little puppy? I can!"

"What a keen nose you have, my child," said Makahwah. She shifted her weight in the canoe, and the bark vessel rocked from side to side. Orios played a few comical notes and Tiwi giggled. Sovana looked up and smiled. Orios looked shyly at Sovana, basking in her approval, but too nervous to keep his eyes locked with hers. Makahwah flipped him on the head with her index finger and pointed to the shore, now glowing in the bright morning sun.

"Keep your eyes away from my granddaughter," she said. "We've work to accomplish this day." Kewahtawa and Teom dipped their paddles in the water, and the canoe moved closer to the approaching lake shore. Hiawatha laughed to himself at his mother-in-law and her no-nonsense approach to life: an approach however, that had helped them survive many a hard winter.

Among our people, power is passed down from mother to daughter. The women own the longhouses and decide which man is fittest to rule, to lead the people in times of great need or in times of calm. Makahwah was a very powerful woman. Her man, Kewahtawa, was once the chief of the Onondaga, but a blood feud with the Seneca caused the death of Tamora, her daughter by her first husband, and Makahwah forced him to step aside for Hiawatha. It is the women who pass the power down from generation to generation. And why not? Do they not give birth to all men and women? This is why the Corn Goddess is not a man. Why the fruits of the earth are sisters, and the growing vines that come back each year are tended by women who know best the ways of birth and death and birth again.

As the sun lifted up over the lake, turning the world to gold, Hiawatha looked behind him and saw the rest of the hunting and gathering party approaching in nine long canoes, gliding in a silver V-formation. Today the men would hunt the deer and the elk, the turkey and the rabbit, while the women would gather the fruits of the earth, the rich berries and herbs of the summer lakeside forest. He half-turned and signaled with his outstretched paddle high above his head for one group of canoes to split to the right side of the shore, and the other group to follow the left. Half of the canoes veered off toward the lush tangle of green brush and tree trunks that marked the beginning of a great forest. The other half veered to the right shore, where a steep incline led up to a large expanse of meadow covered with flowers and dotted with fruit-bearing bushes.

Hiawatha felt the bow and deerskin quiver beside his left leg on the floor of his canoe and his heart was filled with desire for the hunt. He silently said a prayer to the deer spirits to be generous to his people; he said a prayer to the spirits of the forest to guide his footsteps, and to make them silent; he said a prayer to the spirits of the sky and wind to hide his scent and the scent of his companions from the quick nostrils of the deer and the elk; and he prayed to the spirit of his dead wife, Tamora, to look down from the otherworld and smile on today's endeavors.

Memoha's spotted puppy yelped and howled as the canoe scraped the bottom of the shore. Hiawatha stepped over the side into the shallow water and pulled the boat onto dry land. He helped little Tiwi out while Sovana and Seawa gathered the woven baskets from the floor and stepped ashore to join Makahwah, who was stretching her large limbs in the bright morning sun. Memoha was right, she thought. You can smell the strawberries on the wind. Her keen sense of smell told her that pokeberry and yarrow flowered nearby as well. These would be gathered today to make poultices, salves, and headache medicines. Orios and Sovana walked off together toward the winding path that led up the hill to the meadow. He wanted to speak to her, but he could not. There were so many things he needed to tell her, but the words would not come. Instead, he withdrew his flute from its doeskin sheath and began to play a sweet melody. Sovana drew closer to him.

"Orios!" Hiawatha's strong voice commanded the boy's attention. He turned and lowered his flute.

"Yes, Hiawatha?"

"Today you will come with me. We will hunt together in the company of men." Orios' cheeks colored. He glanced at Sovana, nodded goodbye, then ran back down the hillside. In his haste, he tripped on a rock and tumbled head over heels, landing at Makahwah's feet. She grabbed him by the ear and pulled him up. He checked to make sure that his flute was not broken; then, reassured, he ran to Hiawatha's side. Hiawatha put his arm around the boy's shoulders.

"If you want to earn the respect of your people, my son, you must first become a hunter." He led Orios to his canoe. Ever since Orios' father had died four years ago, Hiawatha had tried to fill the void left in the boy's life. Orios had been especially close to his father since his mother had died during his birth.

"Will you teach me to be a great hunter like you?"

"I will do my best, Orios."

"If I become a great hunter like you, then will I gain the hand of Sovana?"

"I think you already have my daughter's heart, Orios. But Makahwah has final say. First gain the trust of Makahwah, and then you will have Sovana as your bride."

"Why doesn't Makahwah like me?"

"She likes you." Hiawatha pushed the canoe off the bank and jumped in the back. He tossed a paddle to Orios up front and motioned him to get moving. "She loves your music. We all love your music. But she is afraid that you will not be a good provider for her granddaughter and the people of her longhouse."

"But why?"

"Because you walk in the woods with your head in the clouds."

"Today I will show her what a great hunter I am!" He pulled a short blowgun out of a fawnskin pouch hanging from a rawhide thong around his neck. "Today I will kill a giant rabbit. A rabbit so great that it will feed the entire longhouse. Its pelt will be so thick it will keep four babies warm on the coldest of winter nights. And everyone will look at the giant rabbit and wonder aloud: 'What great hunter has brought us this giant rabbit? Who is the great man to thank for this gift?' And Makahwah will look at them and say: Orios, Orios of the enchanted flute, has brought this giant rabbit for all to enjoy."

Hiawatha laughed and splashed Orios with a forward slap of his paddle. "What a dreamer you are!"

After a short journey around the edge of the lake, Hiawatha steered the canoe toward the shore. They leapt out and pulled the canoe onto the dry bank. "This is the best summer deer trace in all the land of the Onondaga. Now we will do some real hunting."

Hiawatha led the way down the narrow track into the deep forest. He stopped suddenly. With his deerskin moccasin, he kicked aside the black pebbles of fresh deer spoor. He looked up at Orios. "A buck. Very close." He put his forefinger to his lips. Orios nodded.

They continued on down the path, a path so overhung with a canopy of majestic broad-leaved trees that the shaded ferns were as high as a man's waist. Orios froze in his tracks when he saw through the massive trunks a ten-point buck standing still, looking directly at them. Orios could hear the pounding of his own heart beating within his head. Hiawatha drew a shaft from his buckskin quiver, fitted the hand-carved notch onto his bowstring, pulled the length back to his right cheek, and let go—letting the arrow fly through the forest with a quiet whistling sound. The buck leaped to his right, three feet into the air, and Hiawatha's shaft found its mark just behind the left shoulder, sharpened flint piercing his lungs in mid-flight. The mortally hurt deer ploughed on through the woods for some twenty paces and then hit the ground head-first, the mighty rack of antlers tossing up dirt and dead pine needles.

Man and boy moved in silence to where the once-majestic buck lay beside a tall white pine, his eyes wide and lifeless, his neck twisted. His clouded eyes seemed to Orios to be fixed on him alone. The sight of this dead lord of the forest sent a shiver down his spine. Hiawatha dropped to his knees and motioned for Orios to do the same. He placed his right hand on the buck's shoulder, his fingers straddling the upright shaft of the arrow.

"Forgive us, brother, for this deed we have done today. We are in great need of your meat." Hiawatha's mellifluous baritone filled the cathedral of woods. "We love the life-spirit that once coursed through your blood-paths, the same life-spirit that runs through the blood-paths of all of our people. Thank you for giving us your life, your blood, so that our lives may continue."

A soft wind whistled through the white pine, making a sound like the voices of winged Spirit Beings whispering above him. Orios watched him as he bowed his head and remained still in silent meditation. Then he lifted his head and turned to Orios.

"Bring me that flat piece of bark over there."

When Orios returned with the piece of wood, Hiawatha was unpacking the contents of a small bundle that he had removed from his fawnskin pouch. He took some tobacco from a smaller pouch and sprinkled it on the flat piece of bark. Next, he assembled his fire drill, a small bow with a short, pointed shaft. He looped the string of the bow once around the shaft, placed the point of the drill-shaft on the piece of bark in the middle of the mound of dried tobacco, and began to move the bow back and forth, causing the pointed drill to spin. After a few minutes of rapid spinning, a small plume of smoke drifted up from the mound of tobacco. Orios kneeled over the drill and blew on the small flames. The tobacco caught and Hiawatha added a bit more, causing the aromatic blue smoke to drift heavenward. Hiawatha wafted some toward his face and then toward the face of the buck. He began to chant softly in a rich, deep voice. He spread his arms outward and upward.

"We burn the sacred tobacco to your memory. We offer the holy plant-smoke to your ghost. We honor your strength. We honor your beauty. We honor your brave heart and pure mind. Each time we pass this place, we will remember you, you who gave yourself to us that we might live. Each time we pass this place, we will honor your spirit."

Orios looked up at Hiawatha with admiration. He had found something else about his chieftain to love and respect. And something that he already knew, something that all of the people knew, was reinforced in his mind and heart that day—the creatures of the forest are our brothers and sisters, and, as such, we must treat them with dignity and respect. Those who are killed are giving of themselves; they make a blood sacrifice so that their brothers and sisters, the people, the Onondaga, may live.

Hiawatha stood up and slowly withdrew the arrow from the buck's side. With his stone knife, he field-dressed the deer, and then tied the forelegs together and the hind legs together with two pieces of rawhide. He slung the heavy weight up onto his broad shoulders. They walked back down the path the way they had come to put the still warm buck into the canoe. As they turned around a bend in the narrow path, Hiawatha spied a huge brown hare, frozen on an open stretch of meadow.

"Look, Orios," he whispered softly. "Here is your gigantic rabbit! Take my bow." Hiawatha dropped the gutted buck and gave Orios his bow and quiver. Sensing danger that a mere frozen attitude could not overcome, the hare turned and bounded off across the meadow in the direction of the trees. Orios gave chase, trying to fit an arrow into the bowstring while he ran at full speed. The hare was fast, but Orios would not quit and he kept him in sight.

Hiawatha laughed to himself and continued down the path toward the lake shore. A sudden gust of wind blew across the treetops and the meadow. Crows called in the distance. The wind blew hair into Orios' eyes and he stumbled over a rock in the meadow. He picked himself up and continued running toward the woods where his elusive prey had just entered.

The hare was now out of sight, but Orios knew he would find him. It was his fate, his destiny. He had dreamed of it. He had spoken of it to Hiawatha. And now the great opportunity was put before him. As he ran, he said a quick prayer to the spirits of this wood, and then, twenty feet before him, he saw the hare standing in the shade, large coal-black eyes unblinking, trying to blend in with the grass and the tree trunks. He ducked behind the trunk of a tall oak tree, catching his breath and hugging the bow and arrow to his slim chest.

The spirits of the woods were about to answer Orios' prayer, but not in the way that he had wished for. His destiny and his fate were indeed waiting for him in the strange guise of this timid dweller of the forest. Someone else was also stalking this rabbit. A boy about the same age as Orios, a boy also hidden behind the trunk of another tree on the other side of the rabbit. This boy could have been Orios' twin, his other, his long-lost brother. As his twin was fitting a dart onto his blowgun and praying to the spirits of the woods to guide his missile to the heart of the hare, Orios fitted the notch of the arrow onto the string and pulled the bow back as far as he could. Beads of sweat formed on his forehead and his hands were shaking with apprehension. As in a dream, or in a vision of two split worlds, two dual universes that come together for an instant, both boys stepped out from behind the trees on either side of the clearing. Orios' eyes were fixed on the frozen hare caught between two worlds, hung between two realities. A crow cawed loudly and a black shadow fell across the meadow.

Orios let the arrow loose. It whistled through the summer air like an emissary of doom. It howled like a broken truce. The boy on the other side of the field looked up in time to see what looked like a black hawk's face screaming toward him, yellow eyes becoming larger and larger and brighter and brighter, red and gold feathers fanning out in concentric circles around his crowned and radiating head, the twin slashes on either side of the golden beak bleeding out blood in steady twin streams that poured out behind him, that vibrated all around him, huge gold and red-tipped talons rushing forward now only three feet from his face, and that was the last sight he saw as the arrow struck his chest.

The impact hurled him backwards to the ground and from out of his mouth there came a loud and piercing cry that sounded like an angry raven. Orios dropped the bow and ran toward the stricken boy. He reached his side and dropped down to his knees. He did not know what to do. He put his hand on the boy's chest. Should he pull the arrow out? He tried, but he could not remove it. He looked at his hands covered with blood. Was he dead? He placed his ear next to the boy's mouth, but he could not hear any breathing. The boy's eyes stared at him, but did not see him.

Orios leaped to his feet, blinded by tears that suddenly welled up in his eyes. He turned and ran back the way he came, his legs racing down the path to the lake shore, his mind burning, full of confused images.

"Hiawatha! Hiawatha!" he shouted as he saw the figure of the great leader leaning over the canoe at the edge of the lake in the distance. Hiawatha turned and saw the boy running toward him. Knowing that something was wrong, he grabbed his stone tomahawk from the bottom of the canoe and ran to meet Orios.

"What is it, Orios?" Hiawatha held the boy's arms with his strong hands and felt his slim body trembling. Orios could not speak. He gestured back toward the meadow. His mouth was open, but no words came. Hiawatha shook him. "Take a deep breath, Orios."

Orios managed to breathe in deeply. And then the words came in a rush. "A boy in the meadow. I think I have killed him. It was an accident. I thought he was the rabbit, or the rabbit was there and then he was gone, and the boy was falling with my arrow in his chest . . ."

"Show me," said Hiawatha. And the two of them ran back down the path. When they reached the boy's side, he was already dead. His glazed-over, open eyes gazed sightlessly at the clear blue sky, a look of surprise frozen on his young face. Hiawatha pulled the arrow from his chest and placed his hand on the wound. Blood spurted around and through his fingers as he chanted softly a prayer to the Great Spirit, to the keeper of dead souls in the otherworld, a prayer for the dead boy, a stranger hunting on strange soil.

"Seneca," he said, looking at the markings on the blowgun that lay on the ground a few feet away.

"It was an accident, Hiawatha. I didn't mean to kill him. Suddenly he was there."

"Yes, of course it was an accident. This boy was in the wrong place at the wrong time. Seneca should not be hunting here this time of year. These are the hunting grounds of the Onondaga."

Suddenly, a dart whizzed by Hiawatha's head. He dove for cover, dragging Orios with him. They flattened themselves on the ground among tall weeds and grasses. Hiawatha raised his head slightly and peered through a parting in the grass. Another dart landed beside him, and a loud, crow-like call pierced the still air. Hiawatha saw a painted Seneca warrior on the other side of the clearing, head shaved on either side of a high brush-cut fixed with quills. Hiawatha signaled for Orios to run. The boy half-crouched and ran through the tall grass toward the path that led to the canoe. Hiawatha followed. More crow-calls answered the first. More darts whizzed past them, one of them grazing Hiawatha's arm.

He skidded to a full stop, wheeled, and faced his enemy. The blood pumped wildly through his veins. He felt the strange thrill that always overtook him when he was forced to do battle. Twenty feet away, the Seneca warrior was running at full tilt, placing a dart in his blowgun. Hiawatha quickly removed the stone tomahawk from his belt, took aim, and hurled the oblong stone fitted into the smooth shaft of ash. The deadly missile flipped end over end over end so rapidly that the Seneca had no time to dodge or duck, and it smashed into his forehead with a loud crack, sending a shower of blood and brain out and around his split skull, stopping the man dead in his tracks. He dropped to his knees, and then pitched forward face-first onto the ground, blood pouring out of his nose, his eyes, his ears, and the hole in his forehead.

Hiawatha, exultant, screamed a loud victory cry to warn any other enemies that a mighty warrior was here waiting to deal with all comers. He picked up his tomahawk and freed the blowpipe from clenched fingers. He ripped the bracelet of snake fangs from the fallen enemy's wrist. Trophies of battle that would hang in his longhouse. Two more crow calls split the air.

At the far edge of the meadow, lying in the grass, two Seneca warriors with long blowguns watched Hiawatha turn and jog down the path. Both had shaved heads, save for red-dyed topknots braided with porcupine quills. Their naked limbs were streaked with black and red dye and they both wore snake-fang bracelets on their wrists. One had a nose ring made of hammered gold; the other wore large mica earrings that flashed blue and green in the sun whenever he moved his head. They looked at each other, acknowledging their enemy's strength.

When Hiawatha was out of sight, they crept out of their hiding and rushed to their dead companion's side. The warrior with the nose ring placed his hand on the fallen warrior's heart and chanted a prayer-song to the Great Spirit of the otherworld to take the ghost of their brother into his arms. He sprinkled tobacco on the dead man's bloody head. The other warrior nudged him abruptly. Irritated at being interrupted, he turned to see his companion pointing to the dead body of the boy lying some twenty paces away. They rushed over and dropped to their knees beside the dead boy, brushing the flies away from his open eyes and the blood on his chest.

"It cannot be!"

"But it is. Young Mahtewan." They stared at each other in disbelief.

"Look!" He picked up Hiawatha's bloody arrow that lay beside the dead boy.

"Onondaga."

The man with the nose ring picked up the dead boy and slung him over his shoulder. He had to tell Shadahgoh, war chief of the Seneca nation that his only son was dead. Slain by an Onondaga arrow. It was not a task he was anxious to perform.

Chapter Two

On another part of the lake shore, Memoha's little dog barked as Makahwah dropped a huge handful of plump blackberries into an almost full basket woven from dried corn husks. The girls and their grandmother were working their way across the edge of a meadow ringed around with dense thickets of blackberry bushes. The late morning sun shone on their labor, adding a soft, golden sheen to their arms and hands stained purple with the juice of the berries.

"Grandmother, look," said Seawa, pointing ahead to another bush heavily laden with fruit. "Juneberries!" Makahwah's face lit up as she rushed over to the bush. With her hand on a clump of purple berries, she bowed her head and thanked Sky Woman who brought forth the plants of Turtle Island. Now she could make the important blood medicine that gives strength to a woman's body after childbirth.

Sovana ran up to Makahwah, waving a garland of wildflowers woven into a crown. She placed the crown on her grandmother's head and skipped around her.

"There, Grandmother! You are the corn mother, the summer goddess, the wildflower spirit who brings love to everyone she meets!" Makahwah eyed the young girl askance. Sweet, pretty Sovana. It was hard not to love her. But Makahwah could not help thinking that she was up to something. "What does this one want?" she thought.

"Here, Sovana, look here now. What is the matter with you?

Have you nothing better to do than to make wildflower baubles for old women?"

"I want to see you radiant, Grandmother. I want to see you happy."

"Out with it, girl. What do you want?"

"Grandmother?"

"Yes, child."

"What do you think of Orios?"

"Orios? That young pup? What should I think? I think he needs to grow up. To learn the ways of a man. So that he can one day be Onondaga."

"But he is so sweet!"

"Sweet? Can you live off sweet?"

"Blackberries are sweet," pouted Sovana as she popped a ripe berry into her mouth.

"But you cannot sustain life from berries alone. You need meat and the three sisters."

"Women grow the three sisters. I can plant and harvest corn and beans and squash. Besides, he plays such beautiful music."

"That is his problem. His head is always in the clouds floating with the notes of his flute."

"Grandmother! I love him. I want him."

"You are the daughter of a great chief, Sovana, and the granddaughter of a clan matriarch. You must marry properly. You must marry a man of substance, of influence. Atatarho has come to me recently expressing his desire for your hand for his nephew and protégé, Osinoh."

"Osinoh?" Sovana was truly shocked. The thought of marrying and lying beside the apprentice of the sorcerer revolted her. "But he is so old!"

"He is only seventeen summers old. Every girl in the village would jump at the chance to marry the handsome Osinoh."

"I know, Grandmother. I know he is handsome and a good hunter, but something about him frightens me. What if he becomes stooped and crooked like his uncle."

"Nonsense. He is a fine young man with a great future ahead of him. He will one day become a great shaman like Atatarho. True, Atatarho is a bit stooped."

"A *bit*? He's a hunchback with long bony fingers. They say he eats human flesh and speaks with the dead."

"He cannot help the fact that he was born with some infirmities. But he is not an ogre. He is a sorcerer, a shaman, and as such, he is a very powerful and influential man. Those rumors of man-eating are just that. Rumors. You mustn't believe everything you hear. People who spread these stories are mostly jealous. Jealous of Atatarho's great powers. Yes, he may talk with the dead. And what of it? The dead are always with us." Makahwah waved her large arm in a broad arc. "They are all around us. And there are those among us who are blessed with the power to communicate with those who have gone before us, but who have not left us. Atatarho is one of those blessed men. You should have more respect for him. And as for his nephew, Osinoh, who is being taught the way of the shaman, he will one day be a great man, a great leader in the Grand Council. Just like his uncle."

"I can't help it, Grandmother. He scares me."

"Enough of this nonsense. If the clan mothers and your father decide that you should marry Osinoh, then marry Osinoh you will." Makahwah spied little Tiwi picking the shiny, red berries from a chokecherry bush.

"Tiwi! Don't eat those," she said in such a commanding tone of voice that Tiwi dropped the berries immediately. "You should be looking after your little sister, Sovana, teaching her not to eat poison berries instead of mooning over a silly, worthless boy."

"But Grandmother, it's not fair . . ." The sound of a crow that was not exactly the sound of a crow echoed faintly in the distance.

"Shh," warned Makahwah, a thick finger held up to her lips. The crow call sounded again, sending a shiver of fear up her spine. "Quickly, children, run for the blackberry bushes! Hide! Sovana, get Tiwi. Seawa, Memoha, come with me, and keep your puppy quiet!" The woman and the girls scampered behind and under the bushes, thorns tearing at their deerskin dresses and the exposed flesh of their arms and legs and faces. Memoha held the little dog's jaws shut so that it could not bark, and everyone held their breath and waited as the sound of voices and footfalls became louder and louder.

Blood was running in Makahwah's left eye from a thorn-cut on her forehead. She wanted to wipe it away, but she dared not move, for now she saw through the blood eight Seneca warriors led by a large and forceful man whose eyes, although constantly darting about, seemed blinded by some inner rage. His large head was shaved, save for a topknot pierced by two red porcupine quills and three copper-and-black hawk feathers. Above his large biceps, he wore armbands of black bear fur. The septum of his large hawk-like nose was pierced through with two red quills and he wore heavy discs of blue stone in each distended ear lobe. But the most striking features of this striking man were his legs. He wore only a buckskin breech clout so that his heavily muscled thighs and calves were exposed to the sun. With each step that he took, his enormous calves rippled and bulged. The effect was heightened by long vertical stripes of black war paint that he wore on his legs from the tops of his thighs to his ankles, where they seemed to disappear into his moccasins. He carried a three-foot-long war club in his right hand, a deadly-looking, curved length of carved wood that terminated at its outer length in a round wooden ball the size of two large fists, with bits of sharpened flint embedded around its smooth surface; a perfect weapon for smashing skulls.

"Shadahgoh," said Makahwah in a silent whisper to herself. The notorious war chief of the Seneca, the Great Hill People, the sworn enemies of the Onondaga, was even more awe-inspiring in person than he was in the terrifying stories that people told of him.

Shadahgoh froze in the middle of the field, the muscles of his legs rippling and tensing. He sniffed the air, taking in huge breaths through his hawkish beak, his head darting from side to side like a large bird of prey.

One of his warriors bent over and picked up a blackberry. "Shadahgoh. Look. Fresh footprints."

Makahwah and the girls hidden in the bushes only fifteen paces away froze in horror. They each held their breath in fear that Shadahgoh and the Seneca warriors might hear them breathing. Shadahgoh looked around the edge of the clearing. His eyes seemed to fix on Seawa, who tried to will herself into an invisible spirit of the forest, a dryad whose form could not be seen by the angry coals burning beneath the war chief's painted forehead. His eyes looked away and back to the ground again.

"Women and children," he said in disgust to his men. "These moccasin and foot prints all belong to women and children. We are not in the business of killing women. We look for a man. The Onondaga who killed my son." Shadahgoh's face seemed to burn like wildfire. For an instant, Makahwah thought she could see flames radiating out from his body. The Seneca chief signaled to his warriors, and they ran off into the forest on the other side of the field. Makahwah exhaled a slow sigh of relief as she nodded to the girls and they crawled out from beneath the bushes. Tiwi was shaking as she tried to suppress her sobs. Seawa picked her up and rocked her back and forth, patting her back. Memoha hugged her puppy closer to her breast.

"Did you hear what he said, Grandmother?" asked Sovana. "His son. Killed by an Onondaga man."

"Yes, daughter, I heard."

"Who do you think it is?"

"I don't know. But I'll find out. Come. We'll leave the rest of the berries for the birds. It's time we get back to the lake shore to meet Hiawatha and the other men."

Hiawatha steered the canoe from the rear with swift and steady strokes of his carved paddle, while Orios, paddling in the front, did his best to keep up with him. The deer lay between them on the floor. Orios could still feel the blood on his hands.

"It is hopeless now," he said, hot tears staining his face. "When Makahwah finds out that I have killed a Seneca boy, she will never allow me to marry Sovana."

"It was an accident. You were not aiming for him."

"All the more reason to repeat her familiar chant: 'Orios has his head in the clouds.' Hiawatha, I didn't mean to kill him. And yet he is dead. And now his family will surely seek me out. They will want to exact revenge by killing me."

"They do not know who killed him. This knowledge will remain a secret between only the two of us." Orios turned and looked at him. "Dry your eyes, now. We will go to meet my girls and Makahwah. Be strong. I am with you. The Great Spirit is with you."

As he paddled, Orios said a prayer to the Great Spirit, thanking him for Hiawatha's strength. He said another prayer to the ghost of the dead boy, asking him to forgive him for taking his life. *The dead walk among us,* thought Orios. *The elders say this is so. Perhaps the dead boy is here in the canoe with us now, sitting on top of the deer, looking at me, accusing me.* Orios kept paddling on, but, from time to time, he looked back over his shoulder to see if the dead boy was with them in the elm-bark vessel.

"Paddle faster," said Hiawatha, and Orios snapped out of his reverie. He could see the dim outline of small figures standing on the shore in the distance.

"Look!" cried Memoha. "Grandmother, the Great Mother has heard our prayers!" Makahwah put her hand to her forehead to shelter her eyes from the lowering sun. She could see three canoes in the distance and the outline of Hiawatha and Orios in the lead canoe approaching the shore where they stood.

"We must give thanks." Makahwah closed her eyes, and her

lips moved in silent thanksgiving. The girls followed suit, all but Tiwi, who took the opportunity to grab a handful of blackberries from one of the baskets at their feet.

The next morning, smoke could be seen curling up from the hole in the center of the round roof of the Onondaga council house. Dew still glistened on the elm-bark shingles that lined the vertical walls and the curved surface of the roof. People in and around the surrounding longhouses were all going about their routine daily tasks: skinning deer and rabbit, elk and beaver; scraping and tanning the hides stretched on wooden frames and racks; drying or smoking yesterday's catch of fish; chipping flint for arrow points, tools, and knives. Women with hoes walked in pairs toward the outlying fields of corn and beans and squash.

Inside the council house, twelve men sat on woven hemp mats around a low fire burning in the center of the room. These were the wise ones, the elders, chieftains, sorcerers, and shamans of the Onondaga nation. Hiawatha wore his *gustoweh*, his formal chieftain's headdress—a deerskin-covered, feathered cap with deer antlers on either side. Two eagle feathers, one upright, one dangling down, swirled whenever he moved his head.

Hiawatha filled the bowl of a long, curved pipe. Both sides of the bowl were emblazoned with his personal totem-sign, a golden-yellow sun. He lit a dried reed in the fire and placed the flame on the tobacco, puffing and then exhaling a long plume of thick blue smoke that drifted upward toward the hole in the roof of the Grand Council house.

"Let this smoke show the path of all things. From the earth we journey upward to the Land of the Spirit Beings, the otherworld where the life-force of spirits dwell, where our ancestors dwell, where the Great Spirit and the Creator dwell. The place from where the first woman, the Earth Mother, fell and landed on the back of the great primordial turtle to give birth to our people. Let this smoke heal us as we give thanks for our existence. Let this smoke and this prayer keep the Strawberry Path, the path from the earth to the Sky World, clear.

"We thank the spirit-force of the three sisters who nourish us, the life energy contained in the things that grow in the earth. We thank the spirits of the waters that sustain us, the mist, the rain, the streams, the rivers, the lakes. We thank the spirits of the fish who cleanse our waters and give their lives to us for food. We thank the spirits of the forest who give us their meat and their hides to make us strong and keep us warm. We thank the Spirit Beings who dwell in the sky, the many nations of birds, watching over all the creatures below, keeping all things in harmony; the Thunderer, the four sacred winds, Father Sun and Grandmother Moon. And we thank the Creator, The Great Spirit who dwells beyond the sky."

All the while Atatarho impatiently fingered his bone necklace with his long, crooked fingers and glared at Hiawatha across the circle of seated men. "Could our great chief please explain to us how it happened that the son of the Seneca war chief was killed?"

"The death of Shadahgoh's son was an accident. An unfortunate coincidence. The arrow was shot just as the boy stepped out from behind a tree."

"Is it true that you shot the arrow?"

"The boy was killed with my bow, but, as I have just stated, it was an accident. After the accident, we had to defend ourselves and there was another senseless killing."

"It would not be senseless if we would eat them as in the days of our great-grandfathers."

"We are not man-eaters," said Hiawatha firmly.

"The great chieftain of the Onondaga must learn to cultivate a sense of humor. I was only joking."

"Atatarho joking?" rejoined Teom whose salt-and-pepper hair hung freely about his thin chest and shoulders. "What about those rib bones dug up by dogs when the moon was last full? They were still warm and moist and smelled of the unique aroma that comes only from Atatarho's secret blend of roots and herbs."

"My cousin Teom is very brave to cross the great sorcerer," countered Kewahtawa, who was a respected elder and shaman. "It might be your rib bones we find next." The men around the circle, including Hiawatha, all laughed. All but Atatarho, who glared at Teom, his lips moving as if he were swearing an oath or making a mental note to remember this slight.

"Enough of this talk," interrupted Hiawatha.

"Hiawatha is right," said Atatarho. "As we sit here and make jokes, the Seneca prepare for a blood-revenge against us."

"Revenge? What right have they to revenge? They were hunting on our land. They know the penalty." Kewahtawa's voice was firm and decisive. There were murmurs of assent from the other tribal leaders, all of them respected men in their clans and longhouses.

"Be that as it may. Blood is blood. And as you all know, Shadahgoh is the Seneca's most powerful war chief. And we, or *one* of us . . . ." Atatarho looked at Hiawatha. "One of us has killed his only son, a son that he loved. Do you think Shadahgoh cares whose land his son was killed on?"

A silence descended on the circle of men. Atatarho's burning eyes swept around the circle, pausing to make eye contact with each man. They finally rested on Hiawatha. The chief of the Onondaga stared back at the sorcerer. Some say that if you look too long into the eyes of a sorcerer, your soul will be his forever. Hiawatha felt a cold shiver run up his spine. It now seemed as if Atatarho was reaching down into the depths of his being with those burning, searching eyes. He is trying to read the signs of my soul, he thought, trying to dig down deep enough to uncover the truth buried in my heart. His eyes are teasing out the fiber of my spirit. With an intense effort of will, Hiawatha broke eye contact and looked upward at the smoke billowing toward the hole in the roof of the council house.

Atatarho threw a handful of powder on the fire and a burst

of red cloud exploded upward, making all the men jump. "There will be blood!" he shrieked. "A mighty red flood of vengeance will sweep down upon us all. Look to yourselves! But especially look to your families, your wives, and your children." He began to shake his turtle-shell rattle, chanting in time to the rattling.

The words that Atatarho chanted next were in a language that no one around the fire knew. A spirit tongue. The language of the dead. The language of the beings of the otherworld, the Sky Beings. Slowly, Atatarho rose up. He did not seem to stand as a normal man might, of his own volition, using the muscles of his calves and thighs and feet. But rather, he seemed to be pulled up by some force above his head till he was standing upright. His bent body straight as an arrow, his hunchback gone from sight, he appeared to be two heads taller than he normally was. He was chanting and shaking his rattle faster now, and his body began to quake, to shiver all over like the muscles twitching on a wild creature, an elk or a buck, when they want to brush away insects landing on their backs or sides. His eyes were rolling in their sockets so that the whites showed more than the piercing purple and black. And he began to circle the ring of seated men. He leaped into the air every two or three paces, continually shaking the rattle faster and faster and chanting in the fearsome, unknowable language of the dead.

Sweat poured from the foreheads of the seated men. Some became dizzy and touched their heads to the ground before them. Others prayed to their ancestral clan spirits for protection from the spells of Atatarho. Atatarho ran and leaped around the backs of the council members who were staring straight ahead, afraid to make eye contact with anyone, afraid to speak. The room seemed to spin and the great earth seemed to tilt as if the ancient mud turtle shifted, and everything slid down off his back. Atatarho stood behind Teom and shrieked a loud and piercing scream. Teom's eyes widened and his mouth opened to cry out in terror, but no sound came from his mouth. He gripped his chest and struggled to breathe. The rattling and chanting kept coming in waves and waves of sound like the endless sound of cicadas on a hot summer afternoon building up to a ferocious intensity. Teom tried to stand up, ripping the claw necklace from his neck. He pitched forward onto the ground, and then the rattling stopped, the chanting stopped, everything stopped. All was silence but for the heavy panting of the men around the smoking, guttering fire.

"Look to yourselves! Look to your children!" cried Atatarho as he turned and stormed toward the door of the house. He stopped and turned around, facing the seated men. "I have put a ring of protection around those in this room. Our leaders will be safe. But I cannot do the same for the village, for the longhouses, for all of the Onondaga. I see war. I see blood spilled. Innocent blood. Those who have caused these acts to fall upon us know who they are and what evil they do. There must be atonement." He looked once again into the eyes of Hiawatha. Then he walked calmly out of the round, wooden house.

The men all rushed to help Teom, who lay stricken on the ground. Some were wondering whether it was he who was responsible for the death of the Seneca boy. Why else was he laid low by the great sorcerer's spell? No one else fell to the ground. True, some men came close to fainting. And these were strong men, leaders and elders, many of them seasoned in battle.

"Teom? Can you hear me?" Kewahtawa placed his ear on Teom's chest. He was unconscious.

"He is not dead. His heart still beats."

"We will carry him to the longhouse," said Hiawatha. "He will be safe there, and Makahwah can treat him with herbs and potions." Hiawatha took his shoulders and Kewahtawa his legs, and they carried him out of the council house across the walking path to the longhouse of Makahwah.

"Hiawatha. You know more about this business with the dead boy than you are saying." Hiawatha did not answer Kewahtawa.

"Makahwah knows this too. People talk. The council members all noticed the way Atatarho looked accusingly at you."

"As I have said before, it was an accident. We have no more time to talk of this. We must hasten to prepare for the Seneca vendetta."

"You may not want to talk about it, but Makahwah will. Preparations are already under way for the Feast of Dreams, which I believe to be as important as preparing for the Seneca. Many dream-visions have come to me lately, and much Dream Medicine fills the air. The spirits of our ancestors visit me often in sleep. I must relate these visions to the people. And I must relate them to you, Hiawatha, for they concern you especially."

"Me? How do they concern me?"

"I cannot speak of it now. You will know soon, on the first evening of the Feast of Dreams. Makahwah wishes me to wait till then to reveal the dream-visions and their importance for you and our people."

Hiawatha looked troubled. This was the first that he had heard of these visions. Why hadn't Makahwah mentioned it to him? He suspected some political intrigue was afoot. Makahwah was one of the great matriarchs of the Onondaga who decided who would be chief, which men sat on the Great Council, and for how long. They also had the power to depose a chieftain whom they thought was no longer fit, who no longer could be counted on to lead the people.

Hiawatha and Kewahtawa entered Makahwah's longhouse and laid Teom down on woven hemp mats next to a fire over which Makahwah was stirring a porridge of corn meal. She looked up from the pot.

"What has happened to Teom?"

"It was Atatarho. His chants and spells caused him to freeze up with a seizure of the spirit."

Makahwah put down her ladle and knelt down beside the unconscious man. She placed a hand on his forehead. "He is cold, but he sweats. I will mix a potion. Kewahtawa, you make ready to purge the demon from his soul." Kewahtawa went outside to gather what he needed to perform his medicine chant. Makahwah and Hiawatha were alone with Teom.

"Mother, tell me what you know of these dreams and visions that concern me."

"Son, first you tell me what you know concerning the death of this Seneca boy. It wasn't you who killed him, was it? How could the great hunter and marksman Hiawatha, whose eagle-sharp eye is famous throughout the nation, make such a mistake?"

Makahwah's sarcasm was biting and Hiawatha winced inside. Why indeed was he protecting Orios? What could he stand to gain from shielding a youngster who showed no real promise in the eyes of the elders? A day-dreamer. But he knew why he did it. For his daughter Sovana. She loved Orios, and the young musician loved her. Perhaps he was a day-dreamer, but great spiritual truths and great art came from daydreams, from those who are not afraid of expressing their love through their art.

"I take full responsibility for the death of Shadahgoh's son."

"And you refuse to name the real killer? Do you deny it was that foolish Orios who did this heavy deed?"

"As I have said. It was my bow. It was my arrow. The responsibility rests with me and with me alone."

"Then," persisted Makahwah, "do you take full responsibility for the recriminations that are likely to be visited upon us by the enraged Senecas?" She drew herself up to her full height and threw her head back haughtily. "Do you take full responsibility for the deaths that may ensue from a blood feud, a war of vengeance waged upon our land?"

"I do."

"Then so be it. If it becomes necessary, I will hold you to your word."

Chapter Three

A full moon shone down through the thick swamp trees, illuminating a small clearing. A large fire burned beside a mud-and-stick hut decorated with human bones and skulls. Some called this moon the Dreaming Moon because it was a signal that the Feast of Dreams was beginning. Atatarho was bent over a large clay pot that hung suspended by the fire, stirring its murky contents with a long leg bone for his ladle. The moon glinted in his purple-black eyes and reflected in the black swirling pool he was stirring. His long, loose gray hair was woven with small snake bones that rattled when he moved his head. He wore a long buckskin robe dyed black and painted with signs, symbols, and stylized animal-totems: rabbits, moons, snakes, and bats. He chanted softly to himself. An owl, perched on a pole beside his hut, hooted, warning him of an intruder. He stopped his stirring.

"Who's there?"

"It's me. Osinoh."

"Nephew. You've returned. Well done. What news have you for me?"

Osinoh withdrew a pouch that was hanging around his neck by a woven leather thong. His long, black hair glistened with bear grease and his black eyes gleamed in the bright silver light of the full moon. A sardonic smile lit up his handsome face as he pulled the contents from the pouch.

"Bear claws," he said. "A token of friendship from Shadahgoh." Atatarho snatched the necklace of large claws from his nephew.

"I know what bear claws are, my boy." He rubbed them against his face. "They have a powerful *orenda*. You can feel it running through you like a pure source of darkness and blood. Think of the flesh these claws have torn. The blood that has flowed between them. The creatures dispatched to the otherworld with the strength of these claws."

"I have learned from Shadahgoh's councilors that the great chief is heavy with grief over the death of his son, and he is eager to exact revenge. He sends these claws and this wampum as a token of his gratitude for the information about the man who murdered his boy."

"When does he wish to strike?"

"Now. He is on his way with a war party."

"Tonight? So soon? But the Feast of Dreams begins tonight. Wait a minute. Yes. There will be dancing and dream-telling long into the night. First light will be perfect for his vengeance. Hiawatha is an early riser, and the rest of the village will still be sleeping."

Atatarho continued stirring the pot with the leg bone, an outward, physical action that matched the inner machinations of his mind. "With Hiawatha out of the way, I will be chief, and Sovana will need a strong protector. Makahwah will be more than willing for Sovana to marry you. You will be the strongest warrior in her longhouse."

Osinoh smiled at the bright picture of the future his uncle painted for him.

"Go quickly, Osinoh. Tell Shadahgoh to creep close to the walls of the village this evening. I will see to it that the sentries do not observe him. Tell him that all will be ready for his revenge."

"Yes, Uncle." Osinoh turned and ran off through the swamp, his movements quick and silent as a fox. Atatarho broke into a dance of glee, a joyful dance filled with malice. He was smiling, something he rarely did in public. His tight laughter issued forth from the same source as his smile, a knowledge that his trap would soon be sprung.

"Hiawatha, you are caught like a fly in my web, and I am crawling toward you now. Soon I will suck the lifeblood from your body and eat your heart and destroy your soul. From this moment on, you are mine. And I will laugh and celebrate while Shadahgoh and the people of his longhouse torture you until you scream like an infant. Hear me, oh Great Spirit of the Moon. This Dreaming Moon is now become the Sorcerer's Moon. My time is come. I will be chieftain of the Onondagas. The Great Sorcerer, the great caster of war-spells, will lead the people, and Hiawatha, the weak-willed spawner of girls, the protector of fools, will be utterly destroyed."

Atatarho danced and twirled in the moonlight around his fire in the swamp, the snake bones in his wild hair clicking, the sounds of his chanting and laughing mingling with the croaking of frogs and toads. Inside the stockade walls of the village, the people were already celebrating the first night of the Feast of Dreams.

Sovana emerged from the longhouse of Makahwah, and stopped briefly to smooth out the soft folds in her white deerskin dress decorated with blue and red porcupine quillwork. Satisfied that everything was perfect, she walked toward the fire where Makahwah was ladling out cornmeal porridge in a bowl for Memoha. Her black and white puppy jumped and yelped, eager to be fed as well. Around a large bonfire, the people of the village were seated, eating deer and corn, and telling stories, some nodding gravely, others laughing and joking.

"How do I look, Grandmother?" asked Sovana.

"It looks very nice on you."

"It's not too loose, is it?"

"It fits like the shell on a turtle."

"Grandmother! I don't want to look like a turtle."

"I don't think you have to worry about that, my child," said Makahwah, smoothing down the end of a quill in the intricate pattern woven across the top of the dress. "You look more and more like your mother every day. She would have made you save such a beautiful dress for the festival of green corn."

"But I want to wear it tonight for Orios."

"Orios. Orios is not worth your attention, Sovana. I wish you could see that. Osinoh will be at the feast tonight. Why not pay some attention to him, a young man who will one day be someone?"

"Here comes Kewahtawa! Uncle, do you like my dress?"

"You look lovely, my child. It is a very pretty dress."

"And you look so handsome, Uncle," said Sovana.

Kewahtawa was dressed in his own ceremonial finery. A deerskin leather cap, crowned with many striped feathers hanging down around its rim, sat upon his head, contrasting with his long silver and black hair braided in two strands. His chest was covered with paintings and decorative designs meant to give strength to his dream medicine. In his right hand, he carried a turtle-shell rattle; in his left, an eagle wing attached to a leather handle. His leggings and moccasins were spotted in green dots, and a medicine bundle, made from the entire skinned body of a beaver, hung from the end of a sash that crossed his chest from right to left.

"You are lucky Kewahtawa is speaking at the Feast of Dreams tonight, or I would make you save that dress for a proper occasion." Sovana smiled brightly and started to walk away.

"Sovana."

"Yes, Grandmother?"

"You must be careful from now on. Your father has brought a vengeance down upon our house. You must no longer go into the woods."

"But, Grandmother . . ."

"Have you forgotten how your mother died?"

Sovana did not answer. She looked at the ground beneath her feet, turned, and walked away.

"Why did you have to say that to the girl?" asked Kewahtawa, irritated with his wife for spoiling the first evening of the Feast of Dreams with negative thoughts.

"There is another revenge on our house. No one should forget what happened during the last one. Especially my daughter's daughter. We cannot climb into a hole like a fox and pretend that all this did not happen." Kewahtawa looked away from Makahwah's withering glare.

"How could Hiawatha not have seen the boy?" continued Makahwah. "I only pray that the Seneca do not find out who did this manslaughter."

Outside the high palisade walls that surrounded the village, Atatarho stood beneath the Sentry Tree looking up through the branches at the platform where a guard was dozing. "Hello up there, my brave young fellow! Wake up! The Senecas are coming!" He laughed to himself at his joke as the young warrior, startled, scrambled to his feet on the platform.

"Who is there?"

"Atatarho, shaman and councilor of the Onondaga nation."

"Atatarho! I was not asleep. Believe me. I was only resting my eyes, and listening, yes, listening for any strange noises coming our way through the forest path." There was a genuine fear in the young man's voice. He had heard stories of the powerful spells cast by the great sorcerer. He was young and did not want to spend the rest of his days as a frog croaking in a swamp. They said that Atatarho had the power to make a man's heart stop beating or his blood to freeze like winter water simply by staring or pointing at him.

"I believe you. What is your name?"

"I am Teyan of the Bear Clan, son of Nanowet."

"I know her well. A great mother to her people and a wise woman."

"Thank you for saying so, Atatarho." The sharp sound of a twig snapping broke the night's silence and made the crickets cease their chirping.

"Who goes there?" demanded Teyan. Atatarho turned in the direction of the sound and peered through the moonlit glow of the night.

"It was only me, my boy. I stepped on a dry branch." The crickets resumed their high-pitched chorus.

"Oh. Sorry. I'm a bit jumpy because of all the rumors of war with the Seneca."

"Rumors. Who believes them? Women and children," said Atatarho. "We are men. We do not believe rumors. We believe the evidence of our eyes. Am I right, my boy?"

"Yes sir. Of course you are."

"Are you not going to the Feast of Dreams? The bowls are filled with roasted meats, baked fish, and sweet corn."

"I cannot. I must stand guard all night."

"What a shame. A young man like you not able to feast with his people. To hear the dreams of the elders, to look upon the young girls dancing by the firelight."

"I wanted so to go. I love the Feast of Dreams like no other."

"Then go. I will take your place. I, Atatarho, will stand guard in your stead."

"You would do that for me?"

"Tell your mother that I have taken your place. You can trust me. My shaman eyes see through the dark for miles."

"But don't you want to go to the Feast of Dreams?"

"I have dreams enough of my own. I do not need to hear the dreams of others. Go ahead, my boy. Climb down."

"Thank you, Atatarho. Thank you so much." Teyan climbed down the tree.

"Run along now, and enjoy yourself. While you're still young." Atatarho smiled his toothy smile and fingered the bear claws at his throat as the young man ran off toward the palisade walls of the village. Drums and rattles could now be heard keeping a steady rhythm and providing a backdrop for the chanting voices that began to swell and fill the night air, harmonizing with the regular chirping of the crickets in the grasses around the trees. Atatarho sat down cross-legged at the base of the tree to wait.

The moon was rising higher in the sky now, a full-bellied luminous disc smiling down on his plans, his great plans for the Onondaga people. Under his leadership, they would rise to heights of greatness never seen before. After the weakling Hiawatha was out of the way, then he would lead the people in mighty conquests that would make the Onondaga the rulers of all the other nations of Turtle Island. The Seneca, the Oneida, the Cayuga, and even the fierce Mohawk will all become the subject peoples of the Onondaga nation. It was foretold. He was given this vision thirteen moons ago when the moon was full, just as she is now, on the first night of the Feast of Dreams. But he guarded this dream carefully. He shared his powerful dream-vision with no one. After all, it was granted to him, and to him alone. The Great Spirit of the sky descended to the earth along the Strawberry Path and entered his mind, the mind of Atatarho, the great sorcerer, and the Great Spirit foretold that he, Atatarho, would be a great prophet, that his name would live forever on the lips and in the hearts and minds of his people for generations and generations to come. He would be known as the Keeper of the Flame, the Fire-Leader, the great Shaman Chief of all the nations on Turtle Island.

He leaned back against the tree trunk and stretched his arms out to the moon. He chanted softly in time to the drum beats issuing steadily from behind the village walls:

> "Oh dark spirits of the night,
> Guide my thoughts and words.
> Fire my mind with moonflame!
> Fuse my actions with your might
> That I may prevail and thus fulfill your prophecies . . ."

His prayer was interrupted by the sound of faint whisperings coming from the forest. He leaped to his feet and stared into the moonlit semi-darkness.

"Uncle!" A hoarse whisper floated through the air, making the crickets quit their shrill counterpoint to the incessant drum beats issuing from inside the walls of the village.

"Osinoh?"

"Yes, Uncle." Osinoh's handsome face appeared from behind the tree, momentarily startling his uncle.

"I have taught you well, my boy."

"Look what I have brought you, Uncle."

Shadahgoh stepped out of the shadows. His thick and muscular body was painted in black stripes. The right half of his face was painted red, the left half black. His eyes were burning points set in white, accentuated by the paint and the night. He stood a full head above the skeletal Atatarho, who seemed even more bent beside this tower of muscle clutching his war club. But Atatarho glared at him, fixing him with his reptilian stare, peering through his eyes as if he could reach right down into the bottom of his soul. Shadahgoh shifted his weight from one leg to the other, coughed, and looked away.

"I am here, Atatarho, as I said I would be. I am grateful for the opportunity to exact revenge on my son's murderer."

"Well spoken, Shadahgoh, great chieftain of the Seneca. Climb with me up this lookout tree, and I will point him out to you."

Around the roaring bonfire in the center of the village, men and women danced to the beat of the drums. Everyone wore their finery, long doeskin dresses and leggings decorated with intricate patterns created by sewn cross-sections of dyed porcupine quill. Some of the men wore dyed and decorated doeskin robes draped over one shoulder. The men's hair hung loose with downward dangling feathers, or was plaited with quills and feathers stuck through topknots or a gathered plait at the back of the head. Smaller fires burned at various points in the village where deer and turkey roasted on spits and pots of corn meal, beans, and squash bubbled, stirred by young girls eager to serve the young boys who came back again and again to see them on the pretense of enormous appetites.

At the stockade wall of the village closest to Makahwah's longhouse, Orios was adjusting a round shield of painted feathers on the back of Hiawatha's elaborate ceremonial dress. The buckskin robe draped over his bare shoulder was dyed red and on his chest was painted a resplendent, bright yellow sun. He wore the symbol of his high chieftainship, the feather-covered, deer-antlered *gustoweh*. Hiawatha turned to face the boy and placed a hand on his shoulder. "Tonight is an important night, Orios. Open your ears and your heart to the words of the elders."

"Yes, Hiawatha. I will."

The great chief of the Onondaga and the slender boy-musician, the inadvertent murderer, the boy with his head in the clouds, walked together toward the bonfire at the center of the village. On the other side of the fire, Sovana and Seawa were tending a large bed of burning coals. A line of women with small wooden bowls were filing past them, and Sovana and Seawa, using wooden tongs tipped with clam shells, placed one burning ember into each woman's bowl. As Hiawatha and Orios passed by them, the boy could not take his eyes off Sovana. Her dress was so beautiful. Her eyes were like the soft, deep eyes of a fawn. Sovana met his gaze and their eyes locked. The woman with a bowl standing in front of her cleared her throat loudly, and Sovana jumped when she saw the tips of her tongs smoking from the ember still held between them. She dropped the coal in the woman's bowl and her face flushed a shade of red that matched the glowing ember as her father and Orios walked by. Hiawatha took his place at the head of the circle while Orios went to join the other flute players and the drummers who sat to one side of the fire.

One of the elders passed a burning torch to Hiawatha as the procession of women, each holding a wooden bowl with a burning coal, walked past him shaking the bowls and chanting softly in tune to the drums and flutes. They walked two-by-two up to a circle of large white stones on the ground halfway between the fire and Hiawatha. As each pair reached the circle of stones, they rolled the ember in the bowl three times, and then shook the coal out into the enclosure formed by the circle of stones.

The women took their places beside the fire. Hiawatha looked around at the seated men, women, and children, his people, the Onondaga, and paused. Then he began to speak in his eloquent voice, the voice of a gifted orator.

"As our ancestors did before us, we come together once again under the night sky to share in the Feast of Dreams. Those of you who watch the summer sky each evening know that something very special is happening. Each night many shooting stars and many new dreams are reported. The ancient Sky Beings are falling from their homes and entering into the sleeping minds of our people. This evening we will hear many of these dreams. We will strengthen our minds with the good dreams and free our minds of the bad ones. Only last night, our brother Kewahtawa caught another dream of the holy prophet he calls Dekanawida."

Some of the people shouted their approval. Kewahtawa was a great man among the Onondaga, a shaman and a seer. Some said his mind was growing dim, but even though he was old, most of the people knew that his *orenda* was still powerful and that his visions were pure. Wearing his doeskin robe painted with totem symbols recounting his previous dream-visions and carrying a turtle-shell rattle, Kewahtawa walked slowly toward the circle of stones, its interior glowing with red-hot coals. Behind the circle of stones, the old soothsayer stretched out his arms. The music stopped. Only the crackling of the fire could be heard above the breathing of the seated and waiting people.

After a dramatic silence of ten beats, Kewahtawa began to

shake his rattle. As if on cue, a deep-toned water drum began to rhythmically boom again, followed by more drums, and then joined by the flutes, floating and lilting high above the base line of the drums. Kewahtawa began to chant in the old style, highly ritualized and highly formal.

"I have been in the land of the Great Spirit.
I have been to the land of Great Dreams."

Kewahtawa paused. Then he threw powder across the coals, causing blue flames to leap up high into the night sky. Tiwi and the other children screamed and jumped. Everyone's eyes grew wider.

"The Great Spirit laid his hand
On my head —
And I felt a great wind
Push me from behind. . ."

Kewahtawa shook his rattle to the meter of his chant. At this point he took off his robe and swirled it over the fire causing the flames to leap up higher.

"And the wind pushed me
Through the timeless tunnel
Faster and faster
Till my feet could no longer keep up —
And my spirit was set free
And my spirit raced with the wind
To the end of the long dark tunnel
To the light of many colors. . ."

Kewahtawa passed his robe again over the fire and the flames leapt up in red and blue and yellow hues followed by an explosive noise that echoed in the ears of the seated people. Tiwi and Memoha jumped up from where they sat with the other children and ran to their father. Hiawatha folded them into the crook of each arm and they buried their heads in his chest.

> "And the Great Spirit swirled
> Through the light of many colors —
> And the Great Spirit said:
> 'I will show you the Great Dream —
> The greatest dream of all —
> I will show you the Dream of Dekanawida!'"

Kewahtawa now danced in a trance around the bonfire, shaking his rattle faster and faster to the fast beat of the drums. No longer was he an old man. He had gone backwards in time so that his gray hair now seemed jet in the firelight, and his legs leaped and danced like those of a young man of twenty summers.

Up in the Sentry Tree, beyond the palisade walls of the village, Atatarho and Shadahgoh watched the proceedings. The Seneca chief looked at Atatarho, nodded toward Kewahtawa, and lifted an eyebrow.

"A faker of the worst sort," said Atatarho. "Nice smoke tricks, though, and I think I might be able to use this dream of his to my advantage." Atatarho pointed with his bony index finger. "There is Hiawatha. Sitting at the head of the circle, wearing the antlers."

"Where are his daughters?"

"His daughters?"

"Yes. I will take my revenge through them."

"But I thought you would want to torture and kill Hiawatha, your son's murderer."

"Later," said Shadahgoh. "First he must suffer as I have suffered. Show me his daughters."

Atatarho paused momentarily, taken aback. This was not what he had counted on. He shook himself and regained his composure. "The two youngest, Tiwi and Memoha, are sitting there on his lap."

"Yes, I see them. Which one holds the dog?"

"That is Memoha, nine summers old. Look over there, at the far edge of where the young women sit. The one that is laughing, with the soft skin and the plain buckskin dress. That is Hiawatha's daughter, Seawa."

"Lovely," said Shadahgoh. "Soon that soft skin will rot away like old meat eaten by maggots."

"And over there, the pretty, slender girl in the white dress trimmed with quills. The one craning her neck to look at that foolish young flute player. Do you see her?"

"Yes. Which one is she?"

"That is Sovana, the oldest. If you could spare her, my nephew, Osinoh, who led you here, has his eyes on her."

"That is his problem. I intend to make Hiawatha pay heavily for his crime."

"How many of his children, then, do you intend to take in retribution?"

"How many? I intend to kill them all. He took away all of my children, Mahtewan, my only son, the pride of the Seneca nation. My son's life is worth more than all the lives of Hiawatha's daughters combined. No amount of dead girls could ever equal the worth of my son. So I will take all four of them. I will kill them and scalp them and burn their bodies and feed their cooked flesh and charred bones to my dogs. And you and your people may count yourselves lucky that I do not kill everyone and burn this village to the ground."

Chapter Four

A chorus of voices from the men, women, and children joined
Kewahtawa chanting to the beat of the handheld drums and the
water drums, and in counterpoint to the high-pitched flute notes
rising and falling above them like invisible birds in the night air.
The sweet notes of Orios' flute stood out from among the rest. Or,
at least it seemed so to Sovana, who could not take her eyes off the
boy. In between the chanting chorus of the people, Kewahtawa
created verses that further told the Dream of Dekanawida:

     "From the land of great visions
     Beyond the land of our grandfathers
     Beyond the land of our grandmothers
     Beyond the land of our ancestors
     In the forest of great stars
     Lived Dekanawida.
     And he saw that the stars were wise.
     He saw that the stars knew what they should do
     And what they should not do.
     And Dekanawida lived among man.
     And Dekanawida saw that man was not wise.
     He saw that man knew not what he should do
     Or what he should not do.

     "For the Sky Woman gave birth to a daughter
     On the back of the Great Turtle

And Sky Woman and Sky Woman's Daughter
Walked in circles
On the back of the Great Turtle
Causing the earth to grow.
Then from the east came a mysterious man
Who took two arrows from his golden quiver
And laid them across the sleeping daughter.
And when the daughter awoke
She felt twins growing inside her.
And these twins argued with each other
And fought each other
Even before they were born
So that her belly became a battleground
And the right-handed twin
Slid from Sky Daughter's womb
And she saw that he was good
But the left-handed twin
Gave his mother so much pain
That she died as he pushed his way out
Through her side, beneath her left arm.

And the twins grew up with great powers,
The right-handed twin created
The tall white pine,
The tree that is always green.
But the left-handed twin
Filled it with knots and boles.
The right-handed twin
Created the running river —
The river that runs both ways
So that one may paddle up or down with ease,
But the left-handed twin
Filled it with sharp rocks.

And the twins quarreled, always quarreled,
And so it was when they were full-grown.
To put an end to their quarreling,
They challenged each other to a battle,
The great battle to see who would rule the earth.

And the sun went down and the sun came up
But the battle raged on
And the trees were trembling
And the mountains were shaking
And the blows fell left and right.
Then remembering the goodness
In his mother's pure heart,
And her early death
Caused by his brother,
The right handed twin
Struck a blow so hard
It knocked his brother
All the way through
To the other side of the earth . . ."

The drums crashed and Orios played a long, cacophonous flute-squeal. Tiwi and some of the other younger children let out long gasps of dismay. The adults smiled at their children's innocence, but they also remembered when they first heard this story themselves, the story of their own creation, the story of how the people came to inhabit this place called Turtle Island.

"And so it is that every man has within him
Both good and evil.
No matter how good a person may seem
There is always some evil
That hides in his heart,
Evil that must be controlled

Without the arrows that tear the heart apart
Without the clubs of war
That break the bones of the people
Or the battles
That shake the mountain tops
Or the pain and tortures
Inflicted in the name of vengeance.

And no matter how
Dark the heart,
How black the soul,
No one is entirely evil.
For there is always
A portion of light
That hides somewhere
In a dark corner of the heart . . .

And so it is that the Great Spirit sent
Dekanawida
Into the womb of a woman
Who had lain not with man
And he was born
To walk with the West Wind
And to observe the ways of the people.
And what he saw
Made him weep with sorrow.
And a great pain
Filled his heart.

Then the East Wind took Dekanawida
To the top of a great mountain
Where Dekanawida worked out a plan,
A plan for a new nation,
The New Nation of Man

Where all men are brothers
And the tomahawks are laid down
And the voices of wisdom prevail
And the song of the nation
Is a song of peace and cooperation.

And the Great Spirit said to Dekanawida:
I will send you a great chief
From the far side of the Silver Lakes
In the land of yellow corn
From the people of the hills
From the Clan of the Great Turtle,

And his name is . . ."

Kewahtawa shook his turtle-shell rattle over his head, then leveled it horizontally and turned in a circle, shaking the outstretched rattle at everyone seated around the fire. The drums and flutes stopped. All that could be heard was the crackling of the fire and the steady rattling of the shell. All eyes were on Kewahtawa, including those outside the stockade, high up in the Sentry Tree. All ears were open, waiting for Kewahtawa's pronouncement, including the ears outside the walls, the ears of betrayer and enemy.

"And his name is . . . Hiawatha!"

Kewahtawa pointed the turtle-shell rattle at the seated chief. Tiwi's and Memoha's eyes grew large and frightened as their father jumped back, half-leaping to his feet. The girls moved away from their father who now stood up; they huddled together for protection against the magic of the shaman's spell. A look of shock and disbelief came over Hiawatha's normally calm and placid face. Instinctively he looked over at the seated matriarchs, the Clan Mothers, and he saw Makahwah looking at him, her eyes large and round and glistening in the fire's glow.

"Hiawatha!" shouted the voices of the people seated around the fire.

Kewahtawa continued in the same ritualistic chant.

> "And Hiawatha will teach
> The Laws of Dekanawida
> Across the land of the Silver Lakes
> To all the people on Turtle Island.
> He will preach the good word
> To all the warring nations.
> To the Cayuga,
> To the Oneida,
> To the Mohawk,
> To the Seneca,
> He will bring the teachings of Dekanawida.
> Hiawatha will bring all the nations together
> To plant the Great Tree of Peace."

Many people leaped to their feet around the fire and chanted their leader's name: "Hi-a-wa-tha! Hi-a-wa-tha! Hi-a-wa-tha!" Others chanted the name of Dekanawida; still others repeated the new and unfamiliar phrase that came from Kewahtawa's Dream: "Great Tree of Peace! Great Tree of Peace!" The drums began again, and the flutes soared above them in ecstatic counterpoint, and a new feeling of vital energy and raw excitement filled the air.

The sound of the chanted names of the chief and of the prophet Dekanawida floated on the air outside the village walls and filtered up through the branches of the Sentry Tree, reaching the ears of Shadahgoh and Atatarho.

"You are right, Atatarho. This Kewahtawa is no wise man. He is a woman. His weak mind is filled with weak thoughts of peace. Peace is not the way of the Seneca. We settle our affairs the way our ancestors have always settled theirs, through war. War is a man's way. It is the way of the people."

Atatarho nodded his head, but he did not reply. He was troubled. There was something unsettling, something vaguely familiar about this dream of Kewahtawa. It put him on edge and took away some of the confidence that he had placed in his plans, especially this new turn of events with Shadahgoh. Why didn't he just kill Hiawatha and get it over with? And now a prophet foretelling through a dream-vision that Hiawatha would become the greatest chieftain of all the nations? It was unthinkable. He would not allow it to happen. He needed a backup plan. Some other magic that would solidify his scheme. But, on the other hand, what if Hiawatha were to undertake this ridiculous venture? It would get him out of the picture for some time to come, perhaps indefinitely. He simply could not succeed in such a folly. Or could he? He scrambled down the tree, leaving Shadahgoh alone, and sought out his nephew.

"Osinoh. Come here."

"Yes, Uncle? How may I serve you?" The young man smiled and bent his head in a facetious attitude of servility.

"Don't mock me, boy, or I'll turn you into a toad and grind your bones into a death-potion."

"Yes, Uncle."

"I want you to do something for me. Something that is not without a certain risk. It will take daring, speed, cunning, and stealth."

"Qualities that I possess in ample measure. What would you have me do?"

"I want you to steal something."

"Theft! I'm shocked, Uncle. I thought you held me in higher esteem."

"This is no ordinary theft. I want you to remove something of great importance. Something that is invaluable to those who possess it."

"What is this great treasure you want me to steal?"

"The Great Turtle Shell of the Turtle Clan hanging in Makahwah's longhouse."

Osinoh did not speak for a moment. He breathed in deeply and tried to match the intensity of Atatarho's staring eyes. He broke away and lifted his eyes upward. The full moon was sailing high in the night sky, scudding past dark billowing clouds, creating shadows that made a face seem to appear momentarily on her silver surface. The face appeared to be weeping, or frowning, or perhaps ruefully smiling. Osinoh could not tell. He knew, as everyone knew, that the ancient clan totems contain heavy *orenda*, great spiritual, social, and political capital. The Great Turtle Shell, the symbolic soul of the Turtle Clan, was said to be a descendant of the Great Turtle, upon whose back life for the people began. For this reason alone, the shell held tremendous magical powers.

Finally, Osinoh cleared his throat and said, "This is a heavy deed you ask me to perform."

"It is no heavier than betraying your chief."

"I did not betray him. This is justice. He is paying for the crime he committed. It's better than innocent people in our village paying for it."

"If that's what you think."

"Why do you want to remove the totem?"

"I have my reasons. When you need to know, then I will tell you."

"It seems to me, Uncle, that a crime of this magnitude should have a reward equally magnanimous."

"Name it then. It shall be yours."

"Get me Sovana."

"Ask for something else. You could have any girl in the village. Many far prettier."

"I know that. But I want her. Do you forget our bargain? You said Makahwah 'would be more than willing for Sovana to marry me.' Those were your exact words."

"Very well. I'll make the arrangements myself."

"Do you promise?"

"You have my word."

"And the turtle shell will be returned when all this business is finished?"

"We will return it when you marry Sovana."

"Then I'll do it."

"Good. But it must be done tonight. Everyone is still at the Feast of Dreams. Kewahtawa's vision has worked them all up, and there will be dancing and telling of visions for a few more hours. Go now. Be swift and bold. Do not hesitate. When you have the shell, bring it back to my hut. And make sure that no one sees you."

Osinoh dashed off into the night toward the stockade walls of the village. Atatarho smiled to himself. This was a bargain easily won. *Osinoh knows nothing of Shadahgoh's plans for Sovana. How does one barter for a dead bride? My nephew's reward will be the knowledge that he has played a small but important part in the destiny of his people, by furthering the rise of the next great Sorcerer Chieftain of all the Nations. May he live long enough to tell his grandchildren that he was a warrior who played his part well in the rise of the great Atatarho.*

Osinoh walked toward the sound of the music coming from the center of the village, where the festival was now in full swing. He knew that right now was the opportune moment to slip unobserved into the longhouse of Makahwah, but he had to be certain that everyone was still around the fires, that all were accounted for. Besides, he needed to look at Sovana again. He needed to see her beautiful face; he needed to see the reason why he was about to commit this heavy deed, this act of sacrilege. As he reached the center, he could see the dancing shadows of women and girls thrown across the ground between himself and the roaring fire. The women and girls danced and twirled as they swayed and moved in a circle around the leaping flames. The drums beat out the rhythm of one of the great social songs that always accompanied a festival. The women, young and old, sang and chanted the words in unison as they circled the fire. Orios played a gay and lively tune that matched the joyous lyrics of the women and girls whose song celebrated the oneness of life, the oneness of all creation:

> "We are the source of the people,
> We are the birds in the trees,
> We are the fish in the waters,
> We are the bees of the meadow,
> We are the women who are strong.
>
> We are one with the spirits that walk beside us,
> We are the eagle's mighty wing,
> We are the women who are strong.
>
> We are one with our sisters:
> We are the spirit of the corn,
> The blossoms on the squash,
> The vines of the bean,
> We are the women who are strong.
>
> We are one with the spirits who walk beside us,
> We are the dreams of all our people,
> We are all who have walked before us,
> We are all who will walk in the future,
> We are the flowing rivers of time,
> We are the women who are strong."

As Orios played, his eyes were always on Sovana, and her eyes were on him. As she danced and twirled and sang around the fire, she kept Orios always in her eyesight, and he kept her in his.

She danced for Orios and Orios played the flute for her. It was apparent to anyone who cared enough to notice that these two were deeply in love, and they did not care who saw or watched.

From the shadows at the edge of the crowd, Osinoh saw that their eyes were locked upon each other's. His mind burned with a rage against Orios, this young whelp who could do nothing but play notes on a hollow stick. *Why does she waste her time on him? I will cure her of this affliction that affects her judgment.*

When the music ceased, the women stopped dancing and they all laughed and clapped their hands. Seawa twirled around, laughing and dancing while Sovana was mesmerized by Orios. As the women began to leave the circle, Seawa pulled her entranced sister away from the circle around the fire, for now it was time for the men's dancing. Men, young and old, and boys as well, entered the circle as the drums began to beat again in rhythmic staccato. Orios put his flute down and walked away from the musicians toward the group of young women where Sovana stood beside her sister. She saw him coming and slipped away to meet him.

Osinoh saw this, and his mind became black with a rage against both of them. He watched as Sovana melted up against Orios who put his hand up to her face and brushed a few strands of stray hair back from her eyes. He watched as Sovana strained upward and whispered something into Orios' ear. He saw the sparkle in her eyes and the smile on her face. He watched them looking around to see if anyone observed them. He ducked behind the corner of a longhouse to avoid their eyes, and then he watched them, hand in hand, moving toward the gate of the palisaded village. He watched their backs until he could watch no longer. Then, his face burning, he turned and ran away from the council fires, away from the center of the village, toward the longhouse of Makahwah.

The men were dancing the eagle dance. The sounds of the drums and the warriors' shrill cries faded by increments as the two lovers ran, hand in hand, across the village, through the narrow entrance of the palisade, and across the stretch of open land that led to the forest. And as they ran, they laughed out loud with joy and anticipation. But their laughter was tinged with apprehension. The farther away they fled from the village, the darker the night became around them. They ran past the planted fields of corn and squash and beans. They could hear the wind sighing through the corn, rustling the green arms of the tall swaying plants. And they could see, out of the corners of their eyes, the moving shadows of the three sisters, alive and growing in the moonlight. In the darkness, the tall stalks almost looked human, like warriors, arms open to scoop them up and carry them off.

A noise in the cornrows startled them and they stopped running, their breath choking back down to their lungs, afraid to exhale because the sound might betray them. Then they saw the gleaming eyes of a possum as he clumsily emerged from the dark, secretive foliage. They both let out long sighs of relief, laughed, and began to run again.

When they reached the edge of the forest, they collapsed onto the ground into each other's arms. Breathing heavily, they watched the stars glittering through the leaves of the trees swaying softly above them in the breeze, forming a lacy canopy. Orios leaned up on one elbow and gently stroked Sovana's face. She looked at him with yearning in her bright, glistening eyes. He kissed her on the forehead. Sovana closed her eyes and felt herself transported to a land beyond the clouds. He moved his lips along her forehead and kissed her closed eyelids. She saw an explosion of brilliantly colored lights and moaned softly. He moved his lips along her soft cheek and lightly brushed her lips with his. He cupped her face in his hands.

"Oh Sovana, you're so beautiful. I can't look at you without my heart racing."

She ran her fingers through his hair and down the side of his face, then pulled him closer to her until their lips met. Orios felt an otherworldly music engulf them as he breathed through her, like playing his flute, only now with a divine instrument. He felt her heart beating against his, in perfect tempo as though they had merged as one. And then the soft rhythms began to intensify.

They lay in each other's arms for hours, Orios with his head buried in Sovana's hair, intoxicated by its fragrance, his arms wrapped around her slender shoulders. The odor of musky peach blossoms hung in the still night air. The sounds of the wind whispering through the white pines seemed to speak a magic language in the long and lovely night, and he heard these great white pines whisper his love's name over and over again, calling out to her in hushed tones as if they wanted to hold her in their long-leaved branches or tell her some desperate secret that only they knew: *So-va-na . . . So-va-na . . . So-va-na . . .*

A crow called nearby, breaking the love-spell that wrapped itself around them like soft fur. Orios raised himself up and peered through the woods. Neither of them wanted the dawn to come. But the first gray light was already coloring the horizon and the birds were beginning to sing, joyously greeting the dawn of a new day.

"Listen, Sovana. The birds are singing a love-song for us. They sing of how happy we are and how happy we will always be with each other."

A crow cawed on the other side of the cornfield. Another one answered him. Sovana felt an ominous threat. She had often heard the crows talk harshly, but they had never frightened her before. Orios sensed the danger too. Sovana stood up and smoothed out the wrinkles in her dress.

"We must hurry back to the village. We have stayed too long."

Chapter Five

Morning comes all too soon the night after a great festival. The first gray light of dawn filtered down through the smoke holes in the rooftops of the longhouses of the Onondaga village. The first bright twittering of birds sounded throughout the forest, creating a joyful noise that echoed inside the stockade walls, opening sleepy eyes, causing many to stretch their tired limbs and smile in spite of a lack of rest. There would be two more long nights of feasting. Many were reluctant to rise. They needed to renew their strength for this evening's festivities. Recounting dream-visions and the tales of one's ancestors was hard work. So too was eating and drumming and dancing and chanting many hours into the night.

In the longhouse of Makahwah, Hiawatha lay on his mat on a raised platform with his eyes wide open, staring at the shafts of new light streaking down from the roof to the mat-covered floor. His mind was troubled by the strange dream of Kewahtawa. What did it mean? Why had he been singled out to wander through the world preaching the peace-vision of some obscure Mohawk holy man? It made no sense. If it were anyone but Kewahtawa, he would have dismissed it as fantasy. But Makahwah's husband was famed throughout the nation as a man of true vision, a man whose inner sight was pure.

He liked the idea of this Tree of Peace, even though the notion was an alien one. Disputes between nations had always been settled by armed conflict. It was the Way. It was the age-old struggle that had always continued ever since the twins first fought. But does it have to be this way? Perhaps, as in Kewahtawa's vision, there was a way to end all the bloodshed, the constant blood feuds that take so many lives, that took the life of Tamora, his beloved wife, the mother of his children. Makahwah had never completely forgiven her husband for the small part he had played in the events that led up to Tamora's death in a blood revenge. In the near distance, on the other side of the longhouse, he saw a face staring at him. He jumped up on one elbow as a cold chill ran up his spine. It was the face of Tamora! Those large eyes, like a fawn's, those high cheekbones above full lips and the whole lovely face surrounded by thick and lustrous jet-black hair. How beautiful she was. How much he loved her.

"Hiawatha!" she screamed. "Hiawatha, help me! Save me! They are flaying me alive! Look how they have hurt me!"

The face in the dim and shifting light came closer and he could now see a large, open gash streaming with blood from hairline to chin. The face came closer and closer until it hovered directly before him.

"No! No!" he cried aloud, covering his eyes with his arms.

"Father! Father, wake up!" It was the voice of Seawa, now kneeling above him, her face just a foot away. There was no blood in her hair, no wound on her smiling face.

"Oh, my girl," said Hiawatha as he wrapped his arms around her and drew her to his breast. "I thought you were your mother, coming back to me alive and wounded."

"You were dreaming, Father."

"Yes, yes, it must be. But it was so real." He kissed her forehead. The light was now getting brighter in the longhouse and others were beginning to stir. Women were rising to tend to the fires that needed to be stoked again for today's preparations.

"Father?" whispered Seawa in a trembling voice.

"What is it, my child?" Hiawatha held her face with both of his strong hands.

"What will you do?"

"Do? About what?"

"About Kewahtawa's vision. Will you go away?"

"No," replied Hiawatha. "I will not leave you and your sisters alone." Seawa hugged her father and buried her head in his shoulder so that he would not see the tears welling up in her eyes. Tiwi bounded awake and jumped over to the two of them, clutching a corn-husk doll to her childish breast.

"Father," she cried. "You woke up my doll! She is angry with you! See, she is crying real tears."

Hiawatha laughed and swept the little girl up in his left arm. "Oh my, what a bad man your father is! Here, let me kiss the tears away." Tiwi laughed as her father kissed the face of her ragged doll.

"But Grandmother says that you must honor Kewahtawa's dream," persisted Seawa in a hoarse half-whisper.

"Let Uncle Kewahtawa go find Dekanawida himself. He's the one who keeps dreaming of him."

"Who is Dekanawida?" Tiwi asked in a loud voice.

Across the central walkway of the longhouse, Makahwah turned from where she was rising up from her mat. "Ssh, little one," she said in a loud mock-whisper. "Some of the people are still sleeping." She fixed her eyes on her son-in-law until he was forced to look away. Hiawatha, chief of the Onondaga, was not easily intimidated, but Makahwah was a strong and formidable Clan Mother, and in her cold and steady stare he read the collective will and fierce determination of the people of the Turtle Clan, the most ancient of all clans, whose ancestor was the Great Primordial Turtle upon whose back all life began. Clan membership was determined through the mother's line, so Hiawatha's daughters were all members of the Turtle Clan like their mother and their grandmother, while he, when he married Tamora, left his mother's Deer Clan longhouse and entered into the longhouse of Makahwah.

For this reason, women held great power among the people.

True, men were the chieftains and warriors and shamans, but it was through the consent and approval of the Clan Mothers that the men ruled. If it was truly Makahwah's will that Hiawatha should fulfill the dream-vision of Kewahtawa and leave his daughters and his people to set out on a quest to find this prophet Dekanawida, then that is what he must do. Either that or risk being stripped of all his power by the Clan Mothers.

What bothered him most was that he had not had any dreams of Dekanawida. He had always followed his own dream-visions. If the Great Spirit desired that he should find Dekanawida, why had he not also received a dream or a vision? What was Makahwah up to? Was she trying to get rid of him? After the accidental killing of the Seneca boy, did she think that he was now a danger to the people?

Hiawatha shuddered, then stood up and stretched. He watched as Seawa and Tiwi went to their grandmother to see what they could do to help prepare for the night's festivities. He looked behind him to check on his other two daughters. Beneath a lacrosse stick and a corn-husk False Face hanging on the wall, Memoha was curled up on her mat, her brown, dimpled knees almost touching her chin, still asleep with her black and white puppy lying across her feet. Sovana was nowhere in sight. He glanced up and down the longhouse, but he did not see her. Immediately the face of Orios popped into his mind's eye. Could she have stayed out all night with that scamp? It was a difficult position. He wanted his daughter to be happy, and it was clear that she was in love with the young flute player, the dreamer, the composer of romantic tunes. And he, in turn, in spite of what his powerful mother-in-law thought, loved the boy almost like a son. It was unlikely, thought Hiawatha, that the lad would ever become a warrior. Not even an average hunter. Only yesterday when he watched him practicing his aim with bow and arrow, more often than not he missed the swinging corn-husk target. But, still, there was something about him, something endearing.

He knew what Sovana, sensitive, lovely Sovana, saw in his eyes, the eyes of an artist. But they were so young. His mind traveled back to when he was their age, and he remembered his own love for Tamora. How, every time he saw her, his heart swelled up like it was going to burst apart in his chest. How shy they were with each other the first time. The hot breath and flushed faces, the pounding, burning blood racing through their young veins. They were not much older then than Sovana and Orios are now. What happened? Where did it all go? Tamora, I miss you so much. I feel a vacant ache in a place deep inside of me. A place that is empty. No, not completely empty. Never fully empty; for there is a corner in that place where you will always be.

A scream pierced the early morning air shattering the calm in the longhouse. "Hiawatha!" shrieked Makahwah. People leaped to their feet, frightened awake by the awful cry. Hiawatha turned to where the Clan Mother stood, pointing toward the rafters in the center of the house, a look of horror frozen on her face.

"It's gone! The clan totem is gone!"

Hiawatha looked up to where the huge, ancient turtle shell always hung, suspended from a wide wampum belt, reminding the dwellers of this longhouse that the Clan Mother of the ancient Turtle Clan dwelt here. The sacred shell was a religious, cultural, and political symbol, a sign of the unity and vitality of the Turtle Clan. It was their great talisman, the source from which the nourishing rivers of their power flowed. And much of Makahwah's power was derived from the magical *orenda* that clung to the ancient shell. The shell that was now gone.

Makahwah frantically ran in circles around the longhouse searching every square foot of ground beneath the rafters for any trace of the shell. She tore up every mat, uncovered every pot, and kicked aside all skins and furs. Everyone was awake now and whispering or talking excitedly. Where could the great shell have gone? Could someone have taken it down, stolen a sacred object during a holy festival? It was unthinkable. It must be witchcraft, sorcery. One of their enemies cast a spell, drew the shell to him in the middle of the night. It was the full moon, and the Feast of Dreams, a magical festival when anything can happen.

"Who has taken the shell?" demanded Makahwah in her most authoritative voice. No one answered. She moved from person to person in the longhouse, asking each man, woman, and child the same question: "What do you know about this?" She searched their eyes for any sign of lying, for any signs of nervousness. Satisfied that all told the truth, she turned toward the chieftain, Hiawatha, and raised both eyebrows questioningly.

Hiawatha exhaled and collected his thoughts. "Tonight is still the Festival of Dreams. We will continue with our plans. But before the night is old we will convene an open meeting of the Council. The people will debate this matter and we will jointly determine what course of action to take. I will seek the aid of our most gifted shamans and sorcerers. If we cannot find an answer through the power of our intellects, we may find one through divination, through contact with the spirits who walk among us. One of our spirit brothers or sisters may have seen what has happened." Hiawatha looked at Makahwah to see if his plan met with her approval.

Tears welled up in her eyes and her chin began to quiver. She bit her lower lip in an effort to maintain her composure, but her shoulders began to tremble with the force of holding back the flood of sorrow that threatened to break loose any minute. Hiawatha remembered how Makahwah placed the great shell on Tamora's swollen belly when she labored to give birth to Sovana. He could see in his mind's eye how Tamora hugged the turtle shell to her breast. The *orenda* of the shell had a soothing power that made the birth easier. And then he remembered how Makahwah had held the shell against her own heart when Tamora was buried.

Makahwah straightened herself up with great dignity and cleared her throat. "We will do as Hiawatha counsels," she said. "In good time, we will find out who has done this wickedness. Let us now continue with our preparations for the feast."

As the people of her longhouse, all now fully awake, dispersed to perform their daily tasks and duties, Hiawatha could hear murmurs and grumbling.

"Sorcery. What else could it be?"

"No. It's the Seneca. That's the only answer."

"Yes. The Seneca. Preparing for a blood revenge."

"Hiawatha's fault."

"Killed the Seneca boy."

"Hiawatha . . . Hiawatha . . ."

He picked up his bow and quiver and strode out of the longhouse. Something was shaking inside of him, in a place so deep that he could not identify its source. He would visit Atatarho in his sorcerer's hut of bones sitting on the edge of the swamp. He must make sure that this powerful shaman was present tonight to perform a divination, to speak with the spirits of the dead who walk among us, who are as silent as shadows, but whose eyes see many things that we in the world of the living do not, whose ghost-eyes see things that we will see only when we have joined them in the otherworld, the land of shadows. Often he wished he were in the land of the dead ones. Then he could see and walk with Tamora. They would drift together, their spirits entwined, across the surface of the earth and the waters. They would fly together over the treetops, skimming the uppermost tips of the highest mountain pines, their hearts soaring together, one with the mighty white-headed eagle, inseparable in death. Their lives and love renewed, resurrected in death.

"One day, my love," he whispered. "One day."

Chapter Six

Outside the high village walls, the women worked the fields in the cool hours before the sun would be straight up in the sky. Seawa and Sovana stood in a field of waist-high corn loosening the soil around each plant with long-handled, stone-tipped hoes, just the right size and shape to till the soil without disturbing the precious roots. Each cultivated field was composed of interdependent inter-plantings of the three sisters: corn, bean, and squash. The stalk of the tall and stately sister corn was a support for the climbing sister bean to cling to, to wrap herself around. In the rows between the corn plants with their climbing sisters, grew the low-lying, earth-covering, broad-leaved protector-sisters, the squash. Her canopy of leaves protected the roots, holding moisture in the soil. The three sisters grew together in harmony.

The women sang and talked and laughed as they carefully uprooted weeds and watered their sisters. They not only sang and laughed and talked to each other, they sang to their sisters, the green and golden corn plants. They talked to their sisters, the beautiful, tender, climbing bean, twirling upward, caressing the corn, dancing in the breeze. And they laughed with their laughing sisters, the broad-leaved, cool and shady squash, who hummed a melody of her own, a song of love for the earth and her creatures.

Birds flew in and out of the fields singing. Crows cried their raucous caw. Tiwi lay on her belly beneath the corn plants, among the leafy squash, and watched as a praying mantis swayed like a shaman on a bean leaf, ready to pounce on a beetle. Seawa hoed the mound of dirt at the base of the corn stalk, careful not to disrupt the bean roots. Her hoe unearthed a decomposing fish. She prodded her little sister with the end of her hoe.

"Tiwi. Look at this fish. Someone didn't plant it deep enough. It must be at least this deep." Seawa showed her sister how deep the fish should be placed so it would decompose at just the right rate to fertilize and nourish the soil, providing nutrients for the three sisters. Tiwi continued to stare at the swaying mantis, who suddenly sprang upon the hapless beetle.

"Tiwi! Are you listening to me?" The little girl nodded as she watched the jaws on the green triangle of the mantis' face open and close, eating the stunned beetle. Seawa shook her head in mock exasperation. "You are hopeless, little girl. Do you know that? If you don't pay attention to what I tell you, how can you hope to grow up to be a tender of the three sisters?"

"I don't know," said Tiwi as she stood up, brushed off the dust from the front of her deerskin dress, and ran off to find her sister Memoha, who was rolling in the grass with her puppy beside a stand of tall sunflowers. Bees walked in circles around the intricate mandalas of the huge central eyes of the flowers that shimmered in the golden sunlight.

Four guards were posted around the edge of the cornfield and by the edge of the forest. All the talk of blood revenge and the sudden, mysterious disappearance of the Turtle Clan's totem had made the people nervous, and so Makahwah demanded that warriors accompany the women to the fields to stand guard while they worked. One of the guards, Haka, a wiry, scarred veteran of many battles, was unconcerned with the ill omens that befell the Turtle Clan. He was of the Wolf Clan. Their ancient wolf skin and wolf's teeth were not missing. But, nonetheless, he felt edgy. Many times he thought he saw or heard movement in the forest, but each time he looked, he saw nothing but shadows and squirrels. He became increasingly suspicious when he began hearing the calls and answers of crows, but could not see any of the black birds flying in the fields. There! Another loud caw. And another. They seemed to come from within the forest. Haka removed his ironwood war club from the hemp belt around his waist and moved away from the field to investigate the woods.

Within the village walls, Hiawatha walked among his people. Women were building fires and dressing birds and small game to roast on spits over open flame. Some of the more ambitious young warriors were making arrowheads or ax heads from pieces of flint and stone. Others amused themselves by tossing deer buttons, gambling away what few possessions they owned, or playing *gus-ka-eh*, a game with six black and white peach stones rolled in and tossed out of a wooden bowl. A group of boys were trying to throw a painted javelin through a moving hoop, a game that was too advanced for them, but it was good that they started young. Hand-eye coordination was a skill learned only through continual practice, and its mastery often meant whether your family was well-fed or went hungry. Or whether you lived or died in a conflict with your enemies.

Underneath all of these routine activities, there lurked a hollow feeling. Usually the people went about their daily tasks more joyfully, especially during a festival. But the joy seemed missing now. Word had spread about the bad magic in Makahwah's longhouse. And Hiawatha sensed a certain discomfort or nervousness that some people felt in his presence. Was it this strange dream of Kewahtawa's? Was it the rumor of a blood revenge? Teom, now somewhat recovered from his strange seizure at the last council meeting, sat cross-legged on the ground surrounded by bits of flint and stones. He was attempting to make a flint knife. But each time he bore down on the flint with the antler shaping-tool, it sheared off at the wrong angle.

"I am cursed, Hiawatha. I used to make good knives from flint. Bad medicine is in my eyes. Or my fingers."

Hiawatha sat down beside him. "Here," he said. "Perhaps I can help." He took the sharp piece of antler and the piece of flint from Teom. He folded a piece of deer hide several times and placed it on his knee.

"If you fold the pad like this, and place it on your knee, not your thigh, you can exert more force. Also, it helps if you hold the antler like this, with your thumb on top. That way you have more leverage." Then he began working the antler up and down the edge of the flint, sheering off small pieces at just the right angle. He handed the pad, flint, and antler back to Teom. "How's this for a start?"

"Is there anything the great Hiawatha cannot do?" There was a slight edge in his voice.

"My mother-in-law and her husband want me to start a new nation."

"If anyone can do it, you can. I hear your mother-in-law is making a new pair of snow shoes for you."

"I won't leave my daughters and wander the earth based on the dream of an old man."

"A *wise* old man, Hiawatha."

"True, Teom. I didn't mean to insult one of our elders."

"Dreams are powerful, Hiawatha. Don't ever forget that. Perhaps I will have a dream and the Great Spirit will tell me that we must send your *mother-in-law* in search of Dekanawida." Hiawatha laughed out loud, and Teom joined him, pleased by his joke that lightened the mood within the village walls for a brief moment.

"Teom, what do you think happened to the great turtle shell?"

Teom shrugged his shoulders and looked at the ground. He picked up a piece of flint and ran his rough finger along its edge. "Who can say? Perhaps there is a curse now on the Turtle Clan."

"Perhaps. I will seek the advice of Atatarho." A chill went up Teom's spine at the mention of the sorcerer's name.

"Be careful of that one, Hiawatha. He is a powerful man, but there is a streak of evil in him, something wicked buried deep in his soul. He is no friend to you."

"I'll be careful, old friend. I'll see you later at the Feast. We will hold a special council concerning the missing totem."

Makahwah approached them. "Hiawatha," she said, "we need to talk. Now."

Haka moved through the trees and underbrush in the forest at the edge of the planting field. The laughter and singing of the women and girls grew fainter. It was cooler in the shade of the woods, but, nonetheless, sweat formed on his forehead and on his upper lip. He knew that he was not alone in these woods, and it was not merely the presence of the spirits of the dead. He had thrust his war club through the belt around his waist and had unslung his bow from across his shoulder. He jumped in the direction of a sound of crackling brush coming from his right, and fitted the notch of an arrow on his bowstring. He did not see the blow from a war club that came from behind him and smashed his skull. He dropped like a bag of stones, dead on the floor of the forest. Shadahgoh stood above him and withdrew his antler-handled stone knife from its rawhide sheath. He dropped to one knee, grabbed Haka's bloody hair in his left hand, and made an incision with his knife all the way around his skull, slicing through the forehead and temples. He pulled the skin back, ripping it off the head. Then he held the hair and scalp dripping with blood high above him so that his warriors could see, and beckoned them to follow him to the edge of the woods. He tucked his grisly war prize into his breech-clout waistband, and pointed to two of the young girls in the distance, one straight ahead, tending a corn plant with her hoe, and another, younger one to their right, laughing and playing with a dog.

"Matandah, you and your band take the young one over there by the sunflowers. Dispatch the guard first, but do not lose sight of the girl. We will take care of the others. Move quickly."

Matandah, one of Shadahgoh's war captains, looked at his chieftain through eyes surrounded by large circles of black paint. A red streak ran vertically down his forehead, along the length of his nose, bisecting his thin lips and pointed chin. The whites of his eyes, set off by the blackness, gleamed, and his pupils were narrowed down to pinpoints. He removed an arrow from his quiver and fit the notch onto his bowstring. He jerked his shaved, yellow-painted head in the direction of the girls and began to run, followed by his band of six warriors brandishing stone tomahawks and war clubs.

In the cornfield, Seawa was trying to teach Tiwi not to sit on the young plants. "You wouldn't sit on a baby, would you?" Tiwi shook her head gravely. "Well, that's just what they are, little babies. You must keep your eyes open and be careful of where you step or sit."

"I will keep my eyes open. I will keep my eyes open." Tiwi chanted as she ran to a tree stump and jumped up onto its platform. "Seawa, where is Haka?"

"He's guarding the field, by the edge of the woods."

"I don't see him."

Seawa turned and scanned the edge of the field where it met the woods. A crow cawed loudly. And then she saw the Seneca warriors rushing across the field through the high yellow grass toward Memoha. "Tiwi! Run as fast as you can and climb into the hole of the red fox. Go!" The urgency in her sister's voice frightened her.

"But what if the fox. . ."

"The foxes are gone. Hurry!" Tiwi ran through the corn to where the fox hole was—near the edge of the field. Sovana, and some of the other women heard Seawa's urgent pleas, and turned to see the running warriors. They called to the other guards posted on the other side of the cornfield who came running when they saw their companion posted by the sunflowers drop with an arrow in his chest. Memoha saw it too, but it was too late. As she turned to run back to the corn rows, an arrow from Matandah's bow struck her between the shoulder blades. She felt her insides collapse as another arrow struck her lower down on her back, and yet another pierced her right thigh. She pitched forward, her face ground into the dust. Her puppy yelped and jumped on top of her to play, and a Seneca arrow pinned him to the ground. Seawa ran toward her. Horrified women ran past Seawa in a blind panic back toward the village, screaming for help as they fled.

Sovana reached Seawa and grabbed her by the arm. "Seawa, come on! We must go!"

"But Memoha!"

"Memoha is dead! We must save ourselves! Run!"

Shadahgoh and four warriors were approaching with great speed from out of the forest. An arrow whizzed past Sovana's head.

Hiawatha, Makahwah, and Kewahtawa sat in a small circle on hemp mats in the longhouse, the bright sunshine streaming through the four holes in the roof. Makahwah cleared her throat, and spoke in an even but firm voice. "For many years we have heard stories of Dekanawida and his great laws for peace, but that is all. Only stories. And now, the Great Spirit has sent a message to my husband, Kewahtawa. The message clearly says that you have been chosen to help Dekanawida plant the Tree of Peace."

"Makahwah. Do you know what you are saying? By the time I returned from such a journey, if I returned at all, my daughters would be all grown up."

"Then you can watch your grandchildren grow."

"I must stay here and protect my daughters, or I will not have any grandchildren."

"You must at least travel to the east and see what these new laws are all about. You are only a man, Hiawatha. You cannot go against the will of the Great Spirit."

A great commotion from outside the longhouse made them stop their deliberations. Panicked screams and loud, blood-chilling cries from outside the stockade walls shattered the air in the village. Hiawatha leaped to his feet and ran to the door of the longhouse.

Seawa was momentarily frozen. Sovana gave up her struggle to get her sister to move, and she turned and ran as fast as she could toward the village walls.

Shadahgoh and his men were rapidly shortening the distance between themselves and Seawa. But to her it seemed as though they were running in slow motion. She saw Shadahgoh's huge thigh muscles tense and bulge every time his moccasins touched the ground and sprang back up.

"Memoha!" she screamed, and then she began to run as fast as she could toward the prone, lifeless body of her sister. Perhaps she was not dead, after all. Perhaps she could save her. I must try, she thought.

She kept Shadahgoh's face in her peripheral vision as she ran, but then she saw something that made her stop in her tracks. Running beside him and smiling, her arms open wide, was her mother. Tamora, the daughter of Makahwah, matched the war chief stride for stride. The fringes on the sleeves of her white doeskin dress fluttered in the wind, and her thick, long, jet-black hair trailed behind her. Her eyes exuded love and peace and eager anticipation. Seawa opened her arms to embrace her mother. Shadahgoh and Tamora reached her at the same time.

"Mother!" cried Seawa, as she fell into her warm, open arms, and at the same moment, Shadahgoh's flint-tipped war club slammed into her abdomen. She felt simultaneous stabbing pains of hatred and love. Her mother's face in front of her washed over her eyes in a flood of crimson blood. Shadahgoh swung his war club again, bringing it down on Seawa's face. She felt a terrific shock, and then the universe tilted, and all of life, including hers, was funneled into a small hole somewhere in front of her. Her mother took her by the hand and they traveled through a long tunnel of blood that shone brightly, violet and white, at the very end.

Shadahgoh repeatedly brought his war club down and down and down again on the fragile head and face of the now gone Seawa. Gushes and gouts of blood drenched her dress and splattered the leaves of the trampled corn and beans and squash that only minutes before she had lovingly tended.

An Onondaga war cry pierced the air, and Shadahgoh stopped to look up and see Hiawatha and a band of warriors racing across the field toward them. An arrow zipped past his head and pierced the neck of one of his warriors. Blood spouted upward and the warrior staggered forward and fell, clutching the arrow lodged in his throat. Shadahgoh roared a curse at Hiawatha and the approaching Onondagas.

"Hiawatha! Your blood belongs to me!" Then he turned and ran toward the forest, his men following him. A Seneca warrior, faster than the rest, had caught up with Sovana, halfway between the spot where her sister now lay and where the Onondaga men were running. He sat on top of her and raised his stone hatchet to deliver a skull-crushing blow. Sovana screamed aloud, a scream without words, a scream meant to avert the blow, to forestall the final agony of death. Orios, among the warriors, dropped to one knee, and drew the bowstring fitted with a flint-tipped arrow back to his right cheek. He said a quick prayer to the Great Spirit to guide his missile. His hand, the same one that usually trembled slightly whenever he aimed at a target, was steady now. He sighted along the shaft of the arrow to a spot in the center of the Seneca's naked chest. His fingers released the string and the arrow, and, a heartbeat later, Sovana heard a thump and saw the enemy above her clutching an arrow stuck in his chest. His eyes grew wide with surprise. Then he keeled over on top of her. He reeked of rancid bear fat, and blood was gushing up from his mouth and nostrils. She pushed him off her and got up onto her knees. Orios reached her side and she fell into his arms.

Hiawatha had raced across the meadow, and now knelt on both knees beside his dead and mutilated daughter. He was stunned into sudden inaction. The sight before him was inconceivable. This lifeless corpse was not Seawa. The features of her face were gone, beaten to a raw tangle of blood and bone and torn flesh. It was a horrible nightmare that would soon be over, and he would wake to find his beautiful eleven-year-old girl sitting beside him, laughing gaily. No! This cannot be! It must not be! Hiawatha raised his arms up to the sky as if he were imploring the Great Spirit to reverse this sequence of events, to make this day begin again, to give him back his precious child. He screamed aloud, a long and piercing cry, a wail of anguish from the depths of his being. He clutched Seawa's lifeless, torn body close to him, her blood smearing his face and hair and chest, her spilt life's blood mingling with the salt from the tears that streamed unbidden down his twisted face.

Sovana ran to her father and fell to the ground when she saw Seawa. She threw herself on top of her sister and buried her face in her bloody breast. Orios reached over to put his hand on Hiawatha's shoulder, then pulled back. Tears of shame streamed down his hot cheeks, for he knew that he was to blame. This horrible scene, this tragic waste of life, was all his fault. And Hiawatha, who had been like a father to him, was now paying for his crime.

Teom knelt down next to Hiawatha. "We will avenge the death of your innocent girl."

The other warriors who stood at a respectful distance spoke in assent. "Yes," they said, "Shadahgoh will pay."

Hiawatha seemed to snap out of the grief-trance that held him in its grip. He looked around at the circle of men surrounding him. "I will have Shadahgoh's head! I will feed his eyes to the ravens! His head will adorn the stockade of our village, and the heads of ten of his warriors! The vultures will feed on their entrails!" He leaped to his feet and brandished his stone tomahawk. He ran toward the forest, and his band of warriors, some with bows, some with war clubs, followed him.

Women and children now began cautiously to return to the field, the field that they tended, the field that gave them life, the field that was now the killing field. As she hurried across the planted rows of corn, Makahwah prayed for the safety of her granddaughters. She saw Sovana sitting in the field and breathed a sigh of relief. She smiled and ran to Sovana but stopped dead in her tracks when she saw the lifeless body of Seawa. She let out a piercing scream that seemed to split the sky in half. She grabbed a flint knife from her waist thong and shook it angrily at the sun and the clouds as if she were cursing the world beyond this one for allowing this to happen. Then she pulled a thick length of her long gray hair and sliced it off, wailing and keening loudly. The other women of the village took up her cry and began to wail and keen with her. Seawa was not just the daughter of their chieftain, but a highly respected member of the village. She had touched the lives of all who knew her through her kind and gentle ways.

Sovana raised her head and looked around her. "Where is Tiwi?" Her frightened eyes scanned the field for a sign of her little sister. "Tiwi!" she cried. "Tiwi!"

Tiwi slowly raised her head from the fox hole by the edge of the field. And as she did so, she spied the body of her sister lying on the ground with her grandmother weeping above her.

"Seawa!" she cried as she climbed out of the fox hole and ran toward her beloved sister. Sovana ran toward the little girl. She did not want her to see Seawa's torn and mutilated body. She scooped the small child up into her arms and hugged her close to her breast.

"Seawa! Seawa!" the little girl cried and struggled to get down.

Just as the sound of Sovana's voice calling out for Tiwi echoed in Hiawatha's ears, he and his warriors stumbled upon Memoha's small body lying face down beside the sunflowers, three arrows sticking up from her bleeding back. Her dog lay beside her, pinned to the ground by a Seneca arrow. Hiawatha dropped to his knees beside her. He slowly rolled the child half over.

"Memoha, my child. Can you hear me?"

Memoha tried to answer. "Father?" Her voice was weak. Blood streamed from her small mouth.

"She is alive!" cried out Hiawatha. He thanked the Great Spirit for sparing his little child. But many of the warriors surrounding him knew that she could not live, and they shook their heads or glanced sideways at one another. Teom knelt down beside the dying child and her father, and carefully withdrew one of the arrows. Blood gushed out from the hole in her back. He placed his hand over the wound.

"Father?" asked Memoha. Her eyes were half opened, but glazed over now.

"Yes, my dear girl," said Hiawatha, choking back the tears that now returned to his burning eyes.

"Mother wants me to go now."

"Mother? Where is your mother?"

"There. Beside you."

Hiawatha looked over his right shoulder, then over his left. He saw no one but Teom and his warriors standing all around them.

"I don't see her. Where is she now, my love?"

"There." She tried to lift her arm to point to a spot behind her father, but she could not.

"Good-bye," she said faintly, and then a deep rattle shook her small chest. She became rigid, then relaxed, and her eyes opened wide, a faint smile fixed on her bloodstained lips.

Hiawatha threw his head backwards, his eyes clenched tightly shut. "No . . . no . . . no . . ." he cried softly, praying to the ghost of his wife and all the other Spirit Beings to bring back his child. Teom closed the dead girl's eyes. He put his arm around Hiawatha's shoulder and helped him to his feet.

Inside the longhouse of Makahwah, Sovana placed a large clay pot of clean water next to Memoha's unwashed body. She had just poured out the blood-water from her sister Seawa's body, and watched the blood and water mingle with the earth and the roots of the grasses.

"How quickly the course of life changes," she thought as she adjusted the new pale-white, deerskin dress on Seawa's body lying on a platform beside her younger sister's corpse in the center of the house. It was the way of the people. The way the people showed respect for the dead, who are never really dead. Since they walk among us, thought Sovana, they must be presentable. Their bodies must be clean and they must have new garments to wear. Makahwah had placed a deerskin cloth over Seawa's face. She did not want everyone in the village to see her face the way it was now, destroyed and mutilated. She wanted them to remember her lovely face the way it was just last night when she sat beside her at the Feast of Dreams, a kind and beautiful face, a face that was always filled with love and sympathy.

Drummers sat in a circle at one end of Makahwah's longhouse, their muscular hands rhythmically beating time on their deep-toned water drums to a death chant sung by men and women of the village who had gathered here to mourn the loss of two of their best.

Hiawatha entered the longhouse from the furthest end and walked slowly down the central corridor to the center where Makahwah and Sovana were preparing the body of Memoha. He could not look at anyone. His eyes were fixed on the ground. Tiwi clung to Sovana's skirt with one hand, while the other clutched her corn-husk doll fiercely to her breast as though someone might snatch it away from her. Her clothes and her hands and face were dirty and scratched. She looked up at her father with a confused and solemn expression.

"Mother-in-law? Is there something that I can do?" asked Hiawatha weakly.

"Haven't you done enough already?" Accusation and bitterness were heavy in her voice. She looked up to see the hurt in his eyes and the defeat in his demeanor. "I'm sorry, son-in-law. Go and rest. It will be a long night."

"My mind is spinning. I cannot rest. I must do something or I will go mad."

"Then go and find a new spirit of the False Face. Our house needs to be blessed again."

She looked up to where the clan totem had always hung for as long as she could remember. Now there was only an emptiness. A vacant space left behind where the clan totem-spirits had fled and where evil demons now sought to fill the void. My house is cursed, she thought.

"The old spirits have deserted us. Take Kewahtawa. Go into the forest and find a new spirit for our longhouse." She gestured to Tiwi to come to her. The little girl walked over to her grandmother, her eyes afraid to look anywhere but straight ahead.

"Tiwi, your father needs you now. Go with him and Kewahtawa and help them find a spirit to lead your sisters through the dark forest of the otherworld." She pushed the little girl into Hiawatha's arms. Hiawatha lifted Tiwi up and held her close to his chest. Makahwah turned back to the body of Memoha, tenderly lifting her arm and washing away the blood and dust with a soft cloth made from the tanned skin of a fawn's underbelly. The drums and wailing chants of the death dirge continued as Hiawatha, his small daughter in his arms, and Kewahtawa, Shaman of the Turtle Clan, walked out of the longhouse to seek a new spirit in the forest.

Chapter Seven

At the edge of the swamp, by his hut of mud and bones, Atatarho sat cross-legged, using a hemp-fiber brush to apply a stain made from red ochre dust, bear fat, and sunflower oil to the wooden surface of a newly carved False Face. The features were grotesque. A long, twisted, crooked nose ran almost the entire vertical length of the face and sat above a diagonal downward slash of a mouth that seemed to be grinning and snarling simultaneously. One fang-like tooth, the bulging whites of the eyes, and two beady, protruding pupils further added to the horrific insanity of the expression. Many False Faces were crested and fringed with human hair. But this new mask that Atatarho was fashioning had something unique sewn in among the thick mane of black hair.

Atatarho was a member of the Eel Clan, and he was particularly drawn to reptiles and serpents. He had a large collection of snake bones and snake fangs, and the skins of eels and snakes dangled from the ceiling, ornamenting his hut of bones. In between the shocks of human hair on his mask, Atatarho had cunningly placed the stuffed skins of snakes. Inside these skins were frameworks of supple, specially treated willow branches. Some of the snakes were recoiling upward, curled in a threatening S, their open jaws showing fangs that appeared on the verge of striking. Others reclined downward, partially hidden by the long hair. But when Atatarho put on the mask and shook his head, the snakes seemed to spring to life, bobbing and leaping up and down, outward and backward, making the hair seem like a mass of writhing snakes.

The overall effect was terrifying.

As he slowly worked the stain into the face, careful to avoid the white parts of the fangs and eyes, he hummed and chanted to himself. The hum was the hum of a self-satisfied man; the chant was the chant of victory.

In another part of the forest, Kewahtawa led Hiawatha and Tiwi through a dense stand of majestic and ancient basswood trees. With every step that he took, he shook his turtle-shell rattle in a preordained and ritually prescribed rhythm. Finding the right tree-spirit who would be willing to yield up a face was a very serious and delicate affair. The proper rituals must be observed, and the right words and prayers said before one could take knife and stone chisel to the bark and flesh of the tree, before one could carve (with the tree's permission and with the guidance of the spirit of the tree) just the right features, so that one could lift off of the tree's flesh a mask of grace, subtlety, and spiritual power, a mask that would become a Great False Face with the power to purify evil spirits, a mask heavy with ghost medicine.

Kewahtawa stepped up to a tree and circled it, shaking his rattle and listening intently. He moved from tree to tree, shaking and nodding his head as if he were holding conversations with the resident spirits that lived beneath the springwood, deep within the cambium of the living giants. And the heart-shaped leaves of the basswood trees danced and swayed in answer to the shaman's questions. Hiawatha followed, his mind distracted by the violent deaths of two of his beloved daughters. It is said among the people that a truly wise and heroic chief must have a skin seven thumbs thick. He must be immune to the malicious gossip and criticism of others. He must be immune to the sorrows of his own personal existence, and his only thought must be for the welfare of his people and the well-being of seven generations yet unborn. Hiawatha was neither a wise nor a heroic chief at this moment in time. All he could think of now was the pain caused by his loved ones' deaths. His mind was not on the people and the protection of the earth for seven generations hence; his mind was a raw and bleeding wound throbbing with the ache of a terrible rupture, a violent separation that he still could not bring himself to believe.

He plodded along numbly behind Kewahtawa and Tiwi, who was mesmerized by the conversations that her wise old uncle was having with the trees. She tried this herself, walking up to a stately basswood tree with a curious gnarl shaped like a large nose a little above her eye-level. When she placed her small hand on the knob-like protrusion of bark, she felt an emanation of warmth, and then a sudden surge of energy flowed from the tree's secret veins to the veins in her fingers and hand, and this energy and warmth traveled up her arm and tingled the top of her skull, making her jump with an involuntary reaction. She heard a voice whisper in her ear: *"I am here for you. Take me."* A soft wind seemed to caress her small shoulders.

"Uncle! Father! The tree talks!" Kewahtawa looked over to Tiwi and immediately he could sense that she spoke the truth. The *orenda* of the tree was very strong. With his shaman's eyes, he saw green and violet waves emanating from the trunk where the child's hand still held the protruding bole. The child's body seemed lit up with red and golden flashes. A sparkling light cascaded down from the dancing canopy of leaves high above them, casting a kaleidoscope of shifting designs across her young and eager face.

Children know these things better than adults, thought Kewahtawa. Having been more recently among them, they are closer to the Spirit Beings, and they remember more clearly the words and ways of the otherworldly creatures. He moved to her side and chanted as he shook the turtle-shell rattle. He moved slowly around the tree from left to right, his long gray hair floating in the breeze, asking the tree-spirit to give them a face, to yield up a mask that would redeem the suffering, requicken the dead, and wash clean the evil spirits that had invaded Makahwah's longhouse.

Hiawatha stood as if in a trance and stared at his child and the shaman, barely comprehending what was going on. It was as if he had entered into another dimension, journeyed into another world, the world of stone-dead grief and bone-chilling sorrow.

"Hiawatha!" commanded Kewahtawa in a firm voice. "Bring the tools. It is time to carve the mask."

As Hiawatha moved toward the tree, Kewahtawa took out his fire-making kit and began to make a small fire three feet from its base. As the fire began to burn, he took tobacco out of a pouch that hung over his shoulder and sprinkled dried bits on the fire. A gentle breeze blew in from the east, fanning the flames higher. He knew then that the spirits of the forest were with them. With a hawk's wing, he wafted the smoke toward him and then toward the tree.

"Sister," began Kewahtawa. "Sister tree, within you dwells a strong spirit, a spirit that can heal the evil that has afflicted us. We offer up to you this sacred smoke and we ask you to give up to us the face of the spirit that lives within you. We pray that our knives do not harm you, and with your help we will remove only the spirit-face, not the life-force from your body."

Kewahtawa put the sharpened stone chisel into Hiawatha's left hand and the stone hammer into his right. He pushed him toward the tree, and guided his hands in making the first rough cuts.

A powerful force seemed to take control of Hiawatha's hands and arms, directing them in rapid movements. He was barely aware of his own actions. Some force within him seemed to orchestrate each individual placement of the chisel against the bark and each downward stroke of the mallet. Chips flew away from the bark up into the air, landing in his hair and at his feet. Kewahtawa took the chips and added them to the fire, sprinkling more tobacco and chanting in time to the hypnotic shake of his rattle. Tiwi danced around the tree and helped gather the chips from the ground to add to the smoking fire. Slowly a face emerged from the basswood bark, a face whose features spoke of absolute sorrow and absolute horror. The eyebrows and eyes recalled the expression of someone who has stared long at the frank face of death, the open mouth told a tale of unspeakable sadness and inconsolable grief. Hiawatha and the spirit within the tree, with the help of Tiwi and Kewahtawa, had together created a Great Face of ultimate sorrow, a Face that had stared at and reflected back the pure essence of tragedy.

Hiawatha stepped back from the tree and looked at what he had carved. His hands and his arms were numb as they dropped by his side. His half-naked body was glistening with sweat and his breath came in huge gasps. Kewahtawa stopped his rattling and chanting. His own arm was numb and his voice was strained. Tiwi stopped her dancing. All three stared into the face carved into the side-flesh of the tree. Hiawatha seemed to be staring into his own soul. Tears formed in Kewahtawa's old eyes as he beheld the Ultimate Mask of Sorrow.

"The tree weeps for us," said Tiwi.

A cold chill went up Hiawatha's spine. His daughter was right. The tree had yielded up its tears and had given them a mask that reflected the state of his own anguished and terrified soul. He had merely been an agent. His hands and arms merely the medium through which the tree spirit spoke. It was the tree spirit that had carved this Great Face, the great face of his sorrow and the sorrow of his people. His own anguish and the anguish of Makahwah, the anguish of the Turtle Clan, the clan of his dead daughters, the clan of his dead wife. Hiawatha threw back his head and howled like a wounded animal, a terrifying howl that echoed through the forest and made his daughter scream in fear. He dropped to his knees and chanted a prayer of thanks to the tree spirit, to the spirits of the woods, and to the Great Spirit, the Creator and Destroyer of all things.

Then he and Kewahtawa carefully scored around the large oval of the face, and pulled the carved mask free from the standing tree.

Darkness was falling now in the village of the Onondaga. In the longhouse of Makahwah, men and women lifted up the cleansed and prepared bodies of Seawa and Memoha on platforms, and carried them through the door into the center of the village. Memoha looked peaceful with her eyes closed and an odd little smile of repose fixed on her face. The mutilated face of Seawa, however, was covered with a corn-husk mask, an intricately woven disc that resembled a smiling sun. The men and women set the platforms down in front of the large bonfire that was lit earlier. It was the bonfire of the second night of the Feast of Dreams. A Feast now marred by death and sorrow. The magical festival of dreams had been turned into the Feast of the Dead.

As a dark cloud rolled across the face of the moon, drummers drummed their slow and mournful dirges while flutes cried above them sounding like whispered sighs through white pines. Hiawatha sat at the head of the circle facing the bodies on the platforms. Next to him were Makahwah, Sovana, and Tiwi. From either side of the circle of seated mourners, two single-file lines of men wearing False Faces entered singing and dancing. The masks were terrifying. Crooked noses and twisted grins, bulging eyes and insane features turned and leaped with every dance step of the men wearing them. The Faces were stained a brownish red except for the large white eyes, and the real hair, long and black, flew up and backwards, swirling in the firelight.

They danced around the dead bodies, these men with their frightening visages designed to chase away the evil demons and spirits that might hover over and around the dead girls so that they might swiftly travel the Strawberry Path to the safe fields of the otherworld. One dancer who had not entered with the others now leaped into the middle of the circle, and the mask that he wore was the most horrifying mask that the people had ever seen. Many people gasped and children screamed aloud. Tiwi buried her head into her grandmother's bosom. Even some of the False Face dancers stopped and took a few steps backward as Atatarho danced around the bodies of the girls with two live and writhing golden snakes in his outstretched hands. The snakes that were coiled in the hair of the mask bounced and writhed, their jaws open and their fangs exposed, ready to strike. The crooked and twisted expression on the face of the mask struck terror into the hearts of those who saw it. It seemed to be the Great Mask of Absolute Terror.

Atatarho danced around the bodies of the dead girls, thrusting the live snakes toward them as though the power of the snakes, the venom in their fangs, might have the power to bring them back to life. But the bodies of Seawa and Memoha remained motionless. He spun around several times, and then he leaped up high in the air and came down in a half crouch in front of Sovana. He thrust the snakes out at her face, and she immediately shrunk back, frightened by the double-forked tongues, the vertical black slits of their blood-red eyes and their exposed white fangs. The snakes on the head of Atatarho leaped forward too with every movement of his head. Orios, sitting among the musicians between a drummer and another flute player, dropped his flute in the middle of a note, and tried to jump up, but two of his musician friends restrained him. Hiawatha saw all of this, but did nothing. He sat stoically, looking to the eyes of his people like a still and impervious stone.

The great sorcerer then twirled and turned again performing high leaps and pirouettes that seemed impossible, especially for someone of his years. He was not ancient by any means, but he had some time ago left that time of life when athletic prowess and physical agility were taken for granted. It was as if this mask had given him some secret power over the aging process, had turned back time and returned him to his youth.

He leaped high into the air holding his arms out straight from his sides, the golden snakes writhing, and landed in front of Tiwi who sat in her grandmother's lap. The snakes on his head bounced and recoiled and seemed to lash out angrily at the little girl. He thrust the live snakes out at her just as he had done to her sisters, two dead and one alive. She screamed and tried to run away, but her grandmother held her in place. Makahwah rose up, the little girl in her arms, to face the sorcerer. The drums seemed to increase in intensity. Orios played a high-pitched note on his flute that pierced the air and hung like a phantom shriek above the steady mournful beat of the water drums.

The shaman in his snake mask and the clan mother clutching her granddaughter stood facing each other for what seemed an eternity. Then, like a sun that bursts forth in the middle of a rainstorm, or a lightning flash that rends the sky at twilight, Hiawatha stepped between them. Over his face he wore the uncured, newly carved False Face that he and Kewahtawa had harvested from the spirit of the basswood tree just that afternoon. In each hand he held two freshly cut, four-foot lengths of willow branch, the leaves still green on the supple boughs. He stretched out his arms and brought the willow boughs down on the face of Makahwah and Tiwi to his left, and down across the mask-covered face of the sorcerer. The musicians stopped playing. Everyone around the circle was transfixed by the sight of their chief wearing the False Face of Ultimate Sorrow. The willow branches, extensions of Hiawatha's arms and still-living metaphors of his grief, separated Atatarho and Makahwah. The great clan mother sat back down, still protecting the frightened Tiwi in her large arms. Atatarho backed away to join the other False Face dancers, who stopped their chanting and dancing.

Now Hiawatha began to dance. His slow and sinuous movements around the prone bodies of his daughters on the twin platforms seemed to all the people seated around the fire to be the ultimate outpouring of all the sorrow and grief that had accumulated in the world since the beginning of time. The mask seemed to collect into itself all the tears of all the human beings who ever lived and loved and suffered and died upon the back of Turtle Island. At the same time, it seemed to emanate all the horror and fear that came from not knowing the reason for the existence of evil, the existence of death. Why did our loved ones have to die? Why was it that the innocent suffered at the hands of the wicked?

The Great Tragic Face of Grief hovered over the dead girls while Hiawatha caressed their bodies with the languorous willow boughs dipping and swaying in his hands. Their supple, drooping lengths seemed to spread great green tears of pity and remorse over the stiff corpses of what once had been vibrant living creatures. The joy they had brought to their father and their grandmother and the people of their longhouse and indeed the entire village was now no more, now had turned into a deep and bottomless grief. Orios played a mournful solo on his wooden flute. The tragic notes matched the slow and sensual rhythm of the willow boughs brushing the bodies of the gone girls. The mask of Hiawatha, combined with his languid willow-bough dance and the slow mournful flute-notes, brought forth great sobs from the people of the village. Their faces were wet with tears, tears that flowed like slow rivers of sorrow, rivers that were released in a flood of heartbreaking anguish.

Caught up in Hiawatha's dance of mourning, and staring at the Great Mask of Sorrow, each member of the village recalled the loss of someone dear to them, and the thought of that person and the memory of the loss brought hot tears to their cheeks. Tears also scalded the face of Hiawatha beneath the raw basswood of the Face of Woe, and the False Face seemed to weld itself to his own face, the soft, wet wood melding the features carved on its surface with his own so that, it seemed to him, after he removed the mask, his face would be its identical twin. Voices seemed to spring up in the ears and minds of the weeping people seated around the fire. The voices were the voices of their gone loved ones, and the voices called out to them asking for remembrance. From across the fragile veil that separates this world from the otherworld, the familiar, long-ago voices of dead husbands and wives, mothers and children, fathers and brothers, sisters and uncles called to them, echoing in their ears. So real were some of the spirit-voices that those who heard them called back, spoke to them across the void, told their dead wives and mothers that they had not forgotten them, that they loved them still and honored their memories every day of their lives. This night would be remembered for a long time and it would later be called The Night the Dead Spoke to Us.

The great cacophony created by so many people calling out to their dead ones, combined with the incessant drumming and the constant chanting of the False-Face Men, set up such a din that children began to wail and cry. Makahwah could stand it no longer. She hoisted the weeping Tiwi on one hip and headed back to her longhouse. There were too many spirits set loose in one place. She feared that she and her granddaughter might be sucked into the black whirlpool tunnel that leads to the otherworld, the timeless, shadowy land of the Spirit Beings.

A crack had opened up in the wall that separates one world from the other, and spirits were pouring through that crack into the center of the village. It was becoming too dangerous. As everyone knew, not all of the spirits were benevolent. One had only to look at Atatarho and his Face of Ultimate Terror to know this. The great sorcerer was in his element, leaping from person to person and cajoling, orchestrating the separate conversations that were now taking place with the spirits of the dead. He was like a maestro whipping the players up into a frenzy while Hiawatha continued to dance his willow-branch dance of ultimate sorrow. He too was talking with Seawa and Memoha and the lost mother of the girls, Tamora, whose face he saw clearly hovering above the stretched-out bodies of the girls like a dismembered False Face flying in the moonlight.

"*Hiawatha,*" cried a wailing voice from the face of Tamora. Hiawatha stood transfixed, gazing up at the floating face of his dead wife. Her face shifted back and forth from a translucent youthful beauty, a vital and taut transcendence, to a weeping and bloated mask of decay, a hideous gash running down the middle, cleaving her brow, her nose, her lips, and her chin. Hiawatha screamed and clamped his eyes together so hard a pain lodged in behind them. He opened them and the hideous death mask was back again floating above his daughters. So intently did he focus his sight on the vision of his dead wife that he did not notice the concentrated gaze of Atatarho fixed upon him from across the other side of the fire.

"*Hi-a-wa-tha*," the voice of Tamora cried. The pleading and sorrow in the long, drawn-out syllables of his name was almost too much to hear, too much to bear.

"Tamora! What do you want?"

There was a pause. Tamora's shifting face floated before Hiawatha's eyes. Then a single word that seemed to come with a breath let out through clenched teeth: "*Vengeance.*" The single word was whispered hoarsely as if only for his ears. "You must avenge the death of our daughters. Take their blood as they took ours."

"Yes, Tamora. I will spill their blood upon the ground as they have spilled the blood of our girls. No one will escape the wrath of Hiawatha! For each of our children slain, I will slay five of theirs. Two from every clan, a boy-child and a girl-child, so that all the Seneca will know what it means to slay the children of the People of the Hills."

The face of Tamora seemed to smile—at one second beatific, and at another, cruel and grisly, twisted by the open wound that split her countenance in two. Then she was gone. The drums and the chants seemed louder now to Hiawatha's ears, as he looked around for the face of his dead wife. But she was gone, returned again to the otherworld, the land of the Spirit Beings.

All he saw were the False Faces of the dancers spinning and whirling, and, especially, he saw the malevolent form of Atatarho as he moved sinuously away from him, the snakes on his False-Face bobbing and twisting. All he heard were the trance-like orisons and utterings of his people in communion with the spirits who walked and danced beside them in the moonlight by the fire-glow that cast high and flickering shadows on the ground and on the bodies of his dead children.

Inside Makahwah's longhouse, Tiwi sat solemnly stroking the head of her little corn-husk doll. She looked shyly up at her grandmother, who was stirring a clay pot of cornmeal porridge over a small fire.

"Grandmother?" Tiwi asked, her voice tentative and slightly faltering.

"What is it, my precious?"

"Will my sisters wake up and play with me tomorrow?"

"No, dear. They will not wake up. They are dead."

"What is dead? Will I be dead?"

"Not for a long time," said Makahwah as she put down her ladle and hugged the little girl close to her breast. "Dead means that you live in the land of the Spirit Beings. Only your spirit walks among us, not your body."

"Why did my sisters die?"

"The Senecas killed them."

"Why?"

"Revenge, my child. Vengeance. We took one of theirs. It was an accident, but nonetheless, we killed one of their people, the son of a chieftain, and they wanted our blood in return for his blood. A blood revenge is the ancient way of justice. But a blood revenge never stops. Not until everyone is dead. Revenge is wicked, Tiwi. It is evil."

"What is evil?"

Makahwah shifted her weight, sighed, and placed the little girl on her ample lap. She stroked her hair gently, and hugged her. "In order to tell you that, I must first tell you a story. It is the story of how we, the people, the Human Beings, came into this world, and then, how evil was born out of it."

"In the beginning, many, many ages ago, there were no people; there was not even any earth. There was only water below and sky above. But there were Sky People. They lived way up high in the sky, beyond the great, white clouds. Their world was airy and bright. Light came from a large spruce tree called the Tree of Heavenly Light, and this tree was planted in front of the house of the chief of the Sky People." Tiwi's eyes widened.

"Now, as everyone knows, among the Sky People there was a young and beautiful woman who was the wife of the Sky Chief. She was going to have a baby. Her pretty belly was this big, and round like a melon at harvest time." Tiwi giggled and Makahwah laughed with her.

"But there was a man among the Sky People who liked to cause trouble. Some call him Firedragon. He told the Sky Chief that the baby that was in his wife's belly was not his baby. It was the baby of another man."

Makahwah looked down at Tiwi to see if she understood this last part. The little girl stared solemnly up at her grandmother showing no signs of puzzlement. Makahwah continued her story. "So the Sky Chief became jealous and angry. He pushed over the Tree of Light, causing a hole to open in the ground, a hole that led down to the world of water. He pushed the pregnant woman into the hole and she fell down, down, down toward the waters. Since she was of the Sky People, she could not swim, so naturally she was terrified. But then a large flock of water birds, ducks and geese mostly, saw her falling toward the water, and they flew beneath her, locking their wings together, so that she landed safely on the soft down of their backs. The great flock flew as one bird, gliding gracefully down to where the Great Turtle, master of all creatures, floated upon the deep waters. As they laid her upon his back, Turtle commanded them to dive down to the bottom of the waters and bring up some of the magic earth that had fallen from the hole in the sky with Sky Woman. The ducks and the geese, and other creatures too, like the muskrat and the otter, dove down deep to the bottom of the waters and brought up the Sky-Being earth that had fallen with Sky Woman, and placed it on Turtle's back. The Turtle began to grow bigger and bigger; the light that poured forth from the hole in the sky made trees and flowers grow, maple trees and oak trees, pine and spruce, sunflower and dandelion. The Island on Turtle's back was becoming a lovely place. And on that place, the woman gave birth to a baby girl whom she called Daughter. Soon, Daughter began to speak, and then to walk, and then in a short while she became a fully grown and beautiful woman."

"Like Seawa?" interrupted Tiwi.

"Yes, dear, like Seawa." Makahwah stopped for a moment. She thought she was going to cry. But she collected herself and continued. "Now, here is the way it was. Her mother warned her not to go into the water. But she gave her mother no heed, and, one day, she dove into the water and played in the rippling waves. She swam as freely and expertly as any water-creature, and when she came out of the water, she was pregnant with the seed of the spirit of the great deep."

"Will I get pregnant if I play in the water?" asked Tiwi, a worried look clouding her small brown face.

"No, no," laughed Makahwah, rocking back and forth and hugging the little girl tightly to her breast. "But be careful just the same."

"Did Daughter have a baby then?"

"In fact, she had two babies. Twin boys. She did not know it at the time, but within her belly she was carrying the Good Spirit, Tarachiawagon, and the Evil Twin, Tawiskaron. You see, Tiwi, just like Sky Woman's daughter, we all have both good and evil within us. They are constantly struggling, just as Daughter's twins began to struggle with one another even before they were born.

"While in the womb, one twin said to the other: 'We will not harm our mother. So therefore let us be born painlessly, and enter the world in the natural way.' But the other twin, the Evil One, said: 'Do as you please. As for me, I will go out the nearest and quickest way.' When the time came, Tarachiawagon, the good twin, came out the natural way for children to enter into the world. But Tawiskaron thought he saw daylight under his mother's left arm, so he ripped his way out from a hole he made in her armpit, causing his mother to die a terrible death."

"Why did he do that?" asked Tiwi.

"Because that was his way. It was in his nature to be evil. His birth act was the first instance of evil in the world, because the two twins and their mother are responsible for creation. They are the ancient mother and fathers of the human beings. You can trace your lineage back through time to the birth of Turtle Island, back to Sky Woman and her Daughter and the Two Twins. Do you see?"

Tiwi sucked on her lower lip and nodded as she carelessly plucked a few loose strands of corn husk from her little doll. "What happened then?"

"Well, while Daughter was dying of her terrible wound, she told her mother how she wanted to be buried. She told her to plant her in the ground with her head facing the wind. Her mother did so, and some few days later, corn plants grew from her breasts, so that food could be given to nourish her twins and all the people who would come after them. Ever after this, Daughter became known as Corn Mother. Sky Woman then took her grandchildren to raise them, and, just like their mother, they soon began to talk and then to walk. Wherever the Good Twin went, his Evil Twin followed him. The Good Twin created straight rivers that flowed in two directions so that human beings could paddle up the river and down the river with ease. But the Bad Twin followed after him and he threw rocks in the rivers and made hills that the rivers had to wind around. And he also created waterfalls that went only one way—down, down to sharp rocks below. The Good Twin learned how to cultivate the corn plants that grew from his mother's breasts, so that the corn became sweet and succulent; he created all the animals that were good to eat, the deer, the elk, and the bear, but the Evil Brother who always followed him tried to undo his works by creating the evil and slimy things, frogs and monsters, bats and worms; he created blights and bugs that would descend upon the corn. Whatever the Good Twin created that was good, the Evil one tried to undo it.

"Then Good Creator-Twin created man and woman out of dust and made them sweet and wholesome, careful tenders of Turtle Island, and he created the sun and the moon so that man and woman could see their way through the world, and rain also he created to make the crops grow and the rivers swell. But, his brother, the Evil Creator-Twin put his own evil nature into man and into woman so that sometimes they would quarrel and fight, steal and cheat, lie and kill. And he injected his evil even into the rain so that sometimes it would turn violent, wicked storms lashing the land and drowning the crops and the people, and floods that could take away whole villages.

"Finally, the Good Twin could stand this no longer. He challenged his brother to a duel. They would fight to see who would be dominant over the earth. They went to the very edge of Turtle Island, to where the tallest mountains are, and they fought ferociously. The earth trembled when they tumbled over it. Huge dust storms kicked up by their heels blotted out the light from the sun and also the light from the moon, for they fought both day and night. But neither one was winning, and both were tired from the mighty struggle."

"But someone must win!" interrupted Tiwi. "Does the Bad Twin win? Is that why there is evil in the world?"

"Wait a bit. I am coming to that. The Good Twin, the Creator of good things and good creatures, by a mighty effort of will, summoned up his last reserves of strength and power. He placed his hands on the side of a great range of mountains, and he pushed them so hard that they slammed right up in his evil brother's face knocking him out and twisting his nose all crooked and smashed."

"Like on the False Faces?"

"Even so! Just like on the False Faces. Some of those False Faces represent the Spirit of the Evil ancestor."

"So then did the Good Twin win out over the Evil one?"

"Yes, my child. Tawiskaron yielded. He admitted defeat, and so he became subservient to his Good brother. So human beings are mostly good. But you must remember that Good and Evil both grew in the belly of our ancient mother. So there is always a part of human nature that is evil. That is why evil exists. And why human beings do evil deeds. Now do you understand?" She turned to see her granddaughter curled up with her doll, fast asleep. Makahwah lifted herself up and walked slowly over to her fire, wondering if she herself really understood.

Outside Makahwah's longhouse, beneath the outstretched arms of an ancient tree, Orios sat beside Sovana and tried his best to comfort her as she tried to speak through her tears and sobs.

"I can't believe they're gone. How could this happen? And last night, I should have spent their last night with them in the longhouse. I've slept with Seawa ever since I can remember and now . . . now she won't be there. She was my best friend, we did everything together. And little Memoha, she trusted everyone. Why would anyone kill them? They never hurt anyone. It's not fair! This is a horrible world!" Her whole body was wracked with sobs.

Orios pulled her closer, trying to hold back his own tears and be strong for her. Poor Seawa and little Memoha, and it was all his fault. It was he who killed Shadahgoh's son, and now Sovana, who he loved more than life itself, and Hiawatha, who was like a father to him, were the ones who were suffering for his foolish mistake. He should have been killed instead of them.

"Sovana," he began, hesitantly. "There is something I must tell you."

"What is it?"

". . . Your father . . . did not kill the boy."

Sovana raised her head and looked him in the eye. She saw the last piece of her world come tumbling down.

"No, no, don't tell me!" She pounded her fists against his chest.

An owl suddenly screeched in the tree above them and they both instinctively jumped. In the eerie silence, they heard the loud crack of a twig snapping behind the ancient tree.

"Who's there?" called Orios. The owl cried out again as a shadowy figure stepped out from behind the tree.

"Osinoh! What are you doing here? You were spying on us!" Sovana was angry now. She felt as though she had been violated.

"You killed Shadahgoh's son, didn't you?"

"Don't answer him, Orios."

"No, Sovana. I must. I cannot hide behind your father any longer. It is not fair to him, or to you." Sovana placed her hand on his lips in a futile effort to keep him from speaking, but Orios gently took it away.

"It's no use. Osinoh is right. Yes, I killed the boy with Hiawatha's bow. It was an accident. I don't know how it happened. One minute I was aiming at a rabbit, and the next minute, the boy lay bleeding on the ground."

Tears streamed down Sovana's cheeks. "Then, it is because of you that my sisters are dead?" She tried to choke back the sobs that filled her voice.

"He might as well have killed them himself. His actions led to their deaths." Osinoh moved closer to Sovana.

"Oh, Orios!" Sovana was openly sobbing now.

"Come with me, Sovana," said Osinoh. "I will take you back into Makahwah's longhouse."

Osinoh put his arm around her to lead her away. She looked back at Orios, who stood alone, head bowed in the moonlight. She pushed Osinoh away, turned, and ran back into the longhouse. Orios started to run after her, but Osinoh stepped in front of him.

The two young men glared at one another.

"I warn you, flute-player. If you place any value on your life, stay away from Sovana." The sneer on his lips brought hot blood to Orios' face.

"You don't own her. I'll see her if I choose." He tried to put up a brave front, but he knew that he was no match for the older and stronger Osinoh.

Osinoh laughed. "You really think she will want to see you now? After what you did to her sisters?"

Something in Orios snapped and he flung himself at Osinoh. But Osinoh grabbed his arms, placed his right foot behind Orios' left leg, pushed him down to the ground, and kicked him hard in the pit of the stomach. Orios struggled for breath.

"You're pathetic," said Osinoh. "You fight like a girl."

Orios desperately fought back the tears of pain that were welling up in his eyes. He was on one elbow, trying to push himself up, when Osinoh spat on the ground before him, turned, and strode back into the darkness from which he came.

Chapter Eight

After a sleepless night, Hiawatha gathered the people together in the center of the village. He stood tall and resolute by the war pillar, a post set into the ground standing seven feet high and two feet in diameter. Its surface was battered and hacked, stained with the dried blood of brave men who had been tied up there. Some had survived to become Onondaga. Others had died cruel deaths at the hands of those who mourned for their own dead loved ones. No captives of a mourning war had stood in this place for some time now. The pillar was thirsty.

And Hiawatha was angry. But he controlled his anger so that he might better speak to his people. In his right hand he brandished his stone tomahawk; in his left hand, he held his long war club with the single deer-antler spike at its head. He raised his arms, holding both weapons high above him.

"My daughters are dead!" he shouted. The crowd murmured in sympathy. As he spoke he walked some paces away from the post. "*Onondaga* daughters. Daughters who carried within them the future generations. Dead! Their laughter will be heard no more. Their voices will no longer sing our songs. Their hands will no more tend the three sisters. Their children, *your* children, will not be born. They will lie always beneath the ground with their faces yearning upward."

"Vengeance!" shouted a young man from the crowd.

"Blood!" cried another.

"Kill the Seneca!"

Hiawatha shouted above the calls and cries of the crowd. "Let us revenge ourselves upon these savages. These enemies who creep up to our town and murder our children!"

"Death to the beasts!"

"They are not people! They are not human beings like Onondaga!"

And as the chants and cries became fiercer and more insistent, Hiawatha hurled his tomahawk at the pillar of vengeance. The weapon flipped end over end and buried itself into the post with a mighty crack. The crowd cheered.

"Who will come with me? Who will revenge our people?" He brandished his war club high over his head.

"I will!" shouted a young warrior.

"So will I!"

"I'm with you!"

"I am too!"

And then, pushing his way through the crowd, Orios appeared in front of his leader. "I'm going with you," he said, a look of fierce determination in his eyes.

Surprised, Hiawatha nodded to Orios, then strode over to the mourning-war post, swung his war club with both hands, and buried the antler spike into the scarred wood of the pillar of vengeance. A loud cheer sounded through the crowd.

"Make yourselves ready. Gather your weapons, your arrows, your war clubs, and paint your bodies with the paint of war. We leave at dawn." War cries rose from the crowd as the warriors hastened to get ready. Hiawatha put his arm around the slender shoulders of Orios and led him away toward the longhouse of Makahwah.

Makahwah was not among the crowd that had gathered around their leader to hear his call for revenge. She hung back at the entrance to her longhouse. But she heard. She heard enough so that her heart became heavier than it already was. There was a part of her that wanted someone to pay for the deaths of her granddaughters. But there was also a part of her that struggled against this impulse. She had seen time after time how these affairs always end. Or rather, *never* end. Her first husband, then her daughter, and now her granddaughters. One death called for another death, and that death in turn called for another. And another and another. And so on down through the ages into infinity. The cycle had no ending.

Hiawatha's speech troubled her deeply. He and his war party would take more Seneca lives. And the Seneca would be forced to murder or capture others from the village, perhaps from her own longhouse, perhaps even her remaining granddaughters. And this was something that she could not bear. The killing must stop. This was the import of Kewahtawa's dream-vision, his dream of the Great Peacemaker who would bring an end to this murderous waste of life. And according to the dream, Hiawatha had some great role to play in this vision of peace. But here he was, campaigning for more blood. She watched Hiawatha and Orios approach the longhouse. And she stood in the doorway, blocking their path.

"A fine speech you gave." The tone of her voice indicated that she thought exactly the opposite.

"What would you have me do? Let the deaths of my daughters go unavenged?"

Orios looked at the toes of his moccasins. He felt awkward in the presence of Sovana's grandmother. He knew that the great Clan Mother did not think highly of him. Had Sovana spoken to Makahwah about their conversation? How much did she know about his part in all of this?

"When will the killings stop? When all of us are dead?"

"Step aside, Makahwah. I must fetch my weapons."

"Is there nothing that I can say to prevent you from spilling more blood? What about my husband's dream? Have you forgotten that?"

"His dream is his dream. It is not mine. Let *him* go after this prophet in the sky. I know what I must do. I will have my revenge. Move."

Makahwah glared at him. She looked at Orios and shook her head. "You bring nothing but more blood down on the heads of your people. I want you to remember this, Hiawatha. I hold you personally responsible for any more deaths that occur. Remember my words when you savor the sweetness of your revenge. And you remember too, boy. What is a musician like you doing mixed up in all this bloodshed?"

Orios could not look at her. Instead, he stared at the ground. His face felt hot, and he could feel his eyes burn as if they were about to shed tears. It was all too confusing. He could feel the full force of the clan mother's scorn. Then, without a word, Makahwah suddenly turned and strode back into the longhouse.

Hiawatha put his arm around Orios' shoulder. "Come. Let's go to your longhouse. I'll help you get your things together. We must prepare for a journey of several days and nights."

Atatarho hunched over the clay pot that hung above the fire outside his hut of mud and bones on the edge of the swamp. He was crumbling dried herbs over the pot with his left hand and stirring them in with a carved wooden ladle. The fire glinted in his eyes making them shine brighter and wilder. Deadly nightshade, he thought. Jimson weed. Lovely and deadly. A faint smile flickered across his lips as he continued to stir and as he thought about how things had been playing out lately. Playing out according to his design. Everything was falling neatly into place, just as he had planned, just as he had calculated. The Turtle Clan, the most ancient clan, the clan from which many renowned ancestors had come, was now in disarray, their ancient totem mysteriously spirited away. He laughed out loud and shook his head. And Hiawatha, the great Hiawatha, son-in-law to Makahwah, the Turtle Clan Mother, was falling apart with grief and anger. Soon, and very soon after his next plan played out, Hiawatha would no longer be fit to lead even a band of idiots.

He straightened up, turned, and went into his hut. The skins of animals and snakes hung from the cross poles of the roof, side by side with all manner of drying flowers, herbs, and weeds. Bones littered the edges of the floor. He found a pouch made from a beaver pelt and took it outside to his fire. Inside the pouch were the dried roots of hemlock. He carefully removed two of the dried tubers and dropped them into his bubbling concoction. He continued to stir the greenish-brown liquid slowly and carefully, periodically holding the ladle to his nose to sniff it. A noise in the darkness made him jump. He reached for the stone hatchet that lay by his side.

"Who's there?"

"It's me, Uncle." The voice in the night sounded arrogant and haughty. Osinoh stepped out of the shadows and into the small ring of light cast by the red and yellow fire.

"Nephew! What a surprise. Come sit with me. You seem rather pleased with yourself tonight. What is it?"

"I have news, Uncle. Such news as you would love to hear."

"Have you now?"

"Yes, Uncle. Many would love to know what I know."

"Well, well. This does sound impressive. Tell me."

"I think I ought to make you pay for this news." Osinoh sat back and folded his arms, a smug, self-satisfied smile playing across his lean face.

A darkness descended on Atatarho's features. He picked up a slender bone from the ground beside him and suddenly thrust out his arm, pointing the bone at Osinoh's heart. His eyes narrowed to slits and it seemed to Osinoh as if a line of fire was streaming from the pointed bone toward his own heart. He felt a sudden sharp pain in his chest as if a great black bear were standing on top of him. He could not breathe. He could not speak. He was seized by a terrible thought. He was going to die! Panic filled his entire being. His eyes rolled back in their sockets and he fell over backwards on the ground clutching his chest.

Atatarho dropped his arm, and the pain left Osinoh's body. He gasped, choking as he struggled to breathe air into his lungs.

"Would you like more payment, nephew?"

Osinoh remained silent, unable to reply. He knew that his Uncle was a powerful sorcerer, but, until this moment, he did not know just how powerful. From now on, he would be very careful about the way he talked to him.

"I will tell you my news freely, because you are my uncle and I respect you."

"Good. Let us hear it."

"Hiawatha did not kill the Seneca boy."

"How do you know this?"

"I overheard Orios confessing his guilt to Sovana."

"Orios? That stripling? He killed Shadahgoh's son? I don't believe it."

"It's true. It was an accident. He was hunting with Hiawatha's bow."

"You are sure of this?"

"I am as sure of this as I am sure of the sun rising in the morning."

"How did the girl react to his confession?"

"She was angry with Orios and she ran away."

"Good. Good. And Hiawatha, does he know that his daughter knows?"

Osinoh shrugged. "Perhaps not. He goes to make war on the Seneca. To bring back prisoners in revenge for his daughters."

Atatarho got up and walked back and forth before his fire, thinking. He turned to Osinoh and said, "Go back to the village. Lie low and keep your eyes open. Find ways to get close to Sovana. Court her. Give her presents."

"Uncle?"

"Yes, what is it?"

"You promised you would help me win her."

"And so I shall. Have no fear on that account. She will be yours. I'll prepare a special love medicine. Now go. And if you see or hear anything concerning Hiawatha and his daughter, come immediately and tell me."

"Yes, Uncle." Osinoh got up off the ground and disappeared back into the dark woods as silently as he had arrived.

Atatarho stared into the fire, stirring his cauldron. A smile slowly spread across his face.

Hiawatha and his band of seven warriors were almost out of the country of the Cayuga and were about to enter the easternmost portion of the land of the Seneca. They had been traveling at breakneck speed, running and half-running, stopping only to rest occasionally, to eat a few kernels of corn, or one or two bits of dried maple sap, and to sleep at night. They had covered ninety miles in two days, and now they were making their way through the woods that stretched between the lake of the Cayugas and the lake of the Senecas. The sun was straight up in the sky and the air was hot and humid beneath the canopy of trees in the forest. The warriors were clad only in breech clouts and moccasins. Sweat covered their naked torsos, cooling them whenever a breeze stirred through the trees.

Yesterday, they had skirted the edge of a Cayuga village. They moved quickly, but quietly. Even when they ran full-speed, their moccasins barely made a sound. Whether they trod the sun-hardened ground or the damp mossy carpet beneath the trees, their movements were as stealthy as the mountain lion and as purposeful as the vigilant eagle. In fact, Hiawatha, leading the band in their single-file rush through the wilderness, seemed like an eagle, his eyes, fierce and steady, constantly scanning the way ahead. The two warriors behind him, Tonesah and Honowe, scanned the woods to the right and to the left, keeping an eye out for any threat of ambush on their flanks. The warriors in the rear of the line looked behind to make sure they were not being followed.

Like a flock of geese flying in the sky, or a school of fish in the sea who all move in the same direction instantly, their movements were the movements of one being: each aware, without speaking, of the perceptions of the others. Because of his inexperience with the ways of war, Orios ran in the middle of the line. His legs ached from the strain of keeping up with those before him. But whenever he felt himself faltering, he remembered his act of manslaughter and the pain and suffering that he had brought upon Hiawatha and his family. He especially thought of Sovana. The look of hurt and disappointment that shattered her face when he told her the truth those few nights ago. It seemed an eternity had passed since that night outside of the village. Then he thought of Osinoh, and his mind darkened even further. He saw him put his arm around Sovana's shoulders and draw her close to him, again and again and again. He tried to chase it out of his mind, but he could not. The image lingered there like smoke inside of a longhouse on a still, windless night.

Hiawatha raised his right arm into the air and the band of warriors stopped. He crouched down and pointed to the ground in front of him, to the imprint of moccasins in the soft, damp earth. "Seneca. A hunting party, or perhaps a small war party," said Hiawatha.

"How many are there?" asked Tonesah.

"Four or five," replied Hiawatha.

"They are fresh. Two, maybe three hours past?" said Honowe.

"Yes. We will stalk them slowly, and surprise them at night. When they sit around their fire, we will attack. Remember. Do not kill. We want them alive. No one talks from now on. Hand-talk only. Be vigilant." The warriors nodded to Hiawatha, who stood up, turned, and jogged off, keeping his eyes on the moccasin-print trail and on the path ahead. The warriors followed him, eyes scanning the woods around them, ears open for any sound of Seneca.

Now the day was waning and the darkness was dropping from the sky. Red streaks filled the cloud-scattered western horizon as Hiawatha recognized the first faint whiff of wood smoke. He signaled with his hand, and the warriors dropped to the ground and crawled forward to where he lay.

"As soon as the darkness becomes complete, we attack. Do not kill, unless you have to. This is a mourning war. Our goal is to capture prisoners and bring them back to the village. Tonesah."

"Yes, Hiawatha?"

"Take two men with you and circle around to the right. Keep low. Make no sound. Honowe, you take two and circle to the left. Watch out for sentries. If you see one, take him out. I will approach straight on from this position. Wait till you hear my signal. When I give the signal, two long owl-cries, rush the camp. Strike blows that will not kill. Is that clear?"

"Yes, Hiawatha," said Tonesah.

Honowe tapped Orios on the shoulder and motioned him to follow. Orios and another warrior crawled after Honowe as silently as they could through the undergrowth that lined the forest floor off the beaten path. So this is what the snake feels like, thought Orios as his belly scraped the twigs and moss and dirt. He tried to keep his head down and still see through the deepening gloom. It was almost dark now, but through the brush and the trees, Orios could see a dim flickering of light from the small campfire up ahead. He could feel his heart pounding harder now. He had never been on a war party before. But he had killed. Twice. Once by an unlucky accident, once in anger. He tried to force out of his mind's eye the image of the Seneca boy lying on his back, the life-force leaking out of him, and the other image of the Seneca warrior who was about to kill Sovana when his arrow pierced the man's chest. As soon as he pushed these images aside, they returned with even greater clarity. He squeezed his eyes shut in an effort to banish the pictures from his mind.

A cough suddenly broke the silence in the woods. All the scattered warriors crawling through the brush froze. Only Hiawatha saw whose cough shattered the dark silence of the forest. Some five paces ahead of him was a Seneca warrior standing guard for the hunting party who were now getting ready to sleep. He was a tall, solidly built man wearing long earrings of gold and mica and a nose ring that covered his upper lip. His chest was tattooed with long vertical lines and his breech-clout was dyed green and red. At his hip, hanging from the cord that held his breech-clout, was a stone tomahawk and a long stone knife with a handle made from a wolf's jawbone. His war club hung from a cord slung across his shoulder beside a quiver full of arrows. This man seems more prepared for war than for the hunt, thought Hiawatha. Perhaps there were more of them than he had been able to discern from the prints on the trail. A sound in the bushes made the sentry jump. It came from the right where Tonesah and his two warriors had circled around. Fools! Why could they not keep still? The Seneca unslung his war club and took two steps in the direction of the sound, peering intently into the darkness before him.

Hiawatha sprung like a mountain cat upon his prey and dealt him a blow to the head with the blunt end of his tomahawk. The man dropped like a sack of corn. Hiawatha took out a length of hempen cord from inside of his fawnskin pouch and bound the unconscious man's hands behind his back. Then he tied his legs together. He crouched over his trussed-up captive and peered through the darkness toward the dim flickering of the campfire's dying embers. He could make out the shadowed outline of three men lying on the ground beneath deerskin robes. Off to the right edge of the small clearing was another man sitting at the base of a tree, his hands tied in front of him and his neck and torso lashed to the tree's trunk. His head was shaved except for a topknot. His face and shoulders were bloody and covered with cuts and bruises. But his eyes were wide open. His face was etched with a look of stoic determination. He would meet his fate bravely. But there was something else in his eyes, a searching look, the look of a man who had not quite given up hope.

Hiawatha crept even closer to the clearing. The prisoner tied to the tree looked directly into his eyes. Hiawatha placed his forefinger up to his lips. The prisoner nodded. Hiawatha gave two long, low owl cries. One of the men on the ground stirred. Tonesah and two warriors rushed the clearing from the right and Honowe, Orios, and the other warrior rushed in from the left. The noise of seven pairs of moccasins crashing through brush awoke one of the sleeping Seneca warriors who shouted a loud warning as he snatched up his war club and swung it over his head. The other two Senecas jumped up just as Honowe and Tonesah threw themselves upon them from opposite sides of the clearing. Honowe and one of the Senecas, who had drawn his knife, were locked together in a death duel, hands gripping each other's wrists as they rolled over and over the ground fighting for supremacy.

Tonesah had dispatched his man immediately by dealing him a mighty blow with his war club, the round ball at the end slamming into his solar plexus, knocking him backwards gasping for breath. Orios helped him tie the man up. Hiawatha and the Seneca who shouted the alarm were circling each other, each looking for a weak spot, feinting and then drawing back, testing each other's reactions. The Seneca was bragging and taunting Hiawatha.

"I am Tehgonseh, mightiest warrior of the Seneca nation. I eat Cayuga for breakfast. And I will cut you up, Onondaga, and boil your bones in my cooking pot." He lunged at Hiawatha with his knife in his left hand, his war club held high. Hiawatha sidestepped and swung his club down hard, smashing Tehgonseh's right arm. He screamed in pain as the bone cracked, and he dropped to his knees. Hiawatha brought his right knee up, catching the man full on the chin and knocking him backwards.

"You will have a hard time eating me now with these broken teeth." Hiawatha signaled to one of his warriors. "Tie this blowhard up." He strode over to where Honowe still struggled with his man. The Seneca was on top of him, his knife blade moving closer and closer to his face. It took all the strength that he could muster to keep the blade from cutting him. Hiawatha watched for a few moments longer, then brought his stone tomahawk down upon the Seneca's skull with just enough force to render him unconscious, but not enough to kill him.

"Why did you do that?" Honowe asked as he pushed the man off of him and raised himself up on one elbow. "I almost had him."

"Yes, I could see that. Tie up your prisoner. We will spend the rest of the night here, and return to Onondaga in the morning."

"With mourning captives!" said Honowe.

"The celebration will be great," cried one of the warriors.

"We will avenge Hiawatha's daughters with their torture," said another.

Hiawatha said nothing. He stared at the tied-up Cayuga prisoner who returned his stare.

"What about him?" asked Orios.

"He will go with us through the land of the Cayuga. Then we will let him go."

"But the Cayuga are our enemies," said Tonesah. They have made war on us many times. A Cayuga killed my grandfather." Tonesah was now standing over the Cayuga warrior tied to the tree.

"They have done nothing to us lately. And this man has done nothing at all that requires vengeance. Cut the cords." Tonesah did as he was ordered. The Cayuga stood up, chafing his wrists.

"What is your name?"

"My name is Togahayon. I am a warrior chieftain of the Cayuga people. These Seneca dogs ambushed me while I was hunting on my people's own lands. They were taking me back to their village to torture me for some injury they claim we have done to them. You have saved me from death. How are you called?"

"I am Hiawatha, chief of the Onondaga."

"Hiawatha, what can I do to repay you?"

"You owe me nothing. We will take care of these Seneca for you. The Seneca have done us great injury. But if you wish to repay us, you can give us safe passage through your lands on our journey back home."

"I will walk with you and see that no harm comes your way in the land of the Cayuga. Come to my village, and my people will prepare a feast for you. We will help you torture your prisoners. The Seneca are our enemy too. They attack us constantly. We retaliate, but it becomes more difficult, for their numbers are greater than ours."

"We thank you for the offer, Togahayon, but we must return to our village at once. These Seneca must pay for their crimes against us before the eyes of our own people. That is the way of vengeance, the way of the mourning-war."

"You are right," said Togahayon. "It is the way. But I am still in your debt. Someday I will repay this debt properly."

Chapter Nine

Sovana walked alone down the narrow, well-beaten path that led through the woods to the clear stream. She was defying Makahwah by going out alone during these troubling times, but she had to get out, get away from the sorrow in her longhouse. She knew of a pool surrounded by large rocks that was ideal for bathing, and she needed to be alone now, to float in the clear, clean waters, and wash away all the bad feelings and disturbing emotions that had been weighing her down for the past few days. At times she felt so confused, so helpless. Her sister, Seawa, who she had depended on so much in the past, who was always happy, always dancing and singing, always laughing, was gone. Gone forever. But was she really gone? They say the dead walk among us. They are still here with us; it's just that we can't see them. Was her sister walking beside her now? She turned instinctively to see if anyone was walking behind her or beside her. But she didn't see anyone, only a bright blue jay that fluttered away from his perch on a tree limb. She did not see the dark figure duck behind a tree and hide himself from her sight.

She continued walking down the path, getting closer to the stream. She could just now hear the comforting sounds of the water bubbling and rushing over rocks. And poor little Memoha. The horrible image of her frail, bleeding little body pierced with arrows kept leaping up before her mind's eye. What had she done to anyone to deserve to die such a violent death? Why do these things happen? And then Orios' awful confession. She had loved him so, and, if she were truthful with herself, she would admit that she loved him still. But how was it possible now, knowing that his actions had led to the death of her sisters? Did it matter that it was an accident? And is anything ever an "accident"? Makahwah says that there are no accidents, only fate. Do we bring these terrible things upon ourselves? Her mind was spinning. She wanted it to stop. Perhaps the cold water would freeze her thoughts, banish them, and send them back to wherever they came from.

At the stream's edge, she slipped out of her dress and her moccasins. She tried out the water's temperature with her toes. A shiver ran up her spine, causing little goose bumps to form on her forearms and thighs. But cold as the water was, the feeling was not without pleasure. She moved down a little ways to where a waist-deep pool had formed in a bend of the stream, and plunged herself completely into the water. She remained under the water for thirty seconds or so, holding her breath, and then came up gulping for air, sprays of water leaping from her arms and her jet-black hair. The cold water seemed to penetrate deep into her being, cleansing it and clearing away all bitterness deep inside, easing the sorrow that she carried with her like a stone in her chest. She lay on her back in the water and floated. The sensation was exhilarating, the cool water on her back and the warmth of the sun on her face and her breasts and her belly.

Osinoh peered out at her from the bushes that lined one part of the bank. His mind was on fire. She was so beautiful. He wanted her like he wanted nothing else on this earth. He stepped out from behind the bushes and picked up Sovana's dress, holding it up to his face, inhaling the intoxicating fragrance that permeated every square inch of it.

"Osinoh! What are you doing?"

"Sovana. I cannot help myself. I love you. I want you so badly that at times I think I am going crazy. I followed you here because I wanted to be alone with you, to tell you how much I care for you, to ask you to give yourself to me."

"I came here to be alone. Please put my dress down and go away."

Osinoh continued to rub the soft doeskin of her dress against his face. Sovana swam to the bank and ran up to where he was standing and grabbed her dress. She held it up in front of her, covering her breasts and her belly. Osinoh took a step closer and put his arms around her. He held her close to him and stroked her long wet hair and caressed her smooth wet shoulders and the long curving length of her back. She struggled against him, but his strong arms were overpowering.

"You're so beautiful."

He took her face in his hands and pressed his lips against hers. She felt the warmth of his body flowing into hers.

"No! Osinoh! Stop it!" She tried to push herself away from him, but he became rougher. She struggled to free herself from his grasp. But the harder she struggled, the harder he pressed.

"Sovana, can't you see how much I love you? I must have you."

"A real man doesn't take a woman by force. If you truly loved me, you wouldn't treat me like this." She was angry now, and she struck him across the face with all the strength she could muster. He was shocked, and he let her go, taking a step backwards.

"I . . . I am sorry, Sovana. Forgive me. I couldn't help myself. Your beauty maddened me with desire. I am not a bad man. You must believe me. It's just that I am filled with a great desire for you. Please say that you will forgive me."

"Turn around while I put my dress on."

He did as he was told. "I don't think you are bad, Osinoh. But you act like a bully. You must learn how to behave. You cannot get everything you want by force."

"I am sorry. I promise to be more gentle with you. Do you forgive me, Sovana?"

"I'll think about it." She turned and ran back down the path away from the water, back toward the walls of the village. Osinoh watched her disappear around a bend, his mind filled with pain and regret, his body shaking with love and lust.

The Cayuga are called the People of the Swamp Land. Their territory occupies a stretch of rolling hills and low-lying wetlands between the lower ends of the two Finger Lakes called Seneca Lake and Cayuga Lake. They are a proud people, like all of the peoples of the longhouses, the Haudenosaunee. And their culture was not much different from their neighbors, the Seneca and the Onondaga. There were some differences in the languages they spoke, slightly different words for ideas and objects, differences in pronunciation. But if you could speak Onondaga, you could converse in Cayuga without much difficulty.

As the Onondaga war party with its Seneca captives made its way back along the Finger Lakes trail on their way home, Hiawatha and Togahayon talked of their families and their mutual enemy, the Seneca. Hiawatha found out that they had much more in common than he, or any of his people, had previously thought. They shared the same beliefs about the Sky Beings and the beginning of the humans who sprang from the body of Sky Woman's daughter. Hiawatha had never considered this notion before—that the Cayuga believed in many of the same things his people did, and were therefore a part of Turtle Island, like the real human beings, the Onondaga. But the Seneca. This was a different story. They were animals, savages.

Togahayon agreed with Hiawatha on this point. The Seneca had done many barbarous things to his people. His brother and his brother-in-law were killed by them in one of the many raids they made into Cayuga territory. They were mighty in warfare. And on top of that, they were treacherous. Never to be trusted.

Hiawatha told Togahayon the story of his daughters' cruel deaths at the hands of Shadahgoh and his band of warriors.

Togahayon clenched his fist. "Shadahgoh is the worst of the Seneca chiefs. He lives to kill. He eats the flesh of humans and tortures captives not merely for vengeance, which, of course, is natural."

"Yes, of course," agreed Hiawatha.

"But Shadahgoh tortures for the sheer pleasure of it. He loves to strip away the skin of the skull and pour hot sand on the raw wound. And he loves to see men burn while they are still alive."

"One day I will kill him." Hiawatha's voice was filled with a grim determination.

"If you need an ally in your war against him, call on me. I will gladly aid you, and not just to repay my debt to you, but to rid Turtle Island of this monster."

"That day may come, and soon."

The Seneca captives marched single file in the middle of the war party, tied together by a long hemp cord that stretched from the neck of one to the necks of the others behind them. Their hands were also bound, and they looked forward stoically, accepting the grim reality of the torture and death that awaited them. Tehgonseh, the braggart warrior with a broken arm, overheard Hiawatha's and Togahayon's conversation. He was a very proud man, and he felt that he had nothing to lose, so he spoke.

"What you say about Shadahgoh is not the truth. He is a brave warrior and a great chief. He does not eat the flesh of humans. These are Cayuga lies! He killed this man's daughters to exact justice." He spit on the ground before him.

Honowe, who walked behind him, gave him a cuff behind the ear. "Shut your mouth, you Seneca dog. You will have plenty of time to scream out when we tie you to the stake at Onondaga."

Tehgonseh half turned and tried to spit on Honowe. Honowe gave him a shove that sent him to the ground and pulled down the two captives in front and behind him. He moved to strike him with his war club when Hiawatha intervened.

"Stop this."

Togahayon strode over to the Seneca sitting on the path. "What do you know of this?"

"All the Seneca know that Hiawatha, chief of the Onondaga, killed Shadahgoh's only son. The deaths of his daughters were an act of justifiable vengeance, mourning-deaths to assuage his pain and the pain of our people."

"Is this true?" asked Togahayon.

"Yes, it is true," said Hiawatha. "But the death of Shadahgoh's son was a hunting accident, not murder."

"And I killed him, not Hiawatha." Orios stepped forward, his head held high. "Hiawatha has protected me. I was hunting with his bow, and I shot the boy. It was fate, not my own will that guided the arrow. I did not aim for him. It was not murder."

Togahayon looked at Orios, then to Hiawatha. "But Shadahgoh believes that *you* killed his son?"

"Yes."

"And your people? What do they believe?"

"They also think that I killed the boy."

"Except for Sovana," said Orios. "I told her. I couldn't keep living a lie, letting your daughter believe that your actions brought about the death of her sisters."

Hiawatha took hold of Orios by his upper arms and looked him full in the face. "I am proud of you, Orios. A real man takes responsibility for his actions. I wanted to protect you because in some ways you were still a boy. But now you have become a man, a true Onondaga."

"It was a hard thing to do. But I knew I must."

"How did my daughter take the news?"

"She was upset. Angry. She ran away from me. I do not think that she will want to be with me now."

"We will see," said Hiawatha. "Be patient. I will speak with her."

After one day's journey, the small war party with its Seneca captives reached the village of Togahayon. They were greeted by all of the people who poured out of the gate in the stockade walls to greet their chief, their beloved Togahayon who they thought was forever lost to them. Cheers and cries from warriors and women, boys and girls, echoed throughout the land that surrounded the village. Such was the hatred for their enemy that some old women and young boys picked up sharp sticks and rushed the Seneca prisoners, attempting to stab them or strike them about the head. Togahayon called them off, telling them that these were mourning captives of Hiawatha, war chief of the Onondaga.

Togahayon gave Hiawatha and his men dried venison to take with them on their journey.

"We will meet again. I can feel it here." Togahayon pointed to his heart.

"I look forward to that day. Let us hope that we meet in more happy circumstances."

"Farewell, Hiawatha. May the Great Spirit guide your footsteps."

After two days' journey, Hiawatha returned to Onondaga with his war party leading the Seneca captives, and there was great rejoicing. Sovana and Tiwi rushed out to meet their father. Tiwi flung herself on him, and Hiawatha swept her up in his arms and held her high in the air. With his free arm he held Sovana close to him.

"Father, we were so worried about you," said Tiwi.

"Yes, we were afraid that you would never return." Sovana kissed him on the cheek.

"I am safe, my children, safe and back home. With captives to avenge your sisters."

Out of the corner of her eye, Sovana could see Orios holding the hempen cord that led the Seneca prisoners bound together in single file by three-foot lengths attached to their necks. The four Seneca looked proud and resigned. They tried to show no fear, but behind their eyes, a discerning mind could sense the dread of what they knew was to come. Orios looked different to her, changed in a way that she could not quite identify. Older? Perhaps. But his face did not really look older. He looked her way and she could see the longing in his eyes. She immediately looked away, afraid of her own conflicting emotions. She was drawn to him, but at the same time something pushed her back. It was as if she were torn apart. Her heart yearned for the maker of beautiful songs, but her mind kept recalling the words he had told her that night in the moonlight.

The men and women of the village all came out of their longhouses and crowded around their victorious leader and his war party. Teom and Kewahtawa came forward. Osinoh pushed his way through the crowd and stood before Hiawatha.

"Our great war chief has returned with mourning captives to avenge the loss of two bright stars of our village. Let us cheer Hiawatha, the mighty warrior and chieftain!"

The cries of the people of the village became deafening. And Osinoh cried and cheered loudest of all. He looked at Sovana who looked back at him. He smiled at her, and the way that he looked at her reminded her of the way he looked at her two days ago. She turned her eyes away.

Orios saw the looks exchanged between Sovana and Osinoh, and his blood became hot with an emotion that he had never felt before. His mind seemed as if it were on fire, and there was no water that could ever quench the flames.

"Orios." Hiawatha's voice came to him as if from far away, floating through smoke or fog on a summer's night.

"Orios, what is the matter with you? Wake up." Take the captives to the center of the village and tie them to the pillar by their necks. Honowe, go with him."

"The gauntlet!" someone in the crowd yelled. "Make them run the gauntlet!"

"Yes! Let the old women and children beat them with sticks."

"No! There will be suffering enough for them at the pillar." Hiawatha turned and left the crowd who followed Orios and the war party toward the village center. He wanted to sit in his longhouse for a moment and talk with his daughters. He wanted to wash the dust and paint from his face. As he walked, he hugged Tiwi close to him. Sovana walked by his side.

Makahwah was inside the longhouse stirring a pot of corn and beans with a long wooden spoon. Hiawatha removed his weapons, his bow and quiver, his tomahawk, his war club, and tossed them into a corner. He placed both hands in an earthen bowl of water and splashed the cool liquid over his face. Then he sat down cross-legged on the raised platform by the wall that was his resting and sleeping place. His lacrosse stick and the ceremonial crown with the deer antlers and feathers, the badge of his office as leader of his people, hung on the wall behind him. Tiwi came over and lay across his lap.

"So you're back," said Makahwah. She did not look up from the pottage that she kept stirring, even though it did not really need to be stirred any longer.

"Yes, mother, I am back. I have returned with mourning-war captives for my family and the people of our longhouse to assuage their grief. Orios and my warriors are at this moment tying them up at the pillar of blood."

"I know it is the way," said Makahwah, "but I do not approve of this."

"As Turtle Clan Mother and the grandmother of the victims, it is your duty to make the first blow, to cut the first cut, or be the first to burn their flesh."

"Hiawatha, my son, listen to me. What if I take a burning stick and stab it into the bodies of these men? What if I slice their fingers with a knife? Or pull out their fingernails? Will these actions bring back my granddaughters? Will they make Seawa sing and dance again? Will the pain inflicted upon these men make little Memoha rise up from the land of the Spirit Beings and laugh with us again?"

"No, of course not. But it will ease our pain. The Seneca

inflicted pain on us. Now we inflict it on them, and, in doing so, our pain is eased a little. It has always been so, it has always been the way."

"Well, I will have none of it. Torture them yourself. Remember, though, that the Wolf Clan and the family of Haka, who was also killed that day, need someone to replace him. If there is a brave one among them, one who survives the torture with dignity, perhaps he should be adopted to take Haka's place."

"We will see. What about you, Sovana? Will you strike a blow against these men to avenge the death of your sisters?"

"Are these the men who killed Seawa and Memoha?"

"They may not be the selfsame men who were in Shadahgoh's raiding party. But they are Seneca. Seneca are Seneca. They are all our enemies and the pain that we inflict on one of their kind, we inflict on all."

"I don't know, Father. I think that Grandmother may be right about this. What good can come of it? It will not bring my sisters back to us."

"Won't it make you feel better to make your enemy suffer the way that he made *you* suffer?"

"Why do people have to suffer?" asked Tiwi.

It was a question that Hiawatha could not answer. So he told her what all parents tell their children who ask such fundamental and unanswerable questions. "It's just the way that it is, little one. It has always been so, and always will be so."

"Why? Wouldn't it be nice if no one suffered? If no one killed anyone?" Tiwi looked up at Hiawatha with her big, innocent eyes.

"Here, Father. I made something for you while you were gone." Tiwi handed him a small string of shell-beads about four inches long.

"You made this?"

"Grandmother helped a little."

Hiawatha scooped up Tiwi in his arms and hugged her close to his chest. He kissed her on the forehead, then tickled her on the ribs until she giggled and writhed in his arms.

"Father?"

"Yes, Sovana?"

"Did Orios kill anyone?"

"No, my child, he did not. But he acquitted himself well. He was brave, and he did his part in the raid and the capture of our enemies. Why do you ask?"

"No reason. I was just wondering."

"Ah, I see. Will you come with me to watch the captives receive the justice of fire and blade?"

"I will come with you, but I will not watch."

Tiwi wiggled out of his arms. "Can I come too?"

Makahwah looked at her sternly. "You will stay here with me, little one."

Hiawatha put on the symbol of his office as chieftain, the feathered, deer-antler *gustoweh*, and he and his daughter left the longhouse and walked toward the center of the village. A cheer arose as Hiawatha approached the post where the four captives were tied by their necks, facing outward toward the four directions of Turtle Island. Atatarho was already there, stoking a fire above which hung a large cooking kettle.

"What is this for?" Hiawatha demanded.

"It is for the ritual communion, of course," replied the shaman.

"I do not condone the eating of human flesh, ritual or otherwise. We will give our prisoners the caress of the flames and the kiss of the blade, but I draw the line at eating our enemies."

"It is an ancient practice that many other nations ascribe to. In the old days . . ."

"These are not the old days, Atatarho. I am the chieftain of Onondaga. And I say no. "

Osinoh walked over to where Sovana stood some few paces behind her father. "I have missed you, Sovana. I think of you day and night. Here is something I made for you. I wish you to have it." He handed her a small pouch of soft fawnskin, dyed green.

Sovana held it in her hand and looked at it, unsure of what to do.

"Open it."

She untied the delicate strings that held the mouth of the pouch together and poured the contents out onto the palm of her hand. It was a necklace of white shell beads, and suspended from it was a beautifully carved turtle made from the soft red stone that came from the hills far away to the land where the sun set.

"Oh, Osinoh. It's so pretty, and it has such a powerful *orenda*. I can't accept such a precious gift."

"Why not? To me, you are the most precious person alive. You deserve to have a precious gift. You must accept it. As a token of how deep my feelings for you run. Here, let me put it on you."

Osinoh moved behind Sovana and placed the necklace around her neck. She held her long jet hair up so that he could tie the strings. The intricately carved red stone turtle rested in the hollow of her neck and looked stunning on her. The shade of the stone complemented the burnished gold of her skin. She stroked the shell of the turtle with the tips of her slender fingers.

"It feels so delicate. How does it look?" she asked.

"You look like a goddess."

"Thank you, Osinoh." She threw her arms around him and hugged him.

All of this was not lost on Orios. He did not forget his duties as a member of the war party that was in charge of the mourning rites, but he could not help but let his attention wander to the intimate exchanges between Sovana and Osinoh.

Even though she made a great show over the gift that Osinoh had given her, she glanced as often as she could to where Orios stood in the center of the village guarding the captives. She wondered if he had seen Osinoh give her the turtle necklace, and, in a way, her embrace of Osinoh was partly for Orios' benefit. He pretended that he did not see, and that he did not care what it was that she did, or who she talked to.

Two of the Seneca captives began to sing their death songs.

Tehgonseh, the warrior whose arm Hiawatha had broken, began first, followed by the noble sentry that Hiawatha had overpowered in the darkness of the forest.

> "I am Tehgonseh, mighty warrior am I.
> I have killed many enemies,
> Onondaga too,
> I am not afraid to die,
> Do your worst!
> Tear out my fingernails, burn off my feet,
> I will not cry out,
> I welcome the kiss of your blades."

One of the relatives of Haka, the sentry killed in the Seneca raid, approached Tehgonseh with a red-hot stone knife and jammed it between his legs in the most sensitive part of a man's body. In spite of his braggadocio, Tehgonseh screamed aloud in agony. Others rushed him with pointed sticks and jabbed him in the face, on the feet between the toes, and on the hands. Others wielded clubs and struck his ribs and arms, breaking and bruising his bones.

Atatarho danced a sorcerer's dance around the pole, pointing sticks at the captives and chanting curses that would cause them to have great difficulty in the otherworld.

The other Seneca who sang his death song, the sentry that Hiawatha had overpowered, recounted his life in verse:

> "I have lived a good life,
> Jehahna is my name.
> My mother is Clan Mother of the Wolf Clan,
>
> And in battle I am as fierce as the wolf,
> Many Cayuga have I slain.
> Their scalps hang from the rafters
> Of my mother's longhouse.

I am not afraid to die.
I will go to join my ancestors
Who wait for me in the otherworld.

You can do me no harm
For the Great Spirit watches over me,
He guides my steps as I walk the path of life."

Tehaneto, the Clan Mother of the Onondaga Wolf Clan, listened to the brave song of Jehahna. Tehaneto was the mother of Haka, the sentry who was killed in the Seneca raid that claimed the lives of Hiawatha's daughters. She went to the fire and picked up a stick that was white-hot at the end and walked over to the tied-up warrior.

"Let us see how brave you are when the kiss of flame caresses your thighs." She held the hot stick on his inner thigh. The sound and the smell of sizzling flesh permeated the air in the center of the village. Jehahna flinched, but he did not cry out. He held his head high, a stoic look in his eyes.

Tehaneto needed further proof. "Seneca, do you know what you have done to me?" He did not answer, but continued to look straight ahead.

"You have killed my only child. Now I will have no grandchildren, no one to tell stories of the ways of their mother and grandmother. You must suffer for this crime against me, this crime against the future generations, this crime against my clan." She withdrew a knife and sliced between each of his fingers. The blood flowed freely, staining the ground at the bottom of the post.

Still Jehahna remained silent. His jaw was set in grim determination. Pain was reflected in his eyes, but he made no sound except an occasional prayer to his ancestors.

"Spirits of my father's father, and his father's father, hear me from your place in the otherworld, the world that exists beside ours. Lend me your strength so that I may live up to the nobility of your lives, the nobility of your deaths."

Tehaneto was impressed with the dignity and courage of this warrior. She decided that she would burn his feet so that he could not walk for a while. Then she would take him into her own longhouse, and nurse his wounds, nurse him back to health, and adopt him as her own son into the Onondaga Wolf Clan. He would be requickened as her son, Haka.

The other Seneca prisoners were being tortured in a similar fashion. Some even worse. Hiawatha had cut off the fingers of one of the prisoners. Teom had scalped the braggart and poured hot sand on the raw wound of his head. Other members of the village cut them with knives and burned them with sticks in the most sensitive places so that they screamed aloud in pain. This was true vengeance; this was revenge. Now they were paying for the cruel deaths that their people had inflicted upon the innocent daughters of their leader. Orios took no part in all of this. It sickened him to hurt another person. But Osinoh tortured the prisoners with relish. He wanted to impress Hiawatha, to win his favor so that he would be more disposed to grant him his daughter's hand. He also hoped that his actions of retribution against the murder of her sisters would impress Sovana.

But Sovana could not watch. When she saw Osinoh cut off the ears of one of the prisoners and hold them aloft for all the village to see, the long earrings dangling and bloody, she turned in disgust and ran back toward Makahwah's longhouse. Osinoh and Orios both saw her leave. Osinoh threw the ears in his uncle's cooking pot and ran after her. He caught up to her before she reached the longhouse.

"Sovana, what is the matter?

"How can you do this?"

"Do what?"

"I saw what you did. It was horrible."

"What the Seneca did to your sisters was horrible too, wasn't it? I did it for you. So your grief could find some outlet."

"How will torturing these men, who had nothing to do with my sisters' deaths, help me? How will more suffering bring back my sisters from the otherworld?"

"Of course, you are right. It will not bring them back. But it helps the people. It relieves the grief. By inflicting pain, you dissolve your own pain." He grabbed her by the shoulders and prevented her from turning and leaving.

"Let me go! You're hurting me!"

"No! I will not let you go until you promise to marry me. I did what I did for you. It is the way of our people. I was only following our customs, our ways."

"I cannot marry someone who enjoys torturing another person. You sound like my father. There is too much anger in him, and there is too much anger in you."

Osinoh gripped her arms even harder and shook her violently. "You will be mine. I must have you, Sovana, don't you see that?"

"Stop it!"

"Let her go, Osinoh." Orios stood behind him, a war club in his right hand.

"What are you going to do if I don't, music-boy? Strike me? Knock me down?"

"I will smash your skull in and no one would miss you except your twisted uncle, who even now disobeys Hiawatha's orders and cooks the flesh of our captives." Orios took a step forward and brandished his war club menacingly. "Let her go. Now!"

Osinoh let go of Sovana's arms, and in a flash he grabbed the end of the war club with one hand while he gave Orios a powerful push with his left. Orios landed flat on his back and Osinoh yanked the war club free of his grasp. He raised it high in the air to strike Orios, but as he started to bring it down, Sovana screamed and lunged for the club. When he saw her, Osinoh tried to stop the forward movement of his arm, but it was too late. Sovana took a glancing blow on the side of her head and fell to the ground.

Hiawatha heard Sovana's scream and ran to her. He saw Orios

kneeling by her, and dropped to his knees. "Sovana, how badly are you hurt?"

She felt the knot on her head and said weakly, "I'll be all right."

Hiawatha looked up at Osinoh still holding the war club.

"It's not what it looks like. It was an accident. She threw herself in the way."

Hiawatha stood and glared at him. "Get out of here now," he said, a genuine menace steeling his voice.

Osinoh threw the war club down and stalked away. Sovana raised her head. "Wait!" she said. He stopped and turned around. She pulled the red stone turtle from her neck and threw it at Osinoh's feet. "Here is your token back. I don't want anything from you ever again."

Osinoh's face twisted in a controlled rage as he scooped up the necklace from the dust, turned, and stormed back to the center of the village. Hiawatha and Orios helped Sovana back to the longhouse, where Makahwah made a poultice of chickweed and gave her some soothing white willow-bark tea for the pain.

Sovana lay on her mat while Orios gently stroked her hair.

"Thank you, Orios, for coming when you did."

"Sovana?"

"Yes?" Her voice was husky with expectation.

"I have thought of nothing else but you since I left Onondaga."

"You have?"

"Yes. Sovana, I love you. Can you ever forgive me?"

"Yes, Orios. I forgive you, and I love you too."

They fell into each other's arms and held each other tightly. Orios had never felt such happiness as he felt at this moment.

Makahwah moved farther away, lifted an eyebrow, and looked at Hiawatha for an explanation. Hiawatha shrugged his shoulders noncommittally and left the longhouse.

The people seemed satisfied that the deaths of Seawa and Memoha had been avenged. All of the Seneca captives had been tortured to death, all except for Jehahna. His wounds were severe but not life-threatening. Tehaneto cut him down from the pillar of vengeance and had him carried to her longhouse. He was laid on bearskins, and Tehaneto wrapped his wounds with a poultice made from the wet leaves of chickweed and wood nettle, and she bandaged them carefully so that they would heal. From now on, she would treat him like a son, she would lavish affection on him, she would feed him the best food prepared with her own hands, and if he did not try to run away, there would be a requickening ceremony, and Jehahna would be adopted into the Onondaga nation with the new name of Haka.

Chapter Ten

Atatarho looked at his nephew with disgust. "Get hold of yourself. Weeping like a girl. I will not witness such weakness. Especially from a kinsman."

Osinoh sat at his uncle's feet, fingering the turtle necklace as if it were a talisman that possessed special powers. These shells had touched her slender neck, and this red-stone turtle had rested on the soft flesh just above her breasts. Tears filled his eyes, as he looked accusingly at Atatarho.

"You promised me that Sovana would be mine. I stole the turtle shell and sacrificed my honor for you."

"Be quiet and I will tell you of a plan. A way for you to get your precious Sovana back. That is, if you are man enough to follow through and do as I tell you."

Osinoh looked up at his uncle, the great sorcerer and elder of the Eel Clan.

"Will you do as I tell you?"

Osinoh nodded.

Atatarho took an empty gourd from beside the fire. He dipped his ladle into the pot and poured a measure of the vile liquid inside of the gourd, and then replaced the stopper on the neck.

"Now listen carefully. Inside this gourd is a very powerful potion. A love medicine. I want you to fill the gourd with water and place it near Sovana while she is at work so that she will think it is a vessel of drinking water, and when she is thirsty, she will drink from it. Or place it wherever you can. It does not matter how you do it, but just be sure that she drinks from it. You will give her the love medicine, and then you will court her again. She will forgive you. She will become intoxicated with you. She will forget the girlish Orios, and she will be yours forever."

Atatarho handed the gourd to Osinoh who gratefully took it from his uncle. "Thank you, Uncle."

"Now leave me. I have much more important work to do. The Great Council convenes tomorrow."

Life goes on. Until it stops. Outside the palisade walls of the village, near the spot where her two sisters died, Sovana and the other women of the village tended the crops. She loved the way the bean plants sensuously wrapped themselves around the tall, sturdy poles of the corn stalks, and the way that the large leaf-lobes of the squash shaded the small, growing gourds, keeping the weeds from choking out the three sisters who lived as one. Just as the beautiful, round-bellied squash were growing beneath the shade of their own leaves, she imagined that one day, perhaps soon, her own belly would be round with a child that would come from the love of Orios. She could feel new life all around her, and that thought made her happy.

She glanced down at the pretty little gourd she had brought with her to drink from. It was a pale fawn color, the color of the skin of an orange lily, and striped vertically with light green. It had a cunningly carved stopper made from the top of the neck. She had found it lying beside her when she awoke this morning. Someone had left it there for her to find when she first opened her eyes. It could have been Grandmother, but I bet it was Orios, she thought. It must have been Orios. Lately, he had been giving her little gifts, carvings that he had made or songs that he had composed for her on his flute. Such a sweet boy.

She worked on with her stone-tipped hoe, tending her section of the three sisters. It was hard work and she became very thirsty.

She put down her hoe, reached down, and picked up the little gourd. She carefully pulled the stopper from the neck, placed the gourd to her lips, threw her head back, and took a long drink. The water tasted vile! She spat out what was remaining in her mouth, and tried to look inside the gourd. She couldn't see past the curve in the neck. She sniffed at the opening and turned up her nose. She poured what was left of the water onto the ground and saw that it was a brackish green-brown color, the color of a toad. She shuddered involuntarily, and immediately she was gripped with a stabbing pain in the pit of her stomach. She groaned out loud.

The world was suddenly spinning too fast. Round and round in quick circles it reeled and whirled—the forest, the corn stalks, the wooden palisades, the forest again, and again, and again. Then everything collapsed into blackness as another, fiercer pain ripped through her stomach like a knife blade that was tearing her in two. She thought she heard someone scream. Then she realized it was her own voice screaming.

Women dropped their tools and baskets and ran to her side where she fell amid the corn and bean and squash leaves. She coiled up like a snake, clutching her belly, her eyes shut tight, her face a mask of pain. One of the women took off her deerskin dress and made a stretcher for her and four women carried her back to the village, to the longhouse of Makahwah.

The False Face Medicine Society was called in. Atatarho, Kewahtawa, and others in False Faces, chanted healing songs and danced in a circle around the raised pallet in the middle of the floor of the longhouse where Sovana lay, her face pale and sweating, her eyes and hands clenched together in waves of pain. Her head shook back and forth as she mumbled disconnected words, words that made no sense to the onlookers. The Medicine Dancers shook their turtle-shell rattles and approached her, placing their large grotesque faces right up next to hers, and then retreated, whirling and chanting. The drummers kept up a steady, hypnotic beat.

Hiawatha looked on helplessly. His face brightened with hope when Makahwah looked his way and nodded encouragement. Orios helped Makahwah mix an infusion of herbs, dried mayweed as an emetic and Canada waterleaf as an antidote to poison. Orios poured it into a cup, and Makahwah held it up to Sovana's parched lips. The girl tried to sip it, but she could not keep it down.

"Sovana. Listen to me. This is very important. Tell me what you ate."

"Noth-ing." Her voice was barely a whisper.

"Remember, girl. What were you doing when the pains took you?"

"I drank . . . water . . . bitter . . . water . . . from the gourd."

"What gourd? Where did you get it?"

And then Sovana screamed so loudly that even the False Face Dancers froze in their tracks, momentarily stunned by the ferocity of the pain and terror in her voice. And the sound of her scream was the high-pitched, elongated syllables of one word: *"Father!"*

Hiawatha rushed to her side and placed his hand on her forehead. She was on fire with a fever that burned within her. "Here I am, Sovana."

"Help me, Father. I am dying," she managed to say.

"No! You are not dying. You will soon be well. It is only a fever."

"Where is Orios?"

"I am right here, Sovana, I will not leave you," said Orios as he held her hand and choked back tears.

Hiawatha leaped to his feet and ran to where Makahwah was preparing a poultice of herbs covered in a wrapping of warm nettle leaves. He would place it on her forehead himself. With all the power that was in his soul, he would will her to live.

Atatarho reached beneath the folds of his robe with his left hand and surreptitiously fumbled for something hidden there. He danced closer to Sovana. Hiawatha turned with the warm poultice in his hand to see Atatarho touch Sovana's lips with his left hand.

"Get away from her!" All heads turned in Hiawatha's direction. "Did you see him? It was Atatarho! He poisoned her! He gave her the gourd with one of his foul potions in it!" Hiawatha charged and Atatarho retreated. Kewahtawa and several of the False Faces grabbed him by the shoulders and restrained him. Atatarho removed his mask and looked boldly at Hiawatha.

"Make sure you have proof, when you make such accusations, my friend. Do not blame me for the evil that you have done. When you make blood medicine, blood medicine comes back upon you." He turned on his heel and left the longhouse. Hiawatha struggled to break free, but the other men held him fast. Makahwah glared at him.

"Have you no concern for your daughter? She is dying, and you are raving nonsense. Atatarho is a shaman. He came here with the False Face Society in good faith to perform rituals of healing. I'm ashamed of you. You disgrace our clan and our people."

"Atatarho poisoned Sovana, and I'm sure he had a hand in the deaths of Seawa and Memoha. I cannot prove it yet, but I will, and I swear I will have my revenge on him and on Shadahgoh. I will not rest until they are both dead."

With these words Hiawatha shook off the men who held him back and went to the pallet where his daughter lay. He knelt beside her and took her hand in his own. Her hand was cold and lifeless, and her eyes stared straight up at the ceiling of the longhouse.

While he was vowing vengeance, his daughter had died. He wailed like a wounded animal and pulled at his hair. Makahwah went to the other side of the pallet, closed her granddaughter's eyes, and kissed her on the forehead. Orios threw himself upon Sovana's lifeless body. His tears flowed freely, and for once, Makahwah felt real affection for the boy. She placed her arms around him and comforted him. But he was inconsolable.

She turned to Hiawatha. "Now are you satisfied? How many more deaths will you bring down upon my house? I told you before to leave. I tell you again. Leave this house at once."

All eyes were upon Hiawatha as he rose from his knees and dropped the cold, lifeless hand of his daughter. Her once lovely skin, rosy and golden, was now slowly turning shades of sickly green and deathly blue. His mind was numb with anguish and his body shook with rage. He glared at his mother-in-law who was already washing Sovana's body, preparing her for her death-gown, and cursed her beneath his breath. He walked slowly to the section of the longhouse where his belongings were kept. He gathered up his bow and his arrows. The same bow that had killed Shadahgoh's only son. He cursed Orios, that stupid, foolish boy. He cursed himself for entrusting such a weapon into the hands of an inexperienced whelp. This bow would one day soon send an arrow into Shadahgoh's heart. He picked up his fawnskin pouch and his war club. He placed his deadly stone tomahawk into the belt of his loincloth, and as he did so, he thought "one day soon this hatchet will split Atatarho's skull." This thought was his only consolation as he gathered together his tobacco, his pipe, and his clothes, and placed them all in the middle of a bearskin robe, securing it tight with a length of rawhide. He left his lacrosse stick leaning against the corner. He had no time now for sport. From now on, his thoughts would be bloody; death would be his sport. He slung the robe over his back, cast one final glance around him at the place that he had lived in all these years with his wife, now dead, the place where his daughters had been born, where they had all eaten and played and slept. He cuffed tears back from his eyes with fierce blows from the backs of his wrists.

Hanging on a peg on the wall above where he had made his bed and slept every night, was his *gustoweh*, the fur-and-feather-covered chieftain's bonnet surmounted with deer antlers and eagle feathers, the symbol of his status as chief of the Onondaga nation. He took it down from the peg and stared at it, remembering happier times when his wife and daughters surrounded him and he was the great leader of a great nation.

"That stays here!" Makahwah's voice boomed out so that all in the longhouse, even at the farthest ends, turned their eyes and heads, and looked in her direction. "You have proven yourself unfit to lead the people. You have brought disaster and death upon my family and our nation. By my authority as Turtle Clan Mother, I will help select a new chieftain. Leave the antlers here, for they will rest on another head."

Hiawatha threw the headdress down to the ground. A few gasps could be heard from the shocked onlookers. Makahwah, her strong hands poised with cleansing cloths over Sovana's lifeless body, glared at Hiawatha's back as he turned and stormed out of the longhouse.

Weeks had passed since Sovana's burial rites. Hiawatha did not attend them. But nonetheless, he was there. No one saw him high up in a tree looking down on the scaffold where Sovana's body lay wrapped in furs, surrounded by flowers, medicines, cooking utensils, combs, and other items that she would need for the yearlong journey that her soul would make on its way back to the Spirit World. Hiawatha could not show himself—his humiliation and his anger were too great. Makahwah had cast him out of her longhouse and had even gone so far as to defend Atatarho, a man who Hiawatha knew was implicated in some way in the deaths of his daughters.

Hiawatha had watched Orios weeping and grieving as Makahwah delivered a funeral oration. She told Sovana that the people would always remember her, would always love her, and that they would pray daily to the Great Spirit that her journey along the Strawberry Way would be a safe and easy one. Makahwah told her that she would be remembered at the Great Feast of the Dead, and that they would keep her bones in a special place in her longhouse. Hiawatha watched from his secret perch as a woman from the Bear Clan cut off a strand of Sovana's hair to be offered up to Grandmother Moon, who would add it to the vast cloak of human souls that she was always sewing. He smelled the tobacco smoke and the smoke from the sacred fire that burned night and day by her raised funeral platform. He heard the turtle-shell rattle of Kewahtawa and the old man's prayer-chant that was meant to comfort the girl's soul, her life-force still floating around her body, unsure of where to go, unprepared as yet to make the long journey to her home in the sky. With tears in his eyes, Orios played a mournful dirge that deeply moved the village with its resonant beauty and its sorrowful notes, and made Hiawatha's soul long to die and join his wife and daughters in the otherworld, the land of the Spirit Beings.

Hiawatha had moved outside of the walls of the village and set up a small hut in the forest, a place to cache his few belongings and to sleep after a day of wandering alone through the woods. His friends and his closest advisers were worried about him. They too were saddened by the deaths of his daughters, but they took a more objective view of the grand order of things. Hiawatha was tangled in a spider's web of destructive and malevolent thoughts, and Teom and Kewahtawa had a plan to help him recover his senses, to grapple with his grief in a more manly way. Ever since the people could remember, the game of lacrosse was played as a way to melt bitterness in the hearts of the people. They thought that if they organized a large, village-wide match, and convinced Hiawatha to play, the rigors and camaraderie of the sport would help ease the burden of sorrow that he carried with him like a heavy stone strapped to his heart. Lacrosse was an ancient practice that was as much of a healing ritual as it was a sport. A true warrior and a true Onondaga could not refuse to take part in a large match.

And so these two old friends sought out his hut in the woods. It was not difficult to find, for Hiawatha made no attempt to conceal it, and, in fact, he had not moved far away from the village, since he still had one daughter left, little Tiwi, who stayed close to the skirts of her grandmother. He wanted to keep a watchful, if distant, eye on his only remaining child. But instead of the company of men, he now chose the trees and the creatures of the forest as his companions. They were truer and more honest. They did not argue. They did not scheme for power. They did not poison. Not the way that human beings did. Each night for the ten days that he had removed himself from the village, he threaded his way carefully through the forest to the edge of the swamp where he would hide in the shadows and watch Atatarho. He knew in his heart, in his very soul, that the sorcerer was somehow responsible for the deaths of his daughters. He had no proof, nothing tangible to offer as evidence. This proof was what he sought. And so he hid and waited and watched from a distance the loathsome old sorcerer stir his malevolent, evil-smelling brews while the flames of his fire cast light and shadow on his wicked face.

He returned one morning to his hut, weary from his sleepless vigil. His hair was uncombed and matted with mud. The whites of his eyes were red and his face was swollen with insect bites, bites that he had to silently endure while standing at night on the edge of the swamp, watching and waiting. Teom and Kewahtawa were sitting cross-legged on the ground outside of his makeshift hut. When they saw him, they were shocked. Hiawatha had always taken such pride in his personal appearance. They could not believe that standing before them was the same man they had known and loved and respected as their chieftain for all of these years.

"Hiawatha," said Kewahtawa.

Hiawatha stared at them as if they were ghosts or strangers.

"We have come to see how you are getting along," said Teom. "Do you not know us? I am Teom, your old companion. And this is Kewahtawa, Kewahtawa the dreamer and shaman, your closest adviser."

Hiawatha slowly sat down on the ground in front of the two men. He sighed heavily. "Yes, I know you. Do you think I have gone mad?"

"We don't know what to think, Hiawatha," said Kewahtawa. "We have been worried about you these many days since you left our village. Your sorrow is great. We know. We understand. We have come to help you."

"Help me? How can you help me?"

"We have brought your playing stick." Teom reached for Hiawatha's lacrosse stick that lay beside him and held it up.

"So? What would you have me do? Play lacrosse with the trees?"

"No," laughed Kewahtawa. "We and the Medicine Society have organized a village-wide match. The game is in your honor, Hiawatha."

"Yes," said Teom. "The purpose of the game is to help melt the bitterness in your heart. And in the heart of Orios."

"Orios? What of Orios?"

"He, too, wanders the woods. He will not eat or speak to anyone. He walks the woods playing sad songs on his flute all day and all night."

"I have not seen him," said Hiawatha.

"The woods on the other side of the village, by the lake. He plays and weeps by the water's edge. Makahwah has seen him."

"Makahwah!" Hiawatha spat out her name. "She took Atatarho's part, calling him a great healer. Healers do not poison people."

"Makahwah is my woman, Hiawatha. And she is still your only child's grandmother. She did what she thought must be done for the sake of all the people. She still loves you. Tiwi follows her everywhere, and every day she asks for her father."

"Tiwi," moaned Hiawatha. "Poor little Tiwi. Her sisters gone." Tears were stinging his red eyes.

"But her father is still alive. She needs you. Come to the match. She will be there. She can watch her father, the great Hiawatha, play victoriously in the sacred sport."

Hiawatha stood up, cuffing the tears from his cheeks. "Yes. You are right. I will come. I will play. We must find Orios. He must also play."

Teom and Kewahtawa stood up too, and they both, in turn, embraced Hiawatha.

"Come my friends, let us go. But I must keep an eye on Tiwi."

"We will all watch Tiwi. The whole village will watch Tiwi. And Tiwi will watch us from the side of the field as we play."

A village-wide lacrosse match is a sight that one does not forget. Fifty to a hundred or more men, young and mature, stripped down, painted red, brandishing their sticks, lined up facing each other, and shouting, shouting. The match always begins with shouting, with prayers shouted out loud to the spirits of the earth and the sky: the earth that they run on, kicking up clouds of dust from their racing, stamping feet, and the sky from where the first beings fell, the sky where the ball will fly, soaring high like the eagle, and each man on each team vying fiercely to catch the ball with his stick and hurl it back into the sky toward their goal, or to one of their team members closer to the goal.

Hiawatha played on the red side—twenty-five brave men wearing collars of porcupine quills dyed red. The opposing side facing them wore collars of blue-dyed quills. Teom, who played on the blue team, lifted his stick above his head and shouted above the voices of the crowd.

"We play this match for Hiawatha!" Cheers came from both sides. "We play it so that the strength of the game, the strength of all those gathered here on this spot, will enter the mind and heart of our friend."

"Hiawatha! Hiawatha! Hiawatha!" shouted the players and the spectators who ringed the field.

"We play this game also for Orios! May the strength of all those gathered here, enter into the heart of our young friend Orios, and may that strength become his strength." Teom had found the wandering musician and convinced him to come and join the play, to join Hiawatha and all of his extended family members in the village of Onondaga.

"Orios!" the crowd shouted.

Orios handed his flute to Teom and took the field with Hiawatha's red-collar team.

"Spirits of the Earth and Sky," continued Teom, "join us! Spirit of the Turtle, whose back can withstand all blows, join us! Spirit of the Deer, whose feet are swift, join us! Spirit of the Bear, who is strong and gives mighty blows, join us! Spirit of the Eagle, Spirit of the Hawk, whose wings soar high, join us!"

The sidelines were filled with the women, the boys and girls, and the old men of the village. Makahwah threw the ball from the sidelines and Teom caught it in the netting of his lacrosse stick. Everyone cheered wildly as Teom threw the ball high into the air in the middle of the empty space between the two opposing teams. Pandemonium broke loose as fifty men all rushed toward the middle, their sticks lifted high above their heads, their voices lifted above in fierce cries. The people on the sidelines cheered and fixed their eyes on their favorite players, the sons and brothers, the fathers and uncles, the great and brave men of their clans and longhouses. Tiwi jumped up and down beside her grandmother and tried to pick her father out from among all the half-naked, painted, struggling men, through the huge cloud of dust that so many running feet kicked up.

"Grandmother, where is my father?"

"Down there, in the middle," said Makahwah, but she could not pick him out from all the other running men. "Wait. There! There he is! The one with the ball!" A figure had leapt up higher than all the other men, his stick held higher, and had snatched the hard leather ball out of the sky before a dozen or so others were able to reach it. Tiwi screamed with delight as her father hit the ground, spun round, and ran as fast as a young stag through the maze of men in blue quill collars who rushed to meet him, to prevent him from reaching the goal at their backs. One man, his hair tied up in a top knot and dyed the same shade of blue as the quills that decorated his neck, swung his stick at Hiawatha's legs, but Hiawatha had read the man's intentions, and, without breaking stride, leapt over the stick's horizontal trajectory, hit the ground and continued running toward the goal with a pack of twenty men in hot pursuit. Members of the red-collar team, Hiawatha's team, tried to prevent the blue-collars from catching him. They struck mighty blows with their sticks, aiming for the legs to trip them up. If they did not fall, some opponents turned and struck back, causing them to fall behind in the chase. Hiawatha was closing in on the goal, but two opponents had managed to get there before him, and they stood in front of the post, waiting to block or catch the ball when he made his goal-shot.

Hiawatha stopped suddenly and swung his stick with the ball nestled in the leather webbing high above his head. He leapt to his left as if he were going to fling the ball into the left corner of the goal. The two defenders instinctively moved in the same direction in order to block the shot, but at the last minute Hiawatha shifted position and flung the ball into the opposite corner. The two defenders looked in dismay at where the ball cleanly pierced the planes of the goal lines. A deafening roar went up from the sidelines and from the red-collar team. Orios jumped up on top of Hiawatha's back and all of his teammates formed a tight circle around him, pumping their sticks into the air and chanting Hiawatha's name.

Hiawatha looked over to the sidelines. Everyone was smiling and celebrating the goal. Everyone but one figure, standing alone, intently staring across the field to the opposite sideline. Hiawatha followed the direction of Atatarho's gaze, and his eyes rested on his only daughter, little Tiwi, laughing and clapping beside her grandmother. Atatarho was now walking slowly around the edge of the field with his eyes fixed on Tiwi on the other side.

"Hiawatha," shouted Teom. "You must throw the ball up for play." Hiawatha caught the ball that Teom tossed to him. He whirled his stick four times around his head and let it fly straight up into the sky in the middle of the field. Both teams rushed again toward the center to retrieve the ball. But this time, Hiawatha did not reach the middle first, nor did he come down out of the leaping pack with the ball in his stick. He kept looking for Atatarho, but he could not see him for all of the running, shouting men, waving their sticks above their heads.

One of the opposing team came down with the ball and ran past Hiawatha, knocking him down to the dusty field. The men all followed fast in a pack striking mighty blows. Orios ran over to where Hiawatha was picking himself up.

"Hiawatha. What's wrong? Are you hurt?"

"Atatarho. Where is he?"

"He is not playing, of course. He is too old to play."

"No, not on the field. On the edge. He is going to hurt Tiwi, just as he poisoned Sovana." Orios scanned the field and saw Atatarho kneeling beside Tiwi, his hand on her head, whispering into her ear.

"Hiawatha! Over there!"

"Get him away from my daughter!" Hiawatha screamed as he made a dash for the side of the field where Tiwi stood, entranced by the sorcerer. Orios ran after him, confused, afraid of what Hiawatha might do. But suddenly the mad rush of stamping feet descended upon them, and they were caught up in the momentous surge of bodies contending for the ball.

"Hiawatha!" shouted Teom. "What is the matter with you? Play! Go for the ball!" His teammates pushed him and shoved him along before them, laughing and cajoling and playfully hitting him on the back and shoulders with their sticks.

"Stop it! Stop it! You don't understand! Atatarho means to kill my daughter." And he escaped from the ring of friends and companions who were urging him on. He broke free of the pack and looked over to where he had last seen Tiwi and Atatarho. But they were both gone. His eyes scanned the horizon. Atatarho was nowhere in sight. And neither was Tiwi. He ran to the opposite side of the field and stared as hard as he could through the rising cloud of dust kicked up into the air by forty-nine pairs of running feet. Teom and Orios reached his side and pulled him back, pulled him around so that he was facing the other side of the field. There, on the side of the hill that gently sloped up and away from the playing field, was his little daughter with another little girl gathering wildflowers, skipping, and playing. The sorcerer was not with them. He was nowhere to be seen.

"Look, Hiawatha, she is there. Safe. Playing with her friend. Playing with the flowers." Teom put an arm around his friend's shoulders, and gave him a reassuring hug.

"Yes, Hiawatha, she is fine," said Orios. "Come. Let us play. The game is in your honor. For you. To heal you."

"Yes. Yes, of course. We must play."

The other men had stopped playing. They were all standing and talking among themselves in subdued tones and looking over toward Hiawatha, Teom, and Orios.

"Come, let us rejoin the play," said Hiawatha to his companions. The three of them jogged back to the center of the field.

"What are we waiting for?" shouted Hiawatha with forced jocularity to the men who stood about poised with expectancy. "Throw the ball!"

A great cheer went up on the field and spread to the sidelines. Everyone who had been afraid that Hiawatha was about to do something irrational, everyone who had wondered why he had stopped playing and was running around the field in a confused state, now breathed a great and general sigh of relief. And that sigh manifested itself in a loud and steady cheer.

"Hiawatha! Hiawatha! Hiawatha!"

The ball was hurled high into the air, and for a moment it seemed lost in the glare of the sun, and then no one looked at the ball, for where the ball should have been, where their eyes were directed in the sky, was a great black bird larger than any bird that anyone could remember seeing. Some who tell this story say that the bird was so large that it blotted out the sun. Others are more subdued, and liken the dark bird to a giant vulture, a vulture larger than any that had ever lived and soared through the skies. But all who told this tale agreed that the appearance of the bird was malevolent. It seemed to have flown out of nowhere, out of a hole ripped in the firmament, a creature that had escaped from the otherworld to pierce the texture of this one, bringing doom and discord in its wake.

For a second, no one moved. All were frozen in anticipation of some vast, portentous omen. And then it dived. Dived straight down from its height toward some object on the ground. Only Hiawatha knew what was going to happen next.

"Tiwi!" he screamed, and he took off racing toward the side of the hill where his little girl was picking flowers. She heard him call her name and looked up. She saw her father in the distance running toward her and all the other people of the village turned toward her, looking. She waved. But she also knew something was wrong. She looked up just in time to see a large pair of talons, talons the size of a man's head, streaking toward her, and then she was lifted up and up as a bright hot pain slashed through her small body, making her cry out and then lose consciousness.

Hiawatha was too late. All he could do was stare helplessly at those huge black wings flapping slowly, slowly, almost as if time or life itself were slowing down. And for his daughter, they were. The seconds were spilling from her life like the drops of her blood that fell on her father's face as he stood beneath her and watched the great evil bird climb higher and higher toward the hills. He threw his lacrosse stick at the disappearing dying-girl-and-bird form, but it fell short. He cursed the sky and the spirits of the air, and the entire universe of Turtle Island. As he ran as fast as he could toward the hills where the evil bird had flown, he screamed out over and over again: "Atatarho! Atatarho! I promise you. I will kill you."

The men of the village followed Hiawatha and the path the bird took up into the hills. They spread out to comb the hillside and beyond. After an hour of searching, Hiawatha's heart froze when he heard Teom shout "She's over here!"

When he and others reached Teom, there, on sharp rocks surrounded by tall pines, they found the broken, dead body of his last remaining daughter. Her small skull was smashed in, and her left arm was twisted behind her. Hiawatha picked up the dead and mangled body of his precious little girl, a little girl once so sweet and so innocent, now a lifeless corpse. He kissed her bloodied face and walked back down the hill. And the men of Onondaga, many still carrying their lacrosse sticks, followed him in a surreal procession of death.

Little Tiwi's funeral was the saddest that could be remembered in the minds of the people. The villagers of Onondaga were unsettled by the ominous way in which she died, and also by Hiawatha's reaction to her death. He no longer grieved in a way that was seemly for a man. He carved no mask out of basswood. Neither did he offer up prayers to the Spirit Beings in the otherworld.

Some said that the deaths of his three other daughters, coming so quickly one upon the other, had drained all the sorrow and grief that was in him, and he had nothing left inside of him to bring forth. His tears were all dried up, they said. He had shed them all over Seawa, over Memoha, and over Sovana. And, of course, they added to his first great sorrow, the tragic death of Tamora, his beloved wife.

Others maintained that he was mad. The great tragedies that had recently fallen upon him had unhinged his mind. A mind that was once so clear and pure, as clear as the eagle's eye, and as pure as the great crystal lake. This mind, now, was a swamp. A morass of confused and tangled thoughts. The fact that he had left the village, refused to attend his daughter's obsequies, and took up his solitary wanderings in the forest only confirmed this suspicion in the minds of many. Still others said that he was bent on revenge. A revenge far more terrible than the last bloodletting in the village square. Some said that his "madness" was a sham, that he had a dark purpose and a plan that he would soon put into action. All of the people knew that Shadahgoh was responsible for the deaths of two of his daughters. Eyewitnesses had watched the Seneca descend upon the helpless girls and murder them. All right then, wreak vengeance upon the Seneca and Shadahgoh for these deeds. It was the way. But what of the strange deaths of Sovana and Tiwi? These were not so easily explained, and a path of revenge was not so easily found.

Everyone in the village knew that Hiawatha blamed Atatarho for the deaths of Sovana and Tiwi. Atatarho, the great sorcerer and shaman, the respected elder of the Eel Clan, healer of the sick, caster of spells upon the people's enemies. The notion that he was responsible for the deaths of these girls did not sit well with many in Onondaga. But there were others who saw the logic behind his accusations, if logic could be used to explain what must finally come down to magic. It certainly looked as though Sovana could have been poisoned. And Atatarho was known far and wide as a concocter of mighty potions. And, ever since Sovana's death, the people had noticed a strange rift between Atatarho and his nephew Osinoh, who, as everyone knew, had wanted to marry Sovana.

And what of the death of Tiwi? It was almost too frightening to think of. The great black bird who took her away in its huge talons was clearly not a creature of this world. If it was, it was a creature that no one in living memory had ever set eyes upon. It was a demon-bird, a bird from the otherworld, a ghost-bird, and, as such, it could have been summoned forth by the powers of a great magician, a great conjurer, a great sorcerer. And Atatarho was the greatest living sorcerer. He, and only he, had the necessary power and skill to bring forth such a dreadful creature. But why?

Makahwah and the people of the Turtle Clan longhouse were inconsolable. Within such a short span of time, they had lost the flower of their clan. The four granddaughters of their great matriarch dead. Gone forever. Gone too was the great mind and strength of a leader that they had always relied upon. Hiawatha was lost to them, to their longhouse, to the village, to the Onondaga nation. He wandered the swamps and forests alone plotting revenge. Lurking in the back of everyone's mind was another loss. A loss that seemed somehow to presage the others, to symbolize the disasters that had recently descended upon them: the loss of the great clan totem. The mysterious disappearance of the Great Turtle Shell that used to hang high in the longhouse, a symbol of the ancient power and mythic origins of the people, hovered ominously over the village. Even now, Makahwah often caught herself unconsciously glancing up to the place the shell had hung. And each time she saw the beam that it had been affixed to, she shivered, and her heart emptied out, leaving behind a vacant spot in its place.

The day after Tiwi's funeral rites, Makahwah was staring up at the empty space when Kewahtawa walked over and put his hand on her shoulder. "We must have a meeting of the Great Council."

His wife, the strong mother of her people, looked up at him. Her face looked older now, more drawn and pinched from suffering, but the emotion that poured forth from her eyes made Kewahtawa think of the day he had first seen her, so many, many years ago. She was young then, and bright, quick and slender as a doe, graceful in her movements like a swan gliding on a still lake. Her first husband, Tamora's father, had been killed in a Seneca raid a few months after Tamora was born. Kewahtawa had come from another village to trade furs for seeds. He followed her and little Tamora around for days, moonstruck like a lost puppy, until one day she turned and stared at him frankly in the face.

"Why are you following me around like some motherless whelp?" He could only stare at her dumbly, unaware of how silly he had become in the eyes of everyone in the village. Finally, and with a great effort of will, he managed to speak.

"I cannot help myself. I am drawn to you by some power that I cannot describe. Like an arrow when it is let loose from a bow."

Kewahtawa remembered now, just as clearly as if it had happened only an hour ago, the look of pleasant surprise that melted across Makahwah's young, smooth face. She took him by the hand and said, "Come into our longhouse and sit and talk with my mother and my sisters." And that was how he came to live under the roof of the Turtle Clan, in Onondaga, the beginning of his long and happy life with Makahwah. But now Tamora was gone, and the grandchildren were gone, violently taken away from them. He knew that he must be strong. Not only for Makahwah, but for the whole clan and for the entire village that had adopted him years ago, a village and a nation that was now leaderless. Their once proud and charismatic leader, the great Hiawatha, was now a grief-stricken shell. Driven by anger and rage, he no longer had the best interests of his people uppermost in his mind. His mind was twisted and bent upon revenge. He was a man to be feared rather than followed.

It was up to Makahwah, as the leader of the high Turtle Clan, to pick a new leader, someone who could help the people heal their collective grief. Someone who could help them enter into a new age of peace and prosperity. Someone who could forge new alliances based on mutual interests and trust, based on peaceful exchange and trade, not constant war and bloody, pointless revenge. Kewahtawa knew that revenge begets only more revenge; but he was too old, his eyes too dim, for such a task. The people needed someone with much energy, and someone with great *orenda*. But who?

Makahwah looked up at him. She slowly pulled herself up to a standing position. "Yes. You are right. We must act now. I will call together a meeting of the Great Council and of all the Clan Mothers. We will all meet to determine our future path."

On the following day, the Great Council met in solemn session. The usual in-jokes and glib jibes that peppered the beginning of a routine council meeting were absent from this one. After all that had taken place in the past weeks, words, especially idle ones, seemed useless. More than useless. Words seemed inappropriate. The elders, the chiefs, and the Clan Mothers all sat in silence with their eyes cast down, or searching above along the angles of the roof beams. Some silently prayed to the Great Spirit, the Great Perfector of Minds, for guidance, for wisdom, for inspiration.

Makahwah at last spoke. "I have called you here today, because a grave crisis threatens the very existence of our nation, of the Onondaga people." She looked around the room slowly, carefully measuring the faces and eyes of those who sat beside her in a circle around the council fire.

Tabaldak, the Clan Mother of the Eel Clan, lean and straight as the shaft of an arrow, sat sternly beside the elders and respected people of her clan. To her right was her brother, the great and powerful sorcerer, Atatarho, whose hair was plaited with the bones and fangs of snakes and eels, who wore a necklace of bear claws that hung down about his breast. A great but dark *orenda* poured forth from his eyes which were narrowed to slits.

As her eyes swept to the left, she saw Tehaneto, Clan Mother of the Wolf Clan. Beside her sat her cousin, Tajarta, a large man with a great, kind, sack-like face. He had once been a mighty warrior, as was his father before him. During the warfare long ago between the Mohawk and the Onondaga, Tajarta's father captured the Mohawk war chief and brought him back to the village, where he was tortured and killed. This stopped the Mohawk war. Tajarta inherited his father's warlike skills and killed many Seneca during the hostilities with them in the days of his youth and manhood. He was a proud and noble man, thought Makahwah, but too full of himself and his ancestors' glories in battle to ever be the kind of leader that was needed now, a leader who could bury the war club once and for all. Doubt continued to fill her mind with every face she looked upon. Who was capable of leading them?

"As you know, we have no leader now. Hiawatha, my son-in-law, the father of my dead grandchildren, is no longer among us. He dwells apart in the hidden recesses of the forests and swamps."

A murmuring of commiseration swept over the circle like a breeze that bends the tops of high grasses. And then a long shadow fell across the center of the circle. It was the shadow of a man who stood in the doorway, the sun behind him framing his dark silhouette. All eyes turned from Makahwah to the figure that now stepped into the council house.

"Do not count me out so hastily. I am not dead. Nor am I mad." But Hiawatha's appearance did little to dispel these notions in the minds of the people. Mud matted his hair, taking the place of the crown of antlers and feathers that he formerly wore at these meetings. He was naked but for his torn and soiled breech-clout, and dirt streaked his muscled torso as though he had deliberately clothed himself with the Earth.

"Welcome, Hiawatha," said Kewahtawa. "We have missed you. Come. Sit with the council." And Kewahtawa, gesturing to a place beside him, bade Hiawatha, his old friend, to sit and join the circle. Hiawatha looked around the circle at the upturned faces that gleamed and glowed by the firelight, faces with expressions of awe mixed with pity and apprehension. His eyes came to rest upon the face of Atatarho who sat upright, arms folded across his chest, fingers playing with his bear claws, assuming an air of boredom.

Hiawatha spit on the ground before him. "I will not sit with the man who killed my daughters. Tell this foul toad to leave, and then I will sit with the council."

"But Hiawatha, you know this is not possible. Atatarho is a member of the council. His sister is Eel Clan Mother, and he has every right to be here. As we all do. Do as I bid you. Sit now and listen. Your mother-in-law, Makahwah, has come to address the council. Her speech concerns you, as it concerns all of us."

Hiawatha looked over to where Makahwah sat, a stoic and stony figure, waiting with patience for him to make his move. At last, Hiawatha walked around the circle and sat down next to Kewahtawa.

"Continue, Clan Mother," said Kewahtawa.

Makahwah stood up and moved to the center of the circle beside the council fire. She paused, looking around the room. Then she began.

"As you all know, the longhouse of the Turtle Clan has met with much grief and sorrow. What I have to say now fills my heavy heart with even more grief. With Hiawatha as our chief, the Onondagas have prospered. Our storehouses have always been filled with the harvest of new crops. Our war captains, all trained by Hiawatha, are respected throughout the land for their cunning and bravery. But our once-great chief has changed."

Makahwah paused and looked directly at Hiawatha. Her look was filled with sorrow, with pity, and with love. Hiawatha could not bear to meet her stare. He looked down at the ground before him. Out of the corner of his eye, he saw the antlers and feathers of his *gustoweh* that lay on the floor before Kewahtawa.

Makahwah continued. "His heart is now filled with a dark bitterness, and he no longer walks under the wing of the Great Spirit. This puts us all in grave danger. Sadly, I must ask that Hiawatha forsake the headdress of the Onondaga chief."

Hiawatha continued to stare bitterly at the empty *gustoweh*. All eyes looked to him for his response. Suddenly, he reached over and snatched up the headdress, the sacred badge of office, from in front of Kewahtawa. A collective gasp came from the seated members of the council. Hiawatha stood. He held the crown of antlers, feathers, and deer hide out before him, then walked over to his mother-in-law. They stood facing each other, their eyes locked for a moment in mutual love, in mutual grief, in mutual understanding. He moved the crown forward till it rested on Makahwah's breast.

"Take it," he said. Then he walked back and sat down again beside his old friend.

Kewahtawa cleared his throat of the tears that were trying to choke it. Everyone around the fire was silent and still. Finally, he spoke. "Who does the head mother appoint as the new chief of the Onondaga?"

Makahwah looked down at the headdress, and then she slowly raised her eyes. They were brimming with tears. "The position of chief requires a man with great *orenda*, especially in these troubled times with nations and peoples warring all around us. It saddens my heart to say that my house has no one now qualified to wear the antlers. So I must pass the headdress to the house of my sister clan mother, Tabaldak. As Clan Mother of the Eel Clan, the second sacred clan of our people, it is her duty to find someone to pass on the power of leadership."

Tabaldak rose from her place at the fire, and stood straight, stretching out her lean frame, and she slowly walked over to Makahwah, who fought valiantly to stem the tears that wanted to escape from her burning eyes and stream down her face. But she would not give Tabaldak the satisfaction of seeing her cry. She bit her tongue as she handed over the headdress to her sister clan mother. Everyone in the village knew that there was no love lost between the two of them. Tabaldak had long been jealous of the power that Makahwah had wielded all these many years in the council and among the people. All the council members knew almost by heart the harsh words that had been flung at each other in past council meetings. But still, they respected one another. For all her pettiness and jealousy, Tabaldak was a wise and noble woman. A woman with much knowledge, integrity, and insight.

Makahwah extended the headdress. Tabaldak reached out and placed her two hands on either side of the crown. She felt the smooth sides of the brushed deer hide against her rough fingertips and the feathers that streamed down on all sides tickled the backs of her heavily veined and wrinkled hands. For a moment the two of them stood holding onto the crown. Their eyes locked. Makahwah could not let go. Tabaldak could not force the crown from her hands. Furtive glances and brief, knowing looks were exchanged by many council members around the fire. Finally, Makahwah's grip on the crown relaxed, and Tabaldak held it in her own hands. As she walked back to the Eel Clan section of the circle, she felt an intense surge of power run through her body the way lightning runs through a dark summer night.

"The house of the Eel Clan has only one man who possesses great *orenda*. His powers are known far and wide and they are known by each and every one who sits here in the high council. I speak, of course, of my brother." Tabaldak stopped behind the seated Atatarho, who sat motionless, glaring across the circle at Hiawatha who returned his stare.

"As mother of the Eel Clan, and as a High Clan Mother of the Onondaga nation, I place the sacred headdress of power, the headdress of the Onondaga chieftainship, upon the head of my brother, Atatarho, and I pray to the Spirit Beings that our people may prosper under his leadership."

Tabaldak placed the feathered antler crown on Atatarho's head. He stood up slowly and raised his face to the sky, raised both his arms up to the sky, and chanted in a strong and steady voice.

> "The Mothers have spoken,
> The people have spoken,
> The Spirits of Earth and Sky and Water
> Have spoken:
> New life to Onondaga!
> New power to Onondaga!"

The council members cheered loudly and called his name: "Atatarho! Atatarho! Long life and plenty! Long life and plenty! Atatarho!" The clan mothers chanted, the elders chanted, and all of the council celebrated the decision of the great clan mothers who were descended from Sky Woman long ago in the time when Turtle Island first began.

All but Hiawatha, who alone remained silent, who alone sat and did not rise, who kept his place, staring at the mighty sorcerer who was now the leader of the people. Atatarho signaled with his arms for silence. He cast his right hand toward the fire and purple flames exploded and burst upward and outward. He raised his left arm and pointed to the seated Hiawatha.

"Hiawatha. Your bitterness and hatred is a poison to our society. You must rid yourself of it, or you must leave."

Hiawatha slowly rose to his feet. His motion was deliberate and fluid. He did not use his hands to push himself up from the earth. It was as if he willed his body to stand and it stood. A loud crack of thunder issued from outside the council house, causing some to involuntarily jump. Hiawatha looked around the room as if he were memorizing the expressions on each person's face, as if he were burning them into his memory for some future use. He looked directly at Atatarho, who now wore the headdress that not long ago sat upon his own head.

"You all know me. For many years I worked hard so that you might eat in safety and in peace. I gave my possessions to those who had none. I treated your families as if they were my family. I was your father. I cannot and I will not remain to serve a wicked man, a treacherous man who destroyed my life in order to achieve what he has achieved this day. I am leaving now. I go to fulfill the dream of my old friend Kewahtawa, who dreamed that I would find the prophet Dekanawida. I will find him. And when I do, I will start a new nation, a powerful nation whose magic and *orenda* will surpass yours, Atatarho. And then I will return. And I will have my revenge on you and on your friend Shadahgoh."

With that, Hiawatha left the stunned room. Another loud crack of thunder shattered the silence around the council fire, and a mighty outpouring of rain and hail lashed the roof of the council house.

Part II

Journey to the East

Chapter One

Hiawatha ran through the woods at a frantic pace. His mind was operating purely on instinct. He did not think of where he was going or why he was running. He simply was running, running without stopping. He leaped over large rocks; he crossed creeks jumping from one flat stone to another. What kept him running, what impelled him forward, was hatred. Blind fury was the fuel that ran through his veins. His stone tomahawk banged against his thigh. His ironwood war club and his bow and quiver of arrows rattled against his back with each forward thrust of his legs pounding across dead pine needles and decomposing leaves, leaping over fallen logs, skirting around the trunks of trees. And each time the weapons struck against his legs and thighs and back, visions of blood and screams of death filled his imagination. His eyes were the eyes of a great mountain cat, looking only straight ahead at his prey as pine trees whizzed by and beech trees whizzed by, and hanging vines whizzed by—a blur of green and gray in the periphery of his vision.

He followed an old path, one of the many pathways that existed in those days for trade. People now think that the old ones, the ones who lived before Columbus came, before Champlain and the French came, before the Dutch and English came, they think that the old ones were isolated into small groups who did not know or understand one another. But this is not so. Vast networks of trade existed. Bows made by expert bow makers down along the Natchez Trace were traded for copper mined by the peoples that lived in what is now Minnesota and Wisconsin. Our own people traded mica and quillwork for quahog shells with the people who lived east and south along the endless salt waters. There were many different languages, but there was an international language that served us well for trade and exchange, not only of goods but of ideas. A mighty mega-culture existed in those days all over Turtle Island. And the back of the Great Turtle was lined with well-traveled pathways that ran through forests, that skirted lakes, and that followed the banks of mighty rivers.

But now, on this part of the Turtle's back, the paths were used as war paths. Constant warfare was a way of life among the separate nations. Alliances were easily made in order to raid and hunt the territories of other nations, and these loose alliances were just as easily broken. The Mohawk made war with the Oneida and the Huron; the Oneida with the Cayuga; the Cayuga with the Onondaga; the Onondaga with the Seneca; and the Seneca, the fierce and mighty Seneca, made war with everyone else. It was a cycle of unending quarrels, squabbles, and blood feuds interrupted by lulls, periods of trade and peace on the great highways that ran like arteries and veins across the firm yet fragile body of our mother, the earth. If you looked closely enough along the pathways, you could see picture writing on the trees that told of victories or defeats, the number of scalps or prisoners taken, or enemies killed in battle.

Hiawatha was now running east on one of those highways that extended from the land of the Onondaga to the land of the Mohawk. There, somewhere among the Mohawk people, he would find this great leader Dekanawida, and with his help, he would raise together a huge war party. And that war party would sweep down upon the Onondaga and upon the Seneca with a violent fury. He would smash many skulls himself, and those in his war band would smash many more, and with each tree that he passed in his blind and furious running, his mind filled with visions of broken, bleeding skulls and open mouths fixed in pain.

He could hear the wailings of son-less mothers and new-made widows, and these sounds made his pulse race with dark laughter.

Up ahead, far along the trail, he saw another figure running toward him. A hunter? A trader? Or a messenger from one village to another, from one chieftain to another? Still running, Hiawatha kept a cautious eye on the man. He was relieved when he made out a large corn-husk basket with shoulders straps on the stranger's back, which meant that he probably had wares to trade. However, he was running exceptionally fast for a trader. As he came closer, Hiawatha recognized Oneida quillwork patterns on his moccasins.

The Oneida messenger slowed his pace and studied Hiawatha, deciding whether to speak or not. Perhaps this Onondaga man could give him some information, so he stopped and held up his right hand. "Greetings. I am Garoga, a messenger of the Oneida people. Have you seen any Cayuga in your journey?"

"No, I have not. The land of the Cayuga is far from here. Why do you ask?"

"The Cayuga dogs killed five of our best and bravest men who were out on a hunting party. These Cayuga tricked them into doing their hunting. They promised them many quahog shells, then took their deer and moose and killed our Oneida hunters while they slept. I am on my way to warn the other Oneida villages and encampments, so I must hurry. Good luck in your journey."

As Hiawatha continued his running, he reflected on the strange behavior of the Cayugas. Having met one of their chiefs, Togahayon, he would not have thought that they would stoop to such a lowly act. But perhaps it was not the Cayuga. Perhaps it was the Hurons in disguise. They were often known to raid deep into the Oneida country.

Having run for two days now with little to eat, he stopped by a deep, wide stream and fashioned a spear out of a long elm branch. He built a small fire, and then he carefully waded out into the stream. After a few minutes of peering into the moving water, he decided that he had not the heart to eat. He sank on the ground by the fire and stared into its center, mesmerized by the licking tongues of flame. He heard the sound of someone running, but he lacked the energy to even turn his head in the sound's direction. "Let them kill me," he thought. "I am ready to die."

"Hiawatha!" Orios waved both his arms above his head, smiling and laughing. He ran to where his old friend sat, dropped to his knees, and threw his arms around him.

"Quickly, we must put out the fire." He began stomping on the small embers and burning sticks. "That is how I found you."

"What's the matter, Orios?"

"I have followed you all this while, and I have much to tell you. You won't believe it. But it will justify all of your fears. You were right about Atatarho. And now my own life is in danger. We both are being followed."

"I don't care. I am ready to die." Stunned by the crazed look in Hiawatha's eyes, Orios summoned all his courage and confronted him. "This is not the great and wise leader that I once followed. Your heart has become heavy. And it makes me sad because this heaviness in your heart is my doing. I killed Shadahgoh's son, and caused all your suffering. What I am going to tell you will make your heart even heavier than it already is."

"Nothing you can say or do will make my heart any heavier. Tell me your story."

"Atatarho follows me. Well, not Atatarho exactly, but those in his service. And those in the service of Shadahgoh. For Atatarho and Shadahgoh are in league with one another."

"I knew it! I have suspected this all along, Orios. But how did you find out?"

"I saw something that no one was supposed to see. But come, we must leave. I will tell you my story as we run."

Revitalized by the company of his young friend, Hiawatha felt a new burst of energy surge through his legs. They ran through the forest path that followed alongside a swift-flowing stream, a stream of clear water that tumbled over large rocks and often dropped down in small, foaming waterfalls.

As they ran, Orios told Hiawatha his story. Not long after Hiawatha had left the village, Orios was sitting alone in the woods thinking, trying to sort out what to do with the remainder of his lonely life. After Sovana had traveled the Strawberry Path to join her mother and sisters in the fields of the otherworld, there was a vacant hole in the middle of his chest. To fill this hole, he began to play his flute, something that always eased his melancholy and made his mind stop racing with dark thoughts. Soon after he had begun, however, he was startled by a young man about his own age who plunged out of the underbrush and came upon him. He was so startled that he dropped his flute and jumped back in fear.

"Oh, I am sa- sa- *sorry*," said the stranger. "I did not mean to startle you. Your pah- pah- *playing* was very fine."

"Thank you," said Orios, somewhat taken aback by the halting politeness of this strange youth, who, aside from a stammer, was in all other respects decked out like a warrior. His head was shaved except for a topknot. His face and head were painted red and he wore a roach of red-dyed porcupine quills.

"I am thirsty. Can you show me to the ne- ne- *nearest* running water?"

"Come with me. I will show you a stream where the water is cool and clear."

"Who was this boy?" interrupted Hiawatha as they both ran, their legs pumping at an even-paced gait.

Orios turned to him and said: "I asked him if he were a Cayuga, because the quillwork on his moccasins seemed to be of a type favored by Cayugas."

"No," he said. "I am a Seneca."

"What are you doing here, in the land of the Onondaga?"

"I have a message for Ah- Ah- Ah- *tatarho*. Do you know him?"

"Of course," I replied. "Everyone knows Atatarho. I will show you a shortcut to his hut on the edge of the swamp."

"So this man was a courier from Shadahgoh?" asked Hiawatha.

Orios nodded his head. "Go on," said Hiawatha. "Tell me the rest."

"I guided him through the forest to a path that led to Atatarho's hut and then bade him good-bye. But after he was out of sight, I circled back and crept through the bushes on my belly, like the snake, so that I was within hearing range of Atatarho's encampment. The messenger was speaking to Atatarho. Off to the side, stirring a pot of foul-smelling brew, was Atatarho's nephew, Osinoh."

"Shadahgoh thanks you for your meh- meh- *message*. He vows to stop Hi- Hi-. . ."

"Yes, yes. Hiawatha," interrupted Atatarho.

"Hiawatha. Be- be- *be-fore* he gets to the Mohawks. He will cut off his feet and bah- bah-bring him back to his village to tor- to tor- tor-. . ."

"To *torture* him?" asked Atatarho with a glint in his eye and just the hint of a smile creasing his face.

The messenger nodded his head vigorously to avoid saying any more.

"And then," said Orios, grabbing Hiawatha by the arm as they ran side by side, "Atatarho's owl shrieked a shrill alarm and leaped up from his perch of bone beside Osinoh, and flew across the clearing to where I lay concealed in the bushes. It startled me so, I jumped up and ran back through the brush. But before I ran, I saw Osinoh's eyes and Atatarho's eyes locking with mine, and I knew that they had recognized me. This is why I followed you. Why I have come here. To warn you and to save myself."

Hiawatha stopped running and Orios came to a halt as well. They stood facing each other, breathing heavily. Finally, Hiawatha placed his hands on Orios' shoulders and said, "You must go away. It is not safe to be with me. If Atatarho truly did see you, then rest assured that you are followed. Shadahgoh or his warriors will not be too far behind. You head in that direction down the stream and I will go across to lead them away from you."

"You know they will find me. I am not a great woodsman like you. Perhaps I should end it all. Surrender myself to Shadahgoh. Tell the truth. Tell him that I am the one that killed his son. Maybe then he will leave you alone."

"He wouldn't believe you. He'd only think you were covering up for me. Besides, it's too late for that now. Shadahgoh wants me. And so does Atatarho. They both want me out of the way, so they will have no future threats to their power. But I have my own plans for both of them, and they do not include getting captured and tortured."

"But there must be a way for me to make up for the pain and suffering that I have caused. I know there is something I can do before I die to make up for all of this. To make it up to you and to Makahwah and to all of our people. I am going to stay with you and together we will find the way."

"The way? What do you mean, 'the way'?" Something sounded familiar to Hiawatha's ears about those two small words used together.

"The way of peace. They say that the words of Dekanawida, the prophet, are the words of the Way." Hiawatha looked at Orios and wondered: How did this youngster grow up so soon? And to talk such words.

"You have become quite a philosopher since last we met."

Suddenly, a dart whizzed past his head and landed in the trunk of a tree, a mere foot away from them.

"Quick! Shadahgoh has found us!"

They ran in a zigzag motion, careening in between and around the trees, until they came to a hill above a rushing narrow river. They hit the ground, rolling down the incline as more darts whizzed overhead. Orios leapt behind a large, fallen tree spread across the banks of the river while Hiawatha knelt as low to the ground as possible and fitted an arrow onto his bow. A Seneca warrior appeared on the ridge above them, and Hiawatha's arrow found its mark in the man's chest. He pitched forward and fell down the incline as another Seneca appeared on the rim. His eyes became wide when he saw his companion rolling down the embankment. He saw Hiawatha's arrow streaking toward him in the split second before it found its mark in the middle of his forehead. He let out an angry death scream and pitched forward just as his fellow warrior had done a moment before. Hiawatha screamed too, a scream of victory that celebrated the joy of blood, the joy of victory over one's enemies.

Then he saw the painted face of Shadahgoh and five of his warriors emerge from the shadows on the ridge. Hiawatha turned and did a high-hurdle leap over the fallen tree, grabbing Orios' arm and pulling him to his feet.

"The river! Run as you never have before, and swim as you never have before." Hiawatha dove headfirst into the river and began swimming as soon as his body hit the surface. Orios did the same. Their bodies became like otters moving under the surface and above the surface, one with the white foam of the swift current.

The water was running faster now, and they could hear a mighty roar of water falling down a great distance. One of the many cataracts that dotted the landscape in this part of Turtle Island was just ahead, and they were headed straight for it.

"Swim as hard as you can to the shore," shouted Hiawatha.

Orios fought against the rapidly flowing water, banging his arms and legs against large rocks. Finally, he and Hiawatha reached the shore just before the water dropped off thirty feet down into a narrow gorge of limestone and shale that the river had cut deep into the earth over the course of countless moons. They both lay on their backs on the bank panting and gasping for breath, exhausted from their efforts.

After they caught their breath, Hiawatha said, "Come, Orios, we must keep moving. Senecas do not give up easily." They struggled to their feet and began to run again along another pathway that led away from the water and the gorge and penetrated deeper into the forest.

They ran until the sun had sunk beneath the horizon, then rested by a gurgling stream and waited for the full moon to rise. They worked their way back to the main trail and ran all night. Orios knew that he should have been exhausted, but the night spirits seemed to make his feet light so that he no longer even felt the ground. The sounds of the night comforted him, the cry of the owl, the scream of the panther, and the rustling bats hunting the silver moths of the forest.

Hiawatha stopped and gestured for silence. "Do you hear that?" he said softly. "It's the white pines whispering to each other. They will give us good shelter."

Orios looked around, but he didn't see any white pines. He followed Hiawatha as he ran off the path toward the sound of the whispering. In a short distance they found themselves in a small clearing surrounded by gigantic white pines whose needles made a soft bed on the ground. That night, lying beside Orios in the middle of the stand of white pines, Hiawatha entered into the dreamtime world. He and Orios were continuing their journey to the land of the Mohawks. Shadahgoh and his Seneca warriors were hot on their trail. They were still swimming in the river when they reached a bend where the river widened and the current seemed to gather in its speed. As their heads bobbed up and down in the water, they spied something large and white gleaming downriver on the opposite bank. A canoe! Hiawatha pointed to the canoe and Orios nodded. They swam down towards the opposite shore, and as they got nearer to the canoe they both were overcome with a strange and unfamiliar sensation.

Hiawatha thought he heard singing in the treetops above his head. The canoe now seemed to have a slightly pinkish hue, and the singing intensified. It sounded like a chorus of young maidens singing—singing a song from the Green Corn Festival, a hymn to the Corn Mother Goddess. He rolled over onto his back and looked up to where he thought the singing came from. Instead of maidens in the sky, he saw a flock of geese honking and flying low in a brilliant V above the tops of the trees that lined the banks of the river. The geese were large, but they were not white and black like the geese he normally saw this time of year. These geese were brilliantly hued. Their underbellies seemed to sparkle like chips of mica and crystal stones that, in sunlight, send off all the colors of the rainbow. Their necks were rose-colored and their wings were deep blue with gold and red flecks.

He dreamt then that Orios swam over to him to see if he was all right. Hiawatha pointed overhead, trying to catch the attention of Orios, but when he looked up again, the geese were gone. Instead, a lone eagle circled high above them. It was the largest eagle Hiawatha had ever seen. When they reached the shore, the strange gleaming canoe was only twenty feet away.

"Hiawatha, I have never seen such a canoe. It's massive. It's not made of elm-bark."

Hiawatha nodded. He too had never seen anything like this canoe. They approached the strange vessel cautiously. Hiawatha was unnerved by the singing voices and by the strange, brilliantly hued geese that had sailed overhead. The blood was still racing through his veins from the conflict with the Senecas and the running and swimming. The Senecas would not be far behind them. This canoe could be a godsend, just what they needed to put more distance between them and their pursuers.

Orios reached the canoe first and ran his hands over its surface. "Stone!" he called back over his shoulder. "It is made of stone. And stone that I have never seen before."

Hiawatha knelt down beside the canoe and examined it thoroughly with his eyes and his hands. He could feel it in the dream world, its pure whiteness flecked with pink and rose. The dimensions were in perfect balance and the carving was superb and true. Someone had carved this canoe out of a single large block of stone, the hard stone that is quarried up north by the people who live in the stone hills. He tested its weight by placing both of his hands beneath it and trying to lift it at one end—the way one lifted a canoe to slide it down into the water. It would not budge. Who would have carved a thing so massive, so dense, so beautiful? And why a canoe? A canoe was, by its very nature, light and buoyant, so light that it would float upon the surface of the water as a leaf does. If anyone had the strength to push this one off the bank, surely it would sink to the bottom of the river.

"Look, Hiawatha." Orios was pointing to the inside of the canoe. "Two paddles made of the same stone. And what is this?" Orios clambered over the side of the stone canoe and picked up a feather that lay on the floor. "An eagle feather! And such an eagle it must have come from!" He held it up for Hiawatha to see. It was twice the size of any eagle feather that he had ever seen before.

"It must be an omen," said Orios.

Hiawatha lifted his eyes to the sky, but the eagle was now gone. "Strange," he thought. Have we left the real world? Have we found a rip in the side of time and entered into the land of the Spirit Beings? First, the strange, unearthly flock of geese who sang like praying maidens. Then the eagle. Now this mysterious canoe made of rosy white stone with a huge eagle feather resting in its bottom. His heart was racing when he heard a presence behind him. That is the only way he could later describe the dream-vision experience.

A vibration, a hum, an incandescent glow. If you could hear the sound of fox-fire glowing all around you, or hear the beating of the heart of a star, those might be the sounds that he heard behind him. He turned and saw someone or something approaching them from out of the forest. From out of the deep shade and shadows of the thick trees that lined the bank of the river, a man who radiated a silver-white glow and seemed to glide toward them rather than walk. His thick silver hair shone brightly and flowed down untied and unbraided to his waist. He was dressed in a white deerskin robe that glowed and shimmered. White leather fringes six to eight inches long lined the arms and chest and hem of his robe. Sewn across the front were silver half moons and white and black eagle feathers that dangled down and fluttered in the wind. Huge eagle feathers like the one that Orios now held as he stood dumbstruck in the middle of the stone canoe. He had a high forehead and a slightly curved, aquiline nose. His face was deeply lined, a record of many seasons of joy and sorrow. A white light tinged with shimmering and shifting tones of gold and rose shone forth from the head and heart of this being who came nearer and nearer to where they both stood, motionless, frozen.

"I see you have found my canoe."

He and Orios were speechless. All they could manage by way of reply was to nod their heads.

"Why are you here?" The being, or man—as they now could plainly see that he was a man, albeit a unique one—possessed a voice that was not in keeping with the magnificence of his physical appearance. Although he was not tall—in fact he was rather on the short side—this was the most imposing man that Hiawatha or Orios had ever seen. His intense presence was more godlike than human, but his voice when he spoke did not match this intensity. It was a thin and reed-like voice. Not unpleasant, merely ephemeral. A wispy, whispering voice, a pale and ghostlike voice, a voice more fit for a shadow or a trail of smoke, or a puff of cloud—a gray, evanescent voice that contrasted sharply with his imposing presence.

Orios held up the eagle feather like a talisman against all evil charms. Hiawatha cleared his throat and spoke. "I am Hiawatha, the Onondaga, and this is my kinsman, Orios. We are on our way to the land of the Mohawk to seek the prophet, Dekanawida. But we were attacked and pursued by a band of Seneca led by my enemy, Shadahgoh. While fleeing them we came upon this stone canoe. You say it is yours?"

"You speak well, Hiawatha. Yes, the canoe is mine. And if I am not mistaken you and your young companion are greatly in need of its services."

"How do you mean? What service can a canoe of solid stone

render? It certainly cannot float."

"Hiawatha! Look!" Orios pointed to an opening in the bushes and trees some fifty feet upstream. Hiawatha spun around and saw the end of a long blowgun protruding out between the foliage, and behind that he could make out the shaved head of a Seneca warrior. A dart whizzed past him and struck the side of the stone canoe, caroming off into the river with a splash.

"Quickly," said the old man. "Into the canoe!" Hiawatha was too stunned to argue, so he joined Orios inside the stone craft. Three more darts and an arrow streaked toward them, but the old man pulled out a staff surmounted with an eagle's claw from the folds of his white feathered robe and batted them aside as if they were no more than troublesome insects.

The old man lifted his arms and the staff above his head and waved them about as if he had some unseen purpose. His head was thrown back and his mouth opened and closed as if he were singing. No sound came out of his mouth. But another sound began all around them. It was the sound of a mighty rushing wind. The roaring sound of an immense Flying-Face, a whirlwind. The trees around them began to spin and they themselves seemed to be turning, turning, turning in fast and ever-widening circles. Hiawatha had to sit down in the bottom of the canoe and grip the stone sides because he was afraid that he would pitch overboard.

And then they were above the trees. They could see the thunderstruck Shadahgoh and his Seneca warriors beside the river below them. They were running up and down the bank and pointing at them. Hiawatha fitted an arrow onto his bowstring, pulled the string back to his right cheek and took careful aim at Shadahgoh's heart. At last, he would have his revenge! And then his bowstring snapped! This was something that had never happened to him before. He looked over at the old man standing in the stern of the canoe. The old man's eyes burned and gleamed in their sockets. He slowly shook his head and with his staff he lowered Hiawatha's bow. He then pointed his staff toward the river, and the canoe began to descend, landing on the silver surface as smoothly as any waterfowl landing on a lake or a river. And the stone canoe was floating! Floating by some unknown power down the middle of the river.

"Who are you?" asked Hiawatha.

In a voice so soft that he could barely hear him, the old man replied, "I am Dekanawida."

Chapter Two

Hiawatha awoke with a start from his dream. His heart was filled with a strange mixture of terror, awe, and wonder. The first gray light of dawn was beginning to filter through the white pines and the birds were beginning their joyous songs to a new day. Hiawatha shook Orios who was sleeping beside him. Orios started awake.

"What is it? Are the Senecas here?"

"No. I have just had a marvelous dream. A dream of the future, full of portent." Hiawatha told Orios the details of his dream.

"Dekanawida has visited you in your dreamtime," said Orios. This must be a good sign. He is here to help us."

Hiawatha nodded. He was glad that he too finally had a vision of Dekanawida. But the holy man had not given him any instructions, except that part about the bow. He winced at the thought of it. If Senacas were shooting at him, he certainly had a right to shoot back.

A lone crow call interrupted his thoughts, followed by two more. Hiawatha jumped to his feet and looked around. He said a prayer of thanks when he saw three crows fly overhead. And then they were off again, running up and down the hills until the sun was high in the sky and they came to a wide river. Orios jumped in headfirst to wash the sweat from his body.

"Is this the Mohawk River?"

Hiawatha splashed his face with water. "No. Not yet."

Orios looked around him. "I've never been this far from home."

"This is only the beginning."

"Do you think the Mohawks will be friendly?"

Hiawatha shrugged.

"I've heard that the Mohawks are ferocious cannibals."

Hiawatha smoothed the water from his cheeks. "You can't believe everything you hear. Come along now, we've got to keep moving."

"Do we get to eat today? My dried corn is almost gone."

"Chew it slowly then. Hold it in your mouth as long as you can."

Hiawatha shook out his long hair and tied it back. "Let's swim awhile downstream and then we'll cross over."

As the sun was setting, they ran full steam around a large rock and came face to face with a band of Oneida warriors, who had heard them and were silently waiting for their arrival with their arrows nocked on their bowstrings.

Hiawatha whispered to Orios, "Whatever you do, do not act afraid." Orios tried to swallow, but he had a lump in his throat that felt as big as a fist. A warrior approached them.

"I am Shonon, war chief of the Oneida nation. What are you doing here?"

Hiawatha replied in a respectful tone, "We are only passing through your lands. We are traveling to the east. We seek a man named Dekanawida. Have you heard of him?"

"Of course, everyone around here has heard of Dekanawida. Many people dream of him. But no one yet has met him."

Hiawatha felt a bit more at ease now. "How far are we from the Mohawk lands?"

"If you are a fast runner it is not as far as if you are a slow runner."

Hiawatha smiled at his remark. "We are fast runners."

"Then you should be there in two journeys of the sun."

"'Have you seen any Seneca in the area?"

"Seneca? Yes. We saw Seneca. A small band of Seneca warriors passed by earlier this morning, but we did not show ourselves. We have no war with the Seneca. We are looking for the Cayuga dogs who slaughtered five of our warriors two days ago. We will skin them alive when we find them."

"I wish you luck with your pursuit. We will be on our way."

"Stay and eat with us," said Shonon. "We have plenty of food."

Orios' face lit up. "Do you have fresh corn?"

"As a matter of fact, we have fresh corn from our late planting. It was picked early this morning before we left our village."

Shonon gave a hand signal, and the warriors behind him put up their weapons and began searching for wood for the evening fire.

When Orios bit into an ear of freshly roasted corn, he knew that he had never tasted anything so good. Never had he gone so long without food. It didn't seem to bother Hiawatha. He could go for days without eating. Hiawatha gave Orios a stern look and deliberately straightened his shoulders back. Orios knew that he should sit up straight and watch his manners, but he wanted to ask the question that had been troubling him for some time. "Is it true that the Mohawks are cannibals?"

Shonon shrugged. "In revenge wars, anything is possible. One must reciprocate the tortures done to one's own people. One must pay back in kind. But we have had no quarrel with the Mohawks lately. Dekanawida has had a very good influence on them. They say he has a powerful *orenda*."

"Where is he from?" asked Hiawatha.

"He was born a Huron, but he left his home when he was a young man over some quarrel with his brother. Now his hair is growing white and he still talks of forming a League of Peace. They say he has devised a set of laws that he wants the nations to follow, but it is hard to understand him. Perhaps you will understand him, though. You look like a thinking man. Why do you seek him?"

"Some people in my village dreamed of him. They sent me forth to find him and learn from him." Hiawatha was not inclined to tell these Oneida the whole story or his real reason for seeking the wise man.

After a full meal and a ritual smoking of the sacred tobacco, Hiawatha and Orios found a comfortable place to sleep within view of the fire. No sooner had Hiawatha closed his eyes than he seemed to fall deeper and deeper into a black hole, and he felt the dreamtime world descend upon him again. Through a mist, he saw a large fortified village by the side of a hill. Every other upright pole was crowned with a human skull. A woman with raven hair that hung down straight to her waist opened the gate and beckoned him to enter. There was the feel of death about the place, but he knew that he had to go inside. He felt a strong force pull him through the gate, toward the pulsating drums in the center of this town whose longhouses were all made of human bones.

There he saw three naked men tied to three six-foot tall stakes in a semicircle. In front of the stakes, three large, black stone kettles filled with water were boiling over open fires. The men were heavily bruised and bleeding from open wounds where fingers, ears, and testicles once had been. They tried to look stoic, and, in fact, two of them looked defiant in the face of what had happened and what was to come. But the third, who was younger, was terrified. His eyes wildly darted around like a frightened sparrow. As the smoke lifted, Hiawatha saw that it was Orios. A woman took a long-handled knife whose blade was burning with unquenchable flames, and slowly walked over to the young man.

"You have killed my son. Smashed in his skull while he slept. He was a good and brave man. Now we will see how brave you are. Feel the joys of my hot knife." She placed the flaming knife blade between his legs and held it against his testicles. He screamed out loud a piercing scream in his agony as he watched his body burn.

"Not so brave now, are you? Where is that stoic pride you Cayugas are famed for?"

"But I am not Cayuga! I am Onondaga!" cried Orios.

"Do not cry out!" exclaimed the older captive to his right. "Don't give them the satisfaction of hearing you suffer. Do you want to shame your people?" Hiawatha shuddered and tried to move away, but his legs would not move; some force kept pulling him closer and closer.

With hot brands and sharp utensils the people of this village of bone inflicted hundreds of wounds upon their captives' bodies, speaking as they did so:

"Feel my blade's caress."

"Let my hot knife kiss your flesh."

"Take this stab in the loins for my father whom you have killed."

"My son will never dwell in peace in the land of the dead because of what you have done. Now I do the same to you. I rip open both your thighs with this hatchet and pour hot sand in the wounds."

Hiawatha closed his eyes tight. If only he could get away, but his legs had turned into what looked like tree trunks covered with bark and with roots at the ends holding him to this spot. He looked up again at the tortured Orios. The boy's screams became louder as two women, using sharp knives and clam shells, skinned him alive, pulling the flesh in long strips from his chest and face and back. Hiawatha tried to run to him, but his feet were rooted in the ground. He saw them cut off Orios' arm and throw it into the boiling pot, and then everything became black around him.

When Hiawatha looked up again, Shadahgoh was in Orios' place. Atatarho was standing beside him, holding a long knife that he held out to Hiawatha. Hiawatha felt his hatred for Shadahgoh rise in his throat until he could not swallow. What he thought was so horrible a moment ago now seemed proper and fitting.

He would skin Shadahgoh alive. He would make him suffer unbelievable torment for the deaths of his daughters, for the anguish and torment that he had inflicted upon him.

"Hi-a-wa-tha. Hi-a-wa-tha." The people of the bone-village chanted his name, pounding drums made of human skulls with sticks that were human leg bones. They cried out to him, anxiously waiting for him to exact his blood revenge, his mourning-revenge upon the body of Shadahgoh.

Atatarho had turned into a spinning pillar of flame eight or nine feet tall. His flaming arms reached out of the pillar and in his left hand was a knife. Hiawatha reached out for the knife and suddenly the scene before his eyes shattered into a million tiny fragments as if someone had dropped a huge rock onto the clear reflecting surface of a still lake scattering apart the images of trees and clouds and sky. Shadahgoh was gone. The bone-village was gone. All that remained was the pillar of fire that spun and roared furiously in a clearing surrounded by dark woods. Snakes leapt out of the flames, darting outward quickly and then recoiling inward just as quickly. The knife that Hiawatha held turned into a snake whose mouth spat out flames. The snake arched back its length and turned its hot fury on Hiawatha.

"Get back to where you belong, Atatarho!"

The voice that came out of the dark forest was the same voice that Hiawatha had heard before in the dream of the stone canoe. It was the voice of the silver-haired holy man, the voice of Dekanawida, who now stood on the far side of the clearing, pointing his claw-tipped staff at the pillar of fire.

From out of the center of the burning pillar shot a ball of flame across the clearing at Dekanawida. He sidestepped nimbly for one who appeared so old, and, using his staff, he batted back the sphere of fire as if it were a lacrosse ball. It hit the spinning column of fire causing a small explosion. A demon-howl shrieked from the middle of the hot center as a burning snake leaped out of the flames and streaked like a flaming arrow toward the silver-haired prophet.

In a flash, the eagle claw on the tip of Dekanawida's staff opened up and seized the flaming snake by its neck and shook it furiously. A ball of black smoke surrounded the snake, and out of its center an eagle with a burning snake in his talons flew up and off across the treetops screaming an eagle's victory cry while the snake writhed beneath him.

Hiawatha watched as Dekanawida chanted a song in a language that he did not understand, and as he did so, everything around him in the clearing began turning shades of green. His hair took on a green hue, and the robe that he wore seemed to shimmer with an emerald vibration. The clouds above turned green, the bark of trees turned green, the crimson and gold and orange leaves of autumn turned back to a bright and verdant springtime green. The pillar of fire turned green and no voice issued forth from it. Soon the flames burned lower and lower to the ground and finally it sputtered out with a hiss, and all that remained was a bright green snake that crawled away in quick and looping esses into the underbrush.

Hiawatha felt a gentle hand on his shoulder as he heard a voice that seemed to be calling from far away. He felt himself floating back up from the dark hole he had fallen into. He opened his eyes and saw Orios bending over him. "Hiawatha, you were screaming again in your sleep."

Hiawatha wiped his forehead with the back of his hand and realized that he was drenched with sweat. He sat up. He looked around and was relieved to see that the Oneida warriors had already left.

"I have dreamed of Dekanawida again."

"It sounded like a nightmare."

"It was at first. Horrible scenes of torture. You! It was you they were torturing!"

"Me?"

"Yes. They cut off your arm."

Orios winced. "Then it was Shadahgoh. Then a fierce battle raged between Atatarho and Dekanawida."

"The Peacemaker in a battle?"

"Yes. Yes! This is a good sign. An omen! A good omen of things to come. It means that Dekanawida will help us. He will help us to overcome Atatarho. He appeared to me in my dreamtime again and this time he vanquished Atatarho."

Orios simply stared at Hiawatha and shook his head.

"Come. Let us go. We must find him as soon as possible. He is calling out to me."

Orios gathered his belongings. "Shall we follow the trade path today?"

"No. Not with Seneca in the area."

As they ran through the deep forest, Orios marveled at how Hiawatha could always find his way. He knew that Hiawatha followed the small paths that the deer had made, and then used the path that the sun had taken to correct his course, but the sun was not out today. It was overcast, a blank grayness that made the autumn leaves seem drab and dead. Nonetheless, Hiawatha always knew which way to go.

They stopped frequently and bathed in the streams and rivers. The Iroquois were a clean people who washed every day, even in the cold of winter. Aside from refreshing them, the cool waters took away the human scent that Seneca scouts might pick up.

After a full day of running, they slowed their pace and walked for a while, taking in the majesty of the forest surroundings. Orios came across curious markings on the bark of a tree. It was a pictograph of a stick figure stirring a large kettle and beside it an arrow that seemed to be pointing them in a certain direction. They had never seen tree words like these before and they were curious as to their meaning. They followed the path of the tree drawings, discovering more along the way.

After an hour or so, Hiawatha noticed a faint smell of meat roasting. He looked at Orios and gestured for silence. They moved towards the direction of the scent of cooking, looking all around them for Seneca scouts. After what seemed an eternity to Orios, they came upon a clearing with a small, conical dwelling made from elm-bark shingles. A large clay cooking pot hung over the glowing coals of a fire.

They cautiously walked up to the encampment. A large woman threw back the bearskin covering that served as a door to the hut, and came out, greeting them.

"Welcome. I am Jikonsahseh, the mother of the forest. Many travelers walk this path and I feed them all. If you have hunger, I have plenty to eat. Look at what some nice hunters have left me. Come, sit by my fire."

Jikonsahseh walked over to the kettle that hung above the fire. She spooned out generous helpings of venison, corn, and bean stew onto a wooden trencher with a wooden spoon.

"We'll feed the boy first. He needs some meat on his bones." She handed the trencher to Orios, and he gratefully smiled at her. She prepared another trencher and handed it to Hiawatha. Then she sat down on the ground facing them.

"Thank you," said Hiawatha.

"Yes, we are very hungry." Orios began to eat.

"Wait!" ordered Jikonsahseh. "We must offer thanks first." Orios put his spoon down, embarrassed by his lapse in etiquette.

"Don't be ashamed. It's not a crime to be hungry. But let us thank those who nourish us."

She looked up to the sky and closed her eyes. "We thank you, sister corn and sister bean. We thank you, brother deer. We thank you for giving us your selves to feed us, to make us healthy. And we thank you, our Mother Earth, for creating the plants and animals that heal us and feed us."

Jikonsahseh opened her eyes and looked at the pair of hungry men seated before her. "There now," she said. "Let us eat."

Orios bit into the venison. The warm meat made him feel at home again. He felt his tired muscles, whose energy source had been almost depleted, spring back to life.

Jikonsahseh gave them time to subdue their hunger and then politely asked, "Where do you come from?"

Hiawatha felt a great warmth as he looked into her eyes. "The land of the Onondagas."

A broad smile lit up Jikonsahseh's face. "Then you must be Hiawatha, chief of the Onondaga nation."

"Yes, I am Hiawatha. But I no longer wear the antlers. How is it that you know me?"

Jikonsahseh motioned towards the roasting deer. "It was your friend who brought me this deer. I fed him only yesterday, and this morning he brought me this deer. He wanted to know if you had passed this way."

"My friend? I didn't know that I had any friends out here. What was his name?"

Jikonsahseh looked Hiawatha in the eye. "He called himself Shadahgoh."

Hiawatha set down his trencher and glared at Jikonsahseh. "He's no friend of mine. He wants to kill me."

"Why would he want to kill you?"

Hiawatha reflected a moment. Then he said, "To stop me from finding Dekanawida."

"You know Dekanawida? A great man. Such *orenda*. He taught me not to be afraid. He said that if you are at peace with yourself, there is nothing to fear."

Hiawatha knew that this well-meaning woman could be dangerous, could unwittingly put them in harm's way. "Jikonsahseh? Will you do us a favor?"

"If I can, then certainly I will."

"If you see Shadahgoh again, will you tell him that you have not seen us?"

"The Great Spirit says that we must speak only the truth. That is why I am at peace with myself."

"But Shadahgoh did not tell you the truth. I am not his friend."

"Perhaps you could be his friend?"

"That is most unlikely. You see, he murdered two of my daughters."

"I'm very sorry." She picked up his trencher, filled it from the pot, and handed it back to him. "You must eat for your strength. Tell me, Hiawatha, why do you seek Dekanawida?"

Hiawatha raised his head and sat up straight and proud. "We want to enlist his aid to raise a war party to wreak vengeance upon Shadahgoh and those who conspired with him."

Jikonsahseh laughed out loud, a big belly laugh that bubbled up from the depths of her being.

"Why do you laugh?" asked Hiawatha, annoyed with this woman who seemed to be making light of his story.

"I'm sorry, I meant no offense. But, I know Dekanawida. I know him well. And if you want him to help you raise an army to make war, you are seeking the wrong man. Dekanawida is called the Peacemaker. He is a holy man, a great prophet whose mission in life is to bring together the warring nations into one nation of peace. He won't help you make war."

"How do you know all of this?"

"Many years ago the Peacemaker helped me cleanse my mind. My heart was as bitter as yours is now. A great tragedy entered my life, not unlike the one that has happened to you. But that is a story for another time. I left my village and came out to the forest to live alone, to cover my head with ashes, to spend my life hating all things. But I decided to feed all warriors who passed this way. My reasoning was this: perhaps one of these warriors would avenge the death of my sisters, and that would make me whole. I gained the reputation of one who would feed those who passed this way.

"Hunters who passed by would leave me meat, and in turn, I would feed war parties who passed along my path. I did not think that I was contributing to the endless cycle of war, of revenge for deaths that were caused by prior revenges. Until one day, Dekanawida came by, and he gave me the message of Peace and Power. The Great Message of the Creator. He cleansed my mind and he showed me the way of clear-mindedness, the way of forgiveness, the righteous path of life. He told me of his mission to spread the word of the Great Law that will bring all peoples together so that they will love one another and live in peace, not in constant warfare. He told me that I must not feed the warriors who pass my way, because this was contributing to the continuation of the way of the evil mind."

Hiawatha and Orios looked at one another, and Orios nodded his head. Here was this new concept again. Hiawatha remembered Orios speaking of "the Way." But ever since he could remember, the way of the mourning-war, the war path of vengeance, had been the Way. All powerful men believed in this. Was this man that they sought truly working against the Way?

"I know what you must be thinking," said Jikonsahseh. "This new way goes against everything that our elders have taught. It is a cutting that goes against the grain. But you do not have to believe me. Go find Dekanawida. Let him tell you himself."

"Where will we find him?"

"He dwells now with the Mohawk. Maybe in the village of Tekerihoken, maybe in the village of Gaihogan. I do not know. I hear that the Mohawks are learning from him; they listen to him. But if I know the Peacemaker, he will find you before you find him."

"How can he do that? He does not know us," asked Orios.

"He has great *orenda* and special powers. They say that his father is a Spirit Being, one of the Sky People."

"How is this possible?" Hiawatha placed his empty trencher on the ground before him.

"You will see. You will find out for yourselves. Rest here tonight. Sleep by my fire, and in the morning when you are refreshed, go and seek him out."

Chapter Three

Hiawatha and Orios gathered together their gear, thanked the Mother of the Forest for her hospitality, and began again their journey toward the rising sun. This was the time of the year when the leaves were beginning to array themselves in their bright colors of dying. Bloody crimson and pumpkin orange mingled with varying shades of umber, fawn, and gold to dazzle the eyes of the Haudenosaunee, the People of the Longhouse.

If you have ever been to the land of the Haudenosaunee, what the white people now call upstate New York, during high autumn, then you will know what I am trying to describe. But words, or at least my words, fail to fully capture the beauty of those color-splashed trees that shimmer through that peculiar shaman-slant of light. The air seems charged with a golden glow, an aura, an *orenda* as my people say, of magic, of daytime dreamings, a slumberous enchantment in which the woods vibrate with the last ecstatic pulse of life before winter comes to drop her frosty shroud over the cold bones of the earth.

It was through this shaman-light, through this color-splashed landscape, that Hiawatha and Orios traveled. They met several other travelers along the way, mostly hunters and traders. They stopped and spoke with one trader whose name was Arohanon. He was a Susquehannock, and he was returning from the land of the people by the great salt sea, the eastern edge of Turtle Island. He had with him a great quantity of purple and white quahog shells, shells that could be chipped and drilled to make necklaces and beadwork.

"Why don't we trade something for some of these shells?" suggested Orios. He thought that if Hiawatha could occupy his hands at night when they were not traveling, maybe some of the sadness and anger might be lifted from his soul.

"What have you to trade?" Arohanon looked askance at this pair who did not look at all prosperous.

"We have pemmican, smoked and dried venison that we received from the Mother of the Forest. It is the finest you have tasted. And we also have tobacco, Onondaga tobacco, and fine quality."

"Show me." The three sat down on the ground beside the trail that ran along the banks of a swift flowing stream that tumbled over large rocks and small pebbles. They each brought out their wares. Arohanon brought out his fire drill and they made a small fire. He smoked a bit of the tobacco in his pipe and sampled the pemmican. Hiawatha examined the shells carefully.

"It is good, as you said. I will take three measures of tobacco and two measures of dried meat. And in return you may have a dozen quahog shells."

"No," said Hiawatha. "You will take *two* measures of tobacco and *one* measure of dried meat. We will take *two* dozen shells."

"You are joking," replied Arohanon.

"I never joke."

"Very well. You may take eighteen shells in exchange for two and a half measures of tobacco and one and a half measures of pemmican."

"Two measures of tobacco."

"Done," said Arohanon.

"Good. A fair deal." Hiawatha measured out the tobacco and dried venison while Arohanon counted out eighteen quahog shells.

Hiawatha looked up at the Susquehannock. "You have traveled through the land of the Mohawks, have you not?"

"Yes, of course."

"Have you heard of a man called Dekanawida?"

"Yes," replied Arohanon. "The holy man who dwells among the People of the Flint. Some say that he is more than a man. That he comes from the Land of the Spirit Beings. Why do you ask?"

"We seek him," said Orios. "In what village will we find him?"

"He moves from place to place, staying awhile here, staying awhile there, spreading what he calls his Good News of Peace and Power."

"We have heard of this good news from Jikonsahseh, the Mother of the Forest. So it is not just an old woman's tale to beguile lonely travelers?"

"No, it is true. He says that the way to power is through peace. I myself do not know how it works. It sounds strange, does it not?"

"Yes," replied Hiawatha, "how can you have true power unless you subjugate your enemies?"

"I don't know. Ask him if you find him." With that, Arohanon got up and packed up his gear. "May your road be swift."

"And yours too."

The travelers parted company, Arohanon continuing west toward the land of the Susquehannock, and Hiawatha and Orios continuing east to seek out the famous shaman in the land of the Mohawks. As night began to fall, Orios gathered wood for a fire. They had decided to camp by a clearing on the banks of the stream where they could sleep with the pleasant and soothing sound of running water to soften their dreams. After Hiawatha started the fire with his fire drill, he examined the quahog shells. They were fine ones, white with a good fringe of purple around the outer edge. He took out his chipping tool that he carried in his fawnskin pouch for making arrowheads and a small stone drill. He sat cross-legged with a sturdy piece of buckskin on his thigh and chipped off several bead-like pieces from one of the shells. They flaked off nicely, not too large and not too small, just the right size for drilling a hole through the center. This way he could string them together.

He didn't quite know why he was doing this, or what purpose these shell strings would serve, but the concentrated effort and the manual dexterity required to make these beads seemed to take his mind away from the sorrow and anger that always simmered just beneath the surface of his consciousness.

As they traveled through the forest path that led to the land of the Mohawks, whenever they stopped to rest, Hiawatha continued to make the beads, stringing the drilled ones on a slim strip of rawhide. As he worked, he noticed more and more how his mind seemed at peace just by the mere act of making them and by the presence of a complete string, about eight inches long. It seemed to him, although he did not know how, that the anger and violence, the sorrow and the self-pity that he always carried with him, was transferred into the wampum, the strings of quahog-shell beads.

While Hiawatha worked on the strings, Orios played his flute. Soothing music that matched the songs of the birds that sang in the forest all around them. The flute was Orios' way of easing the ache in his heart for the guilt that he felt over the deaths that he had caused, his way of taming the anguish and great loss that he felt over the death of Sovana.

"Those are fine strings of shells that you have made," said Orios one afternoon while they were resting. "What will you do with them?"

Hiawatha held the string up in the air and turned it over in his hand. The purple shells that he had polished and drilled alternated with the white ones. "To tell the truth, Orios, I am not sure what I will do with them. But they seem to take on the sadness and anger that I feel, to take these feelings away from me and take them on themselves. It's very odd. But that is the only way that I can describe it."

"If it works for you, why could it not work for others who also feel this way?"

"What do you mean?"

Orios reflected a moment, staring at the string of beads. "If we meet someone who suffers as you suffer, or as I do, perhaps giving them the strings could ease their sorrow as well."

"Here, then. Let's try out your theory. I'll give you this string of shells. This wampum string. It already contains some of my sorrow. Let it take up some of yours. Let this string absorb your sadness, as it has mine."

As Orios took the string from Hiawatha, he felt the heaviness in the beads, felt their great *orenda*. "Thank you, Hiawatha. Perhaps it will do for me what it has done for you."

"Perhaps. But right now, we had best cover more ground before the sun goes down."

Early the next morning, as they ran alongside the Mohawk River, they came to an open vista, and there they saw smoke rising from the top of the next hill. Hiawatha stopped. "That must be the first of the Mohawk villages. We must go slower now so that we don't appear to be a threat."

Outside the Mohawk Village, Hiawatha and Orios peered through the underbrush where painted warriors were standing guard around a tobacco field. Women were cutting tobacco and laying the large green leaves on corn stalks on the ground.

The warrior closest to them held a black wooden war club, intricately carved in the shape of a bear's head with its mouth open, holding a round ball in its wooden teeth. He was a big man, tall and muscular, with a deep chest. Six earrings hung from each of his ears. His head was shaved except for a narrow strip of high and stiff hair that ran from the front to the back down the middle of his skull.

Orios whispered to Hiawatha, "He looks fierce."

The fierce warrior, whose name was Gahnaseh, looked in their direction and gave a shrill whistle. His companions came running, following him as he ran towards the bushes where Hiawatha and

Orios were hiding. Hiawatha and Orios stepped into the clearing and held up their hands in greeting. "We mean no harm," said Hiawatha. "We come in peace."

"What are your names and why are you here?" One of the warriors, Wadoh, had an arrow fixed in his bow, and he pointed it threateningly at Hiawatha.

Hiawatha showed no fear. "I am Hiawatha, former chief of Onondaga, and this is my companion, Orios. We seek the village of my mother. She was from the Mohawk Wolf Clan."

"Your mother is Mohawk?"

"As I have said."

"What is her name?"

Hiawatha looked Gahnaseh in the eye. "Mataneh."

Gahnaseh looked at Wadoh and the other warriors. He lowered his war club.

"She was kidnapped by the Onondagas when she was a child. She is gone now. I buried her at Onondaga on the far side of the Silver Lake."

"I remember the name of Mataneh. Your story sounds familiar to me. But there is something I do not understand. If she is dead, why do you come here so far from home? What will it accomplish? It will not bring your mother back."

"Onondaga is my home no longer. I am a wanderer now. I seek allies in a revenge war against Shadahgoh, the Seneca chief, and Atatarho, the Onondaga chief. They murdered my four daughters."

"Now you speak a story that sounds real to me. I am Gahnaseh, war captain to Tekerihoken, a true friend to my friends and a bitter foe to my enemies. I have the scalps to prove it. Have you not heard of me? Many songs have been sung of my prowess in battle. This man beside me is Wadoh. Put down your bow, Wadoh."

The man called Wadoh, not as tall as Gahnaseh, but equally fierce looking, lowered the bow and relaxed the taut bowstring. "Are there others with you?"

"Only Orios here."

Gahnaseh looked at Orios. "Are you a warrior too?" The mockery in his voice was subtle, yet discernible.

"I am a musician and a song-maker," said Orios, holding up his carved wooden flute.

"This is dangerous country and these are dangerous times," said Gahnaseh. "Flutes and songs will not save your life. To survive and prosper, you must learn the song of a warrior." Embarrassed, Orios looked down at the ground and held his flute behind him.

Gahnaseh cleared his throat. "Come, I'll take you to our chief, Tekerihoken."

Inside the palisade walls of the village, a crowd of people waited impatiently for the approach of the two strangers following Gahnaseh and Wadoh. As they walked through the stockaded gates, a surge of people, women and girls, men and children, pushed forward. They looked angry and menacing.

"They are not Hurons!" shouted Gahnaseh. The crowd parted and dispersed.

"We have recently had many deaths due to Huron arrows and tomahawks," Wadoh explained to Hiawatha. "They want revenge."

Gahnaseh went inside the longhouse of Tekerihoken. When he returned, he said, "Chief Tekerihoken will see you now. You will forgive him for not coming out to greet you, but his leg does not work. A Huron smashed it with a war club."

They followed Gahnaseh into the longhouse where Tekerihoken sat beside a fire, his leg wrapped in a splint. "Come sit down. I cannot stand up to greet you properly. My bones are trying to mend themselves. Those Huron dogs will pay dearly when I am back on my feet again."

As they sat down in a circle around the fire, Tekerihoken brought out a long-stemmed, carved stone pipe and carefully crumbled tobacco into the bowl.

"I am Hiawatha, former chief of the Onondagas."

Tekerihoken nodded. "Welcome. I have heard of you. Your fame as a warrior is known across the land." Tekerihoken tamped the tobacco in the bowl down with his forefinger.

"It is good to be in the ancestral home of my mother."

"Yes, Gahnaseh told me that she was from the Wolf Clan. What was her name?"

"Her name was Mataneh. According to custom, she was never allowed to speak of her previous life. I never knew that she was adopted, but when she was on her death bed, she told me of her Mohawk family."

Tekerihoken bowed his head, then looked back up. "Yes. Mataneh. I knew her well. We lived in the same longhouse. We often played together. She was slightly older than me." He smiled. "I remember how she loved to chase the crows out of the cornfield. I am happy that she was not killed that day when she was carried off, and I am very pleased to meet her son."

Hiawatha was moved by Tekerihoken's story of his mother. He watched silently as the chief lit the tobacco with a stick from the fire and puffed deeply on the pipe. He raised it to the sky, then passed it to Hiawatha.

Hiawatha nodded in respect. He took a long puff and blew the smoke towards the open hole above their heads. "Thanks to the Great Spirit for guiding us here and protecting us from our enemies." He looked at Tekerihoken. "It is very good tobacco."

Tekerihoken nodded. "You will not find any that is sweeter."

Hiawatha passed the pipe back to him. "I saw many guards by your tobacco fields. Are they in danger?"

"Yes. Huron scouts were spotted only yesterday. These Huron are very powerful now. Many years ago, they pushed my people out of the Land of the Three Rivers and so we moved here. We have worked hard clearing this land and planting the fields with the three sisters, tapping the maple trees, and tending the earth. Then who should come knocking on our gate but these Huron again, wanting to trade for our corn and tobacco. But we would not trade with them. So they came in the middle of the night and burned our cornfields. And now we fear for our tobacco. Without tobacco, we'll not be able to trade for corn to get us through the winter."

Tekerihoken puffed again on the pipe. "Hurons down here are thick in the head," he said, tapping his finger against his temple. "We gave them many seeds, but they were too lazy to move the trees. They have not studied the plants. They know only how to hunt and fight. The ones up north are skilled farmers. But not these. These people are thick in the head." He raised the pipe up to the ceiling of the longhouse with both hands. "May the Great Spirit protect our fields of tobacco."

"May it be so," said Hiawatha.

Tekerihoken passed the pipe back to Hiawatha. "And why, my son, have you left Onondaga?"

"I was deposed as chief, and the sorcerer, Atatarho, usurped my power."

Tekerihoken was surprised by this news. "We have heard of Atatarho. There are many tales told of him. They say one should not cross his path. I am surprised that the Onondaga would want him as chief."

"He conspired with Shadahgoh, chief of the Senecas, and they murdered my four daughters. I am on the path of vengeance. I seek the deaths of both Atatarho and Shadahgoh."

"Then why look here?"

"I come to find the great leader Dekanawida. To enlist his aid. To help me raise an army of warriors to avenge my daughters and take back my rightful place as leader of my people."

"Well, then," said Tekerihoken. "You may not find what you are looking for. Dekanawida is not like you or me. If a man kills my daughter, I kill his son. If a man kills my wife, I kill his two brothers. But Dekanawida, as long as I have known him, speaks only of peace. I remember once saying to him: 'If you have only

peace, where can you put the revenge? It has to go somewhere.'
He said to me, 'Revenge cannot live in a healthy mind.' And I said
back to him: 'Are you saying that my mind is sick?' And he just
looked at me and smiled that mysterious smile of his."

"Part of me wants to believe in this dream of peace. But surely
Dekanawida must know that we cannot have peace until we get
rid of the evil ones."

Tekerihoken leaned over. "I know it and you know it, but
Dekanawida does not know it. He says that everyone has both
good and evil in them, and if we get rid of the evil ones, we must
also get rid of ourselves. Trust me, if it is a bloody vengeance that
you seek, then Dekanawida is not your man. He has great power,
great *orenda*, but he walks and talks the way of peace. It is his
brother that you want."

"His brother?"

"His twin brother, Adergagtha," said Tekerihoken. "He is a
war chief of the Huron. The same Adergagtha who burned our
cornfields and made many of our women widows. It is hard to
believe that he and Dekanawida came from the same seed. He
is the scourge of the Mohawk territory, and often he comes in
great numbers. All of his warriors wear wood-slat armor and their
blowguns are deadly."

"I have heard of this wood-slat armor," said Hiawatha, "But I
have never seen it in battle. Is it effective?"

"No arrow can pierce it, and it protects the ribs and backs from
war clubs. If you want an army of warriors to march on Onondaga
and take vengeance for the bloody deeds done to your daughters,
you could find no greater ally than Dekanawida's brother. I expect
he would like to extend his territory to the west. And if you
should succeed in striking a bargain with him, it would take him
off of our backs. We would offer to help you, but we need all our
warriors now to stand guard against Adergagtha." He looked at
Orios. "Who are you, young man?"

"I am Orios, the flute player."

"A melodious name for a musician. Come, you must meet others in the village. We will feast as well as we can. We will share with you what little we have, and Orios here will help us make music to pass the time and to lighten the mood. You will be honored guests in our longhouse."

Days turned into weeks and weeks turned into months. Two moons had come and had passed away since Hiawatha and Orios had arrived at the village of Tekerihoken. The charismatic Hiawatha quickly made friends with the Mohawks, who sympathized with his great loss. Even the deer seem to be attracted to Hiawatha and he never missed a shot. The warriors greatly admired Hiawatha's skill with the bow and arrow as well as the stone hatchet. None of them could give it the lightning-fast end-over-end spin that Hiawatha could.

He had given up on his quest to find Dekanawida. From all that he had heard, he knew now that Dekanawida would be of no use to him in his quest for vengeance. The Mohawks were strong warriors who understood his deep need for revenge. They had even promised to help him after they defeated the Hurons. Inspired by Hiawatha, Tekerihoken was now working on a plan with the other Mohawk villages to mount a massive attack on the Hurons to get rid of Adergagtha once and for all, but fate was about to intervene.

Chapter Four

Just after sunrise, Orios and Hiawatha were eating breakfast with Tekerihoken and Gahnaseh in the longhouse of the Wolf Clan.

Gahnaseh watched Orios scrape the last spoonful of corn mush from his bowl. "Would you like to come with me today? I'll show you the ways of a Mohawk warrior." Orios knew that he couldn't put it off any longer. The Mohawks loved his music, but they expected him to be able to fight as well. To be a man in Mohawk society was to be a warrior. He couldn't expect others to always look out for him.

Hiawatha smiled as Gahnaseh took Orios down to his bunk. He reached under the bunk and pulled out his collection of paint. Before long, Orios' face was decorated with lines and swirls of brilliant colors. Try as he might, Gahnaseh could not get an appropriately ferocious look on Orios' face. So he turned his attention to Orios' head. Using clam shells as tweezers, he pulled out the hairs on the side of his head one at a time. Sometimes he inadvertently pulled out more than one, making Orios jump and wince. By the time the sun was straight overhead, Orios had been transformed into a Mohawk warrior. At least in appearance. The sides of his head were free of hair and a three-inch-wide strip ran the length of his skull all the way down his neck where a twisted braid some eight inches in length hung. Three vertical lines of blue paint decorated his right cheek, while the left side of his face was painted red.

Orios followed Gahnaseh across the village, walking behind

him, trying to emulate his stride. Wadoh, who was sitting with Hiawatha and a group of Mohawk warriors in the center of the village making arrowheads, called out to Orios, who carried no weapon. "What do you intend to do when you meet a Huron warrior face to face, boy? Will you sing him to death? Perhaps you will knock him a clout over the head with your flute?" The men all laughed.

Embarrassed, Orios looked at his feet. Hiawatha offered words of encouragement. "But you do *look* like a warrior."

"Here, take this," said Wadoh as he handed Orios a stone tomahawk. Orios took the long supple handle wrapped in deerskin. The oblong rock at the head was as large as two fists. It felt heavy and lopsided in his hand.

"Thank you," said Orios in a subdued voice.

"Swing it twice over your head and bring it smash down on the enemy's face."

"His face?" It had not occurred to Orios that he might encounter an enemy today. Today was only for practice.

"Or his head! You're not afraid, are you?"

"No!" said Orios aloud, but inwardly his heart said yes. He did not like the feel of the heavy tomahawk. It felt like death. As Orios followed Gahnaseh and Wadoh outside the village, he turned back and looked at Hiawatha, who was staring intently at him. Hiawatha wanted to go with him, to protect him in case they were attacked today, but he knew that Orios must fly from the nest at some point. Today would be a good day, for there had been no Huron sighted for weeks. They were probably minding their own business, getting ready for the long winter that was rapidly approaching. And so he waved good-bye to his old friend and companion.

Orios stood at the end of a row of tobacco watching the women harvest the full leaves. One girl, Keteri, often looked at Orios throughout the afternoon, casting sidelong glances his way. She had been swept away by his playing in the village the night before. Orios smiled when he saw her look at him, then pretended not to notice her and tried to look like a warrior. He puffed his chest out as far as it would go, then tensed his muscles so that he looked like a statue. His small muscles seemed to take on a new dimension. He watched the setting sun, relieved that soon they would go back to the village to eat.

Eventually, his muscles could take it no more and he had to shift his position. As he rested his arm, letting it hang loosely down on his side, he felt his flute on the thong around his waist. He was so embarrassed. A warrior did not wear a flute. What must these women think of him? He moved his hand over his flute, trying to hide it in his new warrior stance. He had just perfected the look of his new position when, all of a sudden, he heard a thud behind him. He turned to see Wadoh fall to the ground. Gahnaseh, war club raised, was already running toward the Huron warrior who stood over him. Orios turned his head and saw Huron warriors in slatted wood armor with flaming torches pouring out of the forest. The women were already running toward the village. Orios didn't know which way to go, but the problem was soon solved for him. He felt a crack across the back of his head and that was the last thing he felt before the world turned black.

Back in the village, Hiawatha and the others heard the shouts of the sentries mingled with the screams of the women. "To arms! The Huron are upon us! They burn our tobacco fields!" Hiawatha and the other warriors snatched up their war clubs and their bows and they ran full tilt toward the shouting voices in the tobacco fields. They ran through the gates of the stockades and already they could smell the smoke and see the brilliant fires flaming and flaring up the distant fields in the fading light of the setting sun. His adrenaline racing through his veins, Hiawatha was more than ready to face the enemy. It had been too long since his mind and body had been quickened by the challenge of battle. His blood thrilled to the cacophony of war cries. A superhuman force seemed to propel him as he passed the others and led the way.

The birds already settling in the trees for the evening were greatly disturbed by the barbarous screaming of the human beings. They seemed to confer as a group and then simultaneously flew from the branches and swooped down over the fields crying out harsh warnings and reprimands to the fighting warriors below. The carrion raven and crow came too, cawing encouragement, circling and waiting for a feast. And far away, on a distant hilltop, through the eyes of an eagle, a prophet called Dekanawida watched in sorrow as the blood of the human beings stained the tobacco fields.

Running toward the fields, Hiawatha nocked an arrow onto his bowstring. As they approached the edge of the burning tobacco fields, they could make out the figures of Huron warriors in slatted wood armor wearing high helmets of woven hemp. Many carried torches, and they ran here and there lighting up sections of the field. Others carried long blowguns. Still others had long bows or deadly war clubs. There were at least twenty-five that Hiawatha could see. They must have expected a confrontation because all of them wore the tightly woven, hemp-and-wooden armor. The ones in the distance looked like turtles with their large shell-like, three-paneled back-shields. Flint arrowheads were of little use against this armor.

Hiawatha let loose an arrow and it whizzed through the air, finding its home in the chest of a Huron warrior. He turned in Hiawatha's direction, unhurt by the arrow that now protruded from his armor. He raised the long tube of his blowgun, painted red and decorated with hawk feathers. Hiawatha hit the ground and rolled over three times. The dart landed where he had been standing.

Gahnaseh ran past Hiawatha screaming insults and battle cries: "You filthy Huron devils! We will cut off the tops of your heads!

We will boil your brains in bear fat! We will slice off your toes and feed them to our dogs while you watch them chew your bones!"

Arrows and darts were flying everywhere. It was hard to see anything with the smoke blowing all around them in the failing light of dusk. In the dim light cast by the flames and the red streaks on the horizon, Hiawatha saw Gahnaseh leaping on the back of an armored Huron and riding him to the ground. He struck the man's head repeatedly with his war club. Blood flew up in his face as he screamed exultantly. "Die, Huron dog! Burner of corn and tobacco. Killer of infants and women! Die!" Three Hurons were upon him before he could stand up.

Hiawatha raised himself to one knee, took aim, and let loose an arrow that found its home in the left eye of an armored Huron. But the other two warriors overpowered Gahnaseh. One held him while the other clubbed him to the ground. Then he grabbed Gahnaseh by the top knot of hair and dragged him backwards away from the forefront of the battle. Hiawatha tried to reach him, but he was blocked by an armored warrior with a long war club. The Huron swung at him with all his might, but Hiawatha ducked and threw himself into the man's legs toppling him backwards. He quickly dispatched him with one blow to the face. Hiawatha looked around him, peering through the smoky gloom at the struggling shadows, but it was no use. Gahnaseh was nowhere in sight.

Mohawk and Huron were now fighting hand to hand. Another wave of warriors from the village led by Tekerihoken himself, limping on his still-splinted leg, pressed forward, outnumbering the Huron. Several fell beneath the deadly war clubs of the Mohawk, and even Tekerihoken, in spite of his advanced years and broken leg, felled a Huron with a mighty forehead blow from his stone tomahawk. Hiawatha ran among the Huron giving as good as he got. Twice he was staggered by blows to his shoulders and back. But he knew how to parry with his own club, and he knew how to strike back quickly. Two Huron warriors fell bleeding to the ground from the awful power of his arms and hands that wielded the red and black war club with a single antler spike.

As if some secret but unheard signal had been sounded, the Huron began to fall back, slowly at first, then more rapidly, until finally they were running across the burning fields, turning every now and again to let loose an arrow or a dart from a blowgun. But it was becoming too dark now to take aim, and few of their missiles found human targets. Exhausted, the Mohawk stopped running in pursuit and let them go. And as the smoke cleared, in the last minutes before dusk turned to darkness, they saw that the ground was littered with dead and wounded Huron and Mohawk. Thirteen Huron lay dead and twelve of their own, including two women.

Hiawatha found Wadoh trying to raise himself up on his elbow. Blood poured from a wound at his neck where a dart had struck him. But he was alive, and he would live to fight again.

"Wadoh! My young friend, Orios. Have you seen him?"

"I'm sorry, Hiawatha. He was captured, carried away by Adergagtha himself. Along with my friend Gahnaseh. May the spirits of our ancestors help them!"

"How do you know it was Adergagtha?"

"I have seen him once before. He is a huge man with a scar that travels down his face from beneath his right eye, across his lips, and down to his left chin. A battle wound that he is proud of. He paints this scar red when he does battle. It was this man who carried off your friend."

Tekerihoken reached their side, panting heavily from the exertions of fighting and running on his one good leg. "Where is Gahnaseh?" he asked.

"Taken captive," said Wadoh, "along with the Onondaga flute player."

"We must get them back," said Hiawatha. "I'm going after them."

"Then you too will die," said Tekerihoken. "You are one and

they are many."

"Then so be it. But I will not stand by while my friends are tortured by Hurons."

"First we must tend to your wounds. If they are not properly cleansed, you will die of your injuries instead of your enemy."

They limped back to the village to tend to the wounds of the survivors, carrying those who could not walk. Some had bones protruding through their broken skin. Many others had gashes and contusions on their heads and faces.

The women were already heating water. They had been through this scene many times before. Hiawatha winced as a medicine man from the Bear Clan cleansed his wounds and then applied a reddish-orange tincture. He looked around him and marveled at the expert way the Mohawk surgeons were setting the broken bones, manipulating them into place, and then tightly wrapping them in bandages of woven hemp and corn husks with splints of curved elm bark tied onto the outer layers.

Hiawatha got up slowly and went to his bunk at the far end of the longhouse to gather the supply of arrows he had been making. He would catch the Hurons unaware, perhaps when they were bathing or sleeping. Surely they did not bathe and sleep in their wooden armor. Tekerihoken walked up behind him. "You cannot leave now. The moon will not be out tonight."

Hiawatha continued packing. "I can see in the dark."

Tekerihoken put his hand on Hiawatha's arm, being careful not to touch one of his many wounds. "But the wolves, Hiawatha. You know that the wolves will smell the blood from your wounds. Have you ever tried to fight off a pack of wolves in the night all by yourself?"

"They will smell Huron blood before they smell mine."

"Yes, but they no doubt have already set up a circle of guards for defense. Besides, they know the way and you don't. You have never traveled into Huron territory before. How will you find the way to Adergagtha's village? How can you even find the deer paths at night? You should wait for the first rays of the morning sun."

Hiawatha knew that Tekerihoken was right. "It will be too late by then. Orios is not a warrior. He won't be able to stand up to their tortures."

"Sometimes we must accept fate. If it is the will of the Great Spirit, then Orios must face what he has to face."

Hiawatha sank down on his bunk.

With his good leg, Tekerihoken pushed some of the dried grass on the floor into a heap and sat on it next to one of the fires that were illuminating the longhouse. "Come, Hiawatha, sit by me and we will talk our way through it."

Tekerihoken waited while Hiawatha sat down cross-legged and assumed the position of council, then he continued. "I know how your heart aches, but we cannot afford to lose *you* as well. I would send many warriors with you, but you know what our situation is. We don't have enough warriors here now to defend our women and children in case they attack us again."

"But the hunting parties will be back soon."

"Perhaps. It depends on how far they had to go. They may not be back for several days."

"Then I will go by myself."

"How can you? You do not know the way. There are streams they will walk that will leave you no markings to follow, and they have secret pathways through the thick underbrush. You must have someone who knows the way to guide you."

"But who? You have no one to spare."

"There is someone. He is not here now, but you can go and find him. He is the one you came here to seek. Dekanawida. After all, Adergagtha is his brother. Perhaps he can intercede for you."

"How can I find him?"

"It's hard to say where he is just now. He went into the mountains to pray to the winged spirits, to converse with the spirits of the bird clans. He was greatly disappointed that we would not follow his new way of peace. Actually, he does not call it the "*new* way." He says that it is the *old* way. The way that human beings used to be before we fell from grace and lost touch with the winged spirits."

Tekerihoken stared into the fire. Whenever he thought of Dekanawida, he always felt as though he were there with him. He had not thought of his friend in quite a long time.

Impatiently, Hiawatha asked again. "But how will I find him? It seems to me that it will be much more difficult than finding the Hurons. At least they have a village whose smoke will show me the way."

Tekerihoken smiled to himself. "Dekanawida always told us that when we needed him, to follow his winged friends."

"What does that mean? Am I supposed to follow every bird that I see?"

"No, I hardly think so. I suggest that you head north, straight across the path of the sun, but a little to the right. You will come to a great valley with a river running through it. I expect that you will find some of his winged friends in that valley. The mountain at the end of it is considered a holy place, and the winged spirits who live there often come to the valley to drink its cool waters."

"Have you been there?"

"Many times. But only to the edge of the valley. I wanted to go all the way, but something always seemed to hold me back. Perhaps it was a fear of the unknown. Perhaps I knew that I was not ready. Or perhaps it was because I did not have a pressing reason, like you do now, that I always went around the valley and never climbed to the holy place."

Hiawatha nodded because he understood what Tekerihoken was talking about. Seeing them immersed in deep conversation, Wadoh walked over, his neck bandaged with a poultice of crushed foam-flower roots. The dart had pierced his voice box so that he could not speak in anything but a whisper. He told Tekerihoken that he wanted to be a part of any undertaking that would rescue his friend Gahnaseh. Tekerihoken told him that he deeply appreciated his offer, but that Hiawatha must make this journey by himself.

Early the next morning, before the first rays of dawn, Hiawatha silently left the village and headed on his lonely journey to the North Woods. After a full day of running, he came to the top of a hill overlooking a beautiful valley with a blue-green ribbon of river winding its way from one end to the other. At the far end was the most majestic mountain he had ever seen. He could see birds flying here and there throughout the valley.

He walked halfway down the steep slope, then stopped. Something held him back. He felt a strangeness about the place—an invisible vibration rising up from the valley below. Something didn't feel right. An odd, indescribable sensation caught hold of him. He didn't know why, but he knew that he didn't belong in this valley. His heart was too black with thoughts of revenge. How could he talk with these winged spirits? Some day he would. But not now. He was not ready for it. He must first take care of his earthly affairs, his deep need to revenge the deaths of his daughters.

He sank down on the ground, on the soft needles of a white pine tree and pondered his dilemma. How could he rescue Orios without Dekanawida's help? His only hope was to find them before they reached their village, but he was quickly running out of time and he did not know the way. He needed Dekanawida to show him the way to his brother's village.

Perhaps he could go around the valley and find Dekanawida at the other end. As he studied the terrain, he knew the journey around would take far too long. "Where were these winged messengers to guide him?" Was this just a wild goose chase? Hiawatha jumped at a loud noise in the branches above him. He looked up and there was a golden eagle staring down at him. A large eagle with a powerful *orenda*. The eagle continued to stare at Hiawatha, then he spread his great wings and flew down the hillside. Without thinking, Hiawatha jumped to his feet and ran after the great bird.

He ran at a steady clip down a path that followed an ever-widening stream. The stream flowed into a river, and as dusk began to descend upon the red and yellow tree-canopied valley, a dense fog descended with it. By now, Hiawatha had lost sight of the eagle. He moved carefully through the humid atmosphere, the silver air preventing him from seeing more than a few feet. As he rounded the bend, where the path came close to the small river, he ran into a large pink and white object that blocked the path along the bank.

He could barely discern its shape through the ever-thickening fog. And then he recognized it. The stone canoe from his dream! Exactly the same, and at a bend in the river just like this. Except there was no fog. In his dream, he saw things more clearly.

Hiawatha ran his hand over the smooth, cool surface of the stone. Who would have made such an object? And for what purpose? He sat on the edge of the stone canoe. The dense fog pulled in closer and seemed to swallow him up. Why had he come here? Here he was, lost in this fog-shrouded valley, while his young friend was a prisoner marching to torture and death. He groaned and clenched his eyes tightly as he remembered his dream of Orios at the stake.

From the small pouch around his neck he took out a string of small shells. They were of different colors; some were white and blue and some were white with purple and lavender stripes. His youngest daughter, little Tiwi, had made this string of shells for him before that day when she was carried away by the bewitched bird of prey.

"I will make you pay, Atatarho," Hiawatha said out loud. "I have lost all contact with my former life. And now even Orios will die because of you."

Hiawatha heard a faint noise like geese singing high in the air above him. He looked up but could see nothing. Then a golden light pierced through the fog, and he saw the faint traces of a rainbow—red, blue, green, and golden colors arching above the dark and foggy dusk. He felt a hand on his shoulder, and a sudden jolt of energy shot through his body and lit up the air around him.

He turned and looked up into the luminous face of a man. The same man that he had seen in his dream! A lilac-tinted silver glow emanated from the silver-haired head that framed a narrow, handsome face lined with numerous creases and valleys of joy and sorrow. An intense gentleness seemed to pour forth from this man's eyes and face. Behind those deep eyes seemed to be all the empathy and understanding, all the agony and suffering, all the kindness and humility, all the joy and happiness that ever were and ever would be in this world and perhaps in the next. Hiawatha felt himself choking up inexplicably, as if he were on the verge of crying. He wiped his eyes with the backs of his wrists. He wanted to turn away. But he couldn't. Some force, some magnetic power kept his eyes locked with the intense but gentle stare of this silver-haired man.

"What is it that you seek, my son?"

"I seek the one called Dekanawida," said Hiawatha. His words sounded like nonsense to his ears. He felt his face flush with embarrassment, something that rarely happened to him. But for some unknown reason, he felt like a child in this man's presence.

"You know who I am, and you have found me. But I am not what you seek. Let me tell you what it is that you are seeking."

The old man put his hand on Hiawatha's head. Another jolt of heat and energy flowed throughout his body and his mind. The silver-glowing man then pulled Hiawatha up to his feet. His legs felt unsteady, like a new-born fawn. Dekanawida steadied him.

"Tell me, why am I here?" Hiawatha forced the words out of his mouth. But when he heard them, they seemed to come from someone else's mouth.

"You are here to learn."

"To learn what?"

"To learn how to become a human being."

Cold chills rippled across the surface of Hiawatha's body

and his mind suddenly felt like it was on fire. It was as if he had become a lake and someone had thrown a huge burning rock into the middle of his being, making his blood hot and cold at the same time. He began to shake uncontrollably.

"Come, my son. Let us build a fire. We will warm ourselves. And then you will tell me why you have come these many miles to seek me out in this valley so far from your home."

Sitting by the open fire beneath the stars, Dekanawida looked at Hiawatha. Once again, Hiawatha felt that curious combination of intensity and gentleness pierce down to the depths of his being.

"Why have you come all the way from the land of the Onondagas? What is it you want from me?" Hiawatha strained to hear the voice of the holy man. It did not match the mighty *orenda* of his presence. It was a small voice, a weak, almost ethereal voice, the voice perhaps of a ghost or a spirit.

Hiawatha poked the fire with a stick, making orange-red sparks flare up into the darkness. "The antlers of a chieftain were taken from me and I have been cast out from my people. A sorcerer plotted against me, and with the help of Shadahgoh, a Seneca chief, has killed my daughters."

"Who is this sorcerer?"

"Atatarho, shaman of the Eel Clan, now chief of my people."

"What would you have me do?"

"The tales of your power and *orenda* have traveled the length and breadth of Turtle Island. I have heard of your plan to unite the nations under a Great Tree of Peace. I wish to help you, but it seems to me that we must first destroy the evil ones before we can have peace. I can help you organize the Oneida, the Cayuga, and the Mohawk into a mighty army, and then we will descend upon Atatarho at Onondaga and destroy him and destroy the Seneca who will unite with him."

"Destroy them? Don't you mean 'kill them'?"

"Yes. Of course that is what I mean."

Dekanawida looked up at the countless stars in the night sky. An inaudible sigh seemed to escape from his lips, and a look of sadness crossed the deeply lined features of his face. "You wish me to help you conquer your enemies in battle? What makes you think I would be willing to do such a thing? Do you not know that I am called the Peacemaker?"

"We *will* make peace. After we rid Turtle Island of the evil ones, Shadahgoh and Atatarho, and I am chief of the Onondaga once again. Then we will have peace."

"Do you really think so? Do you not think that the families of Shadahgoh and of all those warriors who surely must die in such a conflict, do you not think that these people will seek out their own revenge upon *you*?"

"Let them try. We will be more powerful than they. We will kill anyone who disturbs the peace."

"Do you not know that peace cannot be obtained by waging war? By killing your brothers and sisters? It is the nature of war to create more war."

Hiawatha remained silent. Finally, he said, "I must disagree with you. We can never have peace with evil men like Atatarho in our midst."

"Perhaps not. But first we must give them the chance to remake their minds, even as you, too, must remake your own mind."

"There is nothing wrong with my mind," said Hiawatha. The irritation in his voice was palpable.

Dekanawida did not reply. Instead, he looked up again into the night sky, studying it as though there were some message traced across the gaps between the stars.

Finally, he shifted his gaze downward and looked at Hiawatha. "Peace cannot live in a mind filled with vengeance," he said.

"Dekanawida, I did not think that we could agree on these matters. But that is not the immediate reason why I have come. Your brother and his Huron warriors attacked Tekerihoken's village. Many were killed, and they took two of our men captive. One was my young friend from Onondaga, who is like a son to me. Orios is a music maker, not a warrior. He will not be able to withstand their tortures."

"I am sorry to hear this news," said Dekanawida.

"I need your help. Lead me to Adergagtha's village so that I can help him escape or try to barter for his release."

"It is probably too late for that."

"That's why I need your help. You can talk to your brother. Intercede for us."

"I have not spoken to my brother in years. And even if I did speak to him, it does not mean that he will listen to me. He has never listened to me."

"But blood should count for something, should it not? Surely there is something that you can do."

"I wish that I could."

"How can you talk of starting a Great League of Peace where warring nations will put down their weapons and speak to one another if you cannot even talk with your own brother?"

"That is how it is." Dekanawida stared into the fire and said no more. "If you will not work for peace, Hiawatha, then you must accept the consequences of war."

Hiawatha became angry and started twisting Tiwi's string of shells back and forth in his two hands, unaware of what he was doing. "Men boast and boast of all the great deeds that they will do, of all the great acts they will perform, but when it comes right down to it, they do not do what they say they will. Even the great Dekanawida."

He spat out the name of the man who sat opposite him as if it were a curse, and, as he did so, the string of shells broke and scattered all over the ground beneath his feet. Hiawatha was stunned by his own actions. The only keepsake of his daughter now lay in pieces at his feet. He stared at the scattered shells, his mind frozen, his body unable to move.

"Let me help you," said Dekanawida. The old man carefully collected the shells from the ground. "May I restring them for you?"

"Why would you do that?"

"You know, Hiawatha, before a man can do good in this world, he must let go of the grief and the hatred in his heart so that his mind will be clear. I will lift the darkness from these shells, for these shells contain the darkness that is in your soul. They have traveled far with you and they have absorbed the blackness that clouds your mind and your heart. I will restring them. I will lift the darkness from them, and they will become words that will restore your mind."

He put his hand on Hiawatha's shoulder. "Then we can talk wisely about what it is that we must do to save your young friend." Hiawatha noticed that Dekanawida's voice was becoming weaker. He had spoken in a soft voice, but now that voice seemed to be getting even softer, wispier, like the voice of a spirit forcing itself to be heard.

By the light of the glimmering fire, Dekanawida restrung the shells. He then stood up and held them up to the sky and uttered words that Hiawatha could not hear. Perhaps he was not even speaking. His finely formed lips moved, but no sound came from them. As Hiawatha watched the prophet perform his ritual, something came over him and his very being seemed to tremble inside like the heart of a small, frightened bird. And then Dekanawida began to chant with a wavering, hypnotic rhythm.

> "Hiawatha is consumed with a grief so deep
> that its pain is like a sharp knife in the heart.
> When a woman is called away by death,
> it is doubly hard. For had she lived,
> she would have raised a family
> to care for our mother, the earth.

> The great evil is that not only have
> Hiawatha's daughters passed on,
> but a long line of expected people has fallen away.
> The many lines of grandchildren
> who would have been born in the future
> are now gone, utterly gone."

Hiawatha felt a stabbing pain in his heart. He began to cry. He could not help himself. It was as if a wellspring of deep and hidden water had been tapped by a long shaft, and the water simply surged upward of its own accord.

The silver-haired holy man placed the restrung shell string that Hiawatha had broken on top of a length of pure white doeskin. As Hiawatha's tears flowed, cleansing his soul, Dekanawida circled the fire. Then he stopped in front of Hiawatha, knelt down, and gently passed the doeskin over Hiawatha's face.

"I wipe away the tears from your face, using the white doeskin of pity."

He passed the skin and the shells over the face, head, and shoulders of Hiawatha whose tears still flowed like rivers that had been too long pent up. Dekanawida chanted:

> "Now do we wipe away your tears
> With a white doeskin —
> Now can you look around
> With peace of mind —
> And see the world around you."

Hiawatha felt his mind open up; his tears stopped flowing as Dekanawida placed a wampum string of quahog-shell beads into his hand. The prophet then placed his hand on Hiawatha's head and chanted some prayers in a tongue that he had never heard. It was the language of the earth, the language of the trees, the language of the bird nations who live in peace side-by-side with their warring neighbors, the human beings. It was also the language that the Spirit Beings speak when they speak with the trees, the earth, and the birds.

He then chanted, "I make the darkness vanish from your eyes and daylight enter your spirit. I beautify the sky. Now, when you look at the sky and your mind thinks, it will think thoughts of love, thoughts of peace. When you look up each morning into the sky, and when you look up each evening into the sky, the sky which the Perfector of our Faculties, the Master of All Things, intended to be a source of happiness to the people of all nations, then shall you be filled with the spirit of thankfulness, the spirit of love for all the people that struggle on the back of Turtle Island."

Holding the shell string in his hand, Hiawatha stared at the leaping flames of the fire, flames that seemed attuned to Dekanawida's every movement. The holy man removed a wampum string from around his neck and held it up towards the sky.

> "When a person is in deep grief
> The ears become blocked
> And the hearing is lost
> So that he hears nothing
> Of what is taking place
> Here on Mother Earth."

Dekanawida placed the second wampum string on top of the length of white doeskin and passed it over Hiawatha's ears. And his ears began to ring and contract, and he felt a great pressure build up in them so that he thought that his ear drums might explode. He clenched his eyes tightly shut, riding out the waves of pain that flooded over his hearing. And then suddenly, as though a floodgate had opened, the wind blew across his ears, leaving in its wake a peaceful lake of silence with beautiful, otherworldly voices drifting languidly across it. Dekanawida chanted again:

"Now do we unblock your ears.
Now will you hear the sounds
As people move all around you.
Now will you hear all things
Taking place on the earth."

Dekanawida placed the wampum string in Hiawatha's hands. He stared at it and felt the *orenda*, the power in the beads surge up his arms, past his shoulders, and into the core of his mind. He was suddenly dizzy, and swayed slightly. Dekanawida steadied him, then helped him to his feet.

Facing Hiawatha, Dekanawida removed another wampum string from around his neck and held it towards the sky.

"When a person is in great sorrow,
His throat is choked up with grief
So that he cannot speak his mind."

Hiawatha's throat began to throb. It became so dry and so parched that he could no longer swallow. The holy man placed the third string on top of the white doeskin cloth and wiped it over Hiawatha's throat and then over his mouth. Hiawatha felt a wet wind enter his mouth and tremble down his throat, relaxing the tensed muscles of his neck and his vocal chords.

"Now do we unblock your throat.
Now will you breathe with ease.
Now will you speak with pleasure
To the people around you."

His throat now seemed like a giant cavern open to the universe. He looked up at the stars in the heavens and opened his mouth as wide as he could. He felt the Spirits of the Sky rush into his body through the open cave that was his mouth, and he felt the fluttering of their wings against his heart, and he felt them filling his lungs with their holy power.

Dekanawida placed the shell wampum string in Hiawatha's hands and clasped both of his hands in his own. Hiawatha shuddered as the energy of a thousand fires seemed to spread throughout his entire body. A warm feeling surrounded his heart which now beat ecstatically in his chest.

He looked up. The night sky was clear and filled with bright, dancing stars, stars more beautiful than he could remember, and there was a crescent moon, a slender sliver of a moon like a silver bow, and around that bow was a large, glowing ring, a ring that was five times the size of Turtle Island, and in that ring were five bright stars.

"Now," said Dekanawida, "your reason has returned. Your judgment is sound again. You have become right-minded, clear-minded. You are ready to help others do the same."

Hiawatha looked up in the tree behind Dekanawida and saw a white-headed eagle sitting on a limb, quietly looking at him. He looked around in the other trees and saw many other birds looking down at him as well.

They slept that night by the Stone Canoe resting on the bank of the river. For the first time in months, the old nightmares were gone, and Hiawatha slept peacefully. He rose early the next morning, before sunrise, feeling like a changed man. He added more logs to the fire, then fashioned a long spear out of an elm branch. He lit a torch and waded in the river, spear in hand. After finding the right spot, he stood motionless and waited for the fish to be drawn to his light. Before long, he had three trout broiling over the open fire.

Dekanawida woke to the sizzling smell of roasting fish mingled with scents carried through the blaze of late autumn's trees shifting and whispering in the wind overhead. He smiled at Hiawatha and said, "You will make a wonderful traveling companion, my friend. Let us eat and be on our way."

He saw Hiawatha's surprised look. "I have changed my mind. You are right. I will go and talk with my brother. I cannot promise anything, but I can try. At least, it will prove to you that I am sincere. For now, let us pray that the winged spirits will give Orios the courage to face whatever it is that he must face."

Dekanawida sat down cross-legged in front of the fire. Hiawatha heard the fluttering of wings as birds flew into the trees all around them. Perhaps it was the smell of the roasting fish that drew them, or perhaps it was Dekanawida, who stretched his arms toward the sky and prayed: "Great Winged Spirits, carry these words on the wind so that Hiawatha's young friend may hear them. Let him know that he is not alone and that we are there with him. If his body must receive blows, soften them, carry him to another dimension of being where his body will no longer hinder him."

The birds rustled and stirred in the trees, and then, as if they were all of the same mind, they rose up together as one, and took flight. "An excellent omen," said the old man, his face crinkling with good humor. "Bird-flight is always a good omen at the beginning of great endeavors."

Chapter Five

Orios groaned aloud as a Huron warrior jerked the leash of twisted hemp looped around his neck. Gahnaseh shot him a stern look of disapproval. And the guard that held his leash jerked it so violently that Gahnaseh fell to the ground. The Huron kicked him in the ribs.

"Wait until you run the gauntlet, Mohawk scum. My wife will slice your ears off before you can get past the women and children."

Orios shuddered at the thought of what lay ahead. If only he had learned to be a warrior, perhaps he would not be a prisoner now. Why did he spend so much time playing his flute when he should have been working on developing his strength and his courage? The first Huron that came after him outside the walls of Tekerihoken's village knocked him over like a stalk of dry corn. The weak cannot survive in this world. Perhaps it was just as well that he would soon die. Now he understood why Makahwah did not want him to marry Sovana. He would not have been a good protector of his wife and the many children they would have had. His neck was bleeding from the constant friction of the tight noose, but the thought of his beautiful Sovana made the pain go away. Sovana. He could see her floating in the clear waters of the Silver Lake. And as he played his flute for her, he could see the waves fanning out from her thighs like cross sections from ancient trees. And then he gasped for air as he tripped and fell down the hillside, his body hanging by his bleeding neck. He could not move, but he knew that if he didn't, the pain would be even greater. He grabbed the leash with his hands to stop the pressure on his neck. When he finally pulled himself back up on the path, the Huron warrior kicked him and knocked him down again. As the world blackened around him, he saw himself flying with the birds, playing his flute. When he came to, he reached to his side and was greatly relieved to find that his flute was still there. Let them have their knives and clubs, his flute was all he ever wanted, and they could kill him for it if they wanted.

The warriors in front continued to harangue the prisoners. "Soon there will be none of you Mohawk left. We Huron will kill you all. The Huron way is the only way. It is the way of the war club."

A large man with a bright red scar crossing his face diagonally from under his right eye down to his left jawbone approached the two captives and their captors. "Do you intend to talk them to death? Shut up with your vain boasting and know-nothing bragging. You sound like two old women."

"Yes, Adergagtha."

"We are sorry, mighty lord."

"Here, give me those prisoners. I will lead them into my town."

Adergagtha, war chieftain of the Huron nation, twin brother to Dekanawida, but nothing at all like the Peacemaker, his shadow in fact, his doppelganger, snatched the neck-leads from the two Huron warriors and dismissed them back to the rear of the procession with a wave of his hand. Orios shuddered when he saw the gates of the village flung wide open and a throng of people gathered at the entrance screaming for vengeance.

Hohknanan, the sorcerer and shaman of Adergagtha's village, stood leaning on his staff, a sturdy length of carved ash surmounted with a stuffed raven's head. His deerskin robe was dyed midnight blue with black raven feathers affixed all over the front, and his long gray hair was littered with jet-black feathers.

"Mighty Adergagtha," shouted Hohknanan. "Your people

greet you and welcome you home after your great victories over the Mohawk animals!" Adergagtha raised one muscular arm high into the air and gestured with the other to the prisoners that he held by the leash. He put one leg behind Gahnaseh's and jerked the leash backwards, making him fall to the ground. The crowd of men and women, old and young, cheered and howled, and then they formed two roughly parallel rows that stretched from the entrance of the palisade and out some twenty or so yards.

"Let them run the gauntlet. Let us see what these Mohawk are made of." Adergagtha dragged Gahnaseh up to his feet and pushed him forward. Gahnaseh held his head high and began to sing his death song in a loud, clear voice. He did not run, but walked steadily as women jabbed him with pointed sticks, piercing his flesh, making him bleed, while men pounded his body with clubs. A blow to the side of the head dropped him to his knees.

"Don't hit him on the head!" a proud, handsome woman scolded. "We don't want him to die now. How can you torture someone who is dead? Hit him on the body. Bruise him, break his bones, make him bleed, but do not kill him."

Gahnaseh tried to run, but there were far too many obstacles. Too many people struck blows and pushed and jabbed. He held his head high and continued to sing his death song, so that the Huron, in spite of themselves, were greatly impressed with his bravery.

"Take him to the stake!"

"We will tear out his fingernails!"

"I will slice his feet!"

"I will flay him alive with clam shells!"

"Then we will see if he still sings his devil-song."

As they led Gahnaseh away toward the center of the village, the men and women in the gauntlet line screamed for Orios to run next before them.

Orios held his flute up above his head. "Please," he pleaded to Adergagtha and the crowd of Huron men and women, "I'm not a warrior. I . . . I am only a musician—a flute player. Why torture one who makes music?"

"If you survive the gauntlet, then we will hear your flute," replied Adergagtha.

"No!" shouted a thin older woman whose hair looked like it was made of steel wires. "Let us hear him play. I want to know how hard to hit him." This was Attignee, mother-in-law to Adergagtha and clan mother of the Wolf clan. Adergagtha was the warlord of this nation of Huron, but Attignee was the power behind the throne.

Adergagtha paused, and then reluctantly nodded. "Play," he said to Orios. "Play for your life."

Orios' lips were parched and his mouth was so dry that it felt like he had been eating sand from the shores of the great salt sea. He placed his flute to his mouth and blew, but a harsh and unmelodious squawk issued forth from the other end. His hands were sweating profusely and the flute slipped out of his grip.

"What kind of music is this?" someone shouted from the line.

"It sounds like a dying duck!" shouted another.

Orios shut his eyes tightly together expecting to feel a blow to the head from a club or a stone. But then, as if in a dream, he saw in his mind's eye a scarlet bird land on a black branch bursting with white flowers. The bird spoke to him in the language of human beings. He said: "Do not be afraid. Play! Play them a song from the land of the winged spirit beings. Make them feel the joy of the spirit world."

Still keeping his eyes closed, so that the vision of the bird would stay with him, Orios placed his mouth on the end of the flute, took a deep breath from way down deep in his belly, and whispered forth notes that seemed to issue from the spirit world. Beautiful music filled the air outside of the Huron village. The birds in the trees stopped chirping to listen, and then they joined in, making counterpointed rhythms with the soaring and floating notes that flowed from the flute of Orios. He played like he never had played before. He did not know where he was. He was out of time, out of this world. He saw only the faces of the winged spirits, bird-like beings who floated and soared before him singing harmonious notes of joy and love.

When he stopped playing and opened his eyes, the men and women in the gauntlet-line were standing still, staring at him. Some even had tears in their eyes. Orios' music had made them forget their anger, their grievances, their lust for blood and vengeance. The notes from his flute took some of them back to a time when they were carefree children, or when they first fell in love by the banks of a stream.

"He must still run the gauntlet!" Adergagtha announced, breaking the spell that enchanted his people.

"Yes," said Attignee. "Son-in-law. You lead him through. Carefully."

Adergagtha pulled Orios behind him grudgingly. The men and women in the line gave Orios blows and kicks, but they were not meant to do him any real harm. His music had deeply moved them, and they sensed that this boy was somehow touched by spirit beings, and they did not want to destroy this manifestation of the otherworld. But still, he was a Mohawk, a sworn enemy, one of the killers of their people. So they were obliged to do something. They landed halfhearted blows. Blows that bruised and cut, but none hard enough to break bones.

When Adergagtha and Orios reached the end of the line where Attignee stood, they stopped. Attignee held up a large round stone in her right hand. Orios looked into her eyes. In the light they looked bright yellow to him, like the eyes of a hungry she-wolf, as she brought the rock down against the side of his head. Blood gushed from the gash in the side of his head as he dropped to the ground like a sack of loose, dry corn.

"Take him to my longhouse," she commanded. "I will personally tend to the boy's wounds."

The stone canoe glided down the river that led to the land of the Huron. Trees, already losing their red and orange leaves, lined the banks, creating a surreal blur of thin and barren color in the periphery of Hiawatha's vision.

The sun shone brightly, and a mist rose from the cold water that was already beginning to heat up in the day's early warming. Birds sang gaily in the sparse branches of the trees and the air held a powerful scent of fresh pine.

Hiawatha steered the canoe around a large rock in the river and then rested the stone paddle on the edge of the canoe. "How is it that you and your twin brother are so different?"

"Who can say? My grandmother says that my mother was impregnated by two forces. By an evil man who planted in her womb the seed of my brother, Adergagtha, and by a Spirit Being, a Divine Ghost from the Land of the Sky People who came down and impregnated her womb with the seed of light. She said that I glowed with a great light when I was born. The father of Adergagtha said I was a demon child, a son of darkness and of evil, possessed by spirits, and for the safety of the people, I must be destroyed.

"So he took me, a newborn baby, and threw me under the ice in the lake. But when he returned to his longhouse, there I was crying beside my mother and brother. Then he took me and threw me into the fire and watched me burn. But when he went back into the house, there I was again, crying beside my brother. He then went outside and dug a deep hole in the earth and came back, fetched me up, took me out and buried me in the hole. But when he returned to the house, there I was again, crying beside my brother."

A bright glow filled Dekanawida's eyes and face as he continued. "Finally, my brother's father determined that he would cut me up into little pieces and feed me to the dogs. He took me outside and drew his sharp flint knife when, all of a sudden, a shadow fell over him and a voice came from the sky and said: *Leave the child alone. Do not try to hurt him anymore. You cannot kill him. He was put here for a great purpose. A purpose unknown to you and even to him, but it will be revealed to all men in good time.'* The voice so frightened him that he left me alone and never touched me again."

Dekanawida laughed. "That story always fascinated me as a child. Needless to say, my brother was not fond of the story, and he was always irritating my grandmother . . ."

Hiawatha finished his sentence for him. "That is why, perhaps, she told it so often?"

Dekanawida smiled that mysterious, knowing smile of his. He repeated a line from the story: "'He was put here for a great purpose.' All men are put here for a great purpose. And you too, Hiawatha, you are here for a purpose. You think you are here to find someone to aid you in your great mission of vengeance, but your mission is far greater than this. Vengeance is the way of the weak, the path of cowards. True courage comes from forgiveness. I will teach you to forgive, because it is only through the path of forgiveness that true healing can take place."

It had been two days since Dekanawida had performed the condolence ceremony, and the great stone that had been in Hiawatha's heart had been lifted. The all-consuming hatred and the lust for blood were gone.

Instead, he had a newfound clarity of vision, a peace of mind that seemed to permeate everything around him. The song of the birds, the light of the sun, even the air that he breathed, now seemed full of a peace that he had never known before. He had been in continual conversation with the Peacemaker for these last two days and nights, stopping only to eat and sleep. And Hiawatha had found that there was more wisdom within this one man than within all of the men and women he had ever known. Hiawatha had decided that the Peacemaker's vision of a Great League of Peace must be fulfilled. They talked long about what needed to be done to bring all the warring nations together, and what needed to be done in order to keep them together.

They talked about a constitution, a set of rules of government and diplomacy, of a Grand Council of Peace Chiefs or Sachems with representatives from each clan of each of the nations that would meet regularly in order to settle disputes through reason and discussion, through peaceful means, instead of through the continual cycle of revenge wars. Hiawatha agreed now with Dekanawida that war is not the way to settle disputes, that war only causes more deaths that need retribution in the future. Acts of violence create more enemies who in turn will seek to wreak their vengeance through more acts of violence. It never stops.

But it *must* stop. He would accompany Dekanawida on a mission throughout Turtle Island, and together they would convince the headmen and the chieftains to bury the club of war under the tree of peace. But Dekanawida's voice became weaker each day; it was hard for him to speak above a loud whisper. And he had done much talking in the last two days and nights. He had imparted the secrets of the Way of Peace and Understanding, the secrets of the Way of Love and the Path of Forgiveness to Hiawatha. He was still an apprentice, but his would be the voice that would speak the words of the Great Peacemaker to the people. He had always been known as a skillful orator among his own people. Together, through Dekanawida's visions and Hiawatha's oratory, they would spread the Word of Peace to the nations.

"We are now in the land of the Huron." Dekanawida pointed with his staff. Hiawatha gazed up at the clear water falling from a flat rock ledge some fifty feet above their heads. The air was crisp and biting, and the sun filtered brilliantly through the thinning red and orange leaves of the trees.

"We are almost there," said Dekanawida. "We will rest here for a little while. We must build up our spiritual strength so we can melt the ice in my brother's heart."

Dekanawida sat down by the waterfall and gestured for

Hiawatha to do likewise. "We used to play here. Many summers ago, when I was a boy, I told my brother stories of the spirits that live behind this waterfall. You see, after our mother died, our house fell apart. My brother wanted the hunting land at Three Rivers, but, as the elder chief—I was born two minutes before Adergagtha—I would not allow it. That was all he talked of—how the corn and tobacco would trade more fairly if the Mohawks lost Three Rivers. He was a fierce war chief and he convinced his men to go against me."

Dekanawida gave Hiawatha a sideways glance to see how he was taking in all of this. The prophet knew that Hiawatha had been a war chief, and he was curious to see how deep his new-found convictions ran. He picked up a handful of dirt in one hand and rubbed the soft black loam between his two fingers. "War chiefs are a very delicate matter, Hiawatha. We need them for protection, but we must structure our League so that they never gain control."

"And how will we do that?"

"We will never allow a representative on the Council of Sachems to be a war chief. Never. If something happens to me, will you promise that you will see to this?"

"I'll try," said Hiawatha. "I'll do what I can."

"Good. Let us go now. We have work to do."

The old man raised himself up on his eagle-claw staff and shook out his stiff limbs. He looked down at the ground littered with brown, rustling leaves that crumbled when you stepped on them.

"These are the dead hairs of our mother," said Dekanawida.

Hiawatha picked up a handful and rubbed them together, inhaling the musky aroma of Mother Earth retreating into winter so that she could rebuild herself once again under a blanket of ice and snow. "Do you think that Adergagtha will take us as his prisoners?"

"Possibly. That was my initial reason for refusing your request to come here. But in the path that we have chosen, we cannot worry about such things. We cannot hope to convert the longhouse nations to the way of peace if we have fear in our hearts. So, let us not be afraid of what may lie ahead. They can only torture us and kill us. They cannot keep us from becoming winged spirits. If it is our time to die, then we will travel together to the Land of the Spirits. I will lead you. So you see, you have nothing to fear."

The Huron were a mighty, water-dwelling people, and, unlike the Haudenosaunee who built their fortified towns and villages back away from the highways of the water, they built their castle-like forts close to the river's edge. Dekanawida's Stone Canoe glided silently and effortlessly down the river toward the fortified Huron town of Adergagtha.

Shouts could be heard from the walls of the town. Warriors streamed out of the heavy entrance gate. Dekanawida could hear the faint cries of his own name shouted from the walls. The canoe glided up on the bank of the river and Hiawatha leapt out first, followed by Dekanawida. "Who are you? State your business," demanded a Huron warrior with three blowgun darts pierced through his left ear. His top knot of hair was piled high and dyed red and yellow.

"I am Hiawatha, the Onondaga."

"The Onondaga are our enemy. Are you always this careless with your life?"

"I come with Dekanawida on a mission of peace and brotherhood."

"He is under my protection, Assiboin. I am Dekanawida, Huron-born and brother to your chief."

"I know who you are. But how is it that you know my name?"

"I know many things."

"So I understand. We also know many things. We have been watching you for the last two days. Come. Follow me into the town."

They followed Assiboin through the gates of the town. Men, women, and children formed a gauntlet so that they might pass through the crowd gathered to see the return of their most celebrated holy man. But this gauntlet was a peaceful one. They were greeted with cheers by some, with stony silence by others. But no one attempted to harm them. An old woman threw herself at Dekanawida's feet and hugged his legs. He lifted her up to her feet and embraced her. He gave her a blessing and she said, "I have prayed for this day to come."

Warriors pulled the woman away. When they reached the center of the town, Adergagtha stepped out of the central longhouse surrounded by guards with war clubs and tomahawks. Below his bare chest, he wore buckskin leggings, dyed red. The quillwork on his moccasins was of the highest quality. He straightened his necklace of bear claws, and draped a bearskin robe over his left shoulder.

"I have brought my brother the gift of the peace wampum," said Dekanawida, holding out a long belt of woven shells and quills.

"Most thoughtful of you, brother. But I have no need of a peace wampum."

"Can we not join hands and bury the bitterness that is between us?" asked Dekanawida.

"I am not bitter."

"Let us sit on the ground then and talk as brothers."

"Sit and talk?" Adergagtha looked to his men standing beside him and laughed out loud. It was a mocking, sarcastic laugh. His men laughed with him. "I say let us run and hunt."

"Hunting is good. But we need food for our minds as well as our bodies."

"Dekanawida grows ever softer in his old age. He should sit and talk with the women." Adergagtha's warriors laughed.

"In order for our children to survive, we must learn to use our minds. I have come to speak with you of a new League of Peace where Huron and Mohawk, and all the peoples of Turtle Island will settle their differences with logic, with their minds, not with the war club." Dekanawida stepped closer to his brother. "Can we sit down and talk about it, if only for a little while?"

"Come into my longhouse. We will sit and talk. We will smoke. I will listen to you, and my councilors will listen to you because you are my brother. But that is all I am promising you."

Adergagtha and his councilors sat on the opposite side of the fire from Hiawatha and Dekanawida. He listened attentively, but from time to time a crooked smile of smug derision crept across his scarred face.

"Each town and village from each nation will participate in the decisions of the League, but at the same time, each nation will keep their own government, their own autonomy." Hiawatha spoke clearly and loudly; his tone and inflections were precisely calculated so that none in the longhouse was offended, none spoken down to, none made to feel ignorant. He relayed the words that Dekanawida spoke to him so that all present could hear.

"What about the land?" asked Adergagtha.

After a brief conference, Hiawatha said, "By birthright, the nations are the owners of the soil they occupy and that their ancestors occupied."

"But that does not account for lands taken in war. What about Three Rivers?" Adergagtha knew that the Mohawk had a prior claim on this disputed land by birthright, land that he had taken through sheer military power.

Dekanawida spoke and Hiawatha relayed his words in a strong and firm voice. "Three Rivers is the birthright of the Mohawk nation."

"It is now our hunting grounds!" said Adergagtha. The air in the longhouse was tense. No one spoke, but the silence was palpable.

"All members of the League will share their hunting grounds."

"Share hunting grounds?" Adergagtha's voice dripped with sarcasm. "What good is it then to say, 'This is our territory'?"

"We must do it for the good of all the people—not just all the people here now, but for the good of all the people to come—the long line of generations that will follow when our bones are dust. If future generations are to prosper, we must think of the future of the Three Sisters. There must be room for the seeds of corn, bean, and squash to grow. We must make room too for the sacred tobacco."

"My people do not poke holes in the soil! Other Huron up north dig around in the dirt. But we are hunters. Three Rivers is our land, and no one else will hunt on it. Never. Not as long as I live and rule. Our Father in the Sky can hold back my anger no longer! You ask Adergagtha to be a woman! To give up his hunting rights so that women can dig in the earth long after I am dead. Do you take me for a fool?"

"I had hoped that my brother was now a wiser man. We can no longer think only of the present. We must think of the future."

"*You* think of the future. I live now." Adergagtha turned to two of his warriors seated against the back wall of the longhouse. "Show them out! It is out of respect for our ties of blood that I let you walk out of here alive."

Hiawatha leapt to his feet of his own accord before the two Huron henchmen could lay hands on him. *This is going to be more difficult than ever he imagined. If Dekanawida's own brother would not be moved at least a little by this talk of the new way, what chance did they have of convincing Atatarho or Shadahgoh?* He helped Dekanawida rise, then turned to Adergagtha. "Before we go, may I ask about the Mohawk prisoners you took from the raid on Tekerihoken's tobacco fields?"

"The prisoners met the fate of all Huron prisoners. They have become revenge trophies for the widows and bereaved mothers that suffered at the hands of Mohawk atrocities against our people."

Hiawatha pressed Adergagtha further. "And the Onondaga boy?"

"The Onondaga boy is dead," said Adergagtha, feigning boredom.

Hiawatha felt the blood rise to his face. He took a deep breath and tried to regain his composure. "May I have his bones for burial?"

"Burial? He is not ready to be buried." Adergagtha laughed. "The Onondaga boy that was is now a Huron warrior."

Hiawatha's eyes widened, betraying the surprise that he felt upon hearing this news. He paused, then pressed on. "May I see him before we go?"

"That is not possible. It would make no sense to him. His past has been erased."

"Would you then give him . . ."

"Enough!" roared Adergagtha. "You exhaust my patience! Get them out of my sight!"

Adergagtha's warriors grabbed Hiawatha by both arms and forcibly pushed him from the longhouse. Dekanawida followed behind.

"What an elaborate scheme my elder brother has devised to finally prove himself right about Three Rivers," said Adergagtha. "I think he has forgotten why he left here running for his life."

More armed warriors joined the pair that forced them out of the longhouse, and this hostile party escorted Dekanawida and Hiawatha to the gates of the town. They were roughly pushed outside and the heavy gates were symbolically closed behind them.

As they walked toward the river's edge, the deliberate slowness that the old man showed in the town of Adergagtha was all gone now and in its place was a speed and nimbleness that belied his age. He moved with the agility of a panther and the swiftness of an eagle as he leaped into the stone canoe and waved his eagle-claw staff over his head. It occurred to Hiawatha that Adergagtha underestimated the power of his brother. And that eventually

Dekanawida must win. Adergagtha and those who rely on aggression and intimidation to achieve their ends might win in the short term. But in the long run, those who rely on wisdom, logic, and the power of the heart must surely win out. No one can withstand kindness. No one can withstand the pure power of love.

The stone canoe left the shore and traveled easily upstream. In its smooth movements, it resembled a swan gliding on a clear lake. All one saw was the V-shaped wake; the source of the locomotion was hidden, like a swan's powerful webbed feet that propel her forward yet cannot be seen on the surface. Dekanawida is also like this, like his stone canoe, thought Hiawatha. What moves him forward, the source of his power, is not something that can be seen readily by human eyes. Nonetheless it is there, beneath the surface, impelling him forward. Could he, could anyone resist this force of nature?

Hiawatha was constantly impressed by the drive and spiritual force within Dekanawida. He was human, Hiawatha knew. He liked to joke, and sometimes had his moments of anger, even of doubt and confusion, but he was also something beyond human, a divine force. Hiawatha could see this in the glow that emanated from his eyes and sometimes surrounded his entire being, and he could feel it in the strong *orenda*, the presence, the bright white and violet aura that seemed to envelop him at times and radiate outward. Then, of course, there were the feats of magic—like this canoe they were now riding in. They would need all the magic and all the otherworldly help that they could lay their hands on in order to perform the tasks ahead of them. How do you change an entire society? How do you erase ways of being, ways of doing that have so ingrained themselves into the fabric of the culture that they were now second nature? It would take much hard work, much luck, and plenty of power from the spirit world. But then, if they could float upon the surface of the waters in a boat made of stone, all things might be possible.

Hiawatha finally felt the full power of Dekanawida's message.

This new way of peace might actually work. He raised both his arms to the heavens and chanted a prayer to the Great Spirit:

> "Oh Divine Spirit of the Universe,
> Lend us your power
> That we may do your work.
> Give us your strength,
> Your wisdom, and your love
> So that we may understand the hearts
> And minds of our people
> And turn them away from hatred
> And blood lust, so that we may
> Give them kindness and forgiveness
> Where there now is fear and distrust."

Dekanawida smiled at him and placed his right hand on his shoulder. "A fine prayer, Hiawatha. From now on, you will speak for me. Your voice is strong and beautiful. You will be the spokesman for the New League of Power through Peace."

Chapter Six

After a day of travel on the river, Hiawatha and Dekanawida were resting on the shore, watching the squirrels at play in the trees, scrambling up and down the trunks and the nearly bare branches. Hiawatha felt a slight vibration. He placed his ear to the ground, listening until he recognized the rhythmic pattern of someone running. Not just one runner, but two fast runners.

He looked at Dekanawida, who nodded and said, "Perhaps you should go and meet them. Invite them to share our fire."

Hiawatha scanned the treetops and the horizon, then took off running, slightly to the north of the direction of the runners. He ran across the floor of the forest, littered with brown pine needles and fallen leaves, red and brown and golden. A steady breeze brought a slight chill to the air and made more leaves cascade down to the ground. As he ran through the swirling red and yellow leaves, he could hear the approach of the runners and he could tell that they were running fast, faster than he had first thought. Hiawatha ran faster and faster, but he could not seem to close the distance between them.

Finally, he stopped and gave three owl cries. He heard the runners stop. He waited and listened but there was no answering cry. He gave another series of cries, but still there was no response. Feeling uneasy in the eerie silence, his hand instinctively went to his side, but there was no tomahawk there to protect him. For the first time in his life, he felt vulnerable, defenseless. Why had he listened to Dekanawida? He should at least have his stone hatchet for defense. It was too late for that now. Whoever it was had heard him, and they knew where he was. As he put his hands to his mouth to give another cry, a head popped up over the rock above him.

"Hiawatha!"

While he waited for Hiawatha's return, Dekanawida contemplated the recent turn of events. For the past several years he had been going from village to village, talking with the people about building a league of peace. The younger warriors usually scoffed at the idea, but some of the elders and headmen listened when he spoke of the possibility of peace among the nations. Hiawatha, however, had been the only one to embrace it. Perhaps it was the Condolence Ceremony. Perhaps that's what had been missing. His thoughts were interrupted by the sound of approaching voices.

"Dekanawida," shouted Hiawatha. "Look who has found us." He stepped into the clearing with two young messengers. "Do you remember Okaiya and Ortekla?"

"Yes, yes, of course I do. But look how you have grown since last I saw you." The two boys smiled.

"Tekerihoken was concerned for our safety and has sent them to see what news they could find. They are very fast runners. Not even I could catch them."

Dekanawida smiled. "They have been practicing their running since they first learned to walk. Tekerihoken once told me they could outrun an arrow." The boys grinned broadly.

Dekanawida waved them forward. "Come over here boys. Sit down and join us. We will celebrate your arrival."

The boys looked at each other, then Okaiya spoke. "We would like to very much, but we must get back to tell Tekerihoken that you are safe."

Hiawatha protested. "But the sun is setting. Surely Tekerihoken does not expect you to run all night."

Okaiya nodded. "I'm afraid he does. But we're used to it."

"We take great pride in it," Ortekla interjected. "We can run three journeys of the sun, stopping only for water."

Dekanawida nodded. "That is most impressive. But since all is well with us, it is not urgent that you return so soon."

"Tekerihoken is very concerned about Hiawatha," said Okaiya. "He will be greatly relieved to know that he has not been killed by the Hurons."

Dekanawida turned to Hiawatha. "It seems as though you already have a following in Tekerihoken's village."

Ortekla's face lit up. "He taught me how to put the proper spin on a flying hatchet. Tekerihoken says that the Huron might have killed all our warriors had it not been for Hiawatha. He does not want to lose him."

"I see," said Dekanawida. "Well, now you will have an even more useful survival lesson from the great teacher. How to fish for your supper. Go with him now, and I will go and find a winged messenger to send in your place. Tekerihoken will get the message even sooner. There are urgent matters that Hiawatha and I must discuss this evening, and we will have an important message for you to take back to Tekerihoken in the morning. If we are to establish the league of peace, we must decide how best to use our time before the heavy snows set in."

The runners looked to Hiawatha for guidance. "Dekanawida is right. Come with me and we will catch some fish for the evening meal." Surprised, Hiawatha and the boys watched Dekanawida leap to his feet and take off at a jogging pace through the woods as if he had found a new source of inner strength and youthful vigor.

In the near distance, a wolf howled a lonely cry. Hiawatha sat by the fire watching the fish slowly roast, waiting for Dekanawida's return. He was tempted to go look for him, but then he remembered how Dekanawida had found him in the dark. Still, he worried about his safe return.

Ortekla and Okaiya amused themselves by playing a gambling game of throwing flat buttons made from cross sections of deer antler. One side of each button was natural, the other side painted black. It was a popular and ancient game of chance. If the buttons came up all black, or all natural, you won. They laughed or cursed alternately whenever one or the other won or lost a toss of the buttons. Hiawatha was not a gambler. He always thought it a foolish waste of time. Especially now when important tasks were to be done. Tasks that demanded attention and perfect clear-mindedness. Tasks whose import stretched beyond himself and his own time. Tasks that affected the future of Turtle Island for generations to come.

Still, he did not berate the two youths. Not everyone was as serious as he, and what good would it do to deprive them a bit of harmless fun? At least they were not killing their "enemies" or torturing war captives. Put in this perspective, a bit of gaming seemed like a harmless channeling of aggression.

"What do you mean, you win?" cried Ortekla. There was a genuine anger in his voice now, not simple bantering and fake moaning as before.

"Just what I said. I win. My toss clearly beat yours," replied Okaiya.

"It did not! I won that toss. You took up the markers too quickly so that I could not see."

"What are you saying, Ortekla?" There was a slow menace in his words. Hiawatha turned in time to see Ortekla draw the stone knife from the sheath that hung around his neck.

"I say that you are a cheat!" And Ortekla leaped upon Okaiya, grabbing his throat with one hand and attempting to drive his knife into Okaiya's heart. Okaiya, however, had drawn his own knife and grabbed Ortekla's knife arm and attempted to drive his own knife home. They were locked in a deadly duel, rolling on the ground, each one trying to force his blade close to the other's body, and each one holding back the knife-arm of the other.

"Stop it!" yelled Hiawatha, who leaped upon the two of them and gave both of them great resounding cracks on the ears with the flat of his hand. He pushed them apart. They tried to charge each other again. Again, Hiawatha pushed them back. He was stronger than both of these two young men combined, and he was not about to take any nonsense from them.

"What is this? Arguing over a child's game? Not just arguing! But willing to take the life of your friend over the arbitrary toss of some deer buttons?"

"But Hiawatha, he was cheating!"

"Liar! I was not! I'll cut off your nose!"

"Stop it!" Hiawatha's roar filled the forest and sent a dozen sleeping birds flying from the branches of the trees overhead.

"By the Great Spirit, I will drown you both in the river if you do not stop fighting over this game!"

Okaiya and Ortekla looked at each other. Then at Hiawatha. Then all three of them laughed at how ridiculous his threat was. He would drown them because they would not stop arguing?

"Is this the great new path of peace that you and Dekanawida will preach?" asked Okaiya. "Stop fighting or we will kill you?"

"No. Of course it isn't. You are right. I sounded ridiculous. But so did you two. Two friends from the same village who would murder each other over a silly game. Make friends again. Now."

"How?"

"You will both beg each other's forgiveness. And then you will exchange knives. Ortekla, you will give to Okaiya your excellent knife with its wide blade and deer-antler handle. And Okaiya, you will give to Ortekla that knife of yours with the fine handle carved from a wolf's jaw. Then you will each have each other's weapons and each other's tools, and it could never be right for the knife of Okaiya to harm Okaiya, nor for the knife blade of Ortekla to draw blood from the body of Ortekla."

The two youths looked at each other momentarily. Then they

sheathed their knives, and removed the thongs from their necks and exchanged them. "Here Ortekla, I give you my knife."

"And Okaiya, I give you mine."

"Now embrace."

The boys embraced and promised each other that they would fight no more. It was a great first victory for Hiawatha. A small step in a new direction. A hint of greater things to come.

He was surprised to see Dekanawida step into the clearing with a bald eagle perched on his right wrist, a magnificent bird with a white head and golden yellow beak. The bird held himself proudly, slowly turning his head in order to keep a sharp eye on all things around him. Dekanawida and the great bird of prey seemed to have some special rapport between them, a mysterious and secret pact that only they shared.

"Meet my friend, Kyree, the clear-eyed, the farseeing one."

Okaiya and Ortekla were too astounded to say anything. They simply stared in awe at the eagle who eyed them warily.

"He is watching you two. If you fight over those rolling bones again, he will know it."

"Where did you find him?" asked Okaiya.

"I climbed up to his aerie, and asked him if he would go with us to be the guardian of the new league of peace that we will establish among the human beings."

"You talked to him?" asked Ortekla.

"*With* him. Yes. The language of the eagle is a difficult one, but this one is special. He comes partly from the Land of the Spirit Beings, and at one time he was a human being himself. So he knows the ways of us ignorant mortals. He knows how frail we are, how easily tempted to wickedness."

Kyree stretched out his wings and screeched loudly. The boys jumped back.

"Let us prepare our message for Tekerihoken." He turned to Hiawatha. "May I have one of your wampum strings?" He removed an eagle feather from his hair, then stared deep into the eyes of the eagle. The other three watched this strange communication take place. No noises were made, only a few eye blinks and head movements. Kyree bent over and picked up the feather in his beak. Dekanawida slowly walked over to Hiawatha. Kyree extended his wings again, then reached with his claw and took the wampum string from Hiawatha.

Dekanawida lifted his arm slightly and the great eagle flapped his wings, bent his powerful legs, and sprang forth from his perch, flying up into the air and over the treetops. They watched him glide across the rising moon toward the village of Tekerihoken.

Tired from their day of running, the boys ate the fish and soon fell asleep. They had always felt a little wary about sleeping in the forest. They preferred to keep running when the sun went down, but tonight they felt completely safe with the great warrior and the holy man standing guard. After the runners had gone to sleep, Dekanawida and Hiawatha sat close by the fire. As they silently stared into the flames, Dekanawida said, "I have been thinking about what our first step might be. Peace can only come by remaking people's minds. And to do that, we need to do more than just talk. I think that it would be a good idea to hold a large condolence ceremony for the people of Tekerihoken's village. A ceremony of condolence might put them in the right frame of mind. After all, how can you rationally discuss building a league of peace when your heart is filled with grief and your mind is full of hate? Where do thoughts of revenge come from, if not from grief and hate? To want revenge, one must still be grieving, still be hating. Is it not true?"

Hiawatha nodded. And Dekanawida continued. "But is there not a better way to relieve the grief? Have we not survived by helping each other? Perhaps we need to give each other more help when we are in sorrow. It should not be the responsibility of each person to work through his or her grief all alone. The whole village must help them. So, I have a plan. We will divide the whole village into two groups, those who are still grieving over some loss and those who are clear-minded. And then we will perform a ceremony similar to your experience by the river when we first met. Does that sound like a good place to start?"

"Yes, it does. But why just Tekerihoken's people? If we are to succeed, we will need the support of all the Mohawk people. They will be the foundation of our league. They are the strongest and the most easterly longhouse of the five great longhouses."

Dekanawida reflected a few moments. "Why not? Yes, of course. It would be even more powerful. A Ceremony of Condolence for the entire Mohawk nation. We invite all the headmen and clan mothers and council members from all the clans in all the villages and towns of the People of the Flint. After the ceremony, we can discuss the plans for a league of peace."

"They will all come to Tekerihoken's village?"

"It's nothing out of the ordinary. They usually get together in the late fall to celebrate the harvest and trade. And Tekerihoken is a respected man among the Mohawk. If the invitation is worded in the right way, I am sure they will come to his village."

Hiawatha recalled his conversations with Tekerihoken. "But will Tekerihoken want to host this gathering for a discussion of the league of peace?"

"I think he will if you ask him. He thinks highly of you."

"Right now, he is thinking solely of defense. Since the last Huron attack, defense has been very much on everyone's mind."

Dekanawida considered this. "A league of peace is also a league of defense, so he may be interested in such a discussion for that very reason."

"Yes, I see your point. And you are right, the Condolence Ceremony is essential. The mourning wars must be replaced with a mourning ritual."

"Yes, and the ceremony must be led by someone with great *orenda*."

"Of course. You must lead it."

"No, Hiawatha. My voice will not carry that far. You will lead the ceremony."

"No. I can't do that. I could never do what you did for me. I am not a holy man. Since becoming clear-minded, I have thought much about my past. My soul has been as black as my enemies. I have tortured and killed and caused the deaths of my own daughters. If I had gone to Shadahgoh in the beginning, with apologies and gifts of remorse, perhaps my daughters would still be alive. If I had listened to the wisdom of my clan mother, perhaps my daughters would still be alive. Instead, I have destroyed everything. I am not an example for other people to follow."

"No, Hiawatha. You are the *perfect* example for people to follow. You are the example of how people can change. For a great warrior, like you, to stand up and lay down his weapons, to speak for the League of Peace—this will have an impact far beyond what I can do."

"The Ceremony of Condolence requires a holy man."

"Haven't you noticed how people always stop and listen when you speak? The gift of your voice is a gift from the Great Spirit. It is only right that you should use it now."

"Dekanawida, there is something I must tell you. I am far more afraid of standing up in front of the whole Mohawk nation and leading them in this new Ceremony of Condolence than I am of fighting the whole Huron nation singl-handed."

"That is understandable, but I will be by your side. Together, we will invoke the Great Spirit to condole the people and to clear their minds. It is our only hope for establishing the League of Peace. Otherwise, the people will talk and talk and compete with each other and fight for their own interests and nothing will ever come of it. They must first be clear-minded."

Hiawatha stared into the fire. The flames were dancing now with a new energy and his mind was spinning, matching the fire's intensity.

"You will be our spokesman now. You can be very persuasive. You even convinced me to attempt a reconciliation with my brother. It was not your fault that it failed."

"But I don't have your great wisdom."

"I will be by your side, Hiawatha, always. I will teach you. And then you will teach the others."

Hiawatha looked up just as a shooting star made a long silver arc across the sky. He turned and looked at Dekanawida. How could he refuse this holy man who could light up the sky to make a point?

Chapter Seven

The following morning Hiawatha rehearsed the message with Okaiya and Ortekla, as the two runners quickly ate. "First, you must tell Tekerihoken that Dekanawida and Hiawatha respectfully request that he host a meeting at his village for the other Mohawk villages to discuss how to best defend their villages. If he agrees, then Okaiya, you will run north to the Mohawk villages and towns of Gaihogan and Oswegon. And Ortekla, you will run south to the towns and villages of Hokenan and Shenandonah. Invite them to the village of Tekerihoken, and deliver the invitations in this way."

He held up a shell wampum string and put his fingers on the first of three purple shells. "Tell them that because of the bloody attack by the Hurons upon your cousins, the Mohawk people of Tekerihoken, Dekanawida and Hiawatha invite you to participate in a new ceremony, a Ceremony of Condolence at the village of Tekerihoken under the light of the next full moon. Do you understand?"

The runners nodded. Hiawatha pointed to the second purple shell. "Tell them that the ceremony will be followed by a council where we will speak of forming a League of Peace for the defense of our villages."

Hiawatha then pointed to the third purple shell on the string.

"And then give them the wampum string and tell them that this is the word that will induce them to come."

Hiawatha gave the string to Okaiya. He placed his fingers on the first shell. Ortekla watched nervously. "Now repeat what I have told you so that I know you understand."

"Because of the bloody attack by the foul and wicked Hurons on your poor cousin, Tekerihoken . . ."

"No embellishments please," scolded Hiawatha. "Repeat the message just as I have spoken it."

Both boys repeated the message word for word until Hiawatha was satisfied that they knew it by heart and would not forget it. The wampum strings would be their memory aids and serve as a pledge for the truthfulness of the message.

Dekanawida then presented them each with an eagle feather. "I thank you from the bottom of my heart for carrying this message. Some day when you are much older, you will look back on this day and know what a great contribution you have made. May the Great Spirit guide your footsteps and light the way of your journey."

When the two messengers had gone, Dekanawida turned to Hiawatha and said, "There is someone that I want you to meet. A very special woman who lives in the woods. We will go to her hut before we return to the place of Tekerihoken."

"As you wish. Shall we leave now?"

"Yes. Help me up. Yesterday's exertions have taken their toll on my old bones." Hiawatha held out his hand for the old shaman to take hold of. As he pulled him to his feet, Hiawatha noticed that he looked older now, and frailer. He seemed so full of energy and exuberance when he arrived with the eagle on his wrist. And this was the curious thing about Dekanawida, thought Hiawatha. He could change forms and attitudes so quickly and so dramatically that sometimes it seemed to him that the old man was in reality more than one man.

The Peacemaker stretched out his arms to the sky, and as he did so, he felt his energy return. "There. That's better. Let's be off! We'll leave the canoe here." And suddenly he seemed twenty years younger, full now of a rekindled sense of purpose. He started off at a brisk pace, and Hiawatha, many years his junior, was hard pressed to keep up with him.

Night was falling now. They were deep into the woods, and the trees were filling up with birds that had come to roost for the night. An owl screeched overhead and bats flitted low in the twilight shadows among the pine and fir trees. In the distance, the flickering of a fire could be seen. "We have reached our destination, my friend," said Dekanawida. "The fire you see ahead comes from the dwelling place of Jikonsahseh, the holy lady of the forest."

"I have met her."

"You know her?"

"I can't say that I know her. But Orios and I stopped here on our way to find you, and she fed us. And told us stories about you."

"All the better. We will stay this evening with her and you will get to know more about her. She will be important for our mission. She loves to tell stories, and she is the best person to relate the events of her past."

Hiawatha could not help but think that the old prophet was up to something. Everything he did had a purpose, and this visit to the hermit woman deep in the woods must have some purpose too.

"I cannot call out loud enough, Hiawatha. Call out to her so that we do not frighten her by our coming."

"Hello! Jikonsahseh!" shouted Hiawatha.

"Who is out there?"

"We are friends who come to speak with you."

"Then come forward into the light and let me see you!"

Hiawatha and Dekanawida stepped into the clearing where a good-sized campfire was burning. A large roast of venison was cooking over a spit, and the juices that dripped into the fire sizzled and crackled. The smell of the roasting meat made Hiawatha's mouth water and his stomach rumble with hunger.

"Who are you? I seem to remember your voice. Come closer."

Hiawatha moved closer into the clearing and the firelight. "My name is Hiawatha. I come from the People at the Foot of the Hill."

"Yes, now I remember you. The Onondaga chief who is a chief no more."

"Yes."

"Good. Onondaga are good. All human beings are good—when they choose to be. When they forget to be wicked. And who is this with you?"

"Don't you remember me, Jikonsahseh? Has it been so long that you have forgotten your old friend?"

"Oh, no! Dekanawida! Can it really be you?"

"It is. How long has it been?"

"So long that I cannot remember, and yet it seems just like yesterday."

"And how have you been?"

"Well. I have been well. I eat very well out here. Can't you tell?" She twirled around showing all sides of her well-fed frame.

"You look wonderful," said Dekanawida.

"But you must be hungry! As usual, your timing is flawless. This roast venison is just about done to perfection. It was a gift from hunters who came by my camp. They leave me tasty bits of game, and I tell them stories of the old times, stories of when the Spirit Beings walked freely among us, stories of my own, stories from my past. You will sit while I bring you roast meat. Then you will eat, and I will tell you a story or two."

Hiawatha and Dekanawida sat cross-legged on the ground around the fire. Jikonsahseh sliced off slabs of deer meat from the joint on the spit, placed them on wooden trenchers, and gave one to each of them. She gave thanks to the deer they were eating and then sat down opposite them.

"Where is your young friend, the musician who was with you when you were last here?"

"Orios?"

"Yes. What has happened to him?"

"He was captured by Adergagtha."

"Your brother?"

"Yes, I'm afraid so."

"The poor boy. I hope he did not suffer too much."

"He was adopted into their nation. Apparently he is Huron now." Hiawatha shook his head sadly. "It is a great loss to me."

"He has a special quality, that boy. Hurons do not often adopt. Ah, well. What story shall I tell you while I watch you eat?"

"Will you not eat with us?"

"I have already eaten. But, since you ask, yes, I might have just a little bite." She sliced off a generous piece of meat and then sat down again.

"Perhaps Hiawatha would like to hear the story of how it is that you came to live out here in the forest all by yourself?"

"Yes, I would love to hear it," said Hiawatha, wiping his lips with the back of his hand. The meat was delicious. He could feel the power of the deer surging through his blood, giving him strength and courage.

"Very well, then. But I must warn you. It is not a pretty story. I once lived in a village, in a longhouse, the longhouse of my mother, Elenwah, of the Bear Clan. She was a wonderful woman, so generous with everything, her goods, her love, her wisdom. I had three sisters, and each was as pretty as a flower that grows on the side of a hill or in the middle of a lush, green meadow. Our father was a great warrior, and he loved battle almost as much as he loved my mother and his daughters. In fact, his name in our tongue means Loves-to-Fight. One day, while he was away leading a war party against the Cayuga to take some prisoners for vengeance, to assuage the grief of his mother's clan, whose people had been killed recently by some of these swamp-landers, my sisters and I were out with the women in the fields around our village tending to the well-being of the three sisters. We were laughing and joking as we often did when we hoed around the corn and the beans and the squash, telling stories on other girls in the village, just playing as young girls will do. A war party of Oneida came upon us. We screamed and ran. But my sisters ran too late.

"I can still hear them screaming as they were being dragged away. I turned and saw my older sister struggling with a tall man. The bottom of his face from the nose down was painted black. My sister's nails raked across his face, drawing blood. The red blood stood out starkly against the blackness of his face. I will never forget the look of helplessness in her eyes as he plunged his knife in her neck and dragged it across her throat."

A light snow began to fall as Jikonsahseh paused in her story, the first snow of the season. A few flakes landed on her gray-black hair and on her cheeks. They melted and mingled with the tears that trickled down her face. She sighed heavily.

"He killed her out of sheer meanness. Out of hatred for us. Nothing more. My sister was the sweetest soul I ever met. She would not harm any living creature. If she stepped on a flower by accident she would cry because she made something beautiful, something living, die. And this man robbed the world of her presence. He made the earth poorer because she was gone."

"What about your other sisters?" asked Hiawatha.

"I never saw them again. I suppose they became Oneida. Or I hoped that they did. I don't know. Perhaps they died. Perhaps they were killed or tortured. Made to pay for someone else's crimes, someone else's acts of murder or revenge. I only hope that they did not suffer too much."

Dekanawida saw the tears in Hiawatha's eyes, and he could see that Hiawatha was deeply affected by Jikonsahseh's story. He knew that he would be. Her story and his were much the same. But he knew that Hiawatha, like most men, believed his story, his anguish, his grief to be unique, unlike any one else's.

"My father, of course, was inconsolable. When he returned

from his own war party with the war captives that he had taken from the Cayuga in revenge for their earlier raid on our village, he tortured them all himself and refused to let any of them live.

"The next day he threw his war hatchet into the post that stood in the middle of the village. This was a signal that another war party was being called for. Loves-to-Fight was going on the path of revenge again. Only this time for himself, not for the grieving widows and mothers of the village. I think he also hoped that he might get my sisters back. But he didn't. I never saw him again. He was killed by Oneida arrows, and his body was cut to pieces and fed to the dogs of their war captain.

"Not long after that, I left the village. I came out here to live by myself. The ways of my people, the ways of my father, sickened me. Always fighting. Always bloodshed. Always revenge for murder and torture. I had enough of it. I wanted to be among creatures who did not murder each other. I wanted to be among creatures who did not torture each other. And here I found that place deep in the forest. Here I live close to my mother, and the forest provides all that I need. Of course, from time to time, some friends stop by to help me."

She looked at Dekanawida with a love in her eyes that comes from a mutual understanding of some great secret that they shared together over the course of many years. "Not long after I escaped my village and came out here, I met Dekanawida. He helped me to forget, no, not to forget, but to deal with my pain, and to forgive the acts of cruelty that were done to my sisters and my father, and those acts of cruelty that my father himself performed upon others. He showed me that we always harvest the seeds that we sow. And that is why my father met such a horrible fate. Because eventually, all the acts that we perform in our lives come back to us later and sit upon our heads."

"Your story is a familiar one to me," said Hiawatha. "I lost a wife and four daughters, and all I could think of was hatred and blood until I met the Peacemaker."

"Did he help your heart to heal?"

"He showed me the path of forgiveness, and he performed a ceremony of condolence that made me whole again."

"In fact, Jikonsahseh, that is why we came here," said Dekanawida. "To ask for your help. Did you hear about the attack on Tekerihoken's village?"

"Yes. Those poor people. How will they get through the winter? Hurons sometimes act crazy in the head. To burn the sacred tobacco like that? The Great Spirit will surely punish them."

"They lost many lives. We are going to perform a Ceremony of Condolence for them. And we want you to come and take part in it. You are widely known and respected by all who pass this way, and your presence will give the ceremony a special power."

"What is this Ceremony of Condolence? What does it do?"

"It wipes away the tears of grief, Jikonsahseh," explained Hiawatha. "It allows those who grieve and who suffer, to become whole again in their hearts without resorting to mourning-wars, without killing and torturing others to assuage their own feelings of sorrow."

"Then I will do it. Not many things could make me leave my retreat in the forest. But this is a cause that is close to my heart. When do we leave? How shall I dress? I no longer have any ceremonial finery."

"That's not important," said Dekanawida. "Wear what you are wearing now. What is important is that you be there with us. You have great spiritual power. If you had stayed within the society of humans, you would have been a powerful Clan Mother. But since you have lived all of these years in the wilderness with the creatures of the forest as your constant companions, you have an even greater power, and one that is needed especially now. You have within you the great reservoir of the power of Sky Woman, the power of the Great Earth Mother. Your presence and your compassion, your wisdom and your prayers, will help others to see how wrong they are to take other lives for the lives they have lost.

Your presence and your prayers will help others to dry the tears of their sorrow."

Snow was falling faster now, casting a white blanket over the ground, clinging to the naked branches in the trees, dusting the long leaves of the great white pines. The wind whispered through their snowy branches and they seemed to nod to one another, and to speak to one another in hushed tones of some great event to come, an event that they would play a great part in.

Dekanawida's voice was tired from speaking so much. From now on, he must let Hiawatha speak more for him. Tomorrow, he thought. Tomorrow. The great work continues. For now, we should get some rest.

The longhouse of Makahwah in the Onondaga village now led by Atatarho bore no resemblance to what it was in the days, not long ago, when Hiawatha was chieftain. Makahwah had to jealously guard all of her possessions and food stores because thievery was now commonplace in the village. Just yesterday someone had stolen her precious and finely wrought combs made from carved turtle shell. These were not just combs for the hair. These combs had a value far beyond their material worth because of their spiritual associations; they were symbolic totems of the Turtle Clan. Things had gone badly for her ever since that day when the Great Turtle totem, the great shell that hung above the middle of the longhouse, mysteriously disappeared. The culprit—if indeed there were a human culprit (for some believed that evil spirits had come and whisked it away to the land of the Spirit Beings)—had never been found. Whoever stole the Great Turtle Shell might also have been the one who stole the combs.

Times were bad. The crops had been mismanaged and blighted. Instead of tending the Three Sisters as they should have been doing, many of the women of the village spent an inordinate amount of time engaged in tortures for mourning-rituals, in grieving, or else urging revenge. As a result, there would not be enough corn and beans to last them through the long winter. And the men of the village did not go out hunting. They gambled and argued constantly. They lay around and quarreled. Three deaths had been attributed to gambling and fighting within the village in the past month. Never before in recent memory could she remember a set of circumstances to match these.

She knew, and many others knew too, but were afraid to say it out loud, that the trouble stemmed from their leader, the sorcerer, Atatarho. His darkness had spread like a disease throughout the minds of the people of the village. Although his official residence was in the longhouse of his sister, Tabaldak, he spent most of his time with his closest advisors huddled around his hut of bones in the swamp, plotting war and planning raids on the neighboring people. Scalps hung from poles all over the central square, and widows and mothers of dead warriors constantly clamored for revenge, for a mourning-war to bring back more captives so that they could ease their grief and pain through torturing those who had killed their husbands and sons.

She walked outside of the longhouse and involuntarily shivered at the first rush of cold air. Soon there would be snow all over the ground, and the nuts and acorns would no longer be found. The hunting would be harder. Hunting deer or elk on snowshoes was an arduous task for skilled and well-trained hunters. It was an impossible one for out-of-shape, lazy lay-abouts. She had no one to hunt for her. Kewahtawa was too old. His eyes were no longer capable of sighting a bow accurately. And Teom and the other men in her longhouse had become cronies of Atatarho. They spent their days by the sorcerer's side drinking strange potions and planning sneak attacks on their neighbors.

She needed to go outside of the stockade to gather firewood for the day's fire. Two scrawny dogs barked at her as she passed the four torture poles on the platform in the center of the village. Human skulls on top of each pole seemed to grin at her and mock her as she passed by on her way toward the village gate. She pulled her bearskin cape closer to her as a chill wind roared down from the hills to their valley.

Outside the stockade walls of the village she passed by the forlorn, broken stalks of the dead corn and sunflowers. They hung like the skeletons of withered old men, gray and brown, brittle, dry, and ugly. Even the black crows avoided their company and went cawing away in front of her. She thought about her two granddaughters who died here, the victims of Seneca revenge. Back then, she thought that Hiawatha had been mad, driven insane by grief when he made those charges against Atatarho, charging him with complicity in the deaths of the young girls. Now, the way things had fallen out for her people and her village, she was not so sure. Lately she had begun to regret her haste in condemning the words and actions of her son-in-law. They were better off when Hiawatha was chief; but in the shape that he was in back then, he could no longer lead. Her mind was spinning again in a cycle of regret, worry, and fear. She regretted the past, she worried about her decision to disempower Hiawatha, and she feared for the future. She did not know how she and the others would make it through this winter.

"I am being punished," she thought as she picked up a three-foot length of dead and dry maple wood. There was not much kindling to be found. Each day she was forced to walk farther and farther away from the village to find enough faggots of wood to burn for a day and a night. She must be strong. If she had to haul back wood eight hours a day in order to keep her longhouse warm, then that is what she would do.

Even though it was cold, the day was clear; there was not a cloud in the sky. So it would not rain or snow. This gave her plenty of time to do her work. And her work right now was the gathering of wood. But why should I have to carry all the wood? Men from the longhouse, even at this moment, sit around a fire casting bones or deer buttons, betting on the luck of the toss. Makahwah lifted a stout stick and shook it. Tomorrow I will take this stick and thrash them about the head until they get up off the ground and help me gather the firewood. The more she thought about it, the angrier she became. Her face was red, and her breath came in short, shallow bursts. I will beat them so hard they will bleed. I will bruise their ugly faces. Those lazy no-goods will feel the wrath of Makahwah!

Makahwah felt a sudden pain in her head. She staggered and took three steps backwards. She could not breathe. Then all was blackness.

Atatarho stirred the large clay cauldron that hung beside his fire. He smiled as he thought of his unhappy childhood and how he had vowed to get even. The many times that he had run into the forest crying from cruel taunts about his misshapen appearance. Until he finally found a friend, his only friend, a large green snake that curled around him as he lay on the forest floor. He brought his friend back to the village, and after that everything was different. The other children ran from him screaming. No one dared to ridicule him again. He had learned how to command their respect through fear. And now, everyone in the village bowed to him.

He watched Osinoh, Gahdonen, and his other war captains enter his hut, reading their eyes for any signs of plots or conspiracies. He kept his friends ever present, to remind his subjects of who he was. He had live snakes tied to and entwined within the long stiff locks of his gray and matted hair. These snakes moved or rested according to the mood of their master. When Atatarho was placid or pleased, they remained still or moved sinuously and slowly about on the top and back of his head. When he was angry, they flared up and bared their fangs and attempted to strike at those nearest them. But they never bit Atatarho. They were an extension of his being, operating as agents of his mood, his temper, his personality.

Osinoh and Gahdonen each wore snake skins woven into their hair in emulation of their sorcerer-chief. Atatarho tasted the broth, frowned, then sat down by the fire and stared to his left and to his right.

"Well?" he asked.

"A party of Cayuga hunters was seen by my scouts two days ago up in the hills by the Lake of the Dead Maidens," said Gahdonen.

The snakes in Atatarho's head stirred and moved about nervously. "Send out a raiding party. Wait until they make some good fresh kills, then ambush them and bring back the meat and the prisoners."

"Yes, my chief."

Atatarho looked expectantly at Osinoh. The silence was broken by the sound of feet on leaves and dead branches. Someone was running toward the encampment. Osinoh and Gahdonen rose to their feet as Tadohnah, one of Atatarho's spies, burst through, panting heavily.

"You are two days late! What news do you bring?" Atatarho, still sitting, glared at him. The snakes on the sorcerer's head reared up and bared their fangs. Tadohnah shrunk backwards.

"Hiawatha is with the prophet Dekanawida."

"I know that already!" The snakes arched their necks and hissed in anger. "Tell me something new."

"They say Hiawatha has become a holy man too."

"Impossible! He is too weak. He hasn't the power to cast spells or to perform magic. These are old wives' rumors."

"I only repeat what I have heard."

"What else have you heard?"

"That Dekanawida teaches him magic." The snakes hissed and arched. "Not powerful magic like yours, great one, weak magic, Huron magic, magic for children and women."

"What does he intend to do with this magic?"

"They say he will cast a spell on the people. Then he will . . . I am sorry, great one, I am only reporting the words that I have heard . . . he will come back to free the Onondaga from your rule."

The snakes roiled and hissed on top of Atatarho's head. His eyes narrowed to twin slits. "Where is he now?"

"In the Mohawk village of Tekerihoken. The Mohawk have adopted him. They hold him in high esteem."

"We must send more spies into the eastern lands," said Gahdonen.

"No!" said Atatarho. "The time for spying is over. I want him dead. But the Mohawk must not know who killed him. We cannot afford a war with the Mohawk just yet. Osinoh?"

"Yes, Uncle?"

"I want you to undertake this mission. I don't care how you do it. But I want it done. And I want it done soon. Bring me back Hiawatha's head."

Chapter Eight

The land of the Haudenosaunee, the People of the Longhouse, lay under a thin white shroud of snow. The sky was a dim gray, and the lacy tops of bare branches could be seen in outline like an ethereal scrimshaw carved upon the sky's pale bone. The people of the longhouse usually stayed put in the winter. They spent their time indoors recounting the stories and legends that had been told to them in their childhood. They told these stories to their children so that their children would, some winter evening, tell their children and their children's children.

Men would sometimes put on their snowshoes and their bearskin robes and go off on a winter hunt, stalking the elk and the deer in their shaggy, thick winter fur; sometimes they cut holes in the ice to fish the frozen lakes and rivers. It was still early in the winter season. So the invitation to a gathering at the village of Tekerihoken to help their Mohawk cousins was accepted without much debate. Since the call had come from no less a figure than the legendary Dekanawida, the holy man of the Mohawk people who promised to talk of an alliance for defense, all the great chieftains, headmen, and clan mothers of the villages in the land of the Mohawk deemed it a good thing to make the journey. It would be a grand opportunity to reestablish clan ties and to strengthen waning friendships and alliances. In these troubled times, with the Huron constantly pressing in upon them, and the Cayugas and Oneida sending out frequent raiding parties, Mohawk people could use all the allies they could get. When one had so many enemies, one could not get enough friends.

Up from the south came the people of Hokenan and Shenandonah. Down from the north came the people of Gaihogen and Oswegon. The clan mothers and the women of the three great clans from each village brought with them their finest doeskin dresses and the men brought all their ceremonial regalia. Many brought arrows and flint arrow points and stone knives to give as gifts or to trade for other items, for the Haudenosaunee were a people who loved to give and also loved to barter.

Along the road to the Mohawk village of Tekerihoken, Osinoh and four Onondaga warriors carried sacks of wares for trading as cover for their real mission. When they reached the top of a hill overlooking the last leg of their journey, they were surprised by the many people filtering onto the main road. They hid in the underbrush and watched a long procession go by. In front, men carried large baskets of corn and tobacco and racks that held freshly killed rabbits and freshly caught trout. The women walked behind them carrying children, food, and clothing. At the rear of the procession, the men of the Medicine Society walked together, carrying their sacred False Faces, some carved from wood, some made from corn husks. Behind the Medicine Society, a group of men carrying water drums and turtle-shell rattles created a pleasing cacophony as they walked. From his hidden vantage point, Osinoh marveled at how similar they seemed to the Onondagas, except for the men, who plucked out the hairs on the sides of their heads.

Intimidated by their numbers, Osinoh waited for two stragglers in the distance, and then gathered his wares to go talk with them. To lessen the threat, the warriors stayed undercover.

"Greetings my friends," said Osinoh. "I have traveled far from home to trade with the people of the great salt sea. Do you have anything you would like to trade? I have some beautiful shell earrings. Let me show you." He spread a small hide on the ground and displayed his wares. One man picked up an intricately carved and polished red stone. He turned it over in his hand, admiring the fine craftsmanship.

"Where are you going?" asked Osinoh. "I've noticed many travelers on the road today."

"We're going to the village of Tekerihoken. The holy man Dekanawida has called us together to form a great alliance."

"An alliance? What kind of alliance?"

"We have no idea, but we will listen to what he has to say. We Mohawks are very independent, so I doubt that much will come of it."

"What would you take for the fine robe you are carrying? I like the Mohawk designs."

"I doubt that you can afford this. It took many turnings of the sun to make."

Osinoh reached into his other bag and pulled out a beautifully carved blowgun. "This, my friend, is from the Seneca. It is easy to carry and deadly to use. From a great distance, hidden in the underbrush, you can bring down your enemies. Oh, and, of course, you will also need this." As he talked, he pulled out five darts, one at a time. "A hand of darts to stop your enemy in his tracks. Is that not worth your Mohawk robe?"

"More." He opened his palms and held up his ten fingers. Then he clenched and opened his hands twice.

"Twenty? Impossible! I have only ten. Ten is a fair trade."

"You drive a hard bargain. I will take it if you also include this stone knife in the quilled sheath."

"Now who drives a hard bargain? Very well, then, it is getting late. I must be on my way, but first I must hunt for my supper." Osinoh collected his wares and the Mohawk robe, bid the travelers good-bye, and walked off.

By the time the people from the south and the people from the north converged upon the village of Tekerihoken, temporary shelters, lean-tos, and huts had been constructed under the guidance of Hiawatha and Tekerihoken to house and shelter all the people. Many would stay in the longhouses of their clan members, but others would have to sleep outside of the longhouses, for there simply was not enough room to accommodate such a large influx of people.

It was unseasonably warm that day, a sign that everyone took as a good omen, and all the travelers had settled in. As the pink rays of the setting sun spread across the sky, the people gathered around a fire in the center of Tekerihoken's village. Men from each of the villages took their turns adding logs to the great fire in the center of the village, making the flames grow higher and higher.

The drummers and flute players, seated off to one side of the growing fire, began to play. Slowly at first, then faster, the steady tempo of the drum beats cast a hypnotic spell on the crowd. As if on cue, the chiefs and clan mothers of the towns and villages, in their finest clothing and regalia, marched in slow procession and seated themselves in a semicircle at the north end of the fire.

Outside the village gate, Osinoh, his head shaved on the sides, and wearing the Mohawk robe over his shoulders, slipped in unobserved as everyone gravitated towards the great fire.

The drums suddenly stopped. A hush fell over the crowd as Tekerihoken, Hiawatha, Dekanawida, and Jikonsahseh walked slowly to the south end of the fire and faced the semicircle of leaders. Tekerihoken looked regal in his deer-antler and eagle-feather headdress. Hiawatha wore a single eagle feather, hanging downward in his long hair, while Dekanawida wore no adornments at all, but he seemed to emanate a soft glow in his white robe with his long silver hair flowing around his shoulders. He ran his palm over the head of his eagle-claw staff, as though he drew power from it. Jikonsahseh looked radiant in her white doeskin dress embroidered with elaborate circles of quillwork. It had been many moons since she had been in such a gathering, since she had fled the company of people to seek solitude in the forest. With Dekanawida by her side, she felt as if she were being reborn back into the community of human beings.

Hiawatha's heart beat faster as he looked nervously at the sea of faces around him. How did he get himself in this position? He had never spoken to so many people, and now Dekanawida was expecting him to create a miracle and change their hearts and minds. Even though he was next to the fire, his hands felt cold and clammy. He wanted to run from the arena, but then the drummers began to drum again and chant rhythmically, and the people began to sway back and forth, up and down, doing an in-place stomp dance.

Hiawatha felt his heart slow down to the beat of the drums. As he looked around the crowd again, he knew that all their hearts were now beating to the same rhythm. He felt his fear slowly dissipate into the ground beneath his feet.

Dekanawida raised his staff high above his head and gestured to the drummers. The drumming stopped except for one water drum that kept the people moving together as one. Dekanawida spoke softly to Hiawatha, who stood on his right side. Hiawatha raised his arms and began to speak to the assembled crowd.

"Brothers and sisters. Sons and daughters. Men, women, and children of the Mohawk Nation." His rich, melodious voice carried far, so that all the assembled people, even those on the outskirts, could hear his words. "You are gathered here today as one people united by blood and kinship and clan ties. The great Turtle Clan is here."

He gestured toward the Turtle Clan, and the three Clan Mothers and three chiefs held up their left arms. The crowd cheered.

"The great Bear Clan is here." All eyes turned to the chiefs and Can Mothers of the Bear Clan with their outstretched arms. The crowd cheered again. Each time the momentum seemed to build as the crowd lost its inhibitions.

"And the great Wolf Clan is here." The leaders of the Wolf Clan nodded to the now roaring cheers of greeting.

Hiawatha motioned for silence. "All villages and all towns are united by clan ties. But during this festival, during this Great Gathering, you will be tied together even tighter, wrapped even more closely like a sheaf of arrows tied tightly with a hempen cord. You will become one mighty Mohawk nation more closely united than ever before, and this will serve as protection for us against our enemies. It will be the beginning of a great and lasting peace, a peace that will descend upon all human beings in the land of the Haudenosaunee. We propose to join the longhouses of the Mohawk together with the longhouses of the Cayuga and the longhouses of the Oneida and the longhouses of the Onondaga and the longhouses of the Seneca to make one mighty Longhouse, the most powerful union of nations ever known or ever seen on the back of Turtle Island."

The people looked at one another in puzzlement and wonder. What did he mean? What kind of proposition was he making? How could these people who had fought each other for years and years—ever since anyone living could remember and even farther back in time—how could they join together except that one might conquer the other? It was a concept difficult to grasp.

Hiawatha saw the looks of confusion on their faces. "I know this sounds strange to you," he said. "But you must believe in me and you must place your faith and trust in the hands of the holy one, Dekanawida. He has never spoken falsely, and these are his words. The people of the longhouse will be united in one vast and mighty longhouse. They will be separate nations, but nations united in a League of Power and Peace, a Great Confederacy that will bind us together and make us so strong that it will be impossible to break us." There were murmurs in the crowd.

Then Hiawatha held up one arrow high over his head. "Do you see this arrow?" The noise subsided. He repeated his question in a much louder tone that got the full attention of the crowd and frightened them a bit. "Do you see this arrow?" He violently broke the arrow over his knee and threw it into the fire. Green smoke burst from the flames.

"Do you see these five arrows?" He held a bundle of five arrows tightly tied together above his head. "Do you see these five arrows that are tied together with a common bond?"

"Yes," replied the crowd.

"Can you break them?" He paused for ten seconds, increasing the dramatic tension already in the air. "Who among you can break them?"

A large muscular warrior from the Wolf Clan stepped forward and gestured for the arrows. He knelt down and smashed the arrows against his knee, but none of them broke. The crowd laughed. A warrior from the Turtle Clan stepped forward and tried his hand at it, but to no avail.

Hiawatha waited patiently as one warrior after another tried to break the sheaf of arrows. He then retrieved the arrows and held them high over his head. "Just as one arrow may be broken over the knee, but five together may not, so will the new League of Five Nations be as unbreakable as five arrows bundled together." Recognizing the wisdom in Hiawatha's visual metaphor, the people murmured among themselves.

"Dekanawida has asked that I speak for him. And so I do. But I also speak for myself. I have known great suffering and great sorrow. As have all of you who have lost loved ones in battle and war. I have known great hatred and a deep desire for blood and revenge. As have all of you who have lost friends and loved ones and desired revenge for your sufferings.

"I have known the taste of murder in my mouth. As have many of you who have tortured and killed war captives in vain attempts to ease the pain of your grief. And I ask you this: What have you gained?"

Hiawatha paused and scanned the sea of faces looking up at him. No one answered. No one knew what to say.

"Let me answer the question for you. You have gained nothing but one thing. You have gained more enemies. You have created nothing but one thing. You have created more hatred.

"You have set in motion another cycle of revenge killings which must be followed by more revenge killings which in turn must be answered back with more bloodshed. A never-ending cycle of vengeance. Is this the legacy that you would pass on to your children and your children's children?"

His voice became louder as the water drums matched his intensity.

"You have become sustainers of murder, the fathers and sons, the mothers and daughters, of blood!"

The drums made one last dramatic crash, and then were silent. Hiawatha paused dramatically and looked into the eyes of the people. There was a deathly silence as though everyone was afraid to move. He nodded to the drummers, and they began again their slow, hypnotic beat.

"But I say to you that there is another way. There is a way out of this swamp of blood and tears. It is the way of the Condolence Ceremony. The path of catharsis and forgiveness. No more will murder and battle-death be answered with more murder and battle-death. In this Great Gathering of the Mohawk nation, something new will happen. A great banishment of tears will occur, and Dekanawida will lead you out of the swamp of misery into the meadows of peace.

"Those who follow in the paths of light through the ceremonies of condolence will be blessed for generations to come by the wholesomeness of their offspring. Those who do not will be cursed by the disease of bloody-mindedness and the curse of hatred and fear.

"I tell you that you no longer need to fear. Great has been your suffering in the past. Great has been your grief in the past for the deaths of your loved ones at the hands of the Huron, at the hands of the Cayuga, at the hands of the Oneida.

"But I tell you that after this Great Gathering, the message will spread, the Great Word of Peace and Power will spread to the other nations of human beings, and they too will join you in the Great Condolence, and never again will like-speaking ones, never again will like-minded ones, never again will clear-minded ones spill the blood of their brothers and sisters."

The people stood still, mesmerized by his voice but uncomfortable with his words, which sounded to their ears like a dream that could never happen.

"All of you who wish to be condoled for the great loss of your loved ones, all of you who wish to leave the old ways of bloody-mindedness behind and step into the light of a new world of clear-mindedness, step forward now and receive the blessing of condolence from Dekanawida and from the lady of the forest, Jikonsahseh."

Everyone remained frozen. Hiawatha's words had moved the hearts and minds of many of those gathered, but they were reluctant to take the first step. Jikonsahseh looked straight into the eyes of her old friend, Chief Gaihogen, and beckoned him to come forward. When the people saw Gaihogen, tall and proud, wearing his bonnet of antlers and eagle feathers, step forward and open his arms out and upward towards Dekanawida and Jikonsahseh, when they saw this, others began to slowly rise and step forward, forming two long lines.

Hiawatha, a bit intimidated by the task ahead, walked over to a birch pole suspended horizontally between two five-foot-high stakes. He ran his hand across a two-foot length of soft, pure-white doeskin draped over the pole. Then he touched each of the three wampum strings hanging beside it. With his hand still on the wampum strings, he said a silent prayer to the Great Spirit to help him cleanse the minds of the people and heal their hearts. And then he turned to the mourners.

"All of you know the great pain of grief. When you lose someone you love, the pain is a sharp knife that cuts deep into the heart. Close your eyes now and remember all the loved ones you have lost because of wars and vengeance . . . your husbands and wives . . . your sons and daughters . . . your mothers and fathers . . . your brothers and sisters." The water drums beat at a slow and somber pace.

"Remember them all, and then think of all the generations of children that will not be born because of their passing." A flute joined the drums, playing a sorrowful melody.

"Now let your tears flow to cleanse your great sorrow."

Chief Gaihogen looked over at Jikonsahseh, her head held high, tears streaming down her face. She nodded at him, and he felt a great gate open for the tears he had suppressed his entire life, tears for his two sons, his father, and his mother. Astonished to see this great warrior cry, other men in the crowd soon felt sympathetic tears rolling down their own cheeks.

"Come," urged Hiawatha. "Those of you who feel his great sorrow, come and mourn his great loss. Join hands now and mingle your tears."

Osinoh, standing on the outskirts of the crowd, out of Hiawatha's range of vision, was surprised when a woman to his left grabbed his hand. A few minutes later, a man standing on his right did the same. Embarrassed, his whole body tensed at the human contact with his enemy. He must be careful not to fall under the spell that Hiawatha was casting. He thought proudly of how he had not cried since his father's death many long years ago, but then he remembered he did cry at Sovana's funeral. At the thought of her, his heart began to soften. He became conscious of the rising tide of grief flowing from one hand to the next, until he, too, was finally overwhelmed. Here he was, a spy in the midst of an enemy village, sent at his uncle's behest. With orders to kill Sovana's father. The world made no sense to him.

Jikonsahseh walked over to Chief Gaihogen and embraced him against her warm body. Hiawatha chanted in his full, melodious voice: "Now do we wipe away your tears."

Dekanawida picked up the pure-white doeskin cloth and the

first wampum string from the birch pole. He gently touched Chief Gaihogen's eyes with the white doeskin cloth, on top of which lay a wampum string. The soft cloth and the calming effect of his gentle hands caused his tears to stop.

Hiawatha gestured to those in the crowd to repeat after him.

"Now do we wipe away your tears," repeated the voices in unison.

Hiawatha continued:

> "Now do we wipe away your tears
> With a white doe skin.
> Now can you look around
> With peace of mind
> And see the world around you.
> Now will you see
> The sons and daughters of your sisters.
> Now will you see them all
> As you enjoy again the clear light of day."

They repeated the chanting ritual with each of the mourners, and then Dekanawida returned to Gaihogen and placed the wampum string in his hand. When he placed his hand on the chieftain's head and chanted the prayers in the language of the earth, the language of the trees, and the language of the bird nations, Gaihogen felt his head swirling in clouds of darkness that suddenly rose and left his body.

Gaihogen then held up the wampum string high in the air so that all the gathered peoples could see it. Hiawatha was surprised by the loudness of the voices that repeated the chant after him:

> "For our witness we now give you
> The Word of this wampum string.
> It now holds the *orenda*
> Of all who sing."

Hiawatha felt the reverberating chorus of voices and the throbbing water drums penetrate deeper and deeper into his inner being. Dekanawida took up the second wampum string, put it on top of the white doeskin, and walked along the line, passing it over the ears of each of the mourners as Hiawatha chanted:

> "When a person grieves,
> The ears become blocked
> And the hearing is lost
> So that he hears nothing
> Of what is taking place
> Here on Mother Earth."

Once again, the people repeated Hiawatha's chant:

> "Now do we unblock your ears.
> Now will you hear the sounds
> As people move all around you.
> Now will you hear all things
> Taking place on our Mother Earth."

Those in the crowd who had not originally joined the mourners now stepped up to receive the condolence from Dekanawida. The chorus grew louder as the flames of the fire leapt higher. The drum beat matched the growing intensity of the people's voices as they repeated after Hiawatha the ritual words of healing. Each time they chanted the words, they felt their common bond of humanity grow stronger and they felt their own beings become one with the shells on the sacred wampum strings.

> "For our witness we now give you
> The word of this wampum string.
> It now holds the *orenda*
> Of all who sing."

Finally, Tekerihoken stepped up to the place in front of Dekanawida. The Peacemaker embraced his old friend as Hiawatha chanted:

> "When a person is in great sorrow,
> His throat is choked with grief
> So that he cannot speak his mind."

Dekanawida placed the third wampum string on top of the white doeskin cloth and wiped it over Tekerihoken's throat and then over his mouth. Tekerihoken could feel the muscles in his throat relax while the chorus sang:

> "Now do we unblock your throat.
> Now will you breathe with ease.
> Now will you speak with pleasure
> To the people all around you."

As everyone sang in the final chorus, they joined hands again. Osinoh took his eyes off of Hiawatha for a moment and listened to the surge of voices all singing in unison the sacred prayer-chant of the new ceremony:

> "For our witness we now give you
> The word of this wampum string.
> It now holds the *orenda*
> Of all who sing!"

The rhythmic staccato of the drums reached a final dramatic crescendo, and Osinoh, moved by the chant-song, forgot where he was, who he was, what his mission was. When the drums and the chanting suddenly stopped, he shook his head. He reminded himself that he was Onondaga. That he owed an allegiance to his leader, his uncle, no matter what happened in the past. What is the matter with you, he thought. You have a duty to your people.

Are you a fool to succumb to this Mohawk magic? He wandered through the crowd, careful to keep Hiawatha, the only one here who could recognize him, in his eyesight. Everything seemed to float as if he were walking through a dream. He saw Hiawatha and Dekanawida smiling and talking with a group of women. Clan mothers, by the look of them. He could do it now if he wanted. The blowgun with a poison dart inserted in its shaft felt warm and urgent against his skin beneath the robe. Just get a little bit closer, and then . . . No. Wait till he is alone. Somewhere outside the village. He can't stay within these walls forever.

The bonfire roared, keeping everyone warm, and the musicians played their drums and flutes with gusto. Food had been prepared earlier. Large roasts of venison, corn breads, puddings, and steaming soup made from mushrooms, beans, and squash were brought out, and there was much feasting. The tobacco that the people of the north and the people of the south had brought with them was shared and smoked. The men of the False Face societies and the men of the Medicine societies put on their masks and danced and sang. They invoked the Spirit Beings who are always present, who always walk among us, to aid them in their new resolve to now live lives of unity. They prayed to the beings of the spirit world to come among them and to help them avoid bloodshed and revenge as a way of life. They prayed to the spirits of their dead fathers and mothers, their grandfathers and grandmothers, to likewise come join them, to walk and dance with them, to aid them in their new path, to help them walk the path that Dekanawida and Hiawatha had shown them.

Later that night, Hiawatha asked the chieftains, Tekerihoken, Shenandonah, and Gaihogen, to gather their clan mothers, headmen, and shamans in an inner circle around the fire. They would now begin to discuss the path that should be taken. A crowd formed behind the seated circle of leaders, and among the crowd was Osinoh, who carefully moved in closer behind Hiawatha.

"Our responsibility is great," Hiawatha began. "And the greatest of our responsibilities is toward our mother, the earth. We must learn how to use our minds so that our children can survive in peace and in happiness. No other animal that walks on the back of the Great Turtle, or that swims in the great sea, or that flies in the air, is as murderous as man. The birds and the beaver, the deer, wolf, and bear, do not kill their own kind. We alone among all living creatures kill our own kind."

Dekanawida, sitting to his right, nodded in agreement as he strung together shells, the beginnings of a wide wampum belt.

Hiawatha continued. "In order to maintain peace and harmony with nature, we propose to form a League of Peace."

Gaihogen, Tekerihoken, Shenandonah, and the other headmen stared at one another, trying to gauge the reactions of those gathered there. Finally, Tekerihoken said, "How will this league be formed?"

Dekanawida talked softly to Hiawatha, and then Hiawatha nodded and replied. "We propose that each clan be represented by a Peace Chief, a Sachem, and that all decisions of the League have the unanimous voice of the Sachems."

"But what if the Sachems cannot agree?" asked Gaihogen.

"Yes," said Shenandonah, "it is not so easy to agree one with another. Look at how our relationships have played out in the past." Others around the council fire conferred briefly and murmured in harmony with these objections.

"If the Sachems are wise men with clear minds, and if we pick men who are so, then through their words they can agree to walk the same path together."

"Hiawatha speaks wisely," said Tekerihoken. "And in an ideal world, I would agree with him. But I am not sure that what he says is truly possible in the real world of human beings."

"It will be possible as long as the Sachems know and honor their duties. The Sachems that we pick must never consider their own interests, but must work only to benefit the people and the generations not yet born. They must be men who truly care about the people. In all their decisions, they must consider the future people to come—for at least seven generations. If they do all these things, then I am convinced that they will be able to find the right path on which all can agree."

There was much head-shaking and animated discussion after Hiawatha's words were spoken. Dekanawida continued to make his wampum belt, his belt of peace, and, to a casual observer, he looked as if he were totally absorbed in this activity and this activity alone. But his darting eyes picked up on all that was happening in every part of the crowd. His ears, still keen and sharp, likewise heard the intent of many conversations. He watched and listened with particular interest to the conference that was being held among the clan mothers.

Tahakahen, the matriarch of the Turtle Clan, spoke with much feeling to her sisters, who listened with respect. But the holy man could not tell if all the clan mothers were in agreement with the words that she was speaking with such apparent passion. Tahakahen stood up abruptly and addressed the council.

"We Clan Mothers wish to know something important. Who is it that will pick these Sachems?"

Dekanawida and Hiawatha conferred with Jikonsahseh. Then Hiawatha spoke. "We propose that our government be built on the houses in which we live. Therefore, we propose that the Clan Mothers, in conference with the women in their houses, select the Sachems to represent their longhouses. And if a Sachem neglects his duties or the welfare of his people, the women can remove him if he does not heed their warnings."

Some of the men looked at each other with raised eyebrows. "I am not so sure that I like this method of selecting the Sachems," said Gaihogen. "The women in my village already have enough power."

Tahakahen glared at Gaihogen, a cold glint in her eyes.

"We must discuss this further among ourselves," said Tekerihoken abruptly. The chief was intent on averting a fierce battle of words. Dekanawida once more whispered into Hiawatha's ear. Hiawatha listened intently, and then spoke aloud.

"The Peacemaker says that in order for our league to succeed, there must be a balance of power. How does this differ from the ancient ways? The ways of our ancestors have always held that the Clan Mothers pick the chieftains of the villages and towns."

"The women already own the longhouses and have control over the fields and the land. They have the power over the food, over the chiefs, and over the children." There was anger in Gaihogen's voice.

"Which is the reason why you men have so much time to sit around and talk," said Tahakahen sarcastically.

"And why you have so much time to make weapons to spill the blood of your brothers," added Jikonsahseh.

Gaihogen and some of the other men held their tongues, but it was clear by the looks on their faces that they were far from pleased by this turn of events.

"The men will do the negotiating," said Hiawatha. "The men will still make the laws, and the men will still make the important judgments about which course of action to take in any situation. But—and this is very important—if the men are to do the negotiating, if the men are to make the laws, if the men are to make the important judgments, then the women must see that it is done for the good of the people. They must see that it is done for the good of at least seven generations to come. And who better to look out for the welfare of the generations to come, than those who give birth to and raise up those generations? The mothers of our children and the mothers of our children's children are the ones who we should trust the most to be the watchers of our people."

"Hiawatha speaks wisely," said Tahakahen.

"Dekanawida is a wise prophet," said another Clan Mother.

"And so is Jikonsahseh, the holy lady of the forest, the friend to the wild creatures who are our brothers and sisters. She too counsels wisely."

"This arrangement will represent a perfect balance of power," said Hiawatha, trying to appeal to the logical side of the headmen and the chieftains gathered around the council fire, men who were feeling put upon by the members of the opposite sex.

"Yes," said Tekerihoken. "A balance of power is good."

"Let us now talk of hunting rights," said Hiawatha. "In order to eliminate the many disputes over our boundaries, we propose that we the people, all the nations, share our hunting lands."

"Share our hunting lands?" asked Shenandonah indignantly. "We people of the southern lands do not share our hunting grounds with anyone." The leaders of the various villages and towns from the south and from the north murmured angrily and voiced their discontent with this radical proposition that Hiawatha was so rash to make. The women, the clan mothers, on the other side of the council fire, looked at the men with scorn and derision in their eyes.

"So like men," said one.

"This selfishness and self-centered behavior is what has gotten the human beings into this mess," said another.

"Look here," said Hiawatha. "In the past, we have said that this is the boundary for the hunting lands of the Mohawk." He drew an imaginary line on the ground and in the air around him. "And that, over there, is the boundary of the hunting lands of the Oneida. But, listen to me, brothers. I say to you that the animals that give us their meat when we hunt them know no boundaries. They roam freely. They are free to travel and eat where they please. We, the human beings, must also be this free. Are we any less than the creatures of the woods and the air and the sea? The Great Creator gave all of us the land, and he made no boundaries for his creations. When Muskrat brought up earth from the bottom of the Great Primordial Sea and placed it on the Great Turtle's back, did he set up boundary stones? Did he place posts on the back of Turtle Island and call this one the boundary of the deer, or that one the boundary of the elk?"

The men listened in silence and inwardly they saw the logic in Hiawatha's persuasive argument. They knew deep in their hearts that he was right.

"But, listen here, Hiawatha. I see the sense in what you say, but if everyone hunts on our land, there won't be enough game left for us." Tekerihoken's objection sounded realistic enough considering how depleted were the storehouses of his village, a village left with few provisions for the winter due to the Huron raids on their cornfields.

"I know that your people are suffering now," said Hiawatha. "But this plan is for the future, to insure that this will not happen again to any of us. Everyone will hunt as close to home as possible. Why, for instance, would Gaihogen or Shenandonah travel a great distance to your land, Tekerihoken, if they have game on their own land? Would *you*?"

"No, there would be no need to," Tekerihoken replied.

"But if they have no game, no deer, no elk, on their own land, and their people are hungry, can you say to them that these are *my* deer and you cannot have them? Why must they fear for their lives and risk death and torture if they must hunt outside their homeland in order to fill their children's bellies?"

There were murmurs of assent and agreement among the assembled men who saw the wisdom in Hiawatha's argument. The women also talked among themselves in excited voices about this bold new plan for the future.

"The deer is a free animal," continued Hiawatha. "Just as we are free people. The deer does not belong to one tribe or one nation or one clan. He is an equal member of the circle-chain of life here on the back of our mother, the earth."

An old woman, who had sat silently listening in the back row of the clan mothers, broke her silence and said, "We respect and live in harmony with our families of deer, the large-antlered bucks, the soft and pregnant does, the tender, spotted fawns. If our hunting lands are opened up to all, then the deer may be abused and leave our lands."

"This is a good point that you bring up, grandmother," said Hiawatha. "The League of Peace that we are beginning to set up here in this place on this very night must see to it that the rights of our brother and sister deer are not abused. Traps will not be allowed and we will take only what is necessary for our people. Before we open our hunting lands to any group of people, they must join our League and agree to all the conditions."

"Once again," said Tekerihoken, "this is a very delicate issue. We must discuss this further with our people."

"And with ours," agreed Gaihogen.

"And ours as well," said Shenandonah.

"Everything will be discussed in great detail with every man and every woman," said Hiawatha as he looked around the circle, making eye contact with each person. We must develop our thinking skills, our skills as clear-minded beings. We must also develop our speaking skills. For the only way to agreement lies in speaking well, in presenting one's thoughts well. So that we can understand one another. If we are to have a peaceful society, there must be a shared understanding among us all."

Dekanawida nodded in agreement and stood up. He held above his head a long and wide wampum belt, the belt that he had been adding shells to as Hiawatha spoke, as the Clan Mothers spoke, as the headmen and chieftains spoke. He raised his weak voice—a voice that sounded more like that of a spirit than a mortal man— so that as many as possible could hear his words.

"You see here before you the great belt of peace which will be known to the future generations as the belt of Hiawatha. It will tell the story of our words this night, a story that our children's children will repeat down through the generations: How men and women achieved a great understanding through the Great League of Peace."

Shouts of approval and assent rose from the gathered men and women overwhelmed by the *orenda* that shone from the face of the Peacemaker. The women joyously shouted their approval. The men joined in, and their voices could be heard far outside the village. Children asleep in the longhouses awoke and smiled at the happy noise. And the Onondaga warriors hiding in the underbrush, waiting for Osinoh to return, were disturbed by this powerful sound of unity.

In the midst of all the shouting, Osinoh stood in the crowd directly behind Hiawatha. He remembered how the great chief had singled out that vapid flute boy and lavished favors and attention on him. Protected him with his own life, even though he killed Shadahgoh's son. I am a better man, a stronger man than Orios. Hiawatha knew that I wanted his daughter. But he snubbed me, passed me over in favor of a weak daydreamer. He stared at the charismatic leader's bare back and thought how vulnerable the great man was now. How easy it would be to plunge his knife into the back of his neck and so stop this man from spreading his dangerous ideas across the land. As Osinoh's fingers wrapped around the bone handle of his knife, Dekanawida suddenly turned and looked him in the eye with a gaze that paralyzed him. The crowd was still cheering and shouting as their eyes locked momentarily, and then Dekanawida seemed to ask him a question with his eyes. Then the old man turned his head once again towards the fire. Confused, his mind throbbing from the loud shouts of the Mohawk, Osinoh inched his way back through the crowd and headed for the stockade gate.

As the shouts subsided, Gaihogen stood up in one movement of his strong legs. "We thank Dekanawida and Hiawatha for presenting their proposals to us. We will have a caucus now with our own people from our individual villages to discuss these proposals, and decide if we can change the old ways and tie our houses together into one great longhouse of peace."

"Good," said Hiawatha. "Think hard about the things that we have said this night. Tomorrow, when the sun is setting, we will meet again in council to hear your decisions."

There was a general bustle and low murmuring of voices as the headmen and chiefs, the elders and the clan mothers dispersed to their own longhouses, to the longhouses of their clan members, who were hosting them during this huge meeting and ceremonial feast, or to the makeshift houses and lean-tos that had been prepared in advance for them. The sun was not long from rising, and a wind swept across the village, blowing through the naked branches of the trees around the palisade walls. A few cold stars twinkled, and the new moon's curved bow could be seen low in the sky, an auger of hope, an omen for new and great things to come.

Part III

The Planting Moon

Chapter One

The setting sun painted the western sky with blood-red streaks as the council reconvened. The assembled leaders took their seats around the fire in the center of the village. Many villagers crowded around the ring of leaders, eager to hear what they would say. Dekanawida filled a long-stemmed pipe with the sacred tobacco leaf. He held it up to the sky and chanted a prayer to the Spirit Beings of the land of the Mohawks, then passed it to Hiawatha who lit it from a burning twig.

"Great Spirits of this Place, accept the smoke from this pipe as a pledge of our faithfulness, as a pledge that we give to one another," he said. And then he puffed slowly and wafted the smoke over his face. He passed the pipe to Gaihogen, and as the chieftain puffed the tobacco smoke, Hiawatha asked him, "Have your people decided if they will join the new league?"

Gaihogen continued puffing the pipe, contemplating his answer. He looked at the faces all around him. He passed the pipe to Tekerihoken, who sat at his left side, and then answered Hiawatha's question. "We have talked long and hard about these matters. What you propose is strange to us. We have our doubts about the success of such an enterprise. However, my people want to live in the Great Longhouse of Peace. But it seems to me that this peace depends upon everyone's participation. If you can somehow assure us that the others will walk the path of peace, then we agree to the proposals that we discussed last night."

Hiawatha looked at Tekerihoken. The chief of the village took a long draw on the pipe and wafted the smoke over his face with his left hand. He passed the pipe to Shenandonah and answered Hiawatha's unspoken question.

"We do not like sharing our hunting grounds with others. But we do like sharing the hunting grounds *of* others." Tekerihoken's jest lightened the solemn atmosphere around the fire. "Let me say this," he continued. "We appreciate what our cousins have done for us by coming here. You bring new light and new strength into our house. My people feel that our brother Hiawatha speaks wisely in all that he says. We are ready to join this new League of Peace. And we agree to all the conditions. If we convince the other four nations to live under the roof of one longhouse, then we will be, like Hiawatha's bundle of five arrows, a strong force to defend ourselves against the Huron and our other enemies."

Hiawatha nodded. "Shenandonah? What do your people say?"

"My people do not like living in fear. We worry each day that some raiding party, maybe Huron, maybe Cayuga, maybe Oneida, will slaughter our people or steal our children. It is not right to live in such fear. We will gladly join the League, and we will work hard to build it and to make it strong."

Shouts of approval rang throughout the village. Those tending the smaller cooking fires stopped what they were doing and looked up. Women pounding dried corn to make meal for bread rested their large wooden pestles and wondered what all the shouting was about.

Dekanawida stood up and showed them the long wampum belt commemorating the first step in the founding of the Great League of Peace. The Mohawk, proud and fierce warriors, would lead the way. As the first to join, they would have a special place of honor as an elder brother in the League. When the other nations saw how they would profit from an alliance with the Mohawk and with each other, surely they too would join the League.

Nations joined with nations in a bond of peace. His dream, his life's work, was now one step closer to becoming a reality. He now knew that he had picked the right man to be the spokesman for the League. Hiawatha had proven himself a skilled and powerful orator. His arguments were sound, with just the right proportion of logic and emotion to sway the people to the right way of thinking.

Tekerihoken stood up and addressed the gathering, indicating with his hands for silence. "Brothers and sisters, grandfathers and grandmothers, sons and daughters, we have one more thing to say before we call an end to this council where we have done much work for the future of our people."

He motioned to his wife Tahakahen, Clan Mother of the Turtle Clan, who stood up and looked around the circle of faces. "Our brother Hiawatha, who has spoken so eloquently the words and thoughts of the Peacemaker, was once a member of the Turtle Clan of the Onondaga nation. But now he is without a longhouse. He is a wanderer on the face of the earth. I say that Hiawatha ought to be a Mohawk. If the others agree, we wish to adopt Hiawatha into the Turtle Clan of the Mohawk Nation."

"Yes, let him be a Mohawk! He will always be welcome by the people in my village," said Shenandonah.

"And he will be welcome inside the stockade of my people," agreed Gaihogen.

"How do the Clan Mothers vote?" asked Tahakahen.

The mothers and grandmothers of the clans conferred among themselves. Then Tahakahen spoke again. "We will be honored to have Hiawatha join our nation."

"So be it," said Tekerihoken. "Hiawatha, step forward."

Dekanawida looked at Hiawatha and nodded his approval. Hiawatha looked up, and he seemed to see his mother in the crowd smiling at him. She had grown to love the Onondaga people, but in her heart she was always Mohawk. Now her son had finally come home. But was he deserting his old Onondaga family? His mind began to spin; then he saw them—Tamora holding the new-born Tiwi in her arms with Memoha at her side, a look of longing in her eyes. He felt a tug on his arm, and there beside him were Sovana and Seawa; they grasped his arms and pulled him to his feet. The others gathered around the fire could not see what Hiawatha saw, but they felt a presence, and they sensed the spiritual communion that was happening in their midst. A silence fell over the crowd. There was no sound at all as Hiawatha walked the path between two worlds. His eyes were misted over as Tekerihoken placed both hands on Hiawatha's shoulders.

"We adopt you as our son, Hiawatha. Your name means 'He who has lost something, but knows where to find it.' You have lost much in your lifetime. A wife, four daughters, a chieftainship, and a nation. But now you have found it, as you always knew you would. You are now a Mohawk, and a member of the Turtle Clan. This is your new home. And wherever you go in the land of the Mohawk, you will always be welcome, and especially welcome in the longhouses of the Clan of the Turtle. Here is my token of good faith, my son." Tekerihoken placed a long-stemmed, finely carved red-stone pipe with three eagle feathers dangling from the bowl into Hiawatha's hands.

Hiawatha embraced his new father, Tekerihoken. Then he turned and embraced his spiritual father, the Peacemaker, Dekanawida, who now stood up and said as loudly as he could in his wraith-like voice, "Hiawatha the Mohawk, you shall lead us all to peace and brotherhood. Your name will be remembered by future generations as the great orator who brought all of the people together. Tonight around this fire we are all Mohawk. But soon, all nations that live in the longhouse will be united in one Great Longhouse. We will all be Haudenosaunee, the People of the Longhouse, joined in our League of Peace and Power, joined in our bonds of brotherhood and sisterhood."

The village rang once again with cheers and shouts of approval. Men cried the cry of the eagle, and the clan mothers cheered their great joy. The noise caught on like a wave across the entire village so that those inside and those outside the walls of the village picked up the cheers and the cries. The noise was so loud that it made the crows in the trees stop calling to one another and wonder what new creature was this that had landed in their midst.

Three weeks after the people of the north and the people of the south had traveled back home to their own longhouses, Dekanawida, Hiawatha, Tekerihoken, and the other chiefs from the north and the south met once again in Tekerihoken's village to plan out their strategy for drawing the other nations into the new League of Peace. Because the day was much colder, and a heavy snow had fallen, they met in the council house, a smaller building separate from the longhouses where the people lived.

Dekanawida had made a map of their section of Turtle Island from the Great Lakes and the Great Niagara waterfalls south to the land of the Susquehannock, and eastward to where they now sat in the great Mohawk valley. He used dried kernels of corn and sunflower seeds on the ground in front of them to show the boundaries as best as he could remember. As a young man, he had traveled over the length and breadth of the Turtle's back.

"This is where we are now, the Mohawk land," Hiawatha said, pointing to the eastern portion of the map. "Up here is the Great Lake of the Eries, just west of the Lake of Ontario. Here is the Great Falls of the Niagara. These southerly lines are the Finger Lakes. And this weaving line of sunflower seeds is the path of the Tenonanatche, the river that flows through the mountain, our own Mohawk River."

Hiawatha pointed to the territory just west of the Mohawk land and said, "This is the land of the Oneida. Here is the Onondaga. Here the Cayuga. And lastly, the farthest away from us, is the land of the Seneca. We all speak the same tongue. There are different dialects and some different words, but we all share the same culture. If one speaks Mohawk, one can converse with the Seneca and with the other nations."

Hiawatha moved his stick along the north, west, and south branches of the Susquehanna River on the map that Dekanawida had illustrated with sunflower seeds. "And here is another great river that unites us. The various parts of the Susquehanna run through all of our lands from west to east. It may be the best path for our journey, our journey to convert the other nations to our new way of living and thinking."

Gaihogen studied the map. "Perhaps it would be wise to talk first with our closest neighbors, the Oneida and Onondaga. If we had them on our side, perhaps the Seneca would be more willing to participate in our league."

"The Senecas are very proud," said Shenandonah. "Will they be insulted if they are not the first to be asked?"

"I think it will be difficult with the Seneca no matter what we do. They are much too proud of their own size and strength to join us," said Oswegon, a chieftain from the north who usually said very little.

"What about the Onondaga?" Gaihogen persisted. "They say that their chieftain is an evil sorcerer, and that the people at the foot of the hills live in great fear of him."

"Yes, and they make war with the Oneida, the Cayuga, and the Seneca," added Shenandonah.

"Is this true, Hiawatha?" asked Tekerihoken. "You are from Onondaga. What do you know about this leader of theirs?"

"What Gaihogen says is true. Their chieftain, Atatarho, is the most evil man I know. He killed my daughters, and he turned my people against me. There is no way that he could become part of the League."

A silence descended on the council house. No one knew how to respond. Finally, Dekanawida broke the silence. "Hiawatha," he began. "Was it the evil in Atatarho that destroyed your daughters and turned your people against you, or was it the evil in your own heart?"

Hiawatha felt his stomach knot up. Why was Dekanawida

attacking him like this? He stared at his mentor for several seconds. Then he said, "You know that it was not my fault."

"Did you not thirst for blood to feed your revenge? Did you not torture men yourself to assuage your grief? Bad crops come from bad seeds, my friend."

Hiawatha tried to hide his discomfort by focusing his gaze on the map. "Let us not dwell on the past, but what is here before us," he said.

"Yes," said Dekanawida. "And what is here before us is Onondaga. We must sit down like human beings and talk with Atatarho."

"I know him," Hiawatha protested. "You cannot reason with him."

"*Cannot* is a word we should erase from our vocabulary, Hiawatha. We can and we will."

"Do you want to contaminate the new league with bad blood? He must be done away with for the welfare of all the people."

"No man will be condemned unless he is first given the Good News of Peace. We will give him this news, and then we will give him a chance to remake his mind. Just as we gave you the chance to remake yours."

Hiawatha said nothing. He had never considered the notion that Atatarho would be given a chance to prove himself worthy of being in the league. It was unthinkable. Atatarho, the sorcerer who fed on human flesh, could never reform.

Dekanawida stared at Hiawatha as if he were reading his thoughts. Then he said, "If we do not believe that our enemies are capable of changing their ways, there can be no hope for peace. Our enemies are people, like us. If we are capable of changing for the better, just as you have changed for the better, Hiawatha, then so are they. We must sit and talk with Atatarho. It is the only way."

"I agree with the Peacemaker," said Tekerihoken. "It is not the good-minded ones that need convincing. It sounds as though we will have to work very hard on this Atatarho."

Hiawatha remained adamant. "It is an impossible task," he said.

Dekanawida looked Hiawatha squarely in the eye. "It is only impossible if you believe it to be so. All humans, even Atatarho, have the potential to be human *beings*, spiritual beings in human form. They only have to remake their minds so that the Great Spirit can flow through them. The Great Spirit cannot flow through those who do not respect and love our mother, the Earth, or those who do not respect and love our brothers who have the same potential as we do to become human beings."

This concept of universal love was new to those sitting around the fire, but they could feel it coming from the Peacemaker, and they liked the feel of it. It gave them a sense of unity, a sense of connection with the Great Mystery of the Universe, the Great Spirit Being who wanted them to be human beings instead of just humans. Hiawatha felt it too, even deeper than the others, for the brotherly love emanating from the Peacemaker seemed to fill up the great vacuum where his heart used to be.

Tekerihoken broke the silence. "Is it agreed, then, that we visit Atatarho?" The other chiefs nodded their approval.

Tekerihoken looked at Hiawatha and said, "Is it unanimous?"

Hiawatha now knew that the path he had chosen would not be an easy one. He had been swept away by the words, but had not yet realized their full import. He sighed, and then nodded his approval.

"Very well, then. It is unanimous. We will extend our invitation to the League to Atatarho and the Onondaga."

"Perhaps we should gain the support of the Oneida first," said Dekanawida. "Then we will approach Atatarho from a position of greater strength. We will send messengers to the other people first. We will offer to come and visit with them and talk about our newly formed League. Then, after our numbers have grown, we will all go together and talk with the dreaded Atatarho."

The next day, the chiefs continued their debate around the fire in the council house. From outside the village gate came a warning cry from a Mohawk runner. The stockade gates opened and closed and then the runner entered the council house. As he tried to catch his breath, he blurted out, "Adergagtha . . . on the march . . . an army of hundreds . . . in wood-slat armor."

"We must stop them before they get here," urged Tekerihoken.

"We must send for help from the other Mohawk villages," said Gaihogen.

"Yes," said Hiawatha, "but they may not have enough time to get here before Adergagtha does."

"Without their help, we are not strong enough to defeat him in an open battle," cautioned Tekerihoken.

"Perhaps we can set a trap for him. I know of a plan that might work." The men all looked at Hiawatha.

"Adergagtha is not easily tricked," said Tekerihoken.

"And the Huron in their armor are mighty warriors," added Oswegon.

Hiawatha looked at the men. "The Mohawk are mighty warriors too. But our special skill is our stealth. We will win not by throwing all of our warriors in the face of all of theirs, but rather, we will win through bravery and cunning. We will think like the fox. And the fox will catch the rabbit."

"Adergagtha is no rabbit," said Dekanawida.

"We shall soon see," said Hiawatha. "Tekerihoken, have your people gather dried cattails and soak them in bear fat."

"Cattails?"

"Yes, cattails. I have seen this done before. We will prevail over their wood and woven armor. We will set a trap for these Hurons that will give us the advantage."

The Peacemaker held up his hand. "Slow down, Hiawatha. Before we proceed any further, we must first send messengers and give them a chance to reconsider their attack upon us."

"I am sorry, Father, but that will spoil the trap. Does the fox warn the rabbit? How can we surprise them if we send messengers?"

"We must first talk with them. It is the Way—the Way of Peace."

"We have already talked with Adergagtha. We gave him a chance to remake his mind, but he wanted no part of it. Now he is bent on destroying us, and our only hope to defeat him is with a surprise attack."

Dekanawida's shoulders seemed to sink under the weight as he thought of all the Huron brothers from his homeland and of all his Mohawk brothers who would soon meet their deaths. "It saddens me to say this, but Hiawatha is right. We have already talked to Adergagtha and he is now the aggressor. We must defend ourselves and our women and children. But we must agree that we will not strike the first blow."

Dekanawida looked around the circle and the chiefs nodded in agreement. "One last thing before we turn this matter over to the war chiefs. Hiawatha speaks as though he is already the supreme war chief. But we have agreed that a Sachem cannot be a war chief, have we not? If Hiawatha wishes to be a war chief, then he must resign his position as a Sachem of the Great Council."

"Without the strength and cunning of Hiawatha leading the warriors, we may not prevail over the Huron," said Tekerihoken. "What will happen to us then?"

"And what will happen to us if we allow Sachems to be war chiefs?" In spite of his weak voice, Dekanawida was a powerful presence, and his passion on this point was strong. "War chiefs live to flex their muscles and show off their power. It is up to the Sachems to see that their power is used only for *defense*. This safeguard will be lost if Sachems are allowed to be the leaders of war. Why have we formed this League? For peace or for warfare?" Although he asked this question to all who were gathered, it was clear that it was addressed to Hiawatha.

After a pause, Hiawatha slowly replied. "For peace."

"So be it, then." Dekanawida looked at the faces of the other

Sachems and each in turn nodded their agreement. "Now let me ask the Sachems one more question. Who knows more about the leadership qualities of a war chief, the Sachems or the warriors who have fought with him?"

"The warriors," answered Gaihogen.

"Yes, it is so," said Oswegon. "If they do not respect a war chief, then they will not follow him."

"Then who should select the leader for the warriors? The Sachems? Or the warriors who must risk their lives in battle?"

"It seems fair that the warriors select their leader," said Tekerihoken. The other Sachems voiced their approval.

"It is agreed then?" asked Dekanawida. The men looked at one another and nodded in agreement.

"Does anyone disagree?" Dekanawida looked at Hiawatha. "It is your choice. Will you remain within the Circle of Sachems, or do you wish to lead others in war?"

Hiawatha paused before answering. The air seemed still and suffocating inside the council house. It was as if everyone present were holding their breath as they waited for Hiawatha's decision. It was a double-edged blade. They needed him on the battlefield now to help defend their village, but they knew that the League of Peace would not become a reality without his guidance.

The tension in the room mounted as the others thought of the approaching threat. Finally, Hiawatha replied. "We must not be blinded by our short-term needs. The temptation for a Sachem to become a war chief will always be there, so a firm precedent must now be set. I want to remain a Sachem. But let me ask Dekanawida this: Is it anywhere in the Great Law that you received from the Great Perfector of Minds that a Sachem who was once a war chief cannot give advice on tactics to a war captain?"

Dekanawida smiled and the tension in the room was dispelled. "No, Hiawatha. I do not recall hearing those words. Advice is a great thing. Go forth and give it."

Late that night, under the cover of darkness beneath a starless, moonless sky, Mohawk warriors wearing snowshoes and laden down with large packs on their backs, slipped out of the stockade and headed toward the makeshift camps that had earlier been erected to house the large numbers of people who had come from the north and the south for the ceremony. In the packs were bearskins and deerskins, and many bags of dried corn. The makeshift village was in a clearing surrounded by pine woods on either side. The men rebuilt the fires that had gone out and wrapped bags of corn and frames of sticks in bearskins and deerskins so that, from a distance, they appeared to be men wrapped in their robes, huddled sleeping by their warm, winter fires. After they had done this to their satisfaction, the warriors bent over and removed their snowshoes. They then replaced them on their feet backwards and walked away through the white drifts of snow. Once in the woods, they hid themselves among the shelter of the low-hanging branches of the pine trees, and waited.

Adergagtha's scouts had returned about an hour before dawn and told him the good news. "The Mohawk sit and lie by their fires sleeping like women. We can surprise them and take many scalps and many prisoners."

"Where are their guards?" asked Adergagtha.

"They are all drowsing by the fires in an encampment outside the gates of the village. The village itself is quiet and still. We will descend upon them and they will not know what has hit them until they see Huron war clubs in their faces. And then it will be too late!"

Adergagtha smiled. The reports of a confederacy of Mohawk all joined together had impelled him to take this drastic war action. He had to stop this union before it started. He knew that his brother was behind this scheme. He shook his head as he thought about his weak brother. Always talking of peace, like a grandmother. Dekanawida had turned the once fierce Mohawk into a tribe of women. Adergagtha laughed to himself. Women mewling of peace were no match for Huron armor and war clubs. Too many had already listened to the foolishness of his brother. He wanted now to do what his father had tried to do years before, destroy his brother. He straightened the wooden armor across his broad chest and pulled his hemp-woven helmet down low on his brow. Half his face was painted black, the other half yellow. The long scar that ran down and across his face and lips was painted a bright red. These were the colors of war, the colors of blood and death. He called forth his shaman, Hohknanan, who had stuffed blue jays sewn all over his bearskin robe by the top of their heads so that they swung around and dangled when he danced and chanted. In his hand he held a sorcerer's staff that was tipped with a stuffed hawk's body. He wore a wolf's head as a bonnet.

"Sing us a war prayer, sorcerer," said Adergagtha. "For we go now to kill our enemy."

The old shaman spun around on his heel and raised his staff into the air. He sang this song, and the warriors repeated verses of it:

> "Now we are made bold
> By the power of our War Song:
> This War Song given to us by
> Aswaregon, Great War God
> Of the Huron!
>
> Our warriors shall be mighty
> In the power of the Almighty
> In the power of the War Medicine
> In the power of Aswaregon
> Who gave us this song:
> This War Song that we sing:
> Hai yai! Hai-yai!"

"Huron warriors, follow me now to victory!" cried Adergagtha as he raised his war club and strode down the side of the hill followed by his army all clad in helmets and armor. Their snowshoes made the earth shake beneath the upper crust of the snow, and the Mohawk hiding in the pine woods could feel them coming in the distance. Wadoh, war chief from the village of Tekerihoken, looked at Dohwahnsah, one of his captains.

"Are the arrows ready?"

"Just as Hiawatha instructed. Wrapped with cattails and dipped in bear fat."

"Good. Have someone make the fire now," said Wadoh. "Then, when they are in the clearing, we will light the arrows from torches, and let them fly." Dohwahnsah crawled off deeper into the woods and gave instructions to a warrior who knelt beside a fire drill and a pile of torches. He placed dried bark shavings and dried moss at the base of the drill where the hole in the board was and began working his drill up and down rapidly. Soon a small stream of smoke rose up from the moss and bark. The warrior bent over and blew gently on the tinder, causing a small flame to leap up. Dohwahnsah placed small twigs on top of the tiny flame which grew in size. Soon they had a good fire from which they would be able to light the greased cattails that were wrapped around the tips of their arrows.

Adergagtha and his warriors came streaking down the slope toward the fires in the clearing below. Huron warriors to his left and his right fitted arrows into their bowstrings, and as they ran closer, they let them fly screaming all the while their Huron war cry: "Hai-yai! The War God gives us victory!"

Arrows pierced the bearskins and deerskins that were supported by frames of sticks. But nothing moved. The enemy did not cry out. More arrows pierced the bags of dried corn that lay beneath the skins, making hollow thumping sounds. And still no one cried out from the camp of the enemy. Adergagtha stopped and looked around. His first thought was that his brother had done some magic here. Magic greater than that of his own sorcerer who stood beside him. Then the pre-dawn sky lit up with shooting flames that soared from the woods toward them, and he realized, too late, that he had been tricked. He, the great Adergagtha, had been led into an ambush.

A flaming arrow struck the wooden breastplate of his armor. Two more hit his hemp-covered thighs, and another struck the high wooden back plate. He was on fire! Flaming arrows hit home all around him. The war cries of the mighty Huron turned into cries of pain and disbelief. All was confusion and chaos. He threw himself down upon the snow-covered ground and rolled about in order to extinguish the flames that surrounded his body and burned the flesh of his face. Others did the same. Those who were not hit in the initial volley of arrows blindly rushed the pine-tree woods on either side of the clearing. But they were met by another volley of flaming arrows. Some dropped instantly. Many stopped in their tracks and hurled themselves down on the snow to put out the flames that engulfed them.

And then the Mohawk charged with their stone tomahawks and deadly war clubs. They descended upon the Huron who were on the ground and beat them senseless about the head and face. Blood, bone, and brains flew everywhere around them, turning the pure white snow into a ghastly pink and black-red blanket of gore. Those who were still standing or unscathed were met by Mohawks in fierce hand-to-hand combat, grappling at close quarters, staving off blows from the Huron clubs and trying to beat through the woven hemp and wood-slat armor. The terrific sounds of wood smashing on wood rang and echoed through the bare branches and the long-leaved pine boughs of the forest, threatening to deafen those in the midst of the battle. The wind screaming through the white pine boughs made sounds that seemed like the voices of a hundred keening widows. Even Osinoh and his small band of Onondaga spies, some five miles away at their new winter encampment, heard the noise, looked at each other, and wondered what else was going on in Tekerihoken's village.

A huge Huron who was missing an ear and who seemed even taller in his high woven helmet aimed a vicious blow at Wadoh's head. At the last minute, he ducked and took the blow on his left shoulder. A white-hot pain ripped through his upper torso, but he swung around low and smashed the man full in the teeth with the round ball of his own war club. The Huron dropped.

All around him, those Huron warriors who were not dead or bleeding to death were writhing in pain in the snow. And as the sun came up, the bright red ball on the eastern horizon matched in hues the flames burning on arrows and armor and the dark, blood-red snow that stained the clearing as far as the eye could see. The stench of burning flesh was heavy in the smoke-filled air, and some charred wooden warriors lay still, their armor burning and melting the snow around them.

Then came the cries from inside the stockade as the gates were flung open and a hundred more Mohawk warriors poured out to put the finishing touches on this army of Huron who would have killed them all. Hiawatha and Dekanawida followed them, Dekanawida carrying his staff with the eagle claw on its tip and Hiawatha carrying the partially finished wampum belt of the newly formed League of Peace.

Adergagtha struggled to one knee and fitted an arrow onto his bow. Half his face was badly burned. "Dekanawida! Your magic and guile have tricked us. Now the bravest die while the cowards live." He pulled the string back to his chin and aimed his shaft at his brother's chest. "You will go to the Spirit World with me!" He let go and the arrow flew straight toward Dekanawida's heart.

At the same instant, Wadoh hurled his war club with deadly accuracy, and the last thing that Adergagtha saw before the world became black was his brother leaping to one side and catching his arrow with his right hand. Adergagtha lay dead in the snow, his body charred and bleeding. Dekanawida broke the arrow over his knee and wept.

The Huron warriors saw their leader fall. Dekanawida held up both hands. "This is a sad day for us all, Mohawk and Huron. Hiawatha, hold up the Wampum Belt of Peace. Offer amnesty and life for all those still living who will join with us in our League. They will become Mohawk, as you have, and live under the Great Tree of Peace that we will establish in the middle of the Great Longhouse, at Onondaga. Offer them this." Tears choked the Peacemaker's throat and his heart was heavy at the sight of so much death and so much pain.

Hiawatha walked among the wounded lying on the ground and those who had been captured, now being tied by the neck and hands with deer hide thongs and hempen ropes. He held up the white and blue Wampum Belt of Peace, and to each man he said, "We offer you life instead of death. We will take you into our villages and towns. We will adopt you as Mohawk citizens, and soon you will be citizens of the Great League of Nations, the League of Peace that we established here, and that we will establish everywhere along the great river valleys of our people."

He stopped in front of one man sitting on the snow and holding his head. He had a nasty gash inflicted by an antler-spiked war club. Hiawatha helped him to his feet, and took a piece of white doeskin from a pouch that hung from his neck. He carefully bandaged the man's wound, and said to him, "With this pure white doeskin I wipe away the blood from your body and I wipe away the blood from your mind. Know that we forgive you. Know that we welcome you as our brother.

"We have the same mother, our mother the earth. We live in the same longhouses, we share the same part of Turtle Island. Why should we not live as brothers?" He said this to all who were around him, all who could hear and could see the Wampum Belt of the Good News of Peace.

"All of you who would join us and become our brothers in the one united longhouse, come, throw your weapons into this fire and follow us into the village, where we will dress your wounds and feed you around our hearths." Hiawatha once again held up the Wampum Belt, and one by one, the wounded warriors limped and staggered to the fire beside him and threw their war clubs and their tomahawks into the flames. And the fire grew bigger and bigger, until it was a roaring bonfire that melted all the snow around it for ten feet, a fire that promised to melt the bitterness in the hearts of men.

Hiawatha moved across the battlefield, speaking to all who could still listen. He paused at a young warrior who lay wounded at his feet. His face was charred and blackened from smoke and the wooden armor was burnt half off of his slender body. Hiawatha lifted him to his feet. And as he did so, he recognized his lost companion, the young man who had shared his sorrows and his travels, the young dreamer and player of the mystical flute.

"Orios! At last, we have found you."

"Hiawatha! I have never left you. You have been in my heart and in my dreams ever since the day I was captured."

"Are you badly hurt?"

"I will live, I think."

Dekanawida joined them and laid his hand on Orios' head. "At last we meet. Hiawatha has told me much about you and your music. I am going to make a new flute for you, my son. A flute that will play the sweet notes of harmony and peace. And you will spend your days with us celebrating through song the joys of brotherhood and the promise of the coming peace of all human beings. You will be our musician, and you will compose the songs for the ceremonies of the Great League of Peace."

The Peacemaker moved on, stopping here and there among the scattered wounded to extend to them his blessings.

"Was that . . . ?"

"Yes. That was Dekanawida."

Chapter Two

There was much feasting and rejoicing in the longhouses of the village of Tekerihoken. The prisoners were treated kindly. No one was tied to the torture stake, no one suffered the blows and cuts at the pillar of blood. Their wounds were bandaged by medicine women and medicine men from the Bear Clan.

Hakonen and her granddaughter Keteri moved among the wounded, applying poultices of Pad-leaf to gashes and rubbing pitch-pine salve on the many burns caused by flaming arrows. Other women held bowls of elm-bark potion to the mouths or placed cloths dipped in tansy-water on foreheads so that those suffering pains in the head would find some relief. Women who had lost sons or husbands in battle looked carefully among the captured to see if any of them could be requickened to replace their dead ones.

Many of the Huron were grateful. Tegonta, a young Huron warrior whose right arm was broken, thought about what Hiawatha had said to them. It made sense to him. Yes, they all *were* brothers, born of the same mother, the earth. Perhaps it was better to be a healthy and happy Mohawk than to watch yourself suffer and die as a Huron. This brotherhood or league of peace that they spoke of seemed a happy alternative. Many of the other prisoners were thinking the same thing as they watched the Mohawk women bath their wounds with salve and the medicine men chant healing prayers. Is it not better to be here in this warm longhouse eating corn and venison than to be bleeding to death in the snow? When you die defeated in battle, thought Tegonta, your soul wanders continually, searching for some relief. You become a vanquished wraith, a bodiless spirit who must search throughout the length and breadth of the spirit world for your killer, to seek revenge. Isn't this more pleasant, lying on a warm bearskin, listening to the music of the drum, the flute, the rattle, and, floating above these instruments, the high sweet voices of girls and women singing songs of good medicine and love?

Shifting his position so that the corn-husk mat he lay on did not aggravate his burns and bruises, Orios played his new flute along with the water drummers, who drummed out a bittersweet rhythm that he matched with high and soulful meanderings. The red-elm flute that the Peacemaker had made for him was a wonder. He marveled at the almost magical way the pitch could shift from a low baritone to a very high tenor without the abrasiveness that sometimes comes with abrupt transitions. Dekanawida had carved a little songbird on the end closest to the mouth piece, and he tried to make it sound like the birds singing in the forest, calling out joyously to one another, in love with the creation that they were a part of.

Keteri stood up when she heard the flute. She knew that it had to be Orios. She was surprised to see him, sitting up among the wounded warriors. She rushed over to him, holding an elm-bark bowl filled with dried chamomile flowers steeping in hot water. Orios put down his flute and looked at her as she knelt down by his side. She dipped a soft doeskin cloth in the bowl and gently bathed his brow. Her eyes were large and dark brown, the softest eyes you could imagine, the eyes of a fawn, and her hair was long and thick, sleek and black like shining obsidian. He tilted back his head and she gently washed the wound on his face. Then she carefully placed the doeskin on his burned shoulder. He winced in pain, then relaxed as he felt the healing power from her hands surge through his body.

"Lay on your back," she said. Orios twitched as her soft hands ran down his chest. She seemed to be drawing the fire from his sides and his legs and transferring it to a fire that was now burning in his heart.

"What is your name?" he asked.

"Keteri," she replied. "Granddaughter of Hakonen, Clan Mother of the Bear Clan."

"Keteri," he repeated. The only thoughts that traveled through his mind were how much she reminded him of Sovana. Perhaps this girl is Sovana in disguise, a spirit in human form. But the touch of her soft hand on his forehead where she dripped the warm herbs and water was all too human.

"And you are Orios, are you not? The friend of Hiawatha captured by the Huron?"

"Yes. How did you know?"

"Many talk of you. They wonder how you survived the tortures of the Huron. They are curious. And so am I. Did they pull out your fingernails?" She turned over his hands and examined his fingers. Her touch sent a warm tingling throughout his body.

"No. They did not torture me much. The mother of Adergagtha liked my music. She took me into to her house and cared for me. She let me do as I pleased as long as I played the flute every day."

"I can see why she would do that. Your music is so lovely. It makes me want to cry. She must miss you, this Huron woman. And now she has lost her son."

"Yes, and they have lost most of their warriors. Those who are not dead are now Mohawk. What will become of her? And of the women, the children, and the old ones of Adergagtha's town?"

"Some other people will capture them," said Keteri as she continued to rub salve onto his bruised legs. "Perhaps the Adirondacks or Mahicans to the north, or the Wampanoags who live by the salt sea. It is the way. If Adergagtha had prevailed, I and my mother and my sisters might have been dragged off to the Huron town on the river to be wives to their warriors, or even to be tortured. Do not feel sorry for them. They would have killed us and tortured many of our people, and your woman protector probably would have led them. Why did you want to attack us?"

"I did not want to attack you. I was forced to. I did not raise my hand against the Mohawk. I lagged behind and hoped that I would be captured. I know that sounds very cowardly, but I cannot help it. It is not in my nature to be a warrior."

"I know. That is what I like about you." Orios smiled at her. He was now thankful for every one of his burns and bruises.

"Turn over and rest, Orios. I will rub your back with herbs and warm water."

Orios lay his head on the pile of beaver pelts and bearskins. He closed his eyes and floated through space under the magic touch of her soft hands.

A week later, Ortekla and Okaiya returned from the mission that Dekanawida had sent them on. They brought back news that Odatsadeh, the Oneida chief, had accepted his offer to come and speak to them about the League of Peace.

The acceptance of the offer was welcome news, for the Oneida were a strong and stubborn people, the People of Granite, and if they accepted the League, then it would make the path easier for the Onondaga to follow. The Onondaga and the Oneida, even though they often raided one another in ritual war-making and captive-taking, were very similar, and they already shared some of the same hunting and fishing grounds.

So they would journey to Oneidatown, to the place of the standing stone, and hold council there. An embassy consisting of Hiawatha, Dekanawida, Tekerihoken, and Orios, together with Ortekla and Okaiya, who would be their messengers and scouts, would travel westward along the Mohawk River in the stone canoe.

The edges of the river were frozen, and ice chunks floated on parts of the river as they made their way west. If they had been in an elm-bark canoe, they would have had a hard time of it. But the rosy-white stone canoe melted all obstacles in its path. The stone canoe was a paradox of weight and weightlessness; it was at once a metaphor and a real granite vessel. Metaphors among the Haudenosaunee are not fiction, are not false, but are real and true.

As they floated above the surface of the ice and water, Orios played a haunting melody on his flute and Hiawatha sang of the coming peace, of the coming good times for the human beings who would live as nobly as do the Sky People. His voice blended together strength and sweetness. It was a bird-song, but one that had the strength and courage of a cougar. In his song, the people would no longer live in fear. They would live under the Great Tree of Peace just as the Sky Beings live under the Great Tree of Light. But even as he sang, he knew that there were many obstacles in the path that led to this goal. Even if they convinced the Oneida to join them, they must, sooner or later, come face to face with his old enemies: the sorcerer Atatarho whose hair writhed with snakes and the fierce war chief Shadahgoh who had killed two of his daughters.

But perhaps the combined forces and voices of the Mohawk and the Oneida, the Flint People and the Granite People, could remake the mind of the dissipated leader of the Onondaga, the man who had worked his evil charms on Hiawatha, the man who had cast a spell on his own people.

As Hiawatha sang in tune with the flute-song of Orios, the old sadness crept back into his heart. He remembered the happier times when the Onondaga lived in peace and security under his leadership. He remembered the kindness of Makahwah, the beauty of her daughter Tamora, and the purity and innocence of his daughters, who did not deserve to die as they did, victims of a twisted sorcerer's spells, victims of an ogre's lust for power. He had to work very hard so that his mind did not turn again to blackness, to dark thoughts of hatred and revenge.

Orios was playing faster now, reaching impossibly high notes full of spiritual intensity as the canoe rounded a bend in the river.

Up ahead, they could see a striking man, tall and straight with long, thick gray hair, sitting cross-legged on a rock. He was sewing up the sides of a wolf skin, making a quiver with a deer-bone needle and thread of gut. He looked up from his sewing when he heard the singing of Hiawatha and the flute of Orios. His mouth dropped open and his hands stopped their sewing when he saw the large granite canoe hydroplaning above the icy river, moving in his direction. He stood up as if to flee, but his legs would not carry him, and at that instant he remembered his dream. A dream about a holy man and a boy playing a flute who came flying across the river with gifts for his people. Is this the canoe and these the people I dreamed of? Have they now come to us?

Hiawatha raised his right arm with the palm extended outward. "Greetings, Odatsadeh, the Quiver Maker. I am Hiawatha, the Mohawk. With me are Dekanawida, the Peacemaker, and Tekerihoken, Sachem of the Mohawk Nation, and Orios, the flute player. We come bearing the gift of Good News to you and the people of Oneidatown."

"Greetings. I have been expecting you. How did you know my name?"

"Our messengers described you well. No one can make wolf-skin quivers like Odatsadeh."

"True. And you . . . you look just as you did in my dream. Leave your magic canoe here by the great stone and I will take you into the town."

The band of ambassadors followed Odatsadeh away from the river, along the path through the woods to the Oneida longhouses. Snow was falling now in large wet flakes, clinging to the boughs of the pines and hemlocks, making a delicate tracery on the bare limbs of the maple, the elm, and the oak. As they walked through the woods, Orios played a cheerful and sprightly tune, and the small winter birds in the trees, the finches, the cardinals, and the long-billed nuthatches, whistled in answer to the call of his song.

Odatsadeh took them into the largest longhouse. He led his

guests to the other side of the fire where he seated them. Messengers were sent to bring the chieftains and headmen and the mothers of the clans. He filled a pipe with tobacco leaf, lit it with a twig from the fire, and passed the pipe to Dekanawida.

When the headmen, the chieftains, and the clan mothers had assembled and had taken their places around the now-roaring fire, Odatsadeh stood up and addressed the gathering.

"My people, these strangers here are the ones that came to me in my dream. I knew they were not evil spirits because they bore gifts, and their *orenda* was pure and strong. That is why, when they sent messengers asking for this audience, this visit, I agreed. They have come for a reason. We should hear this reason. I know that, in the past, many of you have lost sons and brothers to Mohawk arrows and war clubs. Our relationship in the past has not been a good one. You kill us, so we kill you. But my dream was strong. So we will listen to their words."

Odatsadeh sat down and gestured to the Mohawk contingency across the fire. Hiawatha stood up. "My name is Hiawatha. Some of you may know me or have heard of me, for I was once chieftain of the Onondaga. Now I am adopted into the Mohawk nation. But I come to you not as a Mohawk, but as a human being. We are one." Hiawatha gestured with his right hand bringing it forward out from his heart toward his listeners. "You and I are one people. We are the pure people, the human beings, and as such, we should be united into one longhouse—the Great Longhouse of the People. The Mohawk nation will be the Eastern Door, and you, the mighty Oneida, will be the central corridor along with the Onondaga. And the Cayuga and the Seneca will be the Western Door of the Great Longhouse of the People.

"I speak for the prophet Dekanawida, the Peacemaker, who received this vision of a Great League of Peace from the Sky Beings and from the Great Perfector of Minds. His mind is clear, his vision is strong, his *orenda* is pure, but his voice is weak. That is why I must speak his words, so that you may hear them, and so that we may join together in a new way of life—a life of cooperation in politics and in war, cooperation in peacetime and in times of attack. If the Susquehannock from the south or the Huron or Algonquin from the north attack the Oneida, then they also attack the Mohawk. And just as one arrow may be broken over the knee, whereas a bundle joined together may not, so too, the bundle of arrows from the Oneida and the Mohawk will stand firm against all enemies.

"Too long have we made war on each other. Too long have we fed the fires of hatred and revenge. Too long have we satisfied our grief through torturing war captives. I say that this must end. That we join together in a blood-brotherhood, in a League of Power through Peace."

Hiawatha sat down. Odatsadeh looked around at the important leaders of his people. Their faces were somber and unreadable. What this Mohawk had said seemed wise, but it was unlike anything that had been thought of before. "What do you say to this offer, my people?" he asked.

Arenias, a short, wiry man with a bonnet made from many hawk and pheasant feathers affixed to wolf fur, stood up and raised himself to his full height. "I am Arenias, war chief of the Wolf Clan. What you have said is good. But how do we know that you will do as you say? What real ties exist between our people? I am Oneida Wolf, you are Mohawk Turtle or Mohawk Bear. Your family is not my family. How can you make this so?"

Dekanawida smiled and stood up. Hiawatha attempted to help him to rise, but he waved his friend away. "Forgive me, my voice is weak. But my mind is clear. Our two nations, the Mohawk and the Oneida, must be joined through the heart as well as through the mind." The Prophet then drew two large circles on the dirt floor with the tip of his staff. In each circle he drew a sketch of a bear paw, a turtle shell, and a wolf's head. "Hiawatha, tell them about our plan for the extension of the clans."

Hiawatha stood and pointed to the drawings that Dekanawida

had made on the floor. "We propose that we extend our clan system so that the Wolf Clan of the Mohawk Nation are relatives of the Wolf Clan of the Oneida Nation." Hiawatha took Dekanawida's staff and drew a large connecting oval that encircled the two heads of the wolves. "This will be the same with the Turtle Clans and the Bear Clans."

One of the clan mothers raised her voice and asked, "Can a boy of the Mohawk Wolf Clan marry a girl of the Oneida Wolf Clan?"

"You ask well, mother. No. They will not be allowed to marry, for they will be as brother and sister. We have adopted young Orios into the Mohawk Turtle Clan. So, when he marries, he must marry outside of the Turtle Clan, and he will go live in the longhouse of his wife's mother. As a member of the Turtle Clan, he will be welcome, when traveling, to stay in the longhouse of the Turtle Clan in whatever village or town, in whatever nation he may be. One clan, one longhouse, one great league of nations and families."

"So, then, according to your plan, we will all have relatives all across the land," said Odatsadeh.

"Yes, my friend," said Dekanawida. "It will be as it was always intended to be. For we are all brothers and sisters already; we all share the same mother, the Great Mother Earth."

There were shouts of approval and assent at these last words of Dekanawida. Hiawatha held up a large belt of woven shells depicting stylized men holding hands on either side of a central white pine tree. The shells were blue and purple and white.

"This is the Wampum Belt of Peace, the Belt of the Great League of Brotherhood between the Oneida and the Mohawk. We present it to you this day. The wampum contains the words that we have spoken today. It is the symbol of the bonds that exist between our two peoples." He gave the belt to Odatsadeh, who smiled and nodded in acceptance.

Tekerihoken stood up and addressed the assembly. "We have

also brought gifts from the land of the Mohawk. The Mohawk clan mothers and the women of our towns send you seeds from their new corn. It is good and sweet, like the agreement we have reached this day." He gave Odatsadeh a sack of corn. Odatsadeh opened the sack and peered in.

"Red corn. Very nice." He smiled and passed the sack to the others so that they could admire the gift as well.

"Odatsadeh, our new brother, will you join our embassy and travel with us to Onondaga?" Dekanawida's question hung in the air for a full minute before Odatsadeh replied.

"It is true," he began, "that I have ties and relations with the Onondaga. But things now are not so good between my people and theirs. Atatarho, as you know, is a hard man to deal with. Some say he is not even a man. Some say he is a demon from the Spirit World. I do not believe this myself. But he is a sorcerer with great powers, and these powers are not fed by kindly thoughts and notions of brotherhood."

"It will not be easy convincing Atatarho of the value of our League," said Dekanawida. "Hiawatha knows how deep the dark vein runs in his mind and heart. But we must have all of the peoples of the longhouse in the Confederacy or it will not work. That is why I want you to come with us. The more strength of numbers we have, and the more collective wisdom we possess, the better are our chances of cleansing his mind."

Odatsadeh looked at Hiawatha. "You know this man. Do you think it is possible for him to change?"

Hiawatha paused a moment before answering. "I only know this. My mind and heart were at one time as full of the poison of hatred and revenge as his. With Dekanawida's help, I changed. My mind was wiped clean, and I turned from the darkness to the light. If it can happen to me, it can also happen with Atatarho."

"Good. Then I will go with you. We will leave in the morning."

They traveled overland by foot, the brave band of five—Okaiya and Ortekla had been sent ahead to scout and gather information. If all went well, their journey would take them from Oneidatown, at the edge of the lake of the Oneidas, to Onondaga, some thirty miles south and west. In their pouches they carried enough dried corn meal and maple sugar to sustain them for several days. Dekanawida summoned Kyree, the great eagle, who flew high above, sometimes leading the way, sometimes following.

Rim-frost covered the naked branches of the trees, making everything in the woods sparkle in the morning sun like the bright mica found in the mountains. All the colors of the rainbow seemed to glimmer on the fresh and dazzling crust of the snow—chips of red and blue and green, flashes of yellow and purple danced before their eyes. They wore snowshoes on their feet, so the walking was almost as easy as if they were treading upon grass and ground. The pure whiteness of the winter appealed to Dekanawida. Winter is an old man's season, a season of reflection, when great stories are told and retold, and the memories of the ancient ones are kept alive around the fires at night. And it is the old ones who tell the tales, who keep the past alive for the present so that it can be transmitted later to the future.

No one knew how old Dekanawida was. He would not say. Some said that he was one hundred years old. Others thought him twice that age. But he walked with the energy of a man of fifty. True, he could no longer run like a wild buck through the forest, but his limbs were still able to carry him far, and he did not tire easily. His long white hair that flowed in the wind and matched the snowflakes in its brilliance seemed out of place with the vigor of his physical strength. Only his voice seemed to grow weaker with the passing of each new moon.

Dekanawida was glad that he had the strong clear voice of Hiawatha to call forth the great ideas that they now were spreading throughout the land. Hiawatha was also growing in wisdom. He was not just a mouthpiece, an interpreter and amplifier for the ideas and plans of Dekanawida. He now had ideas of his own, and the Wampum belts and strings that he designed were unique chronicles of the councils that had been held and the treaties and agreements that had been made between the Mohawk and the Oneida. This wampum belt of Hiawatha will one day be very long, thought Dekanawida. And on it will be the record of the Great Peace, the record of the Great Law of the Longhouse. Each step they took through the snow-draped forest took them closer to fulfilling the prophecy that had been revealed to him by the Great Mysterious.

The same power that made the stone canoe glide above the river waters, the same power that called forth the great eagle at his command, the same power that allowed him to speak the language of birds was the power that would aid them in their work. This same divine power that was working through the Peacemaker, and now also through Hiawatha, would be the power that they would need to draw upon if they were to succeed in the task ahead, remaking the mind of Atatarho.

As the sun began to dip beneath the horizon, the band of ambassadors found a clearing surrounded by white pine trees, a perfect spot to build a fire and shelter themselves from the night wind. They had covered many miles that day, more than half of the journey. By this time tomorrow, they would be at Onondaga.

As Hiawatha and Odatsadeh foraged in the pine woods for dead limbs and firewood, Osinoh and his four warriors, three miles behind them, followed their large, oval tracks in the snow. They too wore snowshoes, and they had to travel slowly in order to stay far enough behind not to be seen.

"We will camp up there inside that stand of pines," said Osinoh.

"I'll search for some dead wood."

"No. No fire. We can't afford to be seen. Dig down into the snow and huddle together. Only for a few hours rest."

"A few hours?"

"They are seven and we are five. Surprise is our ally. Before the day breaks, we will spring upon them like panthers."

"We will kill them all!" said one of the warriors.

"Remember," cautioned Osinoh, "Hiawatha is mine. I will cut off his head with this knife."

"Yes. It will be as you say. None of them will see the sunrise ever again."

As Hiawatha bent over and picked up a dead branch, he thought about the last days that he had spent in the Place by the Hills. He remembered the look of triumph in Atatarho's eyes when it was announced in council that he would replace him as chieftain. Those wicked eyes surely could not have softened much. He thought about what Orios had told him—how the boy had overheard Atatarho speaking of his deal with the Seneca chief Shadahgoh, whose son had been killed that unlucky day by an arrow from his quiver. Hiawatha knew that Orios still suffered guilt and torment over the results of that fateful arrow. And he now wondered if some sorcery had not been behind this deed. How could Orios have mistaken a rabbit for a Seneca boy? Did the sorcerer have something to do with this first deed that set into motion all the other events? Hiawatha knew in his heart that Atatarho had caused the deaths of his daughters. He had wanted power for a long time. And I was the only one that blocked his path, thought Hiawatha.

And instead of vengeance this is what will come his way. He will be offered a place in the council of the League of Peace. Would he accept? It seemed very unlikely to Hiawatha that this twisted and malevolent old sorcerer would have anything to do with a brotherhood of nations whose aim was to strengthen each other through an alliance of peace. Atatarho loved war. He loved violence and revenge. But, for all his wickedness, he was not a stupid man. He knew which way the wind blew. If he saw that all of his neighbors, strong and mighty nations, had joined together and he was the only one who stood outside, he might very well see the wisdom of joining us. Tomorrow will tell, he thought.

The small warming fire flickered brightly, and the men sat cross-legged around it looking at each other over its flames as they ate their rations of dried corn and maple sugar. After such a long day of walking, this simple meal tasted like the grandest feast ever. Above the clearing, the stars shone brightly in the cold dark sky like bits of ice, like small chips of mica flashing in the heavens.

"Do you think Atatarho will hear our proposition?" asked Tekerihoken.

"No doubt he will hear it," said Odatsadeh. "He has many spies. He probably knows about it already."

"The real question is," added Hiawatha, "will he *accept* our proposition?"

"We will know soon," said Dekanawida. Overhead, the raucous caw-cawing of ravens landing in the trees behind them made them turn their heads. From out of the darkness Ortekla and Okaiya emerged and approached the fire.

"What have you learned?" asked Dekanawida.

Ortekla spoke first. "He knows that you are coming. He has his messenger-scouts too."

"How did you learn this?" asked Dekanawida.

"We listened outside of his bone-hut in the swamp," replied Okaiya. "He was speaking with two headmen."

"Go on," urged Dekanawida.

"He said that he would welcome the opportunity to see the broken-down Hiawatha again. A man who can find no better company than a mad old prophet and a silly daydreaming boy."

"*Mad* old prophet?" Dekanawida shook his head.

"I am sorry. These are not my words. I just repeat what he said."

"Yes, we know. It's all right. Continue," said Hiawatha.

Ortekla continued. "He said that your league was foolish. Blood feuds and revenge wars were the way of the people. He said that he would pretend to be interested, but what he really had in mind was to convert *us* and everyone else in the league to *his* way of thinking. He wants to hang on to the old ways. And even more, he wants to return to the days when all partook of the eating of noble warriors to absorb their strength and appease the God of War."

"Did his council members seem to agree with him?" asked the Prophet.

"Oh yes. They were enthralled. As if under a spell. He said, 'Why should we eat deer and turkey and fish, who have done no harm to anyone? People are evil and should be killed. And when they are dead, then why not eat them?'"

"This will be more difficult than I had thought." Dekanawida walked to the fire and stirred the embers. "I have a plan, but we must rest now. Lie by the fire and sleep. Tomorrow's sun comes soon."

"So Atatarho thinks he will convert us?" said Hiawatha. "It is just like him. His pride knows no bounds."

"Sleep now. We will need our strength for tomorrow's meeting."

In the middle of the night, Hiawatha rolled over towards the fire. Orios lay sleeping. So did Tekerihoken and Odatsadeh. And Ortekla and Okaiya were curled up in the fur of their bearskins by the embers trying to stay warm. But where Dekanawida had been, was only an empty bearskin at an empty place. He was gone. Hiawatha rose up on one elbow and looked around, but he saw nothing. He got up and walked around the perimeter of the campsite, but he saw no sign of the prophet. Perhaps he could not sleep, and he went into the woods to talk with the spirit-beings. Hiawatha decided that whatever the holy man was doing was important and so he wrapped himself back up in his bear skin and went back to sleep.

Dekanawida was in the woods sitting cross-legged beneath a white pine, his arms outstretched, his eyes closed. He saw through the eyes of Kyree the eagle, who was at this moment perched on top of Atatarho's hut. He watched as the sorcerer dragged the body of a man into his hut. Dekanawida could see the slices along his arms and legs, and he saw that his fingernails had been pulled out, and the top of his skull had also been torn back, and his scalp hair was missing. Atatarho dragged the body across the floor of his hut to a large cooking pot from which steam was rising. He raised his hand and looked at the stars framed by the open smoke hole.

"Great Agreskwe, God of War, please accept my humble sacrifice. In life, he was a strong man, not a coward. He faced death bravely and never cried out when the knives kissed his flesh. He had the strength of three men. Now give me his strength and let him live again through me." Sparks popped from the burning wood like fireworks. Atatarho nodded his head in thanks, then fetched a long-bladed knife from the wall of the hut.

He first broke the dead man's arm over his knee, backwards at the elbow. The sickening crack echoed in the close confines of the hut. He then proceeded to saw through the joint. When he had severed the arm, he tossed it into the pot.

Dekanawida could look no longer. He turned his gaze away from the butchery below. The League must prevent this from ever happening again. If you live under the influence of the Evil Twin and his God of War, then other men will be your enemies and you can justify any action you take against them, including torture and yes, even cannibalism. But, if your way of thinking is the opposite, that all men are your brothers, then acts like this one become unthinkable. He lifted his eyes to the sky and saw the beauty of the stars and the waxing moon shining down on creation. The Great Spirit gave them a beautiful home to live in. The earth with her trees and plants and animals was beautiful, the sky was beautiful, but man was not beautiful. Not if he did these acts against his fellow man. All other creatures lived in harmony with their own kind. Something had gone wrong. And it was his life's work to see that the harmony that once existed between men would return. And it must start here, now, with Atatarho.

Dekanawida looked down the hole again through the eyes of Kyree and saw that the sorcerer had finished his grisly work. He waited patiently for Atatarho to gaze down into the pot. After a while, the sorcerer fetched some herbs and an elm-bark bowl from the wall. He walked over to the pot and threw the herbs into the steaming water. As he gazed into the water, he saw a face emerge, the face of Dekanawida. He jumped back from the pot and then looked again, and there, looking back at him, was the same face.

"Who is this looking up at me from the bottom of the pot?" He ran outside and looked around his hut, and then looked up on top to the smoke-hole, to see who was playing this trick on him. No one was there. He looked up and saw Kyree who had flown up to the highest limb on the nearest tree. Kyree stared at him with glowing eyes and Atatarho ran inside to get his bow and arrow, but when he returned, Kyree was nowhere in sight.

He cautiously walked back into his hut and looked again into the water. Once again, he did not see his own reflection, his own face with a head of hair full of snakes, but instead he saw the serene countenance of Dekanawida. The divination of spirits from water was a frequent and powerful practice among shamans and sorcerers at this time. Atatarho himself had seen the future of faraway events by gazing into a pot of holy water. Atatarho stared at the reflection that looked back at him in the water and tried to decipher the message. He felt a warm wave of emotion come over him.

"I have changed somehow," he said to himself. "Is this the way that I look now? My face is not misshapen and the snakes that writhe on my head are no longer there."

He touched the top of his head and the snakes were still there. "This reflection staring back at me must be me as I could be." The snakes started hissing. "Or perhaps some sorcerer is trying to steal my soul." The snakes struck out at Dekanawida's face.

Now convinced of the latter, Atatarho grabbed the pot with

both hands and dragged it outside. The heat on the bottom melted the snow as he slid it away from the hut down a small steep incline and tipped it over. Dekanawida watched from above as the contents of the pot spewed and scattered over the ground, sending coils of steam high up into the night air. As Atatarho gazed at the wretched soup, he recalled in his mind's eye the strange face in the water, the face on the bottom of the pot that looked back up at him. And horror shook his soul to the depths of his being. He had suddenly lost his appetite for human flesh.

Kyree screamed out loudly in the trees above him. The snakes in his hair reared up and thrust their tongues out in agitation. "What does it all mean?" he thought. And for the first time since he could remember, he felt a panic seize him in the chest, and a cold fear gripped his heart.

Chapter Three

Osinoh and the four Onondaga warriors crept through the darkness of the pine forest that surrounded the clearing where Hiawatha and his companions lay sleeping. A smile played across his lips. Dawn was only a few minutes away, and soon the black sky would lighten to gray on the eastern horizon. He stopped and pointed down through the low-hanging boughs.

"There they are," he whispered. The warriors nodded and fitted arrows into their bowstrings. Osinoh jumped as someone in the clearing coughed. Then, through the charcoal-gray air, becoming lighter every minute, he could see one of the party stand up and move toward them. Osinoh motioned to his warriors to stay steady. The man kept coming closer and closer, and then stopped. They could see him now making water on the snow. Someone else sat up and yawned, stretching his limbs.

One of the Onondaga could wait no longer. He pulled his bowstring back to his cheek and let his arrow fly. It found its mark in the heart of Ortekla, who had just finished urinating. He dropped dead instantly without making a sound.

"Fool!" cried Osinoh, for now their ambush had been spoiled, given away too soon, the element of total surprise undone.

Odatsadeh, who had just risen, saw Ortekla fall, and shouted: "Ambush! We are attacked!" He rolled over and fumbled for his bow and quiver of arrows. Hiawatha, Tekerihoken, Orios, and Okaiya all leaped up peering through the dim light of pre-dawn, looking for the attackers. War screams came from the pine trees and two warriors rushed down the slope, one brandishing a war club above his head, the other pulling back his bowstring to let another arrow fly. The arrow whizzed past Tekerihoken's ear, and the Mohawk chief dropped to his knees looking for his war club. Odatsadeh let fly an arrow of his own and it quickly buried itself into the chest of the Onondaga archer.

The warrior with the club leaped on Hiawatha, but Hiawatha was ready for him, grabbing him by the arms, throwing him over his head, and tumbling backwards with him in the snow. They both rolled over to face each other on hands and knees and sprung back at each other like panthers. Each held the other's arms in a fierce struggle of strength and will. Osinoh saw his opportunity now and ran toward the wrestling pair, rolling over and over in the powdered snow that flew everywhere as the sun began to send out blood-red fingers across the horizon. He fitted a dart into his blowgun and looked for an opening in the fierce hand-to-hand struggle.

The two other Onondagas faced off with Tekerihoken, Odatsadeh, and Okaiya. The five men circled each other warily, knives, clubs, and tomahawks in their hands. Orios rushed to help Hiawatha, who was still struggling with his opponent, trying to keep his back away from Osinoh, who had his blowgun to his lips, ready to send a dart at just the right moment.

"Osinoh! What is this treachery?" Taken aback, Osinoh lowered the blowgun slightly as Orios rushed at him. Just then, Hiawatha broke the grip of the Onondaga warrior and swung free. Osinoh inhaled deeply, then blew as hard as he could on the mouthpiece of his weapon. In a split second the dart was speeding toward Hiawatha's chest, but Orios leaped directly into the path of the deadly missile. The dart found its mark in Orios' left shoulder instead of Hiawatha's heart. Before Osinoh could load another dart in the blowgun, Hiawatha was on top of him. He beat him to the ground with his fists, knocking him senseless. The warrior Hiawatha had been wrestling with was about to bring his war club down onto his head when an arrow from Odatsadeh's bow sent him to the otherworld.

Tekerihoken and Okaiya were still circling the other two Onondagas, but when they saw their leader down on the ground, his hands now bound behind him, they realized the hopelessness of their situation. They turned and ran. Odatsadeh nocked another arrow onto his bowstring and pulled it back to his right cheek.

"Stop!" shouted Hiawatha. "Let them go."

Odatsadeh lowered his bow and shook his head. "I could have dropped them both."

"Enough blood has been shed today."

Hiawatha suddenly turned and ran back to the fallen Orios who lay bleeding on the snow. He gently lifted his head up. "You saved my life. By giving up your own." He pulled the dart out of Orios' shoulder and examined the tip. "Poisoned!"

Orios groaned and opened his eyes. "I am dying, Hiawatha."

"Don't talk. Odatsadeh! Tekerihoken! Do you have any healing herbs?"

Tekerihoken rushed over to Hiawatha's side. "No, Hiawatha,"

"I have none either," said Odatsadeh.

"Where is Dekanawida?"

"I am here." Dekanawida emerged from the snow-laden boughs of the pine and hemlock trees and entered the clearing.

"Orios is dying. A poisoned dart."

Dekanawida knelt by Orios' side and placed his hands on the wound. He closed his eyes and chanted softly. The prayer he chanted was in a language that none present had ever heard. A violet-white light emanated from Dekanawida's face and hands, and then spread all over his body and over Orios. They both were glowing with a light that seemed to come from another dimension. And then the light changed to gold. Bright gold light shone forth from the holy man and the stricken Orios. It rivaled the now-risen sun in its brightness. It became so bright that Hiawatha, Tekerihoken, Odatsadeh, and Okaiya had to shield their eyes with their hands.

And then the light faded away. The four men dropped their hands and opened their eyes. The Peacemaker took his hands away from Orios' shoulder, and the wound seemed to have dried up. All that remained was a cauterized scar.

Orios opened his eyes. "Dekanawida! Are we dead? Is this the land of the Spirit Beings?"

"No, my son. We are all here in the land of the living. You too."

The four men looked at each other in wonder. No one said anything. What could one say? No one wanted to break the spell that hovered over them.

Dekanawida looked at Osinoh, whose legs and hands were bound. "Who is your captive?" Osinoh stared back. He too was in awe of what had just taken place. What kind of man was this, he thought.

"Atatarho's nephew." Hiawatha explained what had happened.

"What will you do with him?" asked Dekanawida.

"I don't know."

"He should be punished," said Tekerihoken. "Ortekla is dead. He must pay for this offense."

"Yes," agreed Okaiya. "He must die to avenge our friend."

"Have you forgotten so soon what I have taught you?"

"But this boy was murdered! Is no one to be held accountable? In this new world of yours is no one to pay for their misdeeds?"

"No. Wrongdoing will not go unpunished. But let us try to put into practice now the great lesson of forgiveness."

"What will you have us do?" Hiawatha looked at his mentor, his teacher, his spiritual father.

"We will do first to the nephew what we will later do to the uncle." Dekanawida bent over and put his hand on Osinoh's head. "We will heal his mind."

After they buried Ortekla and the two warriors, they offered up tobacco to the Great Spirit, praying that their journeys along the Strawberry Path to the Land of the Spirit Beings would be quick and easy ones. Dekanawida and Hiawatha then held a condolence ceremony for Osinoh. Tekerihoken, Okaiya, Odatsadeh, and Orios were both the mourners and the clear-minded. They repeated the prayer-chant that Dekanawida and Hiawatha recited to unblock the eyes, the ears, and the throat of Osinoh so that he could once again see the light that darkness had obscured, so that he could hear the beauty of the world all around him, and so that he could speak the words of forgiveness and truth.

Osinoh was greatly moved by the ceremony, and he wept. He thought of Sovana lying on her funeral bier, a victim of his uncle's poison. She was the only thing he had ever truly wanted in his entire life, and his uncle had poisoned her. Why? His uncle said that it was an unfortunate accident, an interaction with some other herbs she may have taken, but for the first time in his life, he did not believe his uncle. So why did he still obey his uncle's every command?

Since the burial of the dead, their funeral ceremonies, and the remaking of Osinoh's mind had taken up the greater portion of the day, Hiawatha decided to spend the night at this same spot before facing Atatarho.

After eating their frugal supper of corn meal and maple sugar, they banked the coals of the small sleeping fires, and they lay down, curled up in their bearskins, drifting off to sleep. Hiawatha's mind was full of apprehension for what they would face tomorrow. Something about the sudden conversion of Osinoh to the new way of thinking troubled him. Was it this easy? Would his old enemy, Atatarho, be so easily converted? He was puzzled by the events of the day. Dekanawida was a great prophet and a wise seer. He did not doubt that. The words of the ritual were strong medicine, and he knew in his heart that they contained the power to change the darkest of hearts. But Osinoh seemed to give himself over too easily, too quickly. His head and his heart filled with these nagging thoughts, Hiawatha finally drifted off into a shallow, uneasy sleep.

When they awoke in the morning, covered in a blanket of newly fallen snow, Osinoh was gone. Snow had covered over any tracks that he might have left, so they did not know in what direction he ran. Hiawatha looked at Dekanawida, searching his face for some explanation. The Peacemaker shrugged his shoulders in resignation. These things happen, he seemed to say.

"I'm not surprised," said Odatsadeh.

"No doubt we'll soon see him by his uncle's side," said Tekerihoken.

"Okaiya," said the Peacemaker, "run ahead and announce our visit to Onondaga. Even though Atatarho already knows a party approaches, we will adhere to protocol and have our visit formally announced."

Okaiya quickly gathered together his gear and took off running, his snowshoes throwing up great sheets of powder behind him. Following him high in the sky was Kyree, his dark wings and golden beak flashing through the morning's brightness.

Hiawatha chanted a prayer of thanksgiving to the Great Spirit, the life-giver, the mysterious force behind all living things. He raised his arms to the sky and faced the rising sun.

> "Oh Great Spirit of the earth, of the sky, and of the
> waters, We thank you for giving us another day.
> We thank you for the deer and the birds of the forest,
> We thank you for the sun and the moon in the sky,
> We thank you for the clear waters of the rivers and lakes,
> We thank you for the fish that love them
> and that give themselves to us to sustain our lives.

For all things that crawl and walk and fly
and swim upon the back of Turtle Island,
we thank you.

Bless our journey for peace
And bless our mission this day."

"A fine prayer, Hiawatha," said Odatsadeh. The Oneida chief was not a holy man, but he had a deep reverence for the earth and all its creatures, and the dawn blessing and thanksgiving chant had touched his heart.

"Thank you, my friend. We have important work to carry out this day, and so we have need of all the divine assistance we can summon forth."

"Well spoken," said Tekerihoken.

They packed their belongings into their fawnskin pouches, put on their snowshoes, shook the snow from their bearskin robes, flung them over their shoulders, and followed the running footprints of Okaiya and the high, gliding path of Kyree.

As they walked steadily onward, Hiawatha turned to Dekanawida, and asked him in a low voice, so that no one else could hear, "Where did you disappear to last night?"

Dekanawida looked at Hiawatha and said in his whisper of a voice, "I had some errands to run."

"Errands?"

"Yes. The work that I did last night will make the way smoother when we deal with Atatarho."

"Dekanawida, I must tell you this: The Great Wampum Belt of Peace will not be finished."

"It is not finished now, certainly. We have three more mighty nations to convince."

"No. That is not what I mean. We cannot finish it because we have no more shells to make it with." Hiawatha showed him the fawnskin pouch that the blue and white quahog shells were kept in. He turned it upside down and inside out. "We have used them all, and the belt is not finished."

Dekanawida thought for a while. "I know of a small lake which is not far out of our way. On the bottom of this lake you will find all the shells you will need to finish the wampum belt." He looked all around him, then pointed in a direction more westerly, but still heading south towards Onondaga. "We will go this way." Dekanawida led the band across a broad field that, in the summer, is covered with wild flowers and running strawberries, and the others followed, making good time in their snowshoes.

After walking at a brisk pace for two hours, across fields and through pine woods, the band of seekers came to the edge of a small lake that was frozen around the edges, but whose central surface was crystal clear. The blue sky and white clouds could be seen on the mirrored surface, and on that smooth and sparkling surface floated a large number of ducks of all species. Many of these species of ducks were familiar to the men, like the green-headed mallards with their brown-colored mates. Some, however, no one had ever seen before.

"What strange and lovely ducks," said Orios, pointing to the ones on the outermost edge of the lake. "I have never seen ducks with golden heads and purple beaks. Their eyes flash like mica and their red feathers shine like hematite. What kind of ducks are they?"

"You are right, Orios. They are not ordinary ducks."

"I have been to this country before," remarked Odatsadeh. "But I don't recall this lake. I too have never seen birds such as these. Do you have these birds in the country of the Mohawk?"

"Not that I have noticed. They are extraordinary," answered Tekerihoken.

"These are spirit ducks from the other world and they possess great power," said Dekanawida.

"Where are the shells?" asked Hiawatha.

"Watch and see." The Peacemaker raised his staff high into

the air and made three circles with it. He chanted prayers in the language that only he and a few others could speak, the language of bird spirits, the winged messengers of the Great Mysterious. The wind picked up from across the lake, sending snow flying into their faces, and the golden ducks began speaking the same words that Dekanawida chanted. Only the birds and he knew their meaning. The lake seemed to whirl, to move in a counterclockwise direction. And the ducks began to swim in the opposite direction. Slowly at first, then faster and faster as the lake began to spin faster in the other direction. Soon the birds in the middle of the lake, the common ones that the men knew, flapped their wings and lifted up into the air. They flew upwards in unison and made for the south. Then the golden ducks, the spirit ducks, lifted up from the surface, flying in the opposite direction, and with them they took all of the water from the central region of the lake. It looked like they held the ends of glistening, water-colored deerskins in their beaks and the water held together as if it were a different, more solid element, and when they had flown away, the bottom of the lake bed was dry.

"There are your shells, Hiawatha," said Dekanawida. He pointed with his staff to the middle of the lake, which was now dry, and to the bottom, which was littered with pure white and blue shells that sparkled radiantly in the sun.

Hiawatha ran down to the lake and walked out to the middle; he bent over and gathered up the shells. Orios took up his flute and played a hymn to the beauty and mystery of nature and the spirit world. When the natural world and the spirit world are brought together by a holy man like Dekanawida, then one sees and feels the power and the majesty of creation, the miracle of life at its fullest. All of this he tried to put into the song that he composed and played to commemorate this moment. The notes he struck were haunting and intense, full of the anguish and bliss that is the true essence of the soul of nature. For nature has a soul, just as human beings do. All things that live have an eternal spirit in them, a spirit-force that compels them to continue on and on into the generations and never to die. It is our mother the earth's way of keeping us alive. Because, if there were no more trees and no more lakes and no more birds or fish, if there were no more clean air to breathe, then all of life would cease to exist.

Odatsadeh and Tekerihoken stood in awe of the great powers of the Peacemaker and of the wonders of the world that they lived in. When things like this can happen, how can there be any other thought but for peace and for the betterment of the world to come? They watched Hiawatha gathering up the glistening shells from the bottom of what had once been a lake and they shook their heads in amazement.

"Dekanawida, how is it you can work such wonders?" Odatsadeh asked. Tekerihoken had known the Peacemaker longer and had often seen evidence of his powers. So he simply stood silently by and waited to hear the answer.

"I do nothing," replied the prophet. "The Great Mysterious does it all. All these things are happening around you all the time. But we, the human beings, are too blind to see them. I simply reveal the workings, the daily miracles of the Great Mystery to human sight." Dekanawida shrugged his shoulders as if that was all that there was to it. Nothing more. Pay attention, and you too will see the miraculous.

Hiawatha returned to the bank of the lake with his fawn-skin pouch full and overflowing with pure white and purple shells. "Look! These will make the belt complete. I have never seen such beautiful shells." He showed them to the men and smiled at Orios, who stopped playing to admire them. The wind began to pick up again, and they could hear ducks in the distance coming closer and closer.

"Let us continue on our journey, now, my friends," said Dekanawida. "The ducks will bring back the lake, and all will be as it once was."

As they approached the palisade walls of Onondaga, powerful feelings of nostalgia mixed with anxiety swept over Hiawatha. They were crossing the fields where his daughters were murdered by Seneca arrows. The dried stalks of dead corn looked like stubble on a white face, and the few remaining stalks of withered sunflowers that had not been taken in stood hunched over like forlorn old widows praying to the ghosts of their ancestors. A deathly, shroud-like pall hung over the fields and over the town behind the high stockade walls. These dismal sights only added to the emotions that made Hiawatha's heart pound like a water drum, and he thought it might burst through the walls of his chest and scream out his fear and his horror.

Dekanawida sensed Hiawatha's panic and put his arm around his shoulders. "Be strong; be brave," he said. "This is the moment we have worked day and night for. All of your life leads now up to this moment, this meeting with Atatarho. You must swallow all fear. You must destroy all hatred within your soul. For you are now going to do the greatest deed of your life. Hiawatha, my son, today you are going to forgive your enemy, and pledge your kinship and your undying brotherhood to this man who has wronged you."

Hiawatha swallowed hard. His mouth was dry and he could find no words with which to speak. Dekanawida placed his left hand on Hiawatha's abdomen. "Breathe from down here. Breathe deeply and let me feel your breath push out my hand away from your stomach." Hiawatha breathed in the air slowly and deeply. And as he did so, the beating of his heart became slower and the fear subsided.

"Breath is life. Fear is death. Breathe deeply of the life-force around you, and you will never walk in the pathways of fear."

As they drew near the gates of the walled town, two messengers came out and spoke the traditional greeting. "Who are you? And where are you going?"

Hiawatha took a long, deep breath, exhaled slowly, then replied in a clear and strong voice, "I am Hiawatha the Mohawk, formerly chieftain of Onondaga, now part of an embassy of peace. Here is Dekanawida, the prophet, also called Peacemaker. In our embassy are the great Mohawk Sachem Tekerihoken, and the great Oneida chieftain Odatsadeh. Some in this town may recall Orios, formerly Onondaga and now Mohawk. All of us are members of the Great League of Peace. We are here to speak with Atatarho."

The two messengers nodded, and one of them said, "Follow us. Atatarho has been expecting you." They led the party through the familiar gates and across the avenues of longhouses. There was no one out except warriors standing by each longhouse. Atatarho had ordered everyone to stay inside their longhouses. He did not want them to see Hiawatha.

Hiawatha was shocked to see how dismal the place looked. Snowdrifts hugged the walls of many of the longhouses. There seemed to be no attempt to clear the snow from paths that lead from one house to another. There were holes in many of the longhouse walls, and filth littered the snow-bound streets of the village grounds. In many longhouses, no fire seemed to issue forth from the smoke holes, and in most, only one or two feeble streams of smoke wafted lazily from the roofs. Hiawatha involuntarily shivered, thinking how cold the people inside them must be, huddled beneath hides and bearskin robes.

They passed the longhouse of Makahwah, and it looked the most run-down of all. Was she inside? Was she still alive? This was once his home, the place where he slept and played with his daughters, where he ate with his family, where, in happier times, he made love to his wife. It all seemed now as if these events took place in a former lifetime, and that they happened to someone else. This shabby, broken down longhouse with rude patches covering rotting bark, and snow threatening to collapse the roof, surely could not have been where he had lived and loved and led his people.

Off to his right, he saw the place where he and his boyhood friends had played the game of snow-snake, hurling long hickory spears down a narrow chute of ice to see whose "snake" could go the farthest. He remembered how Kewahtawa had taught him how to hold the snake properly so that it would skim the ice chute without hitting the sides. He had not thought of this in a long time. The place of the chute stood empty now. No boys were outside playing the game he had loved in his youth; in fact, no children could be seen anywhere. He heard a child crying from inside one of the longhouses and a dog barked somewhere off in the distance. But aside from that, the snowbound village was silent and still.

The messengers opened the door to the council house, which was surrounded by warriors. None of them would look him in the eye. His heart began to pound again as they walked into the dim light of the interior, the familiar place that Hiawatha had many times held council in, where he sat with the deer antlers on his head and made decisions concerning the welfare of his people. The messengers took them each by the arm, according to the approved protocol, and sat them down on the side of the small, smoky fire that was opposite from where the shadow of a man stood with his back to them. No one else was in the room. Dekanawida sat in the middle, then Hiawatha to his right, and beside him, Odatsadeh. Tekerihoken was seated to Dekanawida's left, with Orios beside him. No one spoke for what seemed an eternity. The sorcerer still stood in the shadows with his back to them.

"Bring more firewood," commanded the voice from the other side of the room. The messengers went outside and returned shortly with firewood which they heaped upon the fire. The flames shot up and lit up all the corners of the council house. Atatarho turned and glared at Orios. His face was a scowling mask, and the snakes on his head reared and hissed, flicking their tongues out continually to identify each new scent in the room. Orios instinctively jerked backwards as if someone had struck him across the face. The sight of the malevolent sorcerer was worse than he remembered. The snakes hissed in his direction.

"I know you. You are that useless boy who does nothing but skulk about playing tunes on a wooden flute. You spied on me once. Are you here to spy on me again?"

Orios was so frightened that he could not speak, so Hiawatha spoke for him. "No one is here to spy on you. We are here to offer you the greatest gift that can be given. We are here to offer you our friendship and our brotherhood."

"Friendship? Brotherhood? What kind of trick is this?" Atatarho threw down his hand toward the fire and the flames exploded upward, shooting up bright purple and green tongues of flame that licked the rafters of the house. He turned his piercing gaze to Hiawatha. "You expect me to believe that you bear me no ill will? You must take me for a fool!"

Just then an eagle screamed, sounding as if it were in the same room with the men. It was the same eagle cry that Atatarho heard in his hut two nights ago—it brought back the fear and terror that gripped his heart when he tipped over the pot on the hillside. He turned his head and saw a great eagle's head on the shoulders of the man who sat to Hiawatha's left. The eagle screamed again and its feathers and golden eyes slowly dissolved into the face of a man, a bright and luminous face, the face that he had seen looking back at him from the bottom of the pot! He covered his eyes with both hands. The snakes on his head reared up and hissed, and roiled, and bit one another, striking out at the air in front of them and at Atatarho's own hands.

"I am Dekanawida," said the Peacemaker in a whisper of a voice, so low that it seemed as if no one could hear it, but they all heard it clearly, especially the Onondaga shaman. "Sit down now, and we will talk." Atatarho obeyed the voice and sat down heavily, crossing his legs beneath him. He took his hands away from his face and looked again upon the face of Dekanawida.

The Peacemaker turned to Hiawatha and nodded to him to begin. "It is true that in the past you have done me harm. But that is in the past. My heart is healed and my mind is clear. I forgive you and offer you the bond of my friendship."

Atatarho shook his head in disbelief. Hiawatha continued. "What I offer you, however, is something far greater than the bond of my friendship. What I offer you now is the bond of the friendship of the Mohawk nation."

Hiawatha looked at Tekerihoken who nodded and said, "It is so. I speak for my people who are united, whose longhouses now are all as one. We pledge our bond. We wish to be brothers with the Onondaga, not enemies." He smiled as he gazed deeply into Atatarho's eyes.

Hiawatha continued. "We offer you now not only the bond of our friendship and the friendship of the mighty Mohawk nation, but also the bond of friendship with your neighbors, the Oneida, the great Granite People."

"It is as Hiawatha says. I, Odatsadeh, chief of the Oneida nation, pledge the bond of friendship to the Onondaga people."

"And soon enough, we will offer you the pledge of the Cayuga and the Seneca," said Hiawatha.

Atatarho rose to his feet. "I am no boy easily tricked. I have seen pledges and bonds and treaties come and go like the shifting winds. Talk of friendship falls easily off the tongue. How is this pledge of yours any different from those that failed in the past?"

"Atatarho speaks wisely," said Hiawatha. "Let me try to explain. We five nations share the same customs, the same clans, and the same beliefs. But we continually wound each other. Each nation makes the other weak. Our League of Peace will make all of the nations strong. If the Huron or the Susquehannock attack the Onondaga, they are not simply attacking the Onondaga. They attack all five nations."

Hiawatha paused and pulled five arrows from his fox-skin quiver. "Here are five arrows. One arrow for each of the Haudenosaunee nations. If I bundle them together so, and try to break them over my knee, I cannot." Hiawatha placed one arrow over his knee and snapped it like a twig. "Alone and broken. Destroyed utterly.

This fate awaits the nations now who fight themselves and their enemies. We must break this cycle now, so that we stand firm in our alliance not to make war on each other, and to make war only on those who attack the League.

"If we do not do so, then we will destroy each other through the endless cycle of blood feuds, and our children's children will suffer the torments of a life with no hope. If we continue these acts, there may be no children's children. And then who will tend our mother, the earth? We have been given many great gifts from the Good Twin, the grandson of Sky Woman. We must not throw these gifts into the fire or bury them in a pit. We must band together as one people and bury the weapons that we use to make war on each other into a great pit that has no bottom. And then plant the Tree of Peace above it."

Atatarho sat motionless and stared at the fire. He could feel Dekanawida's gaze burning inside him. All the hurt and pain, both physical and emotional, from his long-forgotten youth welled up inside him, overwhelming him and threatening to unbalance the carefully propped up hatred and anger that kept his mind and his soul together. He shifted his gaze from the fire and looked into Dekanawida's eyes, and he felt for the first time that someone cared about him. He felt the darkness that was his constant companion begin to fade into something lighter, something that had been touched by the first rays of the sun. He felt the bitterness inside him start to melt away like ice on the edges of a river's bank at the end of winter.

He filled a long-stemmed, red-stone pipe with tobacco, lit it from the fire, and smoked, letting the smoke rise up to the rafters. He then passed the pipe to Hiawatha. "What you say is strong and makes much sense, but it goes against everything I have seen in the past. I cannot believe that someone will not turn on me." The snakes on his head started to roil and coil themselves around each other.

Atatarho's eyes suddenly took on the yellow glow and slit pupils of the snake's eyes, the snakes that were lashing their black, forked tongues out at the air, all the while hissing and spitting. "Say I give my bond to this League of yours. What is to keep you from banding together against me? What is to keep you from attacking me while my guard is down and destroying me so that you can become stronger?"

"Trust," replied Hiawatha.

"Trust?" hissed Atatarho. "Why should I trust you? You have every reason to want revenge from me. Perhaps this is simply a ruse, a scheme to catch me unawares and then destroy me."

Dekanawida spoke in a soothing voice. "Your mind is sick. It is twisted by the snakes of evil-thinking. With these snakes in your hair, you cannot tell good intentions from bad ones. We will now comb the snakes from your hair."

Dekanawida produced a hair comb from inside of his bearskin robe. It was a wide bone comb with long teeth and two intertwined snakes carved on top of the horizontal handle. He handed the comb to Hiawatha. "Rise, Hiawatha, and comb straight this man's mind."

The comb seemed to jump from the Peacemaker's hand and into Hiawatha's. Atatarho took two steps backward, the snakes leaping and hissing on his head. Dekanawida raised his eagle-claw staff and pointed it toward the sorcerer, and, as he did so, some power seemed to grab Atatarho by the upper arms and hold him in place. He could neither move his arms up nor move them down.

Hiawatha slowly walked around the fire to where Atatarho, the man who had done such harm to him in the past, stood frozen, motionless. His eyes darted about in fear, and the snakes reared and hissed, striking out more furiously than ever before.

Orios and Tekerihoken sat in their places, too stunned to move or to make any noise at all. Odatsadeh had to force himself to breathe, while Dekanawida held Atatarho in place by sheer force of will. Hiawatha extended his arm and moved the comb to within an inch of the snakes, who reared back when the two carved snakes on the comb came alive and jumped off the handle and onto Atatarho's head. They twisted and twined and wrestled with the snakes on the sorcerer's head, subduing them and straightening them.

"Now!" said Dekanawida.

And Hiawatha brought the comb down into Atatarho's hair, and pulled it through, and with the first pass through his hair, two snakes were caught in the teeth of the comb. Hiawatha pulled them out and flung them into the fire. They made a ghastly noise of hissing and exploding gases, a green and yellow light expanded from the flames that reached now up to the rafters, filling the whole house with a dreadful sulfuric smell. Atatarho screamed loud and high as if someone had pulled out one of his fingernails.

As Hiawatha brought the comb down again and again, more snakes became tangled in the comb and were flung into the fire, exploding and hissing. Atatarho's eyes darted about and sweat dripped from his face and chest.

As the snakes were pulled from the old sorcerer's hair and flung into the fire to be sent back into the spirit world where they belonged, Atatarho seemed to be getting younger. His body was becoming straighter, no longer twisted and misshapen as before. His eyes were losing their yellow cast, and the deep furrows that lined his face and his brow were smoothing out now.

Two more snakes remained in Atatarho's hair, and these were the most stubborn. They reared back and struck out at Hiawatha, who ducked aside just in time to miss their venomous bite. Hiawatha brought the comb down hard upon the top of these two demons, saying, "You twisted creatures who poison the mind, I make you straight with this comb. I send you back to your pit. With this comb, I comb straight the mind of this man who has lived too long under your spell. He created you from the poison of his soul, and now I cast you out!"

The snakes on the handle of the comb reared up and leaped upon the snakes in the sorcerer's hair. They wrestled and twisted and hissed and entwined; they bit and struck out at each other. All the while this battle was taking place, Atatarho's mouth remained open in a soundless cry, a look of horror stamped on his face, a face that was changing before everyone's eyes.

"Out! Now!" Hiawatha pulled the comb hard through Atatarho's hair and yanked the twin demons out, casting them into the flames that exploded up in a white and yellow gaseous ball that emitted horrible shrieks of pain as if someone was suffering the most awful tortures ever devised. From the ball of gases that now reached halfway up to the ceiling, a face suddenly and momentarily appeared. It was the face of Atatarho with his yellow eyes and his hair full of snakes, jaws wide open and fangs dripping blood. Fire shot out of the snakes' mouths, and in that fire multiple images of Atatarho's old face shimmered and glared.

And then it was gone. Only smoke and a smell of sulfur remained. Atatarho, his hair combed free of the snakes, his body untwisted, his face made straighter, fell backwards upon the ground, and shook violently for three minutes. Then he fell into a deep sleep.

Chapter Four

Inside the Turtle Clan longhouse, Makahwah bent over a pot of old corn porridge she was stirring. Her one good eye wandered up to the cross beam in the center of the house where the clan totem, the great turtle shell, used to hang. Her thoughts traveled back to the days when Hiawatha was chief and the laughing voices of her granddaughters filled the longhouse. A heavy sadness filled her heart as she remembered how little Tiwi would watch her cook deer stew and ask her questions about why things were the way they were. She no longer knew the answer to these questions.

A hand on her shoulder broke the spell of her reverie, and she looked up to see the deeply lined face of Kewahtawa smiling over her. "It has come to pass, old friend," he said. "My dream of long ago has come to pass. Dekanawida and Hiawatha are here. People say that they have converted Atatarho to the way of peace."

"Can it really be?" said Makahwah. Her voice rose in pitch with a new excitement that she had not felt for years. "Are they really here? I am not dreaming this?"

"No, they are here. Hiawatha is here. Orios is here. And the holy man I dreamed of is here. So in a way it is a dream, a dream come true. There is to be what they are calling a Ceremony of Condolence, a ceremony of healing for the whole village tonight."

That night the people gathered together in the Grand Council House. Hiawatha saw many faces he recognized and greeted them all with kindness and love. He clasped hands with Honowe and Tonesah, the two warriors who were with him when he brought back Seneca prisoners to Onondaga. The thought of what he did then saddened him.

His spirits were lifted when he saw his old mentor, Kewahtawa, and his life-long friend, Teom. They embraced, and tears of joy mixed with feelings of regret welled up in their eyes. But it was the sight of Makahwah, the mother of his gone wife and grandmother of his gone daughters that moved him the most. At first he did not recognize her. Teom pointed her out to him. He had not seen her since he had left the village, and he was shocked at how frail she looked now compared to the days when she ran the clan as a strong matriarch. She had lost much weight and had to walk with the aid of a long, forked stick propped under one arm. The stroke had left half her face paralyzed, and her iron-gray hair had turned completely white from the shock of her attack and the subsequent illness. He hugged her and she hugged him back so hard that it seemed she could not let go. Tears streamed down her weathered face, marked with deep lines of sorrow and pain.

"I have returned to you, Mother," he said.

"How often I have prayed to the Great Spirit for this day, Hiawatha. And now you are here. You must never leave us again."

Orios' flute that night never sounded as soulful or as sweet, full of the mournful notes that complemented the wiping away of the tears, the unblocking of the throat, and the wiping away of the blood. So much blood. The purpose of the ceremony was to heal the wounds of the people of the town who had lived for so long under the tyranny of blood feuds and the tyranny of the snake-haired sorcerer.

It also was held to requicken Atatarho, to send the old wicked man to the otherworld and change his powers of darkness to powers of light, then give him a new life with a new title, that of

Tadodaho, the Firekeeper and Spiritual Leader of the One United Longhouse. It was held to open his ears so he could hear the message of Peace, the message of the Great Law of the Longhouse; to open his eyes to the beauty of the world all around him, to shut out the darkness and to open him up to the light; to unblock his throat so he could speak words of truth, words of health and respect. And it was held to purify his mind, to make him clear-minded and to fill him with the one quality necessary to be a Sachem of the League: right-mindedness.

Hiawatha led Makahwah and Kewahtawa to places of special honor on either side of Dekanawida. It was, after all, the prophetic dream of Kewahtawa long ago at the Feast of Dreams that began the journey that led to this moment. Makahwah stopped and embraced Orios, tears streaming down her cheeks. As she walked to the front, the young song-maker played his flute especially for her.

Tekerihoken led Atatarho to the condolence place in front of the fire, and the members of his village followed behind him. Hiawatha explained the Great League of Peace to the assembled members of the village, who were happy once again to hear the restored man who used to wear the antlers and hold high council when times were better and their storehouses were full.

After the white doeskins and the wampum strings had been passed over Atatarho's eyes and ears and throat, after the clear-minded ones and the mourners had sung the songs as Dekanawida and Hiawatha had shown them, Hiawatha handed the wampum strings to the former chief, saying, "Now your eyes have been wiped clean so you may see the truth. Now your ears have been wiped clean so that wisdom and the words of your people can enter them. Now your throat has been made clean so that you can speak truth to your people. We give these strings of wampum as a record to the people of this town that you are not the man that you once were. They will prop up your minds and the minds of your children to come, the unborn whose children's children will remember this day and will tell the story of these events around the winter fires for all times to come.

"And now we install you as the new chief, with a new name and a clean mind, a chief called Tadodaho, who we will ask this night before his people to join us as a Sachem in the Great League of Peace, the Great League of the United Longhouses, and to give his pledge as assurance. We have lifted up your mind, and we ask now that you show us your face."

Atatarho stood up and turned to face the crowd. He smoothed his new sleek hair with his hands and touched his rejuvenated face with his fingertips. "The old Atatarho is dead! No longer do I have the snakes growing from my mind. The Peacemaker has shown me a new way. I am a new man." Shouts of approval and cheers rang throughout the winter night around the blazing fire.

He signaled for silence and turned to Dekanawida. "But before we agree to join, we need some further assurance, some further proof of the merits of this new League of Peace. You spoke of a Great Law. Tell us about it so we may fully understand."

The Prophet stood up and moved closer to the crowd. "Tadodaho is a great man who knows much of the laws of the forest. But there is a greater law, and that law is this: We must live in peace and harmony with each other and with nature here on the back of the Great Turtle. All the animals of the forest know this law, all the animals except for human beings. The deer does not kill his brother deer. The bear does not scalp or eat his brother bear, even though they may live on different sides of the river. This is why we have formed the League of Peace.

"Our brothers who live scattered throughout the forests and along the lakes and rivers of Turtle Island have agreed to abandon their feuds and their revenge wars, and they have agreed to reform their minds and unite together. Listen now to the words of your brothers." Dekanawida walked over and whispered to Tekerihoken.

The Mohawk Sachem cleared his throat and moved forward. "I am not the skilled orator that Hiawatha is. I am not the holy man that Dekanawida is. But the words of Hiawatha and the Peacemaker entered into my heart and into the hearts of my people. I will try to speak for them. My people of the Mohawk nation have joined the new League of Peace. We have put away revenge and deceit from our minds so that our new minds will be healthy. Peace can only spring from a healthy mind, one that is as clear-sighted as the eagle and one that is as pure as the mind of our mother, the earth. When trouble happens, or an emergency occurs, we have agreed to meet together to talk things out and to come to wise agreements instead of taking up the war club against one another. We may need the war club some day, but we must deliberate together before we take it up. This way, all nations will prosper." Tekerihoken turned and walked back to his place. Dekanawida walked over to Odatsadeh and led him by the arm to the orator's spot.

"My people of the Oneida nation have also joined the League of Peaceful Power. We have agreed that we must do now what is best for the ongoing generations of our families. Before any action is taken, the chiefs of all the nations must meet and decide if that action is in the best interests of seven generations to come. And so it is that I stand here in front of you today joined in peace with my brothers, the mighty Mohawk and the great Oneida. I hope to stand now with you, Tadodaho, as a brother of the Great Longhouse."

The proceedings were interrupted by a messenger who came to Tadodaho and whispered into his ear. He turned to the crowd and to Hiawatha and to Dekanawida and said, "News of this League of Peace travels fast. The chief of the Cayuga town that borders our hunting lands, Deskaheh, is outside our gates with an embassy from the Cayuga nation. He requests to be heard."

Hiawatha looked at Dekanawida and read the barely perceptible smile that came from the Peacemaker's eyes. Hiawatha shook his head and smiled to himself.

"What do you know of this, Hiawatha?" Tadodaho asked.

"Nothing. I assure you. It is as you have just said. Good news travels fast."

Deskaheh and three warriors who accompanied him were led forward toward the center of the square. Tadodaho offered them tobacco, and they smoked from the long-stemmed pipe, fanning the sacred incense over their faces. Deskaheh was a striking man in appearance. He wore a fur bonnet with a high crest of multicolored feathers, hawk tails and pheasant tails that cascaded downward all around his head. His eyes were dark and piercing and his nose was thin and straight. His earlobes were heavily distended by rings and jewelry that hung down to his shoulders. He held himself with a dignity that only a man who knows his own worth could muster. His warriors were equally impressive, and they carried no weapons in their hands.

"Welcome, Deskaheh. What brings you so far from home on a winter's night?" Tadodaho's tone was a strange mixture of respect and irritation. There had been many skirmishes in the past with war bands from his village.

"Greetings, Onondaga. I have come to deliver a message from my people, and from the people of Togahayon, high chief of all the Cayuga. For some time now we have heard these rumors about the founding of a League among all the peoples from the Genesee to the Mohawk Rivers. For too long now we have fought in wars against the Onondaga and the Seneca. The blood of my brothers was drained here in this very spot, and the blood of your sons stains the ground of my village. We have heard that the prophet Dekanawida proposes a way to end this bloodshed. We wish to hear this message, for we are tired of the endless cycle of war.

"You must not think us weak. As you know, we are brave and fierce fighters. And we will fight if we must. We only come to hear what Dekanawida proposes. Have you, Atatarho, joined this league?"

"The old Atatarho is dead. I have been requickened as Tadodaho. And this ceremony and meeting tonight is to decide if the Onondaga will join the league."

Dekanawida held up his hands and stepped forward. "Welcome, Deskaheh. You are right to want to know more. This shows the clear-mindedness of a reasonable man. Reason is the only thing now that can bring us all together. Thinking and discussing is always the superior path. They are the best ways to solve disputes. What have warfare, blood feuds, and revenge done for your people in the past?"

He stopped and looked around at the circle of faces. His voice had become stronger in the past few days and a new sense of urgency accompanied his movements and gestures. At times, he seemed like a man who knew his time was limited, and therefore must make every word and every action achieve the utmost.

Makahwah rose to her feet. "Blood feuds have destroyed my family, and destroyed my clan," she said. Her half-paralyzed face reflected in the firelight contained all the agony and tears that the way of war had inflicted upon her body and mind in the past few years.

"You all know me. I was once a proud mother who took care of her clan. And then the blood wars came. And they took away my daughter. But that was not all." She looked at Hiawatha with her one piercing eye. His soul shriveled and shook inside of him. Tears of bitterness steamed in his eyes. "The revenge feuds also took my four granddaughters. These wars have stolen the future! They have robbed me and you and everyone of who knows how many unborn faces! They have robbed me and you of who knows how many protectors of the earth, of who knows how many future guardians of the three sisters, the givers and sustainers of life. The future went away, and with it went the Great Turtle Shell totem, the ancient relic that hung proudly from the rafters of my longhouse. This was given to us by the Spirit Beings to protect us and to guide us. But when it went away, our leader's senses went away too.

"Now he has come back to us, and he has brought with him

the Peacemaker who will help us install the Great Law, the Great Peace. Kewahtawa dreamed of this. In the Festival of Dreams he told of the Peacemaker and told how Hiawatha must seek him out to aid our people. We did not know how or what this meant back then. But now the dream is fulfilled. Hiawatha returns with the Peacemaker. And we must not let this chance to change the future slip through our fingers. Let us join the League now!"

Loud cheers rang through the square. Makahwah had barely spoken three words at a time in the past year, and now she let loose this flood upon their ears. And what they heard gladdened them. Deskaheh was clearly moved, and he had to fight back the tears that clouded his eyes. He too had suffered in the past.

Dekanawida called for silence. "Makahwah speaks powerful words full of reason and emotion. Tadodaho, if you join with us, we will have a strong chain that cannot be broken, a chain that Deskaheh will add Cayuga links to, and make even stronger. You will be the center link that binds us all together."

Hiawatha could see that something was still holding the old sorcerer back. It is not easy to break with the past. Old ways of thinking can hold one back forever. He had to intervene quickly before the magic of this moment was gone forever.

"Tadodaho," he began, "Look around you at the delegates of the three nations, the sachems and chieftains of the Mohawk, the Oneida, and the Cayuga." He glanced at Orios, and the young musician understood. He placed his flute to his lips and began to play a haunting and mystical tune, one that reached down into the depths of the soul, colored with notes of pomp and ceremony. As if on cue, the drummers took up a ceremonious rhythm, and they played low and slowly in tune to a soft chant that the women began to take up.

Hiawatha pointed to the sachems. "They have all agreed to offer the message of Peace and Power to you, and they will give you the office and the power of the Firekeeper and spiritual leader of our people. They want you to use your great powers for the good of the people."

Dekanawida dropped to his knees and opened the palms of his hands outward toward the Onondaga chief. Odatsadeh and Tekerihoken did the same, and, after a slight hesitation, Deskaheh and his warriors also went onto their knees in ritual homage and ceremonial abeyance to Tadodaho, who, if he joined the League, would be the Firekeeper, the central fire of all the five fires in the one, united longhouse. The old sorcerer's eyes widened in disbelief.

Hiawatha walked closer to him. "Onondaga will be forever, for all generations to come, the heart and soul of the One United Longhouse. It will be the center, because it is the center, and it will be the place where the fires of the Great Law will burn always. And the Tadodaho will keep the fires burning for the sake of the unborn who will be coming our way." Then Hiawatha dropped to his knees.

Atatarho, who was now reborn as Tadodaho, drew himself up to his full height. No longer was his spine twisted, no longer was there venom in his heart. He had been touched. Moved by some divine power, the power of love, the power of truth as told in words and in song. He put his hand on Hiawatha's head, then lifted him up and embraced him. As he wiped the tears away from his face with the back of his hand, he moved forward to the kneeling sachems. One by one, he lifted them to their feet, and grabbed their arms in friendship.

Chapter Five

As the days passed and warmer weather was approaching, Dekanawida, Hiawatha, and the other sachems spent their time as guests of the town of Onondaga. The people of the longhouse are by their very nature great lovers of oratory and debate. Each sachem had to be heard, and it was understood that none could interrupt until he was done. The clan mothers too were an important part of the debates and deliberations over each item of business.

Dekanawida looked around the circle of seated men. This process of bringing together the minds of the nations had been every bit as difficult as he had expected. It would take more than magic and miracles from the spirit world to bring together all these huge egos into one agreeing mind. But it was a task that he was more than willing to do. The human beings could not continue to settle their difficulties by blood revenge. The price had become too high. And these men and women, the leaders of their people, knew this as well. But working through words and ideas to settle their differences was new to them and was taking time.

The deliberations—not always calm—went on for two long months. Many laws were made and many fine points were debated and decided upon. The number and names of each Sachem from each nation—except, of course, the Seneca, were decided upon. The number of Sachems that sat in the Council determined the number of votes that nation would have. It was a tricky negotiation, and one that was based on population and the political realities of the present moment. It was a fact that some nations were stronger than others, and some nations, like the Onondaga, needed more placating. The Mohawk, who would be guardians of the eastern door, would have nine Sachems, and they would be given the distinction of Older Brothers. The Oneida would also have nine, but they would be given the title of Younger Brothers. The Cayuga would be given one more Sachem—they would have ten—but, since they were later to join, they would be, with the Oneida, called Younger Brothers.

The Onondagas, the powerful warriors once led by an evil sorcerer, but now converted by the power of truth and love, would be given the largest number of Sachems, fourteen. They were the central glue, the central Firekeepers of the league, and since the Great Tree of Peace was to be planted at Onondaga, they were also given status as Older Brothers. It was decided that when the Seneca joined they would be given eight Sachems, but, as guardians of the western door of the Great Longhouse, they would also be given the title of Older Brothers. In Grand Council meetings, the Older Brothers, the Mohawk, the Onondaga, and the Seneca, would sit on one side of the council fire, and the Younger Brothers would sit on the opposite side. An elaborate protocol of speaking back and forth between both sides of the fire was finally worked out after much debate.

As Atatarho thought about his new role as a Sachem, his mind turned to his nephew. *What has happened to Osinoh? He was here at the beginning of our deliberations, but then he did not return from his last hunting trip. He hoped that he was alive and well and would return home soon to take part in their new community.*

The cold, short days of winter began to lengthen and warm. The snows melted, and purple crocus flowers began to sprout up in the meadows whose grasses were beginning to grow greener. Slowly, the miracle of regeneration began to take place again as it always had in the past. Small, tight buds on the trees began to open up and burst forth into flowers. Many birds that had flown south for the snow-filled months returned now to build nests in the trees that would soon be filled with bright green leaves. The time of the Planting Moon would be soon upon them, and so the women busied themselves by sorting out the seeds of corn and bean and squash that they had gathered in last autumn's harvest.

One afternoon early in the new season of rebirth, when there was still a slight chill in the air and the sun shone brightly through the buds on the fruit trees—the apple, the pear, and the cherry— that were just beginning to flower with sweet promise, Orios walked alone through the wood playing a song on his flute. It was a song full of hope, full of bright notes of renewal, full of the promise of bursting life that was the essence of this new season. His heart was full almost to bursting with a joyful love for all of life, for the golden rays of sunshine that filtered through the tiny new leaves and bursting buds on the trees, and for the greening floor of the forest sprinkled with small wildflowers. The joyous love-songs of the birds mingled with the rising and falling notes of his flute as he strolled along the well-worn paths of his boyhood creating new hymns of praise to Mother Nature and the Great Creator of all things, the Great Mysterious, as Dekanawida called him, the Great Perfector of Minds.

He paused in his playing and sat down beneath a maple tree whose tiny, bright green leaves were just beginning to unwrap themselves from the buds on the branches. It was an old tree with a large, round trunk. The tree had given them sweet syrup last winter, and, as he laid the back of his head against the bark, he could feel the urgent stirrings of new life that were breathing and growing in the living tissue of the new growth, the springwood. He could feel the pulse of the tree-spirit beating and throbbing against his own flesh, and a warm feeling of joy and bliss coursed through his veins. It made his heart swell and his throat ache and choke. He placed the flute to his lips to begin a new tone-poem to the goddess of life, to the goddess-spirit of this tree that he felt so close to now. And, as he played, he thought of Keteri, the Mohawk girl who nursed his wounds last winter, who reminded him so of Sovana. Where was she now, he wondered? Was she sitting under a maple tree thinking the same thoughts about the beauty and wonder of nature, about the great plan of the Creator of all things? Was she feeling the awe that he felt now for the life-force that came anew each spring? Was she, perhaps, thinking about him?

But what he heard next sent an ice-cold wave of fear through his blood. It was a familiar caw-caw-cawing sound, the sound of a human voice imitating the crow-call, and he remembered that sound, that dreadful sound that ripped out from the past. It was the same crow-call signal he had heard on that fateful day when the arrow from Hiawatha's bow had found its mark in the heart of Shadahgoh's son. He could see the dying boy's face vividly now, as if it were right in front of him, the young handsome face contorted in death's agony. It was also the same terrible sound that had echoed in his ears on the day when Hiawatha's daughters were brutally murdered by Seneca arrows and war clubs. Orios jumped to his feet.

"CAW! CAW-CAW!" The sounds ripped through his heart like a sharp knife, and he turned and ran, ran as fast as he could back toward the palisade walls of the town, his eyes burning, his heart on fire with fear.

Orios ran into the Council House, startling the gathered leaders who were deliberating a fine point of the new law. He stood in the center of the room, shaking, unable to catch his breath. Hiawatha rushed to his side and grabbed him just as his knees were beginning to buckle beneath him.

"Orios! What is it? You look as if you have seen a ghost from the Spirit World."

"Sen-" Orios was choking and gasping for air. "Sen-a-" Looking into Hiawatha's eyes, he took a deep breath and composed himself. "Senecas. I heard their war signals. They are close."

Atatarho leaped to his feet. "We must fortify the town. I will call my war chiefs together." The other leaders responded in similar fashion.

"No!" said Dekanawida. "This is just the occasion that we have been looking for. We will not make war with the Seneca. When they arrive, we will welcome them at the woods' edge and we will invite them to join us as the fifth member of the League."

"And what if they don't?" asked Tekerihoken. "We are not ready to do battle with a large war party. My Mohawk are many miles from here. The Oneida and the Cayuga likewise are not prepared for war."

"I will send my messengers to see how many they are. But no matter how many, we will not engage in battle. We will offer them the high place at the Council that they deserve. Leave it to me and to Hiawatha. Put your faith and your trust in us, my brothers. This is not a threat. This is the opportunity we have been waiting for. The time is at hand. Soon we will plant the Great Tree of Peace, and we will bury the stone hatchets and the clubs of war in a hole beneath it, a bottomless pit that leads all evil away into oblivion."

The men all left the Council House talking among themselves. Atatarho, who had forgotten momentarily his new role as Tadodaho, remained with Dekanawida and Hiawatha.

"Forgive me, Dekanawida. I forgot that a Sachem of the council cannot also be a war chief. My first impulse was to take up weapons to defend the village against attack. It is a habit that will take some time to break."

"You have done nothing to be ashamed of," said Dekanawida. "Your impulse was a good one. To defend one's people is the first duty of a great leader. But, even though the Seneca do not know it yet, they are not our enemies. They are our brothers and our natural allies. Our job now, this day, is to show them the truth of this statement. Even though they come with the war club held high and with their bowstrings taut, our words will enter into their hearts, and they will drop the club, they will unstring their bows, and take up the wampum string that we shall offer them."

"You are wise, Dekanawida."

"The wisdom that I speak is within you as well, Tadodaho. That is why I have chosen you to keep the fire of the Great Longhouse burning. And here, where the eternal fire shall burn, is where we will all come together in a Great League of Peace."

"It is a great day," said Tadodaho.

"It will be when it is done. But we have work to do now. Come, let us make preparations to meet our guests."

Chapter Six

The huge war party of the Seneca rested on the crest of a hill. They sat cross-legged beneath the bright green trees, or crouched low, their backs to the pines. Below them they could see the rim of the lake, the Silver Lake of the Onondaga. They had been traveling for two days, moving mostly by night. Now they were here. To call this gathering of Seneca warriors simply a war party, however, would not do it justice. It was a small army. The best and bravest of the Seneca all painted and armed for war. Their number was over two hundred, enough warriors to crush Onondaga.

Shadahgoh's face was painted black from the lips down and red from his cheeks upward to his brow. The sides of his shaved head were also painted red, accentuating the yellow quills that decorated his braided topknot. His muscular body was stripped but for his breech-clout, and his entire body was painted in black and red stripes that seemed to vibrate angrily when he moved.

He turned to Skanyatei and Nishah, war chieftains of two other powerful Seneca villages. He brandished his war club, and said, "Today, my vengeance will be complete. We will destroy all of our enemies in one glorious afternoon. Thanks to information provided by Osinoh, once an Onondaga, now of the true people, the Seneca, I now know who the slayer of my son is, and I will finish today what I started in the past. Today I will personally cut off the head of Hiawatha, and I will lead the real killer of my son, this flute player called Orios, back to my village. My son's mother and his sisters, and I, and the people of my clan, will torture him so exquisitely and so slowly that his death will be remembered as the greatest mourning-revenge ever to be achieved by our people."

Shadahgoh and the other war chiefs nodded toward Osinoh, whose hair was now shaved on the sides leaving a red-painted strip on the crest, and whose body was painted for war. In his hand he carried an antler-spiked war club.

"The Onondaga have become weaklings. My uncle has given himself over to all the nonsense about peace that Dekanawida and Hiawatha have filled his ears with."

"I cannot believe our good fortune," said Nishah. "Chiefs of the Mohawk, Oneida, and Cayuga, all together under the longhouse of Onondaga."

"We will kill them all," said Skanyatei. "We will hang their heads from our palisades."

"Our people will celebrate us in song for many generations to come, and the Seneca will be the masters of Turtle Island." Shadahgoh looked up in the sky as if he were searching for some omen written in the patterns of the morning clouds.

"Call for Kawtawda, our shaman. I would have him read the signs in the sky." Nishah nodded and jerked his head toward a warrior who stood some few paces away from them. The warrior ran toward the rear to fetch the Seneca soothsayer.

"I believe the omens to be good today," said Skanyatei. "Just look at the sky. Clear and full of gold clouds."

"Something is too right about it," said Shadahgoh. "I do not trust days that look too perfect. I will seek the advice of my shaman."

Kawtawda limped slowly toward the group of chieftains. His long, thin gray hair, braided with snake bones and crow feathers, blew limply in the morning breeze. He wore deer-hide leggings sewn all about with the jet-black feathers of the crow, and his tattooed upper body was bare. The tattoos on his old wrinkled chest were made after the old way, long, downward-pointing triangles—twenty in number—that ran a girdle round his body and those upward and downward lines stretched from his lean old belly to his withered neck. Over his left arm he carried a robe made from raven feathers, a robe that he clutched to his body with a hand that carried an elm-bark rattle.

"I am here, great one. What would you have of me?" The old man leaned on a staff crowned with a stuffed raven's head and peered at the war chief, seeking some directional clue in his blank, cold gaze.

Shadahgoh stared at the shaman with a glare that pierced to the bone. "Study the sky, old one. Tell us what omens you read. But study them carefully. I do not want lies. I do not want flattery. I want the truth. What does the nature of the moment yield up to your sight?"

Kawtawda was surprised to notice Shadahgoh's flint-studded war club trembling in the war chief's hand. He withdrew his medicine bundle—an otter skin with head and tail intact—from within the folds of his raven-feather robe, and carefully withdrew the contents, laying them out, side by side, on the ground. He looked up at the sky and chanted softly, a chant that no one understood except for him and the Spirit Beings. He gathered up a handful of snake fangs and raven bones. As he chanted, he cast the bones into the air and watched how they dropped back down to the earth. He shook his rattle and chanted again. Then he took out some dried tobacco, held the crumbled leaves in the palm of his left hand, and blew out bits of it to the four corners of Turtle Island, bowing and chanting as he did so. Rising up from bowing the fourth time to the south, he saw something that astonished him.

"Look!" he cried, pointing his raven-head staff at a shape flying towards them. Shadahgoh and his retinue followed the path of Kawtawda's staff with their eyes.

"It's an owl!" shouted Osinoh. "And in daylight!"

"What does it mean, shaman?" demanded Shadahgoh.

The old man paused. Then, softly, he replied. "Death."

"Death? Whose death?"

The old man shrugged. "A Great Horned Owl flying in daylight is an omen of death. That is all."

"Then the omen is good," said Nishah. "It means death to the enemies of the Seneca."

"Yes," said Shadahgoh. "It means that we are the bringers of death, does it not?"

Once again the old shaman shrugged. He would not say yes. He would not say no. "It is a portent of death. Death for someone or some thing."

"Some *thing*? What do you mean?" In spite of himself, a cold chill crept up Shadahgoh's backbone. He shrugged off the feeling and brandished his war club above his head. "The time for talk is done. Let us carry out the message of the owl. Now we bring death down upon Onondaga."

With his club, he motioned his warriors to follow him, and he began to run down the crest of the hill towards the woods that fringed the palisade village.

Dekanawida motioned to Hiawatha and to Atatarho to join him in sitting upon the ground. The newly requickened leader of the Onondaga, the Tadodaho, the Firekeeper, looked puzzled.

"Excuse me for my ignorance, holy one. But tell me how we can save our people from death and destruction by sitting cross-legged on the ground while the Seneca swoop down on us and club us like rabbits?"

Dekanawida motioned again for them to sit down. "There will be no clubbing today. Orios?"

"Yes?"

"Play a soothing tune on your flute. Something to quell the savage lust and to keep fear from rising to the surface."

"I will try, Peacemaker. But I must admit that my hands tremble a bit."

"So long as your heart does not tremble, then all will be well."

When Hiawatha and Tadodaho were seated, as were Tekerihoken and Odatsadeh, who had joined them, Dekanawida said, "We will greet them at the woods' edge. We will greet them with tears in our eyes."

"Tears, holy one?" asked Odatsadeh.

"Yes. Real tears. Our tears will be the tears of grief for the death of Shadahgoh's son. Our tears will be the tears of understanding, the tears of empathy for the pain and suffering that he and his family have felt. Our tears will be the tears of grief for all of the sons and brothers and fathers of the Seneca nation who have died at the hands of Onondaga, Cayuga, Oneida, or Mohawk."

"I see," said Hiawatha. "The tears will be like the Condolence Ceremony. We will be the mourners." Orios' flute soared in the air above the sachems, the notes taking on a life of their own, notes of sorrow, notes of sympathy, notes for the grief of suffering people.

"Not only the mourners. We will also be the clear-minded ones. We will send our message of peace and compassion into their hearts with a song."

"So we will sing too?" asked Tekerihoken.

"Yes, we all will sing and chant the Three Bare Words of condolence, the most important words of all: 'Tears, Ears, and Throat.' For the water of sympathy that flows from the eyes unblocks the blindness of sight. The ears too must be open to our message, so that they may hear the truth, and for that reason, Orios will play his beautiful flute. The whole village will chant and sing the notes of condolence while Hiawatha speaks the words of condolence. Our throats will be open, so that theirs may be unblocked and open too, so that they too may speak the words of truth, compassion, and peace."

"Listen," said Hiawatha. "I hear them coming." The men became silent and focused their hearing towards the direction Hiawatha was pointing. Deskaheh, the Cayuga chief, placed his ear to the ground and listened.

"By the sound of their feet, there are a hundred warriors or more."

"Let us go. Now we will walk to greet them." Dekanawida rose to his feet with an ease that belied his years. "Keep playing, Orios. Play as you have never played before. The future of our people depends upon it."

Orios followed the Peacemaker, playing slow and mournful notes, sometimes high and seeming to soar above the trees, flying with the songbirds whose melodies matched his own, sometimes low, the sonorous notes seeming to roll across the tops of the small grasses, striking chords deep into one's being. The others followed too, walking slowly and with great dignity in spite of their fear. This was, after all, something quite new to them—to meet one's enemies with no weapon in either hand. To greet someone who is coming to kill you with words of friendship and brotherhood, words of love and peace.

Hiawatha walked the proudest. He felt no fear. He believed completely in the message of universal brotherhood among the nations, and he was convinced that those dreams, the dreams of the Peacemaker, the dreams that started long ago with the dream of Kewahtawa, would today become a reality in the waking world.

Behind them came the entire village walking in groups of five and six following their respective Clan Mothers. Makahwah, using her stick to support her, walked with great solemnity, the remnants of the Turtle Clan behind her. She had believed in the dream long before anyone else had. She had urged Hiawatha to find the Peacemaker according to Kewahtawa's dream. And now, it was she who began the singing. She lifted her face to the sky and began to sing a song of her own device, but a song that echoed the teachings of Dekanawida. She matched her pitch and rhythm to Orios' flute.

"We are crying,
We are crying out,

We are crying out tears for you.
Our tears will flow forever
From the rivers of our eyes.

We know your pain
We feel your pain
For your lost son.

Your pain, oh Shadahgoh,
Is *our* pain too,
Your pain, oh Seneca nation,
Is *our* pain too. "

And the people of the village, the men, the women, the children, all began to sing with Makahwah, to sing the chorus of this new song of tears:

"We are crying,
We are crying out,
We are crying out tears for you . . ."

It seemed all one voice, one voice made of many voices just as the vast sea is made of many drops of water, one voice made from the individual voices of young men and old men, girls and boys, young women and old women, all singing, all crying tears of empathy.

The procession was now halfway between the walls of the village and woods, and the singing people led by the Peacemaker, Hiawatha, the Sachems of the Four Nations, and Orios playing the flute to the tune of the new song of condolence. They crossed the cornfields as yet unplanted, those same fields that Sovana and Seawa tended with their sister villagers, the same fields where Shadahgoh and his war band had attacked and killed Seawa and Memoha.

Hiawatha felt a twinge of anger color his brow, but as he

listened to the song his people sang, the old murderous feeling was replaced by another, a deeper, more profound one, one of eternal sadness for the continual state of violence and hatred that resulted in so many useless deaths, so much grief, and so much sorrow. As if from a mountain spring, from the very depths of his being, hot tears clouded his eyes and flowed down his face like two salty streams.

Odatsadeh placed his arm around Hiawatha's shoulders to steady him, and Hiawatha, in turn, gripped the Oneida chief's hand with his own, a strong grip of brotherhood, of unity, of solidarity in the face of danger. Tekerihoken, the proud Mohawk, walked beside Dekanawida, and he threw his head back and lifted his strong voice to the sky singing in unison with the people behind them, "We are crying out tears . . . for you . . ." For *all* of you, he thought, and for all of us who have suffered by our own foolishness in the past, suffered the slow death of many emotional cuts. And as he sang, real tears sprang to his eyes, and he cried real tears for the first time since he could remember, perhaps when he was a child or a very young boy. Now the tears ran down his face and he was not ashamed. Tears streamed down the faces of everyone who marched, of everyone who sang, of all who were both mourners and clear-minded ones.

Shadahgoh heard the singing when they were fifty feet from the woods' edge. He slowed down his pace and signaled to his men to proceed with more caution. This was something he had not expected. Singing? Where were their warriors, pitiful as he knew they would be? Have they become such weaklings, such cowards, such women that they could not send out even a small party of armed men to defend their village? As they walked through the dense woods, he began to pick out words from the great wordless chanting that now filled their ears. "Tears . . . crying . . . grief . . ." And then he heard his own name sung, and his puzzlement turned to a strange feeling that crept up the back of his spine like fingers of ice.

Shadahgoh and his war chiefs kept moving toward the edge of the woods, looking from side to side, expecting an ambush. But none came. Only the singing growing louder and clearer. And when they reached the woods' edge, there in front of them, some twenty paces or so from where they stood, was the entire village of Onondaga and not one of them carried a war club, a stone tomahawk, or a bow. Hiawatha, Atatarho, three other chiefs wearing the *gustoweh*, the feathered bonnet of high office, and the flute-boy called Orios, his son's murderer, stood beside a powerful-looking old man whose long, gray hair blew sideways in the wind, and whose bare torso was in remarkably good shape for someone of advanced years. The man held both his arms out above and in front of him, palms turned toward them in ritual greeting.

And then Shadahgoh noticed something that made him involuntarily shiver. Everyone who stood before him was crying. Tears streamed down their cheeks. Hiawatha's face was wet from tears. The chiefs that flanked him had faces lined with little streams that ran from their eyes. Even Atatarho stood there with great rivers of tears flowing down his face. Shadahgoh was shocked by how different the powerful sorcerer looked, his weaponless hands stretched out before him in supplication, a look of peace on his face in spite of all the tears.

"We greet you with tears at the woods' edge," said Dekanawida.

Then Hiawatha said, "We, the people of Onondaga, together with leaders from the Oneida, the Cayuga, and the Mohawk, greet you with the Three Bare Words of the New Covenant: Tears, Ears, and Throat. We greet you with tears. The tears are in our eyes because we grieve for you and we are filled with sorrow for all the suffering and death that your people have gone through. Our ears are open to hear your words, and we wish to open *your* ears so that you can truly hear our words of brotherhood and peace. We open our throats to you. We sing a song of condolence, we cleanse our own throats so that yours may be unblocked, so that your throats may sing with us and speak with us the words of truth given to us by the Great Mystery through his agent on earth, Dekanawida."

Shadahgoh was dumbfounded. He did not know what to say, nor did he fully believe his eyes and his ears. Far from being unblocked, they seemed completely stopped up so that he could not talk, could not hear, could barely see; he knew not what senses to trust. Dekanawida stepped forward, holding in each hand strings of wampum.

"Today you will help us plant the Great Tree of Peace. We will all be brothers in the League of Peace and Power. These strings of wampum will prop up our words."

"Peace is for women and children. I have come to exact my revenge. I know who killed my son. Him!" With his war club, Shadahgoh pointed to Orios, who had stopped playing his flute.

A still silence filled the air. Dekanawida looked at the Seneca war chief with pity and love in his eyes. A powerful *orenda* poured forth from his entire being. "Your son entered into the Land of the Spirits by an unfortunate accident. His life was not taken in anger. Why now would you stain his memory with the blood of those who are guiltless?"

"Who is guiltless? We are all bloody. And the bloodiest shall inherit the earth." Shadahgoh raised his war club and was about to bring it down on the head of the Peacemaker, when someone in the Seneca ranks pointed up to the sky and shouted, "Look! Something is eating the sun."

While they were talking, it had become darker; slowly at first, and then more rapidly, the sun's rays were being blotted out by some strange power in the heavens. Now half of the sun was covered up and a huge shadow was falling across the land.

"Your anger has caused the sun to die," said Dekanawida. "When light and clarity go out of this world, then darkness and obscurity replace it."

Shadahgoh looked in awe at this sight never seen in his

lifetime or in the lifetime of his people. He trembled visibly. His brave Seneca warriors behind him were all babbling in a chaos of confusion and fear. Even the shaman, Kawtawda, dropped to his knees and raised his raven's head staff up to the blackening, darkening sun.

And then the Great Horned Owl came. Screeching and flying low, he flew almost in the face of Shadahgoh. Dekanawida straightened out his left arm, and the Great Owl wheeled around his head and perched on the holy man's wrist. Shadahgoh trembled. The sun was now almost entirely blotted out. Only a small sliver of light remained as the Great Owl blinked his large yellow eyes at Shadahgoh. The war chief dropped his weapon and then dropped to his knees, lowering his face to the dust.

When the sun was eaten entirely, and darkness at noon settled on the land of the Onondaga, the sound of many voices singing could be heard coming from the east of the village. With accents sweet and pure, the high voices of women and children came drifting through the trees:

> "We are the Mohawk,
> Turtle, Wolf, and Bear are we,
> We come to Plant the Tree
> With our brother and sister Oneida.
> We follow Dekanawida,
> The Holy Prophet of Peace.
> We come with our Grandmother,
> The Planting Moon,
> To the Ceremony of Unity
> To build the Longhouse of Peace.
>
> All is dark
> We cannot see.
> Evil has eaten the Light,
> Day is turned to Night,

> But we see in our hearts:
> We see the golden fire of truth
> With the eyes inside our minds."

And from the southeast came another chorus of voices, many voices lifted in song:

> "We are the Cayuga,
> Turtle, Wolf, and Bear are we.
> We come to Plant the Tree
> With our brother and sister Mohawk
> Our brother and sister Oneida
> Our brother and sister Onondaga
> Our brother and sister Seneca.
> We follow Dekanawida,
> The Holy Prophet of Peace.
> We come with our Grandmother,
> The Planting Moon,
> To the Ceremony of Unity
> To build the Longhouse of Peace.

And when all these singing voices came to the same spot, surrounding Dekanawida and the Sachems of the New League, surrounding the people of Onondaga, surrounding the mighty Shadahgoh prostrate on the ground, surrounding the silent and speechless Seneca army, the sky began to lighten. Little by little, the sun was being reborn, shedding his beams of bright light on the heads of the people below, on the bright green leaves of the springtime trees, on the new grasses, and on all the creatures that walk and swim and fly on Turtle Island.

Dekanawida motioned with both arms for the singing to cease. As he did so, the Great Owl sprung from his arm and flew into the depths of the darker forest. Then he raised his face to the sky.

"Look, my people. Up in the sky. The Sky Beings are giving

us back the Tree of Light, which is the Tree of Life. Clarity is born again. Clear-mindedness is born again. We all now will see again with clear vision. We will see clearly the path that we are to walk. The old ways that we used to walk, the ways of darkness, the ways of killing for vengeance, of bloody mourning-wars, of dark torture to avenge other killings, these old ways are dying with the dying darkness in the sky. We are being reborn just as the sun is now. Now we are all ready to receive the Good News of Peace and Power."

The Peacemaker looked down upon Shadahgoh, who knelt on the ground before him. He took the Seneca war chief by the arms and lifted him to his feet.

"Shadahgoh. The Great Owl of Death flew this day, a day that became night and then day again. Death was foretold to you this morning. And so it is. Today you have died. You will be requickened, reborn under a new name. We will hold a Great Condolence Ceremony for you and your people. You will be reborn as Shadekaronyes, Level Skies, and you will be the Guardian of the Western Door of the Great Longhouse. You will be one of the Fifty Founders of the Great League. And you will never die. Down through the generations to come, someone will always bear your name, will always sit in high council, and will always guard the west from invasion of enemies."

The death and rebirth of the sun, the tears of the Onondaga, and the mass coming together of what seemed to be all the peoples in Turtle Island singing as with one voice, had a profound effect upon the soul of Shadahgoh. The experience had struck deeply into the core of his being and had shattered him utterly. He repeated the name softly to himself. Shadekaronyes. A wave of calmness like a soothing balm swept over him. As he repeated his new name over and over, he felt a golden light encompass his body, and tears began to pour forth from his eyes, cleansing his soul. He looked up at Dekanawida.

"What must I do, holy one?"

Dekanawida looked at Hiawatha and gestured with his right arm. "Accept Hiawatha as your brother. He is one of the Fifty, a Sachem from the Mohawk nation, a Sachem of the League of Five Nations.

"And you, Hiawatha, accept Shadekaronyes as your brother. He also is one of the Fifty, a Sachem from the Seneca Nation."

Hiawatha opened his arms and took a step toward the Seneca chief. Then Shadekaronyes slowly raised his arms and took a step toward Hiawatha. The two men, once bitter enemies, grabbed each other's forearms and embraced. As he felt the muscles of the Seneca war chief gripping his own, Hiawatha felt a surge of the old anger returning to his heart. Here was the man who pierced the body of his little girl with arrows, who beat Seawa's face into a bloody pulp. Leaping in front of his mind's eye was the mental image of Memoha lying in bloody grass, Seneca arrows sticking up from her small back, her little black and white dog dead beside her. He tried to erase it from his mind, but the image grew larger and larger.

Likewise, in Shadahgoh's mind the image of his dead son laid out on a funeral bier, his mother and his sisters keening and weeping, Kawtawda and the False Faces dancing and rattling around his lifeless body, leaped into the space behind his eyes.

The two men gripped each other harder and harder, and the same thought jumped up in their minds. Shadahgoh reached for the stone knife that hung from a sheath around his neck and Hiawatha reached for the stone knife that hung from a hempen cord about his waist. Each man instantly knew what the other intended to do, and each man restrained the other from reaching his weapon. It was a struggle of wills as much as a struggle of sheer physical force. Their eyes locked, and each man recognized something alien and something familiar. It was as if they were twin brothers, one good and one evil, only each man could not say which was evil and which was good.

Osinoh ran forward from the Seneca forces. Even though the

death and rebirth of the sun and the combined forces for peace had a great impact on his being, he wanted to help his new guardian, the Seneca war chief. When he saw Orios, his old rival, he stopped in his tracks and pointed his war club at him. "This is all his doing!" he shouted to all the people gathered. "He killed Mahtewan, but everyone thought it was Hiawatha. This led Shadahgoh to exact his revenge upon Hiawatha by taking his daughters."

Hearing his son's name, Shadahgoh dropped his hold on Hiawatha and looked at Osinoh. "He speaks the truth. He led us to your village and Atatarho pointed out Hiawatha's daughters."

Orios shook his head in disbelief. "You did that? But why? Now she is dead," said Orios. Tears welled up in his eyes.

Osinoh moved closer. "I loved Sovana. As much as you."

"Her spirit is still here, watching us. She does not want others to die like she did. She wants you to do the right thing so that her death will bring a better life for the generations to come."

Osinoh felt the hairs on his arms bristle as they did when he first held Sovana. He felt a hand on his shoulder and jumped. He turned and was surprised to see a warm light coming from the reborn Tadodaho. He hardly recognized his uncle. "I am sorry, Osinoh, for the pain I have inflicted on you. Please forgive me." He had never seen tears in his uncle's eyes before, and he felt his own tears of regret and forgiveness stream down his face. Tadodaho pulled him into his arms.

"Play, Orios," said Dekanawida.

And Orios played a mournful dirge, an elegy for Sovana, for Seawa, for Memoha, for Tiwi, for Mahtewan, the son of Shadahgoh, and for all those dead because of revenge. The notes that he played pierced the hearts of all the men and women and boys and girls who were there. Some were moved to sing songs of their own device, songs in memory of their dead dear ones, songs that matched the notes of Orios' flute.

Tadodaho took the war club from his nephew's hand, raised it above his head, and with a mighty swing flung it down hard against the base of a tall, white pine tree. A loud crack like the voice of an angry Thunder Being caused all to stop singing. The men, women, and children all stood in awe as the tall white pine tree toppled over, leaving a huge, gaping hole.

Tadodaho, Dekanawida, Hiawatha, and Shadahgoh ran over to look down in the hole. There, entangled and clinging among the roots, was a large turtle shell. Twenty feet below it was a rushing underground river that seemed to run as fast as the great falls at Niagara and roared with the sound of a hundred mighty rivers.

"Makahwah! Look! It is the Clan Totem, the Great Shell of the Turtle Clan!" Hiawatha ran to Makahwah and led her to the edge of the great fissure in the earth so that she could see for herself.

Makahwah's knees went limp and she fell to the ground reaching toward the Great Shell. She had never thought to see the Great Shell of her clan again. So many terrible things had happened to her family and her clan since that night when the totem disappeared. Tears filled her eyes, and she wept aloud for the bitterness of the past and for joy that the source of power and magic for her clan had now been rediscovered. She stood up and looked at Hiawatha. "How did it get there?"

Osinoh looked at the ground and then up at his uncle. He then stepped forward. "I took it. The night of the Feast of Dreams many moons ago, when Kewahtawa spoke his dream of Dekanawida. I took it and buried it here beneath this tree."

"But why?" asked Makahwah.

"I told him to do it." Atatarho's confession brought a chilling silence over the crowd.

"But we trusted you. We made you our chief. We put our future in your hands. Why did you do something so terrible?" Makahwah was hurt and angry.

Atatarho studied the dust on his moccasins as he searched his mind for an answer. "I suppose it was for power. No one ever liked me, even as a child. They could not bear to look at me. So I called on my inner spirits and learned to be a sorcerer. I needed power so that the people would respect me. But the power of a sorcerer was not enough. I was jealous of Hiawatha's influence. I wanted his power. Destroying his clan seemed to be the first step in that direction. I am sorry, Mother. I was a different man then than what I am now. Hiawatha and Dekanawida combed the snakes from my soul and straightened my mind so that I now see with a clarity of vision that was then clouded by the darkness of evil thoughts. Forgive me, Makahwah." And then he leapt into the hole.

The crowd gasped, thinking that Atatarho had leapt to his death, but when they looked into the dark hole, they saw him hanging onto a long, white root trying to reach for the turtle shell. He swung there perilously for a moment above the abyss below, above the rushing underground river that ran down to the bottomless regions of the underworld. He held onto the long root with one arm, and with the other he stretched as far as he could, reaching out until he had a firm grasp on the great turtle shell. He tucked it under his left arm and tried to climb out of the hole, but he came to an impasse, a place where he must use both hands and drop the turtle shell or fall down into the abysm of rushing water. He looked up at the crowd gathered around the edge of the hole, a look of supplication mixed with resignation in his eyes.

"Someone do something!" ordered Makahwah.

A Cayuga man ran to Hiawatha, a long hempen rope in his hands. "Do you remember me?" he asked. "You saved my life once. Seneca warriors had me tied to a tree. But you walked with me to the land of my people and saw me safely home."

"Togahayon!"

"Yes. I have brought my people here to help install the Great Peace."

As he bent down over the edge, an unwelcome twinge of hatred crept back into Hiawatha's heart when he saw his old enemy helpless and now at his mercy. *I could kill him now by simply doing nothing,* he thought. *A painless revenge.*

Dekanawida was suddenly standing beside him. He placed his hand on Hiawatha's shoulder. "We are all brothers now. Old enmities are forgotten. Save your brother, Hiawatha. Or do I need to comb the snakes from *your* hair?"

Hiawatha, with the sheer force of his mind, made the feelings of hatred and revenge become as small as a flea, a flea that he stepped on with his deerskin moccasin. He grabbed the rope from Togahayon, tied a large loop at one end, and flung it down to Atatarho. Togahayon and he held fast onto the other end.

"Atatarho, put this rope around your waist and hang on. We will pull you up."

Atatarho gripped the shell beneath one arm, and with his free hand managed to slide the loop over his head and under his arms. Hiawatha and Togahayon then began, with great effort, to pull the rope. Shadahgoh rushed to help them. "Let us pull the old man up," he said. Hiawatha smiled as he felt his old enemy right behind him helping him pull his oldest enemy back to safety.

A great cheer went up from the crowd when Atatarho scrambled over the edge of the hole and stood up, holding the Great Turtle Shell of the Turtle Clan high above his head. The cheers of joy came from the throats of Mohawk, of Oneida, of Onondaga, of Cayuga, and from the throats of Seneca too. They were mingled together and blended so that no one could tell which one was a Mohawk, which a Seneca, what voice belonged to an Oneida woman or what voice to a Cayuga boy. They were one people now.

Tadodaho, who was once Atatarho, walked over to Makahwah, who stood surrounded by the people of all the nations, all intermingled, all cheering, all made glad by the strange and exciting events of this day. The newly appointed Firekeeper held the sacred shell in both hands with great care and reverence, and then he extended his arms, offering the shell to Makahwah, returning to its rightful place the most ancient relic of the most ancient clan.

Makahwah accepted the shell. And once again the people opened their throats, lifted their voices, and cheered with one united sound of affirmation. Tears of joy welled up in her old eyes. Her heart felt as if it would burst with all the surging warmth that swelled in her breast. She clutched the shell close to her heart, and she felt a sensation that she had not felt in a long time: she felt complete, whole, fulfilled. She felt once again like a Clan Mother.

Chapter Seven

Dekanawida walked up to a rising of the ground a few paces from the uprooted tree. He lifted his arms high into the air, calling for silence. It took some time for the great crowd of people to subdue their feelings of elation and excitement. But the Peacemaker was patient. He had waited all his life for this moment. Now his dream was about to become a reality. When the people finally settled down, he bade them sit upon the ground.

Dekanawida paused a moment, then he held above his head a long and wide belt of wampum. He slowly turned so that all sitting in a semicircle around him could see the intricate symbolic design. In the center was a stylized pine tree. It was flanked on either side by two rectangles and all five designs were joined together by horizontal lines or "paths." He motioned to Hiawatha sitting next to him. Hiawatha stood and faced the people.

"The Peacemaker wishes me to speak for him. He holds in his hands the Wampum Belt of the League of Peace and Power. This Belt will prop up the words that we speak today. It will serve as a symbol of the peace we make this day for the future generations. See the White Pine Tree in the center. This is the Tree of Peace, the Tree that is on its side over there, the tree that we will replant this day. See the Longhouses on either side of the Tree, two on each side. These are the Longhouses of the Seneca and Cayuga, the Oneida and Mohawk, all joined together by the Great Tree of Peace here at Onondaga, the central fire of the One Great Longhouse."

The people lifted their voices in loud approbation. Among the crowd cheering and chanting their approval was Keteri, the same young woman that Orios had been daydreaming about earlier that morning. Her gaze was fixed on Orios. She was so proud of him, sitting in a seat of honor between Tekerihoken and Tadodaho.

"Before the Fifty Sachems are installed and given new names, names that will never die, like the Great Peace itself, the Peacemaker wishes to see a commitment, a sign that we will no longer lift the war club against one another.

"See the hole in the earth where the tree has toppled? The hole where the Great Turtle Shell was restored. Dekanawida wants all warriors who carry weapons to throw their clubs and tomahawks into the abyss so that the swift-moving underground river will carry them all away into oblivion.

"Rise now, brother warriors, and, as a symbol of your commitment to the Great League of Peace, cast your weapons of war into the waters of the abyss."

One by one the warriors rose from their places, and followed their war chiefs in single file up to the edge of the yawning hole left by the uprooted pine tree. Led by the Mohawk chieftain, Tekerihoken, all the men who had come that day from the eastern door of the Great Longhouse cast their weapons of war into the hole. Large, ball-headed war clubs, antler-spiked war clubs, stone tomahawks, all were thrown down into the great hole and into the rushing underground river that took them away, never to be seen again.

Then the Seneca, fierce and proud warriors, one by one went up to the edge of the abyss and cast their bloodstained war clubs into oblivion. Shadahgoh himself threw down his enormous and infamous flint-studded war club, a weapon that had sent many men to the Land of the Spirit Beings.

Odatsadeh, the Quiver Maker, led his band of Oneida warriors up to the hole to cast away their war clubs and blood-red tomahawks. Then Deskaheh and Togahayon led the Cayuga warriors who walked solemnly up to the hole, and, one by one, they threw their weapons down into the swift waters that carried them away forever.

Finally, Tadodaho led his Onondaga warriors to the uprooted pine. The war club that he held in his hand was intricately carved—the curved handle representing the body of a snake, culminating with a round ball protruding from the open jaws of the serpent. The ball of this old weapon was stained dark red from the blood of its former victims. Tadodaho held it ceremoniously high above his head so that all could see. Then with a loud cry he flung it down into the pit, where the rushing waters carried it away to a place where no living man could go. Then he withdrew his long stone knife from its quill-work sheath, a knife that had cut off the scalps of many Oneida, many Cayuga, and had severed the limbs and sliced the flesh of many men at the torture stake. This too he cast down into the pit of darkness, consigning it forever to the realms of the deep. From now on he would be a man of peace, a sachem, a leader with skin seven thumbs thick who would work only for the betterment of his people and the people to come for seven generations.

After the last Onondaga warrior, Tonesah, had flung his feathered war club into the pit, Hiawatha spoke to the multitude gathered at his feet. "The Peacemaker enjoins us never to forget this day. Because if we always keep today in our minds, then we will not lapse back into the old ways, the ways of the mourning war and the revenge torture. If one man or one woman or one nation has a grievance against another man, woman, or nation, then that grievance should be brought to the Grand Council of the Fifty Sachems. They will deliberate and decide through unanimous vote what the right course of action should be.

"And to prop up these words so that they will never be lost, so that they may be spoken by our children's children down through the generations yet unborn, Dekanawida has devised another belt of wampum to be kept here at Onondaga beside the Belt of the

Great Peace."

Dekanawida held up an intricate circle of shells with fifty strings of shell beads attached to the interior circumference and hanging down toward the middle to make another, smaller circle in the center.

"This is the Great Circle of Wampum. It symbolizes the fire that will always burn here at Onondaga. The fifty strings are the fifty sachems who will sit around the Great Council Fire. This Great Circle will be the official sign of our new government—all are equal, all are joined together in an unbroken circle."

Dekanawida placed the Circle Wampum on a mat that was spread before them. He signaled to the Clan Mothers who sat to the right of the rise that he and Hiawatha stood on. They each came forward, bearing deer-antler headdresses. Dekanawida spoke to Hiawatha, and Hiawatha called out the names of the Fifty. One by one, as their names were called, they walked up to the Peacemaker, and the Clan Mother of their clan—Turtle, Bear, Wolf, Heron, Hawk, and Eel—placed on their heads the antlers that signified their role as leader, one of the Fifty Sachems of the Great League of Peace.

All the while, the mystic music of flute and water drum, of rattle and voice, provided a backdrop for the auspicious ceremony, a ceremony that was being created extempore. No one taught the words and rituals to Dekanawida and Hiawatha; no one taught Orios and the other musicians the notes to be played and sung. They came from the Great Mysterious, the Creator of All Things, the Great Force of the Universe, and it filled their hearts to bursting so that the words and the music and the songs had to come out and spill themselves into the rarefied atmosphere.

As the last man to receive the antlers of authority returned to his place and sat cross-legged on the ground, Dekanawida spoke again into Hiawatha's ear.

Hiawatha turned to the crowd. "Dekanawida now wishes to plant the Tree of Peace. And we plant it here, in your territory,

Tadodaho, the Onondaga nation, the central fire of our Great Longhouse. All of you Fifty Sachems, and all of you warriors and war chiefs, come forward, and let us raise this uprooted pine tree. Let us replant this tree, this Tree of Peace, this Tree of the Long Leaves with four white roots that reach out to the four sacred directions, to the four corners of Turtle Island, roots that reach out into infinity, touching the lives of all who live and all who will live. Follow me, and let us put our backs and our hearts into it."

A great cheer went up and all the men who were able, the Fifty Sachems, the warriors and the war chiefs, even the young boys, all rushed toward the great white pine that lay on its side. They took places in between the long branches all along the trunk, from the wide base to the more narrow top. At Hiawatha's signal they all lifted with a mighty effort. But they only managed to raise it halfway, up to a forty-five degree angle with the ground. The men strained with the effort to keep the giant tree at this level.

Then came the women. Young women and middle-aged women, teenage girls and elderly clan mothers, grandmothers and young mothers still nursing their babies. They all rushed to the men's aid. Keteri found Orios among the Onondaga men, and she wedged herself between him and another young warrior.

"I think you men need the help of strong women," she said, giving him a shy look.

"Keteri!"

"I came with my mother's clan to help plant this tree."

"I was thinking of you this morning."

"You were?" She looked him full in the face. Their eyes met, and everything stopped for them.

"Hey, you two! Quit dreaming and help us raise this tree!" The older woman behind them shot Orios and Keteri a hard look that was followed with a wink and a smile. "There will be time enough for lovemaking after we have done this day's work." Keteri's face flushed and she felt hot. Orios too was embarrassed, and, with a quick look at Keteri, he put his shoulder to the tree and pushed with all the rest of the people.

With the combined effort of all the people, the men, women, and children of the Five Nations, the tree began again to move upward, slowly at first, then,as everyone pushed harder and harder, the great white pine finally righted itself. The weight of its long branches and sturdy trunk made it drop into its hole and settle there with a thunderous sound and a spreading cloud of dust.

The people gasped out loud and let out cheers of approval as they cautiously backed away from the tree and looked up at it in awe. It was truly magnificent—a long-branched white pine standing some fifty arm-lengths tall.

Dekanawida raised his arms up to the sky and said, "Let us give thanks to the Creator of All Things for the gifts that are bestowed upon us this day. It is my wish that a Prayer of Thanks be said before the beginning of any ceremony, any meeting, or any social event. We must never take for granted the blessings that greet us each day.

"I ask our sister, the lady of the woods, the first to practice the New Way of Peace, Jikonsahseh, the Mother of the Nations, to come forward and lead the Thanksgiving Prayer."

Jikonsahseh slowly climbed to the top of the rise and stood beside Dekanawida and Hiawatha. The intricate porcupine quill-work on her white doeskin dress glittered in the slanting rays of the late afternoon sun. Her long gray hair blew freely in the breeze. She was trembling inside with nervous apprehension. Sensing her unease, Dekanawida put his arm around her shoulder and gave her a reassuring hug. He nodded, and the lady of the forest lifted her face to the sky and opened her throat to the people.

"Let us join our minds together, and give thanks to the Great Mother—the earth who sustains us. Let us join our minds together and give thanks to our Mother's daughters—the three sisters: corn, beans, and squash. Let us join our minds and give thanks to the first fruits—the wild strawberry. Brothers and sisters, let us join our minds together to give thanks for the plants and grasses that heal us, that make us whole."

Jikonsahseh continued listing the gifts of the Creator that all people should give thanks for, the sun, the moon, the wind, the rain, all the fish in the waters, and all the animals in the woods. And as Jikonsahseh prayed forth her litany of the wonders of Nature, the wonders that the people should give thanks for, men and women began to join in and reply to her prayers by answering in chant-song:

"Let us join our minds and give thanks!"

Everyone was deeply moved by the thanksgiving prayer that they had created with Jikonsahseh, and she herself was moved the most. As she stood next to the Peacemaker, her heart was full to bursting, and tears of joy streamed down her face.

"The Peacemaker says that now we are all spiritual warriors," said Hiawatha. "Warriors of the rainbow. Here are arrows from each of the nations, a Mohawk arrow, an Oneida shaft, an Onondaga arrow, a Cayuga, and a Seneca. Each has been dyed a color of the rainbow. Red for Mohawk, Orange for Oneida, Yellow for Onondaga, Green for Cayuga, and Blue for Seneca. Just as the colors of the rainbow are separate but united, one blending into the other so that there is no real distinct border, so too are the five nations. You are autonomous nations, yet you are one. Your strength is in your unity."

Dekanawida motioned to Atatarho to join him. Atatarho stepped forward. He stood straight and tall, proud of the antlers that crowned his head, the sign and symbol of his office. "It is now time to light the fire. The fire that will not be extinguished, the Great Central Fire of the One United Longhouse. Light it now, Firekeeper of the new League of Peace, and make sure that its flames do not die out, that the light we have shed on the darkness today will burn forever with the same intensity. This is your charge and your duty."

Dekanawida put his hands on Tadodaho's shoulders. "And when it comes your time to join our ancestors in the Land of the

Spirit Beings, your name will remain among the living, and you will be remembered always. You will be reborn, requickened in the body of another good-minded man chosen by the Clan Mothers. Keep the fire free from dust and dirt. Keep it free from things that crawl in the night. Keep it clean and free from dark and evil thoughts that might lead our people astray."

"I will, Peacemaker." Tadodaho embraced Dekanawida. He then picked out three young men and left with them to return to the village, and there, at Onondaga, they built the Central Council Fire that would burn forever, lighting the way toward the uncertain future.

"One thing remains to be done before I am gone," said Dekanawida.

"Gone?"

"Gone where?"

"Why are you going?"

"Where are you going?" The crowd murmured and asked these questions aloud to their neighbors and to the Peacemaker himself.

Dekanawida held up his hands to quiet them. "My work here is nearly done. I must go now. I must return to the Land of the Spirit Beings from where I came. But I will not leave you alone."

Then Dekanawida let out a loud and shrill eagle cry, a cry that pierced the sky whose clouds were now streaked and splashed with gold and vermilion, rose and crimson. The sun was huge and low in the sky, and it shone a bright and fiery red.

The Peacemaker's cry was answered by another eagle cry. The people looked up into the brilliant sky, and there, high above them, coming from the west, framed against the flaming ball of the sun, was a large eagle soaring towards them. His wingspan was at least five feet, and he soared gracefully and cleanly through the sky, his clear and quick eyes constantly watching the terrain below.

The Peacemaker cried out again, and the great eagle soared closer and lower until he reached the clearing where the nations were gathered. Dekanawida held out his left arm for a perch and the eagle landed on his wrist, folded his wings, and stood erect and proud, eyeing the crowd assembled around him.

"This is my old friend, Kyree. We have known each other for many years now, and often he has been my eyes, seeing great distances and traveling far and wide as my emissary and guide. Now he will be *your* eyes, *your* guardian, *your* protector. He will sit atop the Great Tree of Peace, and he will watch with his keen and clear vision. He will watch for trouble on the horizon. He will see evil approach. He will know when the Great Peace that we have established this day is in jeopardy, and he will warn you. He will act as my eyes. He will act as my voice. Listen to him, my children. Pay heed to his warnings. Watch for anything unusual. Be vigilant. For I must tell you that hard times will come.

"I see a great threat coming from the future. I see strange men with strange ways, men whose minds are unclean, whose ways are not the ways of righteousness. Watch for this danger. Tell your children, and enjoin them to tell theirs, and so on down through the generations, so that when this trouble comes, the people, those whose faces are still in the ground, will be ready."

The Peacemaker voiced another, softer, eagle-cry, and lowered his left arm momentarily, then raised it suddenly like a springboard. Kyree, the Great Eagle, spread his wings and bent his powerful legs, and at just the right moment, lifted off from Dekanawida's arm and climbed into the air, flying straight up, circling the Tree of Peace four times, each time looking in the direction of the four white roots, the East, the West, the North, and the South. Then, he gracefully settled on a long-needled limb, very close to the top of the tree, and he perched there, spreading his wings.

"My children," said the Peacemaker, "brothers and sisters, sons and daughters, mothers and fathers, my work here is now done. The rest is up to you and your children and your children's children.

"I must leave you now and return to the Land of the Spirit Beings. I will walk out alone into the woods. No. Do not follow me. I must go alone. When I find the right spot, I will cover myself with elm bark, with maple leaves, with the leaves of the pine, and I will bury myself under the ground, so that I can keep watch on the foundation of the Longhouse. I will be with you always to prop up the house and to prop up the minds of the people."

"Don't leave us, Dekanawida!" the people pleaded.

"I am not leaving you. I will be in all things around you. When you see a butterfly land on the petals of a flower, that will be me. When you see the eagle circle the sky watching below with clear-sighted eye, that will be me. When you pick and eat the wild strawberries that bless the carpet of the earth in the spring, you will be picking and eating me. I will be in the wide V of geese in the autumn. I will be in the grass, in the trees, in the scales of the fishes, in the waterfalls and rivers great and small. I will be in the eyes of the beaver, the shell of the turtle, the velvet antlers of the deer, the warm fur of the bear. I will be in sunlight at daybreak and moonlight at midnight. I will be the whispering of the warm winds in your ears.

"Today you are given the light. But as you have seen, the sun can be taken away. Darkness came today at noon and blotted out the light of the sun. There will be, must be, times of darkness ahead. This is as it should be. Just as the other side of joy is sorrow, so too, the other side of light is darkness. One does not exist without the other. For this reason, I know that there will be times of darkness, times of trouble, ahead. If you need me, call for me in the bushes. Call for me in the woods. I will hear. And I will return in your hour of need. Keep my spirit alive in your hearts to prop up your courage, to prop up your souls. I will be with you until the end of all the days."

Dekanawida turned to Hiawatha, his brother in the great vision that had now finally become a reality. "Good-bye, my friend. May you live a long and happy life. Remember, even though you cannot see me, I will be walking beside you. May your path be a straight one with no obstacles in your way."

Hiawatha could not speak. His eyes and throat were choked with tears. He embraced the Peacemaker, the man who had saved his life and who had saved the lives of countless others who live now and who would live in the future. Dekanawida gently pushed Hiawatha away.

"Do not be sad. I am returning to my home. Celebrate the living." He swept his arm out over the multitude of people, Oneida, Seneca, Cayuga, Onondaga, and Mohawk, all one people now. "Be strong for them. They will need your wisdom and courage in the years to come. Live your life so that when it is time for you to join me in the Land of the Spirit Beings, the people will celebrate your name and tell their children the story of your life."

Dekanawida grasped Hiawatha's arms firmly one last time, then he turned and walked down the slope of the hill they were standing on, and slowly walked into the woods.

The people did not follow him, for they knew that this was his wish, this was the way he had chosen. But their eyes followed him. The eyes of Makahwah followed him. Odatsadeh's eyes followed him. Tekerihoken's eyes followed him. The proud eyes of Shadekaronyes followed him. The eyes of Orios and Keteri, who now stood together, hand in hand, followed him as he became smaller, disappearing into the woods. The eyes of all the people whose lives the Peacemaker had touched followed his dim figure, now becoming only a shadow in the gathering dusk that was quickly becoming darkness. The eyes of the people were filled with reverence and sadness. Not tears, because Dekanawida would not have wanted that, but instead, a bittersweet feeling, a joyful melancholy, came over the people. Melancholy for the passing of the Peacemaker, but joy for the peace that was his legacy.

This is how the story was told to me by my grandfather, who heard it from his grandfather, who heard it from his. Some people tell the story differently. They may be right, I don't know. I only know what I have been told. Perhaps there is no wrong version and no right version, but simply different tellings and retellings of the same story, the story of the Haudenosaunee, the People of the Longhouse, the story of Dekanawida, the Peacemaker, the story of Hiawatha, the great leader and orator, and the story of my own ancestor, the flute player, Orios, who married Keteri the Mohawk girl, and so started a line of generations that ended in me.

Does it matter which version we tell? Perhaps not. What matters is that in a time of great need, a time of blood and murderous revenge, a time of continual warfare fueled by the darkness of vengeance, a prophet came, and he showed the people how to live in peace with each other. The people and the nations no longer made war, one against the other. But the Peacemaker was right. Hard times were ahead, but no one then could foresee how strange their world would become.

Author's Note

The events in this story are based on the myths, legends, and oral traditions of the Haudenosaunee. Dekanawida and Hiawatha are historical persons, but other characters, like Orios and Makahwah, are the product of my imagination. If you are interested in reading more about the League of the Iroquois, the following list is a good start.

Selected Bibliography

Arden, Harvey, and Steve Wall. *Travels in a Stone Canoe: The Return to the Wisdomkeepers*. New York: Simon and Schuster, 1998.

Atwood, Mary Dean. *Spirit Healing: Native American Magic & Medicine*. New York: Sterling Publishing, 1991.

Barreiro, Jose, ed. *Indian Roots of American Democracy*. Ithaca, NY: Akwe:kon Press, Cornell University, 1992.

Barreiro, Jose, and Carol Cornelius, eds. *Knowledge of the Elders: The Iroquois Condolence Cane Tradition*. Ithaca, NY: Northeast Indian Quarterly, Cornell University, 1991.

Carey, Kenneth X. *Return of the Bird Tribes*. Kansas City, MO: UniSun, 1988.

Colden, Cadwallader. *The History of the Five Indian Nations, Depending on the Province of New York in America*. New York: William Bradford, 1727. Ithaca, New York: Cornell University Press, 1958.

Fenton, William N. *The Great Law and the Longhouse: A Political History of the Iroquois Confederacy*. Norman: University of Oklahoma Press, 1998.

_____. *Selected Writings (The Iroquoians and Their World)*. Lincoln: University of Nebraska Press, 2009.

Foster, Michael K., Jack Campisi, and Marianne Mithun, eds. *Extending the Rafters*. Albany: SUNY Press, 1984.

Graymont, Barbara. *The Iroquois*. New York: Chelsea House Publishers, 1988.

Greene, Alma (Gah-wohnh-nos-doh). *Forbidden Voice: Reflections of a Mohawk Indian*. London: Hamlyn House, 1975.

Herrick, James W. *Iroquois Medical Botany*. Syracuse: Syracuse University Press, 1995.

Hyde, George E. *Indians of the Woodlands from Prehistoric Times to 1725*. Norman: University of Oklahoma Press, 1962.

Jennings, Francis. *The Ambiguous Iroquois Empire: The Covenant Chain Confederation of Indian Tribes with English Colonies*. New York: W. W. Norton, 1984.

_____. *The Invasion of America*. Chapel Hill: University of North Carolina Press, 1975.

Johansen, Bruce E. *Forgotten Founders: How the American Indian Helped Shape Democracy*. Boston: Harvard Common Press, 1982.

Lyons, Oren and John Mohawk, eds. Preface by Daniel K. Inouye, Forward by Peter Matthiessen. *Exiled in the Land of the Free: Democracy, Indian Nations & the U.S. Constitution*. Santa Fe: Clear Light Books, 1998.

Mann, Charles C. *1491: New Revelations of the Americas Before Columbus*. New York: Alfred A. Knopf, 2005.

Morgan, Lewis Henry. *League of the Ho-de-no-sau-nee or Iroquois*. Rochester: 1851. Carol Publishing Group Edition, 1984.

Richter, Daniel. *The Ordeal of the Longhouse: The People of the Iroquois League in the Era of European Colonization*. Chapel Hill: University of North Carolina Press, 1992.

_____. *Facing East from Indian Country: A Native History of Early America*. Cambridge, MA: Harvard University Press, 2001.

Parker, Arthur C.; William N. Fenton, ed. *Parker on the Iroquois.* Syracuse University Press, 1968.

Parker, Arthur C., ed. *Myths and Legends of the New York Iroquois.* Museum Bulletin 125. Albany: The University of the State of New York, 1981.

Snow, Dean R. *The Iroquois.* Oxford, UK and Cambridge, USA: Blackwell, 2001.

Tehanetorens (Ray Fadden). *Roots of the Iroquois.* Summertown, TN: Native Voices Books, 2000.

______. *Legends of the Iroquois.* Summertown, TN: Native Voices Books, 1998.

Tooker, Elisabeth. *Lewis H. Morgan on Iroquois Material Culture.* Tuscon and London: The University of Arizona Press, 1994.

Wall, Steve. Wisdom's Daughters: *Conversations with Women Elders of Native America.* New York: HarperCollins, 1993.

______. *To Become a Human Being: The Message of Tadodaho Chief Leon Shenandoah.* Charlottesville, VA: Hampton Roads Publishing, 2001.

______. *Shadowcatchers: A Journey in Search of the Teachings of Native American Healers.* New York: HarperCollins, 1994.

Wallace, Paul. Foreward by Chief Leon Shenandoah, Message from Chief Sidney I. Hill, Epilogue by John Mohawk. *White Roots of Peace: Iroquois Book of Life.* Santa Fe: Clear Light Books, 1996.

Weatherford, Jack. *Indian Givers: How the Indians of the Americas Transformed the World.* New York: Crown, 1988.

Willoya, William, and Vinson Brown. *Warriors of the Rainbow: Strange and Prophetic Dreams of the Indian Peoples.* Happy Camp, CA: Naturegraph Publishers, 1962.

You will find Iroquois and pre-Columbian art,
cultural artifacts, and educational resources
at the following museums:

<u>*Museums*</u>

Akwesasne Museum
    321 NY-37, Hogansburg, New York

Cayuga Museum of History and Art
    203 Genesee St, Auburn, New York

Eiteljorg Museum
    500 W Washington St, Indianapolis, Indiana

Iroquois Indian Museum
    324 Caverns Rd, Howes Cave, New York

Museum of Native American History
    202 SW O Street, Bentonville, Arkansas

National Museum of the American Indian
    Fourth Street & Independence Ave SW, Washington, DC
    1 Bowling Green, New York, New York

New York State Museum
    260 Madison Avenue, Albany, New York

Oneida Nation Museum
    W892 County EE, De Pere, Wisconsin

Seneca Art & Culture Center
    Ganondagan State Historic Site
    7000 County Road 41, Victor, New York

Seneca Iroquois National Museum
    814 Broad Street, Salamanca, New York

Six Nations Indian Museum
    1466 County Route 60, Onchiota, New York

Jack Ramey is a poet, author, performer, and English professor at Indiana University Southeast. His poetry books include *Eavesdropping in Plato's Café, Death Sings in the Choir of Light, Burnt Almonds*, and *The Future Past*.

His documentary on William Blake won an Aegis award for best educational film.

In his early years, he studied to be a priest at the Passionist Fathers Seminary, then became a member of the counterculture and read his poetry in Santa Cruz, San Francisco, Eugene, Victoria BC, and Kent OH. His one-person show, *Dark Is a Long Way: An Evening with Dylan Thomas*, ran for two years at the 13th Street Theater in NYC, at the Odyssey Theater in LA, and toured the country.

As a student of anthropology at Kent State, he wrote a paper on Lewis H. Morgan's *League of the Ho-de-no-sau-nee or Iroquois*. Since then he has continued his lifelong fascination with the People of the Longhouse, which led to the creation of *Turtle Island*.

He frequently posts poems and reviews at the Springwood Press *Poetry & Art Gallery*: springwoodpress.org